Alien Earth

By
Greg Burke

Edited by Spike Y. Jones

*To: Anne
How nice to meet you
And thanks for your
support!
Greg Burke*

Alien Earth

Alien Earth copyright © 2002 by Greg Burke. All rights reserved.
First printing in hardback edition, 2002.

Published by Golden Pillar Publishing, P.O. Box 2531, Elk Grove, California, 95759. http://www.goldenpillarpublishing.com
Printed in the United States of America.

ISBN 1-890305-34-0

Greg Burke

Acknowledgements

Special thanks go to my wife Julia for her unconditional support. I dedicate this novel to her with all my love.

Thanks to the following for technical help and proofing:
Fran Brender, the Burkes: Adam, Ed, Julia, and Shirley, Charlie Daniels, Janice DeLong, Joe and Mabel Konopa, Jeff Mankin, Tim Nicholson, Cindy and Dan Via, and Robert Workman

Thanks to the many science fiction writers whose water I cannot carry, but whose spirit and vision I greatly admire and aspire to emulate.

Alien Earth

They're Here!

Tears crept from the corners of swollen eyes and flowed slowly down dark complexioned silky skin. Beads of sweat formed on a taut forehead and upper lip. Toned hands and legs started to twitch noticeably. There was rapid motion beneath fluttering eyelids. Irregular breathing stopped suddenly.

With a lifesaving gasp, Del woke in a panic and frantically threw off her damp covers. It was pitch dark and she was momentarily disorientated as the nightmarish experience flooded over her consciousness again. But it wasn't a nightmare! Everything...no matter how unbelievable...was true!

She buried her head in her hands and sobbed through eyes that should not have been capable of making more tears. Through blurring tears, she glanced at the alarm clock by her bed: 2:37a.m. Exasperated, she flopped backwards and stared blankly at the inky blackness of her ceiling. Too many sleepless nights were catching up with her and her active mind would not let her body rest. *"How could this happen? Why is it happening? What can I do about it? What can I do or anyone do at this point?"*

Del reviewed the indelibly etched chain of events of the past two weeks for the thousandth time. Sometime in the middle of a clear February 22 night, the visitors started landing and began their takeover of Earth. It was not impossible to know where on the planet it had started nor did it really matter at this point.

By the time Del had woken up, her world had changed unbelievably and dramatically. Whether this was better or worse for the world was yet to be determined. Personally for Del it had been much for the worse.

* * * * *

Adelle Summers recalled hearing the civil defense sirens around 1:00 a.m. In Cocoa Beach, Florida, that could mean a lot of things from severe weather to missile launches gone awry. When they didn't stop after 15 minutes and the incessant barking of her neighbors collie didn't let up, she sat up, threw off her covers, and, naked as usual at night, keyed the small bedroom TV where chaos was being played out on all channels.

Newscasters were wide-eyed and frantic with reports coming in from military and civilian sources. There were conflicting reports of missiles launched from unknown origins, meteors falling in several countries, huge asteroids on approach to Earth, and, of course, the inevitable UFO sightings. It was crazy and downright hard to believe, but panic was in the air and Del came fully alert, trying to take it all in.

Then, suddenly the local news station went dead; not a test pattern, just static as if some plug had been pulled, right in mid-sentence cutting off some scientific guru who was trying to elaborate and speculate on what he'd just seen. Del quickly switched news channels. Hysteria was reaching a peak as normally calm anchors tried in vain to report and explain what was clearly a rapidly occurring series of bizarre events.

The sirens stopped and the sudden lack of noise was like being plunged into a vacuum. The collie next door was no longer barking. She glanced at her window and then back at the now totally frazzled news anchor only to see the national channel go dead, just like the local channel.

The last thing she remembered hearing were snippets of "invasion forces," "spaceships," "no word from the military," "no comment from the State Department or President at this time" and "communication disruptions nationwide and around the world." She watched the static for 30 seconds, and then realized she'd been holding her breath the whole time.

She gulped some air and turbo-flipped through all 47 news channels only to get static. The remaining 450 channels were mostly static except for movies and "infomercials," but within a span of 25 minutes, everything was dead.

She turned the TV off and her condo was still and quiet again; just the repetitive and soothing surf in the background. It was too quiet, unnerving actually. This dizzying turn of events made it hard to think clearly as she sat stiffly on the edge of her bed trying to absorb the possibilities.

Turning on the clock radio by the bed resulted in a full dial of static on AM, FM, and short-wave bands. Living alone had delighted her for years, but in this circumstance the growing feeling of isolation started to panic her. She clicked on the bedroom light and rose without dressing to call her mom, her best friend and confidante since Dad had died.

"I have to talk to someone about this!" she ordered herself. The effort to reach the phone drained her immensely. Perhaps it was shock or disorientation at what she has just seen and heard. Slowly, incredibly slowly, she activated the phone on her computer. Her hands felt

numb as she keyed the number. *"What is going on?"* She heard the first ring as the power failed and she was plunged back into darkness and seemingly an even deeper quiet.

With backup power on the computer, the phone icon was the only light in the room. Then, it faded too, leaving her to listen to the clicks as the phone connected. Unbelievably the phone went dead as well. That raised hairs on her neck because in all her 29 years, the phone had never gone dead during power failures. It was the one constant you could count on in a world full of daily technological surprises.

Her head started hurting and the numbness in her hands spread like a drug to the rest of her body. She started to hear a reassuring voice telling her to, *"Go to sleep,"* and saying, *"Everything will be all right."* The darkness around her was deep and her condo was deathly quiet. The only sound was her shallow breathing and the voice in her head, which kept repeating its calming message.

Her headache increased, as did the volume of the voice. She detected a slight smell of ozone for an unknown reason. Del found she could still move about, albeit very slowly, so she trudged like her feet were in molasses to the bedroom window. She had to see what was happening outside.

With the sudden power outage, isolation set in and she looked up for the reassurance of a starry sky on this clear night as she drew open the blinds, but clouds must have rolled in quickly because nothing showed, not even a flicker. Then some starlight began to peek through the clouds.

Even as she brightened at the notion, the lights appeared to move and grow quickly in size, splitting up, moving in different directions at incredible speed. Some were now moving closer and their glare brightened like a hundred spotlights to the point Del had to shield her eyes.

The lights, the voice, and her headache reached a crescendo, causing her to stagger slowly back from the window and fall onto the bed. She felt her consciousness blur and narrow as the white light dimmed and then disappeared altogether.

* * * * *

Back in the present and still staring at the pitch-black ceiling, which was as dark as her recent memories, Del began to chill outside her covers. Rather than make a useless attempt at sleeping, she got up, put on her red terry cloth robe, and walked to her bedroom window, finger stroking the snarls from her shoulder length brown hair along the way.

She brushed aside the curtain and looked out over Cocoa Beach from her modest fourth floor condo. Even at night, condo backlights revealed foamy waves steadily rolling shoreward and crashing in a constant untiring rhythm.

Flotsam and assorted dead seafaring animals gathered at the shoreline of the coquina shell beach, but no one stirred, no life of any type could be seen. It was an eerie sight for sure. Here, on a Florida beach at this time of year and this time of night, college students on spring break should still be over-indulging in beer and rum drinks and be seeking just one more form of entertainment before crashing for the night. Instead, the beach was silent. Another reminder of how much even simple things had changed.

Her thoughts were tugged back to the events of the 'morning after' as her deep brown eyes stared gloomily and blankly at the beach below.

* * * * *

She remembered waking up at 6:20 a.m. to her favorite classical music. Another great day! Strangely, though, her room was lit up like it was noon. Wondering why she was sprawled crosswise and undressed on top of the bedspread, a few seconds passed before her brain was flooded with last night's occurrences.

She lept for the phone key on her computer but never made it as her knees buckled, her head reeled, and she fell in a heap on the floor. Choking back nausea, she wisely moved a bit slower and things stopped spinning and churning.

Not really hurt by her fall to the soft carpet, she reached carefully upward, keyed the phone to call her mother, and got nothing. The speaker was silent. Evidently that plug had been pulled on her life. Glancing around she saw the light by her bed was on; reminding her there had been a power outage.

Questions raced through her head. *"How could it be mid-day at half past six in the morning?"* Despite the power outage, her clock was battery powered so it wouldn't have been affected. In fact, that clock had saved her from being late to work several times when power had failed. *"What had really happened last night? Was it some sort of hoax? Had something seriously gone wrong in the world as the news channels had reported?"*

Without being able to talk to her mother, her boyfriend Alan, or anyone else by phone, she quickly lost her main way of communication. So used to talking to people remotely via speakerphone or voice chat on the computer, it was like losing one of your senses. Del felt the hair rising on the back of her neck...again. It was hard to think straight with so much going on.

She felt dizzy. Whatever had happened to her the previous night and moments before, she hadn't completely recovered. She climbed slowly onto her bed to steady herself and gather her wits. Her fingers clutched the covers in frustration.

"OK," she told herself, *"Calm down. Think this through. Take stock of the situation. You're a grown woman, one of NASA's top trauma nurses, and a neo-natal specialist for the upcoming space station families. You have one of the most analytical minds God ever made according to your late father and many associates."*

She closed her eyes, took several deep breaths, and relaxed her tense muscles and mind. Immediately she felt more steady and focused and immediately she started hearing a calming voice telling her to turn on the TV or radio. Even through the fog of last night, she recognized that voice.

It was the same one that had told her to go to sleep and that everything would be all right. "Well everything isn't all right!" she yelled at the wall, feeling better for saying something yet also feeling a bit of a headache for her effort. The voice faded instantly, to her surprise, but it didn't go away entirely.

Trying to calm down again, she forced herself to relax. The voice kept repeating the need for her to turn on the TV or radio and grew in volume to the level of someone having a normal conversation with her across a table.

Del had never had an experience with ghosts or poltergeists, but she knew that those were supposed to be external experiences, whereas this voice was coming from inside her own head, nearly identical to her own thoughts, and it was hard to dispel. She quickly verified this by plugging both ears so tightly it hurt, only to hear the same soothing voice continue its compelling plea.

"This is too strange," she complained, standing up in defiance. The voice diminished to her relief. *"What the heck is going on?"* she wondered. Stubbornness was one characteristic Del cherished. Like two sides of the same coin, though, it had both good and bad results in her life. Today, at this moment, she was glad to be a thinking (and stubborn) person. Rather than follow this voice she rebelliously got up with all the steadiness she could muster, donned her robe, and walked to the beach window.

What she saw broke down her resolve, for at mid-day she saw nothing of humanity; no people, no boats, no surfers, no walkers, no joggers, no sun worshippers, no passed out spring breakers. She quickly ran down the short hall to the living room and the front of her condo and looked out onto Route A1A, the main road into and out of Cocoa Beach. Incredibly, she again saw nothing. Not one moving car, tourist, or shopper.

Her mind screamed the kind of scream one has when they realize they must be trapped in the ultimate nightmare. Like in the old TV show "The Twilight Zone" when you realize you are the only person on Earth. Almost in a panic, she looked up and down the road in case she was being too hasty. Sadly and slowly, she confronted the truth.

Something had happened. Cocoa Beach, Florida at least, and perhaps the rest of the world had changed. Remembering what she saw and heard the previous night drove home the realization that whatever happened must be dramatic and probably for the worse. It wasn't just a dream. Thoughts of her mother drifted into the forefront, increasing her worries.

She keyed the TV remote in resignation. *"What's so damned important the voice wants me to know about on TV?"* she griped inwardly.

In half a second, she started to get answers as the big screen snapped into focus. The president of the United States herself was addressing the nation in what was obviously a serious speech from the Oval Office. Del had missed the intro but listened intently to what followed.

"...alarmed. We have new friends who have traveled a great distance to live among us. I am as shocked and surprised as you are to find out we are not alone in this universe. So much has happened since last night that many of you, like myself, may feel confused, upset or even a little panicky. Please relax, though, as our new friends have assured me they mean us no harm and are here to help us.

"Like never before, I am awed by what little they have told me and I can personally assure you that a great event has occurred that will improve the lives of every human being on Earth. I'm confident a lot of changes for the better will occur in all our lives in the near future and for many years to come. Together, we must accept the changes this momentous situation brings to America and this planet.

"Some of you may have already met our new friends, who call themselves the Quazzga. Much more will be revealed about them soon, but they are a shy unimposing people who will be staying away from us in the short term to ensure their privacy and allow us to adjust to their presence. Again, much will unfold in the near future and I will be busy serving this great country and making sure a peaceful coexistence can develop.

"You may also be feeling disorientation and some physical discomfort may last a couple days. It's an unfortunate but harmless result of our friends' arrival..."

Being skeptical as well as stubborn, Del never took things at face value. Her eyes narrowed as she scrutinized President Griffith and listened between the lines.

Frances Griffith was a striking and beautiful woman of 38, with short-cut curly blonde hair, green eyes, milky white skin, and a cover-girl complexion. Her meteoric rise to the presidency was so unprecedented and her popularity so overwhelming, she left her competitors in the dust despite a peacenik reputation.

Her forthrightness and folksy wisdom had reminded Del's Father of Ronald Reagan, and she had a decisiveness and tenacity that Dad said would have rivaled Margaret Thatcher. Best yet, she got the "will of the people" done which is what drew supporters to her like moths to a streetlight.

Del always listened when President Griffith spoke because she could understand her soft-spoken and direct manner of speech and could feel the honesty in her words. As the president continued, though, warning flags went up; this was not the same president she had grown to respect.

Oh, she spoke straightforwardly enough and she was captivating, but Del could tell the president wasn't quite herself and wasn't quite telling the whole story. She'd heard much clearer and better-delivered speeches that were done in the heat of crisis. Something was amiss.

Her mind raced with questions. *"Are we talking little green men? Why would "friends" come in the middle of night causing power to fail and people to lose consciousness? Where is our expensive military hardware and protection? Why should we accept these beings and why the need for changes? And what about that damn voice?"* which she now heard repeating, *"Relax. Listen. Relax. Listen."*

Other things bothered Del as she watched more closely. The first was the slender man with dark glasses dressed in black pants, tie, and coat just at the edge of the screen. She knew most of the president's staff through the news but had never seen this foreboding character standing stiff as a board, body and face squarely turned towards Griffith. Bodyguards usually looked at the audience; this was no bodyguard.

The second was the automatic way President Griffith spoke, as if she was being manipulated or was under the influence of some drug.

The third was that the whole thing just didn't ring true, as if this was some giant scam, perhaps the greatest scam of all time. Finally, she got the feeling the listeners were being manipulated as well.

"Of course we are!" Del yelled as she smacked her head, momentarily drowning out the voice. Thinking to herself, she could only come to some hasty conclusions, conclusions that would require more answers for proof, but for the moment best summed up what had happened.

Yes, we have been visited, but probably not by friends. Yes, this was a surprise, but probably not as much as the government is letting us know. Yes, there will be changes, but probably not for the better. No, this was not mankind's finest day.

President Griffith was finishing her speech and for the first time, Del didn't trust what she heard nor was she compelled to action or support, as had always been the case in the past. "I'll keep you fully informed as things develop," said the president.

"Yeah, right," Del said sarcastically. *"So far so bad,"* she concluded. The feeling of isolation and loneliness was growing with each passing minute. Then the president dropped a bombshell drawing Del's attention back with a jolt.

"...circumstances warrant this next action," continued Griffith, "In order to protect everyone, martial law must be implemented nationwide. I regret the severity of this executive order, but believe me it is necessary to avoid undue panic and give us the necessary time to adjust to this historic occasion.

"As of this moment, The United States will undergo a temporary nationwide shutdown. Martial law is now in effect. No one is to move more than 100 yards from his or her homes for any reason unless authorized or directed to do so by local and national law enforcement agencies.

"Stay where you are now is the best advice. Those who have found themselves away from home must seek residence in the nearest town. I ask you good people to be understanding and house these travelers temporarily.

"There will be a television blackout for the next 24 hours at least. Telephone and Internet services have been temporarily suspended for an as yet undetermined period of time, except for 911 calls. Remember to use 911 calls for grave emergencies only.

"Radio transmissions will be jammed. Power, water, medical, emergency, and sanitation services will continue, and the appropriate state and local authorities are being contacted about the details of this unusual though necessary action. Police and our military specialists have been ordered to imprison any martial law violators and take any and all necessary steps to maintain national order.

"Your cooperation will make sure no one gets hurt. Rest assured our country is safe as similar martial law orders are being implemented worldwide. The United States has not been alone in this experience. For perhaps the first time there is unity among our nations to meet this unprecedented challenge.

"Please try to relax, even though many of you will feel alone and even frightened. If you have loved ones close by, enjoy this time together without all our technological intrusions. If you are alone, visit quietly with a neighbor, read a book, do a puzzle, or catch up on your sleep. Treat it as a national vacation period by yourself or with you family.

"Do not worry about loved ones in other areas of our country or world. For the moment, they are on their own. All of us will be safe if we stay calm and follow these martial law guidelines. Again, I will keep you posted as things develop. Thank you in advance for the patience and understanding you *must* have for the next few days.

"I also ask you to help each other as needed, sharing food and perishable items. Plan on at least three weeks of martial law though we anticipate it will be much less.

"One last item of business my friends. It is now 1:27 p.m. Eastern Time. Some of your clocks may have been affected by last night's events; mine was. Take care. Trust me to look after your best interests as you have done so well this past year. Trust in yourselves. Trust in each other. God bless.

"Whoa! No way!" said Del shaking her head vigorously in disbelief, bringing back some of her earlier dizziness and headache. But the president had spoken and surely her word would be law this day. This was totally unreal. Like Alice down the rabbit hole, humans were in for some adventure.

Del was more certain of deception now by her beloved president than she could ever have believed possible. *"Would even a normally untrustworthy Congress address this issue? Could they?"* she wondered. Change was definitely in the air with no turning back.

The voice in her head was now repeating, *"Calm down. You have new friends. Change is good. Relax."* It was soothing, and it was very compelling, but bullheaded old Del found she could consciously push this voice aside and concentrate her energy on what to do next. Yes, what to do next....

Greg Burke

* * * * *

Clutching at reality, Del stared out her window at an empty nighttime beach and recalled how unprepared she was for the changes that would come, and how helpless she would be as things unfolded.

All those years of UFO reports that were denied by the government came flashing into her mind. While never having a personal experience, some of the evidence had been convincing or at least highly suggestive that perhaps we weren't alone. It was hard to form a solid opinion based on the wide-ranging stories involving aliens or friends as the president had called them. Worse yet she realized in retrospect, she was one who trusted the government sources and would have wanted more proof herself from all the UFO theorists to back up their claims.

And now age-old questions came to life. Could the world handle the knowledge of aliens without a massive upheaval beyond anyone's control? And if not, how would that be handled? Guess she was seeing the results of one way to handle those questions first hand. She thought the current answer stank. It was not a fun process to watch.

Whatever one had believed up until now though was of no consequence because the question was moot. The events of recent weeks were certainly no hoax. The time for speculation had passed because extraterrestrials were actually and incredibly here among us. And like most big events in life, one can never predict with any great certainty what things will be like after the event until it has actually happened. And the wilder the event, the greater the uncertainty.

Trauma

Still unable to sleep as she continued to reminisce, Del decided to leave her room and walk outside to the beachfront balcony. The early March chilliness struck her quickly but brought her senses fully awake, acting like a sharp slap in the face to temporarily make her forget her fears and tears. The cold feel of the sandy carpet on her bare feet, the smell of the salt air, the perpetual incoming breeze, and the chorus of churning waves reminded her she was not dreaming, that she was indeed alive.

Moreover, and still more puzzling, she was in control of her life when everyone and everything else was being controlled. Wrapping her robe tighter to ward off the worst of the chill, she sat down on her aging white plastic chair next to its small white plastic table. Wiping nearly dried tears from her cheeks, she continued to recall the past, hoping against hope to make sense of it all and find a few answers to her growing list of questions.

* * * * *

After President Griffith completed her speech, the TV went dead, just like the previous night. To be certain, she turbo-flipped through the channels and came up with nothing but static. Keying the phone, her Internet connection, and then the short-wave band of her radio revealed the president wasn't a total liar. She glanced at her watch, which now said 7:03 a.m. She shook her head at the mystery of it all.

What could affect clocks and make her lose almost six hours? What could put her out like a light as that experience the previous night had? Her computer clock also read 7:03. A quick stroll around the condo showed equally unreal time figures. Even if the power was out for seven hours, it wouldn't explain why her battery powered bed clock read the same time. "Forget it," she said to no one. She would just have to put this anomaly on the back burner. There were more pressing problems at hand as she decided what to do next.

First, she had to take stock of the situation. Having practiced many days responding to emergencies involving astronauts, NASA support personnel and their families, she was quick to check the basics. She had plenty of food to last at least a week, though she had hoped to get some fresh greens for a salad tonight. No big deal now.

Water and power were still on so she would have heat or AC depending on what the weather did over the next couple of days. She could also cook, bathe, and wash clothes. *"Hey, half the world still doesn't have it this good,"* she mused, so even in a state of emergency she was pretty well off. With travel restricted, she didn't have to worry about gas.

With all the basics taken care of, she could move to the next priorities: what to do with her time and how best to assess this situation. She was not the type to watch a dozen videos with a couple bags of munchies and unlimited rum and cokes, though right now would be the best chance for mindless entertainment and a bit of inebriation she might get for a while.

She loved to read and had several good books to enjoy, but that didn't strike her fancy either. What she really wanted to do right now was figure out what the heck was really going on.

With basically no chance at getting information from the usual sources, Del would have to improvise, perhaps even use some old fashioned methods like actually talking to other people. She might only get a localized picture and opinions, but this was no time to sit back and take this matter passively. Besides, it wasn't her nature to be an abstract observer.

She took a long hot shower, the kind that empties the water tank, to gather her strength and wits. It gave her time to realize she had more questions than answers. She grabbed a quick breakfast food bar and got dressed in black jeans, a gray sweatshirt and sheepskin slippers, the first warm things she could find. It was supposed to get up to 55 degrees so this should be fine.

She was only going next door anyway to visit Bud and Renee Stephens and get their take on this whole mess. A quick glance in the hall mirror showed that her haggard hair and face were barely suitable for public viewing but she didn't really care. Del reached for the door and jumped as someone knocked at the same time.

While not a safety freak, every door at this complex had a peephole and Del used it occasionally. This was one of those occasions. Hopefully it was someone she knew. A quick glance through the lens showed the full figures of a policeman standing next to another man sans insignia, but dressed in black pants, turtleneck, and dark glasses, not too dissimilar from the man she'd seen nearly off screen with the president.

Alien Earth

The officer reached up to knock again as she stepped warily backwards. The triple rap on her thankfully solid door was followed with an, "Open up the door, Ms. Summers. This is Officer Roy with the Police Department on national business."

She threw back the fear that was quickly rising and opened her door as nonchalantly as she could muster. Neither man moved towards her although she instinctively took a defensive stance.

"Come with us now, Ms. Summers. You are needed at the NMC," said Officer Roy. "You will get more information when you get there.", he added. No "How do you do?" or other greeting, just a flat, stoic directive.

Officer Roy, a pudgy man in his 40's, had blue eyes with a hint of sparkle that indicated he once had a sense humor. He did nothing to introduce his companion and it was evident this rather sober looking man had no intention of introducing himself.

His mirrored glasses reflected her direct glance at him. She could sense no emotion, and felt chilled by his stone-like presence. Thin purplish lips on his somewhat gaunt face made for quite a contrast between the two men. The voice in her head urged her to do as they asked. That in itself was selective, and weird.

Surmising they wouldn't take no for an answer or even give her a chance to freshen up or stall before heading to the NASA Medical Center, she nodded with exasperation and said, "Let's go then."

Officer Roy turned and walked down the corridor, a short distance down a wide blue paisley-carpeted hallway to the elevator. The man in black said nothing, looked directly towards her with those mirrored glasses, and made a waving gesture indicating she needed to go ahead of him. "You go ahead, I'll follow," offered Del, but he frowned, said nothing, and repeated the gesture. Not wanting to rock the boat at this point, she quickly complied and nimbly caught up with Officer Roy.

They were only at the elevator a moment when it opened and all three entered. Thinking she could get more answers from Officer Roy than Mr. Black, she asked if he had heard the president's address.

"Yes," was his direct and non-committal answer.

"Way to go Del!" she chided herself. Even in Counseling 101 they taught you to ask open-ended questions if you really want answers. So, she switched gears and asked the officer what he thought about what had happened.

Instead of revelations, he looked her in the eye and said solemnly, "I am glad we have new friends."

Seeing the glazed over look in his eyes, she knew she was beat for the moment, Del decided passive observation would be her best data gathering tool. In fact, flags were going up telling her to cool it, act like a chameleon, and blend in as best she could.

The trio rode in silence to the first floor, disembarked, and walked briskly to the white, mid-sized patrol car parked directly at the main entrance. Her companions remained very stone faced. They encountered no one during their short exodus in what would normally be a busy complex of residents, especially as they walked through the commons area.

Her building contained many young professionals like herself, a few small families, and, of course, an excellent group of retirees, which meant someone was up and active at all hours.

Officer Roy entered on the driver's side and Mr. Black opened the rear door for Del, waving her roughly inside. She got in and he got in behind her, requiring her to scoot over to the other side.

Upset at this rudeness, she shot a few mental daggers his way although even real daggers probably wouldn't have fazed him. This entire ordeal was seeming more like an arrest or abduction than an escort. *"Perhaps this is an abduction! And here she was just going along for the ride!"* she worried, panic rising.

"Easy, Del," she ordered herself inwardly, and floodgates of fear were held back. *"You won't get info from these two. Nor does it appear you can get away. Let's just play this out for the moment and make nice."* Besides, Officer Roy appeared legit and the car unquestionably belonged to Cocoa Beach's finest.

Mr. Black was a total anomaly and beyond figuring out for the moment since he didn't appear to be much of a talker. Like all patrol cars, the back seat doors could not be opened from the inside. Rather than get anxious about the situation, she accepted what she couldn't change...for the moment.

The ride to the NMC in the Kennedy Space Center was deathly quiet with no radio and no conversation. Del dared not break the silence, again just wanting to observe developments. Of course, the voice kept up its never-ending repetition of calming encouragement.

Watching out the window for the short 15-minute trip, she noticed things were really quiet, with only other police cars and some military vehicles on the road. Pretty eerie in a town as busy as Cocoa Beach should be at this time of year. She absently wondered what the spring breakers were doing under martial law. It was unlikely the snacks and booze would last long before they had to do something.

As they approached the NMC, however, there was a chaotic convergence of police, military, NASA, and emergency vehicles and a hell of a lot going on. Before she could determine what was happening their car jumped a curb and stopped short of the mass of vehicles.

Officer Roy opened the door for Mr. Black who turned and motioned for Del to exit, again having to scoot over to use the same door. Officer Roy said, "Report ASAP to the ER desk for your assignment."

Del started to protest. After all, she wasn't dressed properly for duty, this was her day off, and this wasn't her shift. Once here, though, she knew what her job as one of the top trauma nurses and neonatal specialist was, but felt certain in this state of emergency she'd best see what was specifically needed of her before making any assumptions. At least she'd be getting away from these two, especially creepy Mr. Black.

A little less apprehensive now that she was at familiar work surroundings, Del moved quickly to the ER entrance, taking in the bleak situation that indicated a lot of injuries that needed fast action on everyone's part.

Glancing back she saw Mr. Black continuing to watch her without expression, perhaps making sure she'd go inside. As she turned back to the ER, Mr. Black turned away as well, apparently satisfied with her actions. Stealing a final look before she entered the door, she watched them speed away, probably on some new bizarre errand.

All of a sudden the voice changed from obedience to her chauffeurs to, *"Help these people. Stay calm. Do your duty."* "This is so odd," she said aloud, out of earshot of the busy paramedics and hospital personnel closer to the entrance. There was no question this voice was compelling on many levels of her psyche. Being a health care professional, she would do what the voice asked anyway, but it was amazing how influential the words could be. *"Gotta figure this out when I get a free moment,"* she mused.

Once inside the ER, it was just like a regular shift when an emergency had occurred. Her mind switched instinctively to the focused excitement she had to have when seconds count between life and death, at least to the patient with a laceration needing stitches, or suffering a coronary, stab wound, or a burn.

She moved to the familiar desk and presented herself to the head nurse on duty. "Hey Rachel!" she exclaimed, glad to see a familiar face and a human who *would* talk to her civilly.

Instead of the camaraderie she expected from a confidante and long time drinking buddy, Rachel turned around without any welcoming sign of recognition and said, "Del, you need to prep now for... team 2... to handle multiple burn patients in Trauma Room... E, then F as needed."

If Del hadn't known better, she'd have thought Rachel was a stranger and hooked up to some computer the way she talked so levelly and without emotion. Shock? Drugs? *"Not the Rachel I know,"* concluded Del. Rather than stir the pot, Del felt this would have to wait. Perhaps Rachel had been traumatized by this whole ordeal.

"OK, Rach...I'm on it," Del replied evenly. The strangeness of the encounter needed analysis, but it would have to wait as she went on duty.

Shedding the slippers, washing up, and donning scrub shoes and a yellow smock, Del entered Room E. She had expected burn victims from a fire or accident injuries, but was totally unprepared for someone who was clearly a radiation burn victim who was in shock and fading fast.

"What the hell's going on?" she burst out, but the two attending physicians continued to spew a host of orders which made her forget what she was seeing and just obey the commands. So like a computer herself, she processed the orders into automatic action in order to save the patient. Years of practice allowed her entire body to move in concert with the physician's orders to ensure the rest of the medical orchestra completed this number to the benefit of the patient.

In the end, it was futile, as withering patient after patient died despite their best efforts; first in Room E, then in Room F, and back and forth in a constant procession. Out of 26 people brought in during the first hour she started work, only three were alive 13 exhausting hours later, and those few might not make it another day or so. God knew what was happening in the other rooms. More questions, few answers.

"You'd have thought someone exploded a miniature nuclear bomb or that there was a nuclear accident at one of the power plants with what I'm, seeing," she wondered. It was certainly not something they normally saw at the NASA Medical Center. But the damage was not typical of radiation exposure and surely no atomic explosion had occurred to her knowledge. The burns were mostly on faces, necks, and hands, with the rest of the body under the clothing unharmed and the clothing itself undamaged.

Some of the patients babbled about bright lights, saucers, and such. Many were just hysterical with pain or acted half crazed by what had happened to them, whatever that was. Moreover, she got the impression these were civvies, not NMC types. The only thing that made sense was these poor souls were injured and were being treated; any other attempt to connect the dots failed.

At one point, Brian Richardson, a burley anesthesiologist, never known for an opinion on anything except what the Miami Dolphins should do to win the Superbowl, piped up, "This is a bunch of bull!" and, "President Griffith and this whole invasion is intolerable!" and, "What's with the voices in my head telling me what to do?"

Actually, the wording was a bit more colorful and his tirade more forceful, but the effect was immediate as uncomprehending colleagues stepped back, distancing themselves physically, heads bowed and eyes averted. Suddenly two men in black stepped forward out of nowhere to apprehend Brian. Del could swear that one of the men just touched Brian's neck with a needle like instrument and he slumped immediately as if shot dead.

They carried his large limp form out so fast; she hardly had time to believe it had happened at all or to launch a protest of her own. The voice was now saying, *"Continue your duty. Help these people. Stay calm. Stay focused."* While pressured to do just that, Del was easily able to resist, if she chose to.

Looking around her, however, she could see that everyone else *was* totally influenced because they went back to work as if nothing had happened to their close friend Brian. He might not have existed at all judging by the reaction she witnessed. There was still some small talk, but only about the serious and deadly business at hand. It was like working with a bunch of robots rather than the talkative and amiable people she had known for over six years.

After about 20 hours, the shift ended. Del felt like the walking dead but not just because of the long shift. The cumulative effects of all that had happened since she had awoken had exhausted her physically and mentally. And she was hungry, too! Heading for the nearest snack machine, hoping for a fresh Snickers bar, she ran into Officer Roy.

"Let's go," he said, as if she knew exactly where that was. Not surprisingly, lean Mr. Black was there, too.

Throwing her arms up in surrender she said, "Gotta change, boys," and headed to the locker room without asking their permission. She toyed with the idea of staying in the locker room. *"Would they wait forever outside or come in and get her?"* she wondered. Sighing, she knew the answer and donned her clothes quickly.

A glance in the mirror confirmed she looked like hell. Not caring about her appearance at this point, she exited the changing area. Both men were waiting patiently outside. She then led the way; correctly guessing their car would be right out back.

The ride home was as quiet as the ride in. She noticed several fires off to the west across the bay towards Cocoa and Merritt Island and also heard what sounded like gunfire and explosions near tiny downtown Cocoa Beach as they rode home.

"What's going on out there?" she exclaimed.

"Not your concern ma'am," replied Officer Roy as he shot her a look saying she ought to know better than to ask such a question.

Paying attention to the voice, which she now found, could be tuned into but not totally tuned out, she heard, *"Mind your business. Relax. Do your duty. You are in safe hands."* Mr. Black also looked questioningly at her for many long moments, then appeared satisfied and turned his eerie gaze away to stare straight ahead.

"Yep, just another day at the office for these guys," she realized. Yet she knew this was no ordinary day and whatever was happening wasn't good for those involved, especially her. She felt different, disconnected. She wasn't playing up to script that's for sure, and she instinctively knew it. *"Del, tread lightly. Watch your step,"* she chided herself.

Sandpiper East was a welcome sight. Officer Roy let her out, she thanked both men for their hard work, much to their heavy silence, and walked away into the commons area, not turning back to acknowledge whether they stayed or left.

She entered the elevator, hit the fourth floor button and once the door closed nearly collapsed in relief at having survived this whole day, glad to be away from watchful eyes. As much as her brain demanded analysis and answers, her body demanded food and rest. Except for emergencies, she was typically an early to bed person.

Del's apartment was unchanged. Nothing dramatic had happened in her absence, at least nothing noticeable. All this government takeover stuff made one a little paranoid. She would keep her senses alert.

First thing on the agenda: a couple eggs, toast, and some juice. While cooking, she keyed the kitchen TV and got static. The radio provided nothing coherent either "Had to try anyway," she muttered with exasperation. At least the clocks were working. Whew, 5:12 a.m.!

The hasty meal satisfied her hunger so she quickly showered, a longer and hotter one than she had wanted to take, but it felt so good to linger and try to relax. She was asleep as soon as she hit the bed. No dreams or voices intruded on her much needed respite.

Loud knocking on the door woke her up with a start.

"Doesn't anyone know how to use the doorbell?" she said wearily. She threw on her robe and walked in slow halting zombie like steps to the door. Glancing at a clock, she knew why she still felt tired: 8:40 a.m!

A bit irritated, Del started to open the door, but hesitated and looked through the spy hole. Immediately she grew less irritated and more concerned because it was another policeman standing on her doorstep.

He knocked again as she stood silent deciding what to do. "Ms. Summers, this is Officer Lynch with the Police Department on national business!" he called through the door.

Del recalled Officer Roy had said the same thing.

Tuning in the voice, she heard, *"Trust him. Follow him. Do your duty. Start your day."* Not trusting the voice one bit, Del opened the door to see what the agenda was for this day.

Officer Lynch was older and a lot grayer than Officer Roy, but in fit condition. He wasted no time in saying, "Get dressed. We'll be leaving for the NMC in five minutes."

Del knew better than to protest or ask questions. She motioned him in, but he replied stoically, "I'll wait right here."

Closing the door and shaking her head in dismay and fatigue, she threw on proper work clothes this time and grabbed a food bar as she passed the kitchen. At least she'd have some food if not sleep.

Officer Lynch marched ahead to the elevator and once outside opened the left rear door of the squad car to let her in.

"No Mr. Black today," she mused. *"Wonder why not? Am I being trusted more or is there some shortage of escorts?"* Mr. Black and his look alike buddies gave her the creeps anyway, so she felt grateful for small favors.

Venturing some conversation, Del asked, "What's new in the world today?"

Keeping his eyes on the road ahead Officer Lynch started to open his mouth. Listening to the voice in her own head, Del guessed what he would say and wasn't disappointed when she moved her lips silently to match his words; "You will be briefed when the time is right." While these officers didn't look like clones, they certainly acted and spoke like them.

The deathly silent ride, no music or even cop chatter on the scanner, allowed her to take in the morning surroundings. While she was quick to wake up and shift gears into action, her body was feeling the sleep deficit. "If I can just close my eyes on the way," she yearned.

Just as she was about to get comfortable and grab a few winks she saw a saucer shaped object approaching from the northwest which then passed by quickly out over the ocean towards the south. Her view was obscured as it came between her and the rising sun, and then it was gone.

Incredible that anything could move so fast! Its size was hard to judge not knowing the exact distance, but her guess was it was twice as big as the Goodyear blimp. She'd seen some of the best this country had in military hardware at the air shows in Pensacola and was privy to some secret stuff as well, but this was clearly something extraterrestrial.

"Hey, did you see that?" she barked at Officer Lynch.

Stone faced and staring straight ahead, he replied, "See what ma'am?"

"Might as well have asked the seat cushion," grumbled Del. *"Wow, my first actual encounter with a flying saucer! Finally nice to see some evidence that what the president said was actually true."*

Tuning in the voice brought her these words, *"You've seen nothing. Think of your duty."* She was definitely going to have to figure out how the voice could change so often and be so damned manipulative. *"How could they be so person specific?"* she wondered.

She was wide awake now with the excitement of the flyby, but her enthusiasm diminished like dousing a fire as they approached the NMC. Emergency traffic had lessened to be sure though she could tell a lot was going on.

"Gonna be a busy day," she whispered softly.

The car stopped and she impatiently waited for Officer Lynch to open the door. He started to say something, but she interrupted, "I'll get my assignment at the ER desk. See you later. Thanks for the ride."

She could tell this response confused the officer, but he shrugged and got back in the patrol car. Amused at herself for beating him at his own game, she headed towards the ER like a good little girl.

Once inside, her predictions came true about the busy day. Rachel was at the desk again, making her glad she wasn't the only one with a tiresome schedule.

Looking up from her desk she blandly read Del's assignment, "Team 1.... Rooms A and B, Doctors are prepping now."

"Gee, such warmth makes me really feel needed," she muttered away from the head nurse. Not at all like the fun loving and personable Rachel she had known. Not that any of her other friends showed her any recognizable emotion, good or bad. It was as if personalities had just been switched off. *"Time's a wasting,"* she knew, *"Can't spend moments wondering about personalities. Better scrub quickly."*

Today's casualties were totally different. They included real burns, not radiation burns, and a variety of gunshot wounds of a serious nature but probably not fatal. Del was reminded of the fires and gunshots she heard the previous night and made the connection. Del was no dummy.

Was this civil unrest and vigilante justice or was this some government crackdown? Recalling the president's words and how her escorts of the previous night had ignored the shots, Del opted for the latter.

After assisting with several burn patients in Room B, she entered Room A to assess the next case and was shocked to find Brian Richardson prepping the patient with a general anesthetic.

"Brian, how the hell are you? What happened last night anyway?" Del was dying of curiosity, but in an instant knew she would get no answers.

Brian looked up with blank eyes and said, "I don't understand what you are asking Del. This one will be ready in a minute. Nothing happened last night."

The fire in this mans eyes and soul had definitely been extinguished. Dumbfounded, she walked behind him to get to her equipment table and glancing back at him to confirm it really was Brian she noticed the fresh scar on the back of his neck, as if someone had punctured his skin and performed some minor surgery.

Opening her mouth to ask about it, she quickly shut it again so hard her teeth hurt and sucked in any beginning comments. *"Steady Del. Easy does it."* Observe, listen, ask questions, then act was what her father had taught her. If only she could follow his wisdom without panicking first; it was clear she had a lot of observing to do.

A check on the voice's message produced a repetition of, *"Do your duty. Help these people."* She closed her eyes, turned her head, and willed herself to focus on her duty, wondering if she had any steady grip on reality.

Brian had definitely changed since last night. She glanced furtively at him as she gathered up the instruments she would need for this procedure. It was clear he didn't care. No normal chitchat, no extra motions, just an unswerving focus on his task at hand. There wasn't any music playing either. Brian always had Led Zeppelin going at deafening volume until the docs arrived.

Concentrating on the job at hand was easy with the compelling voice and years of training. The problem was that sometimes you failed to actually notice the patient other than as some mass of flesh being worked on in an assembly line fashion.

Del fancied herself as a bit more caring than most other health care professionals, but with all that had been happening to her these past couple days, she found herself less concerned than normal, especially since she was spending so much energy keeping herself sane. Eventually, though, like the dawning of a new day, her senses came awake, slowly starting to reveal to her that something was not normal about these patients.

What finally struck her was their behavior. No matter how serious the wounds, the patients were too calm. This was highly unusual because in all her years of ER experience, even the toughest of patients cried out a little, and some were down right hysterical or even mean with wounds of the severity she was seeing now. Also, most had already received advance triage before they got to her so while they needed serious treatment, none were in danger of dying.

These inconsistencies nagged at her as the hours went by. When she rolled one teenager over to examine an exit wound on his shoulder, she was startled to see the same mark on his neck as she had seen on the "new" Brian Richardson. Then it hit her like a cold slap in the face: *"These people have been surgically altered!"* Whatever had happened to Brian must have been done with these people too. *"Gotta know more. Gotta have some confirmation! Don't jump to conclusions!"* roared her brain.

She staggered out of the room and surreptitiously examined a few patients in the hall awaiting admission. Each had the same mark! In nearby radiology, she pulled up X-rays of all the patients who had injuries showing the neck region.

Crystal clear on each X-ray was a small, opaque capsule shaped object the size of a BB imbedded in the brainstem of each and every patient. In her short years as a nurse she'd seen thousands of X-rays and there had never been anything like this. The mark on the neck and the capsule in the X-rays could not be coincidence. Some X-rays showed another capsule near the hypothalamus. This could only have been placed through the nose, which would explain some of the nosebleeds she had seen today.

Her deduction was that this capsule or capsules must alter people mentally, perhaps physically as well. *"Between the voice apparently controlling most people like Rachel and the neck surgery dominating those who questioned authority like Brian, things are looking very grim indeed for someone like me,"* surmised Del. "My God!" she muttered in near silence, voice and body shaking with fright, *"What happened to these people? What is happening to us?"*

Nausea swept through her in an instant, weakening her legs and making her swoon in the hallway. Thankfully the women's locker room was just around the corner. She held her hand to her mouth and hugged the wall with her shoulder and head as she moved as fast as possible towards escape and refuge.

The door had barely been pushed open when the nausea hit her full force. No one was in the room to witness the mess, which made Del grateful. She circled around and leaned against the wall, sinking slowly to sit down. Despite feeling sick and fatigued, she had to get a grip on herself so she could face this new discovery.

"Ohmygod, ohmygod," she kept thinking. *"What am I going to do? How can I get through this? These people are changed, probably forever. How am I going to blend in?"*

Rachel burst in, giving Del very little time to gather her thoughts, "Are you OK?" she asked. "I was concerned when I saw you leave the area." Del sensed more suspicion than concern in that voice and knew she had to handle this situation with caution.

Wiping her messy mouth in embarrassment, it was easy to reply, "I'm just not feeling well. Must be the flu or something. Sorry."

Glancing around and observing Del's pallor, Rachel appeared somewhat convinced.

Del added, "Let me clean up and get back to work."

Unthinkable to let a sick person work with patients, she worried Rachel was about to agree, then gladly heard the nurse say, "No. You shouldn't be here. I'll get you an escort home. Let me know when you're ready to go."

Rachel left quickly, leaving Del to lower her head and let out her breath with relief, the taste of vomit and bile lingering horribly in her mouth. *"A stick of gum would be nice,"* she wished. The need to get out of here now was overwhelming. There was too much to comprehend. She had to force herself to breathe, feeling suffocated by her circumstances.

Del's shift ended early after working only nine hours due to "sickness". With what she'd seen, looking and acting sick was no problem. Her brain buzzing and body still not quite recovered, she hardly noticed who escorted her home or anything else about the trip for that matter. She simply stumbled inside, up the elevator, and into her condo. Flopping onto her bed in frustration and fatigue, tears came easily as did an uneasy sleep.

Greg Burke

New World Order

Del awoke that third morning sprawled across her bed, again. Still dressed in yesterday's clothes, she felt stiff, as if she had slept restlessly and on the floor instead of in her very comfortable bed. Her eyes felt puffy and her mouth tasted awful. Then she remembered why.

It wasn't quite dawn judging by the low reddish light tendrils glowing through the window. Squinting through swollen tear dried eyes, the clock read 5:51a.m. Her first inclination was to catch some more winks before the inevitable escort service arrived. Her second inclination was to run away before then. The third, and most practical inclination was to get up and face the day, again trying to make sense out of a living nightmare, meeting the day on her terms.

There was never enough time to sort things out with the rapidly occurring events. Plus, the fact she was swept up in work, not having the luxury of the president's temporary vacation to figure out some clear course of action, didn't help.

After witnessing both physical and psychological alterations to her friends and most other people she had met, one thing was crystal clear: she wanted to remain Adelle Summers in mind, body, and soul and would do whatever it would take to stay that way.

The sheer loneliness and craziness of her situation threatened to overwhelm her, but she fought back her flood of emotions, instead focusing on the dawning of a new day as a dike against madness.

Not knowing how much time she might have before being called to duty, Del decided to do some analysis. A quick check of radio, TV, and computer operations confirmed the national emergency was still on. So much for that.

"How about this voice thing?" she asked out loud as she walked to the kitchen and brewed some fresh coffee. Tuning in, the normal litany of, *"Relax. You have new friends. Everything will work out. Do your duty."* could be heard.

With just a few days of practice, she realized she could ignore these commands altogether, though they always gnawed at her consciousness. The voice gave general and helpful commands, obviously meant to keep order and pacify the listener. But while compelling, she found she could fight it off.

Other people reacted like they were hardwired and had been given a computer command. She felt more like a child given a parental command as the words penetrated to the depths of her brain, but as an adult, she could decide whether or not to obey. The reason why she was different was the real mystery here.

Perhaps, like most natural attributes, there was normal variation, the bell curve, at work here with a few people being very influenced, most people being heavily influenced, and a few people, like herself, being influenced very little.

She never cared much for being like everyone else and was glad for this difference. What scared her about being in the minority was this minority was completely unacceptable, judging by what had happened to Brian and the injured patients.

Was the government orchestrating this whole mess? Or was it "our new friends"? Without taking a poll or interviewing the president directly, Del was certain it was both. That meant she had to keep up some act of normalcy, probably forever, never letting on that she wasn't one of the gang. *"Gee, lucky me,"* she thought sarcastically.

The fresh coffee smelled and tasted good, the hot cup warming her all over and clearing her groggy head. Realizing she wasn't influenced as much as others and that she'd have to keep up an act to survive didn't settle things in the least.

"What kind of life will this be?" she wondered. She thought about the Jews caught in Nazi concentration camps and how many of them hung on to survive against incredible odds, hoping for an end to their horror, but not knowing if that would really happen.

Her situation was analogous, except she was in a golden prison. For the most part, she had the freedom to live her few off duty hours as she chose best and what was asked of her so far was no more than her regular job though for much longer and irregular hours. No, the Jews had had it far, far worse than she could imagine, so certainly she could hang on to some hope and figure out a way to make things better again.

She was about to step out onto the balcony and enjoy the sunrise when she heard the voice pipe up louder than normal with what sounded like a special announcement.

"Wake up. Turn on your TV or radio. Listen carefully," were repeated in a more insistent manner than usual. Indeed, she felt extra pressure inside her head with this message. No doubt everyone would be listening whether they wanted to or not.

Del forced her mind to accept the inevitable bad news from the president or maybe even the aliens themselves. "Rise and shine, world," she said as the golden sun broke over the watery horizon, a sight she never failed to enjoy.

Not wanting to miss anything important like the last time, she immediately keyed the TV. "Stand by for an important presidential address." was on the first 35 channels she scanned and was no doubt on the hundreds of others. Channel 2 was her favorite so she flipped there and waited.

Her coffee was growing cold. Topping it up while she watched the TV out of one eye brought it back to a satisfying temperature. Six long boring minutes passed before President Griffith's impeccable personage filled the screen from the Oval Office. Del sat down to watch, her mind keen and wary this time. In what she figured was a stroke of genius, she had the mental clarity to key the omnirecorder.

"Good morning my friends. Sorry if some of you are getting up earlier than usual. Your patience and understanding these past few days has been greatly appreciated and very necessary. Now it's time for some explanations and answers."

Almost as loud as the president's message was the voice imploring Del to, *"Listen to your president. Do your duty,"* along with the usual, *"All will be better. You have new friends."*

"We have entered a new era on this planet with the coming of the Quazzga. World governments have known about them for some time, although to avoid panic and undue fear, nothing was ever admitted because our knowledge was incomplete, specifically why they were here and what would result from meeting them. Some of you have even met with them in what hopefully was a pleasant experience. With their arrival, however, we now know they are truly our friends and are here to help us in many ways. In fact, I now realize our future is brighter than ever.

"The Quazzga are a very old race, related genetically to us, and far advanced in technology. They have come a great distance, sending their best and brightest to assist us at a time when we really do need them to keep this planet and its people safe and productive. In short, they are here to help us make Earth the paradise it should be for us today and for our children in the future.

"As you might guess, they have traveled through space to accomplish this and will be living among us in remote areas. There are about 5 million of our new friends waiting in orbiting ships and now on our planet. They are choosing uninhabited or rural areas to set up their new homes. You will be meeting many of them in your daily affairs in the near future. Please welcome them, as they are here to help and have only our best interests in mind.

"Naturally, their presence necessitates changes in the way we do business as a nation specifically and world as a whole. I'm confident you will find these changes for the best. Since the beginning of time, people, towns, cities, countries, and alliances have fought each other for a hundred thousand different reasons. Until now, there was little hope we could ever unify as a world and move the human race ahead to greater achievement.

"With the coming of the Quazzga, the world can now be united under one government and in the past 48 hours, the leaders of every nation on this planet, including myself, have taken the unprecedented move of pledging support to a worldwide system of government.

"Many details need to be worked out to make this as smooth a transition as possible, but the Quazzga have assured us that a world government will work and is necessary to our mutual future. Their plan is so simple it makes me wonder why we didn't do it a long time ago.

"One reason is that we weren't looking at the big picture in a global sense. By continuing to foster individual and nationalistic pride we kept everyone on this planet from enjoying what was easily within our reach to accomplish.

"Some specific actions have already been taken to secure our future. The first is the standing down of *all* military forces in *every* country. Nuclear weapons have been disabled by Quazzga technology. Planes have been grounded and ships are returning to port.

"It is time to turn weapons of destruction towards peaceful use and concentrate those resources on more beneficial purposes. Weapons that cannot be turned toward peaceful purposes will be destroyed. We are entering an era of world peace where we need not fear attack from without or within. This is a great victory for mankind. No one has been injured who has followed orders.

"The second step is the creation of a world bank pooling the assets of every country. There will be a unified currency in the near future. We have long tried to balance our budget and erase its deficit. As of this moment, all national and international deficits are eliminated due to the pooling of funds.

"Stock markets will remain closed until funds are liquidated and individual assets are transferred to the new World Bank. I'm not a genius about these matters so the details remain sketchy but you should consider these changes for the better and relax, trusting that unparalleled good will come of this.

"The end goal will be the global restructuring of economies so the standard of living for every human being in every country is raised. No one need go hungry or have to scrape out a living. In addition, by raising the standard of living worldwide, there will be more global productivity. Everyone will have meaningful work, including those now dependent on government support. Handouts for nothing are a thing of the past.

"Current aid packages will be phased out as beneficiaries become employed. The only exceptions will be children and young adults in school, disabled persons, and the elderly who are unable to contribute. These world citizens will need our continued support. With the changes being implemented, we will finally have the resources for all these people.

"The United States of America will continue to exist in name and will play a major role in the new world order, helping people around the globe as we always have, and continuing our leadership in making the world a better place for all people.

"The elements of our Constitution, established by our wise founders, will finally come to fruition as a way of life around the world. We will remain a free people within the limitations of the new world order that keep us from hurting each other and that require each individual and the world at large to be the best it can be.

"Within our country you will see many transformations involving our economic and political structure. There are too many details to go over at this time, but the goal is to make the necessary modifications that will support the new world government and improve all of our lives. Our basic framework will remain unchanged as we engage in life, liberty, and the pursuit of happiness, following the moral framework, which founded this great country. Your elected officials, including myself, will continue to serve you as liaisons and contacts should individuals need anything specific.

"Our multi-party, argumentative system of government, however, is now obsolete. This will be refreshing to many of you, I'm sure. We have new priorities now and will be serving you as well as the greater good.

"Some of you will be changing jobs in the near future as we restructure non-productive industries and businesses in favor of those that serve the greater good and provide the useful products and services of a global economy. Please be understanding and calm during the coming weeks. There will be *more* jobs and *secure* jobs for more people than ever before. In addition, every effort will be made to keep people doing exactly what they are now in the same locations. Be patient. Everyone will have work and training and relocation credits will be issued for the few who need it.

"You will be glad to know martial law is being eased so phones, Internet connections, television, and radio are now in operation. Enjoy, and sorry for the need to restrict these services. Please understand that phones and Internet access may be jammed for a while and expect delays, as no doubt there may be some system overload.

"Many of you have some catching up to do with friends, coworkers, and relatives around the country and world. You will find many format changes on the Internet, TV, and radio that are in the best interest of all our citizens, mainly the elimination of violent, demeaning, pornographic, criminal, and immoral programs as judged by most Americans and our wise new friends the Quazzga. Unfortunately, we must still restrict travel to within 100 yards of your current location unless instructed otherwise by local or national law enforcement officials.

"That's about it for now my fellow citizens. I'll be talking to you this way every few days as more information becomes available. I apologize that I cannot answer your many questions directly.

"I again ask the huge favor of you to trust in my judgment in fulfilling your needs and those of our country as a whole. I also want to reiterate that these changes are absolutely wonderful and will improve our lives immensely. Thank you for your time and continued patience."

Del's fingers keyed the phone instantly. Like a radio call-in contest winner, she wanted to get the jump on everyone else before the lines jammed up. Analysis of the incredible words she just heard would have to wait; her mom came first.

Several days of isolation had been enough. Four impossibly long rings were answered with a congenial, "Hello?"

"Mom, this is Del, how are you?"

Del nearly cried with relief to hear her mother speak, but her relief died as she heard her say nonchalantly, "I'm just fine, Del. So great to hear from you after these past few days of peace and quiet. Isn't what's going on just wonderful? We have new friends and our President is doing a great job handling this. How are things at work?"

Her mother was never as conservative as her dad, but change didn't come easy and she couldn't imagine Mom just accepting aliens among us and a new world order in one fell swoop as just another ordinary day.

"I'm OK, Mom," Del said as calmly as she could, sadly realizing even her mother was under the influence of the voice and she no longer had the same woman to talk with.

Del desperately needed someone to talk to who could help her digest and make sense of recent events. It obviously wasn't going to be her usual and best source. "Work is fine and yes, things appear to be working out for the best," she lied hesitantly.

Her usually astute mother, who could read through and would question any hesitation sign of dissembling, didn't even acknowledge Del's verbal transgression. "Glad for you and glad for the world dear. Are you eating OK?" her mom continued.

Her words had no real warmth, though, confirming Del's suspicions. Usually they could talk for hours and like Del, her mom enjoyed discussions between the lines of news stories, with thoughtful reflection upon what was really happening, not just taking things at face value.

Sadness, frustration, and despair were welling up inside Del and the start of tears was imminent. "I'm eating just fine, Mom," she stammered. "Glad you are happy and that you got some rest."

Her mom didn't even pick up Del's telltale emotions and responded, "Well, thanks for calling. I must get hold of some friends to share the good news. Bye."

She stared unseeing at a picture of her parents made just eight months before he died, a giant 20"x 30" laser etched stone portrait. The abruptly ended phone call was a distant memory. Minutes went by before she could pull herself away. When she did and raised her coffee cup automatically to her mouth, she realized the coffee was as stone cold as the portrait. Setting the cup down slowly, she wiped new tears from her eyes.

"Some new world order!" she shouted and shot her middle finger at the TV and no one in particular. The changes disgusted her. World peace yes, world slavery no! She wished she could throw up everything Griffith said. This really sucked.

There had been no one to talk to at the NMC and now her mother was out of the picture too. She shouldn't have been surprised that even her mother would be influenced, but she was disappointed. She'd hoped being able to resist the voice was a genetic thing. Guess not.

So, dreading the outcome, she made her next call to Alan. They had been dating for the past eight months and had become real close friends, real close. Alan had just about all the attributes she was looking for in a lifetime partner. He was smart, funny, considerate, honest, and made her feel good in so many ways. She had never felt as good about anyone or herself before. He was one who could make someone forget about every high school or college flame. Just thinking about him as she started to make the call made her tingle and brought up memories of his face, smile, smell, and touch.

Del crossed her fingers and hope rose as the line was answered in one ring. "Hello, this is Alan," was the automatic response, which didn't answer the question screaming in her mind.

Hesitantly, but still enthusiastic, she blurted, "Alan, this is Del. Are you OK?"

"Sure am," was his mildly buoyant response that still didn't answer her question. Then he continued, "It's been quiet the past few days which has been a great break from the office, but I'm excited about what has happened and am anxious to help in any way the president wants."

That iced it and another avenue of help was closed. Still hopeful of something, wanting to be sure of her conclusion, she probed, "Alan, how do you feel?"

He answered quickly and she hung on his every word for a possibility. "Del, I'm just dandy. Thanks for your concern. I'm just glad we have new friends. We can all relax. If we get a chance, let's get together for dinner."

"Yeah. Sure. That would be great," she replied slowly, her balloon of hope deflating, "But I've been pretty busy at the NMC. If I get a chance, I'll give you a jingle. Good luck Alan."

His only parting words before hanging up were, "OK. See ya," spoken without warmth or affection.

Sadly, her conclusion about Alan wasn't wrong. He'd been a fighter, but not anymore. He hated Griffith too, which had been about the only bone of contention they had agreed to disagree on. So, Alan was just spouting the party line now like so many other people she had talked to the past few days. *"Damn!"* was the only word her brain could come up with.

Looking closer at the TV, she noted President Griffith was gone, replaced by some ancient looking TV show. It showed a beautiful collie who looked vaguely familiar but she couldn't place the name. Thinking she must have keyed into Family Favorites TV, Del decided to see what else was on.

In 20 minutes, she had the answer and could again only shake her head in disbelief. News, sports, soap operas, music videos, religious shows, and movies were out, as were commentary and public opinion shows. Not a single premium or pay per view movie was available checking the TV log. Comedies, fitness, weather, wildlife, educational, and what she could only interpret as ancient family type shows were available and had filled much of the programming space formerly occupied by shows she could no longer find.

"Damn!" she said aloud and smiled inside at the irony of it all. Certainly there were more important things going on that merited her attention, but even still, she was going to miss the upcoming college basketball tournament. Clearly, censorship was part of the new world order.

It was 8:42 a.m. when her door chimed. Not knowing what to do next or what would happen to her, she had showered and dressed for work, all the while mulling over the unbelievable things she had seen and heard. The chime was welcome because that meant a friend or neighbor instead of the door knocking police from previous days. It was probably the Stephens from next door.

With a hopeful smile, she quickly opened the door. The NMC uniform caught her eye first, then the recognizable face of Dan Bryers, the base shuttle driver for medical staff. Her smiled relaxed a bit as she said, "Hi Dan. Wasn't expecting to see you."

Glancing over his shoulder she confirmed that he was alone. Dan was usually the type to look over a girl's body before addressing her, but all she got were eyes staring directly at hers and, "Time to go, Adelle. Are you OK today? It was reported you went home sick yesterday."

Not being able to feign sickness and avoid another day in the NMC hell because she obviously looked fine, Del gritted her teeth and said tersely, "I'm fine. Let me grab my stuff and we'll get going."

Introductions

Two other NMC staffers were picked up along the way. Like Dan Bryers, both were clearly under voice control, or VC as Del dubbed it. She remembered VC had once been used when referring to North Vietnamese in the Vietnam War, but in this situation, saw no parallels between these VC and the ones in the history books except perhaps Americans had felt the Vietnamese were brainwashed into communism.

At any rate, Del pondered how one could tell the difference between VC, shock, and normalcy given the present situation. While one could never be completely certain with various levels of shock, generally one couldn't perform normal duties and would be very withdrawn. VC people on the other hand, performed regular and detailed tasks and were not withdrawn, just focused. It was like dealing with someone who had nearly died and whose life was now so changed they had new priorities and goals.

Another characteristic of VC people was a dulling of expression and emotion; they adopted a more serious posture. Her mom was the most animated person she had heard in days, but even that conversation was far less emotional, and certainly more abrupt, than it would have been before.

Fakers like her would be hard to spot and the unacceptable danger in revealing herself to a VC person would make any contact risky. A wave of nausea rose as she remembered the altered patients at the NMC from the day before, a yesterday that felt like years before. She swallowed with distaste and calmed herself.

Del felt certain she could tell the difference between VC and a normal person like herself, but that opportunity, if it arose again, would have to be approached slowly and with great caution. One thing she realized was strongly in her favor was having made it this far, through the worst of it she hoped.

Another thing in her favor was that VCs were only superficially suspicious, like the police early on. Once she played along, it was assumed she was VC also. Still it would take constant work on her part not to let her guard down. She couldn't afford to be cute, even just for the fun of it.

So, rather than engage in pointless conversation with her three traveling buddies, she gazed out the window, continuing her inward analysis. Things appeared fairly normal as they traveled north except for the lack of traffic and beachcombers. The hotels appeared empty judging by the paucity of cars in the parking lots. *"What happened to all the tourists that were here?"* she wondered silently. It was another question that would have to go unanswered as they pulled up to the NMC complex. Judging by the emergency traffic, it would be another busy day. She steeled herself inwardly and outwardly to handle whatever came her way.

Once inside, Del checked the duty roster and was at her assignment 40 minutes without being told what to do by Rachel. When she did bump into Rachel, she sensed a suspicious gaze, which then changed to approval as Rachel moved back to the nurses' station.

"I'm fine today, Rachel," she said to the departing form. While never close, Del had enjoyed the friendly, talkative, yet businesslike fellow nurse. Now, she was just businesslike with a Gestapo flair. Del would have to be *very* careful around Rachel.

Today's patients were a repeat of the day before with burns, gunshots, some broken bones, and again chillingly calm victims. Without looking, she could guess they had all been altered. Several cursory and nonchalant examinations confirmed it. It sent chills down her spine and she said a silent prayer for the lost souls.

She dubbed these patients SA, for surgically altered. During the next five hours, she worked without a break, doing her normal excellent job, keeping pace with her VC co-workers. Her external actions echoed the voice that repeated the litany of, *"Do your job. Help these people. Relax."*

One patient, elderly, well dressed, yet looking like he'd slept outside a couple days, arrived unconscious with head trauma and little else. He was Lou Rollins from Tampa according to the chart. While reviewing his X-ray prior to treatment, she noticed the lack of a capsule in his neck. Cynically, she theorized he was probably VC anyway.

He regained consciousness while she was checking his eyes and she instantly knew that was not the case. His dark brown eyes had fire and life in them, even in his dazed state. Big, fine-boned and dirty hands reached up and grabbed her head roughly. He blurted out with dire urgency, "Help me!"

Del stepped back in panic and quickly glanced around the treatment room to see if anyone was watching. It was empty but three of the walls had windows and she could see other doctors and technicians busy outside, for the moment oblivious to this new development. She looked back to the man who was wide-eyed and intent on her. He pleaded rapidly, "I don't want to end up like the others! Miss, you've got to help me. They're killing people who fight this invasion or turning them into zombies! God, you're not one of them are you?"

Realizing she wasn't discovered, but afraid he'd get hysterical and attract attention, she said in a forceful yet reassuring low tones, "Calm down, Mr. Rollins, and be quiet or we're both in trouble. Lay back now and let me examine your injury and you can tell me what's going on while I work."

"Finally," she figured, *"a few answers from the outside."* He relaxed a little, resting his head back on the exam table, and looked at the ceiling, wincing as she cleaned his scratches and cuts. *"This is no street bum,"* she realized, studying his nice clothes, Rolex watch, and many-carat ruby ring.

He looked over, and in a calmer low tone said, "I'm not like the others, you know. I hear the words in my head, but I can choose not to follow the commands. I don't believe the lies we're being told by the words in my head or by the president herself. I tried to avoid trouble the first couple days, but I have to do something!"

His hands started gesturing wildly and his voice was starting to get louder so she held a hand to her lips and his mouth closed before he could say another word, although his urging eyes indicated he had a lot he wanted to say.

Hearing him speak, she would normally have thought him stark raving mad, but Del knew exactly what he was talking about. "You have to stay calm, Mr. Rollins. There is nothing I can do for you right now, but you must relax. Perhaps we can get help together but you have to play along."

"No!" he shouted, nearly spitting at her in anger and throwing her hands away in the process. It was clear he was panicked now. "Let me out of here! We have to fight! I didn't work hard all my life in this great country only to see it go down the tubes to some aliens! You're sounding just like those damn words in my head!"

Wishing he would shut up and thus protect himself from being discovered, Del backed up to close the door and give them a little privacy, her back to her colleagues so they wouldn't see her mouthing calming words to Mr. Rollins, while she frantically searched for a way to help the first normal person she'd seen in days.

He was getting off the table, ignoring his painful injury and the trickle of blood down his sideburns when he froze, looking over her shoulder.

The door burst open shoving her rudely aside. Officer Roy and his companion man in black rushed past to subdue her patient.

Before she could protest, Rollins grabbed a tray full of instruments and flung them across the room. Del ducked and covered her face, but was spared any injury as the tray's contents hit Officer Roy and Mr. Black. Mr. Black deflected the sharp instruments like a ninja and in one lightning fast motion was able to touch Rollins on the neck. He collapsed instantly, dropping like a stone into Mr. Black's arms. Just like Brian Richardson the other day, Del knew what would happen to this poor man. Laying him on the gurney, the two men wheeled the patient out.

Officer Roy said, "Sorry about the trouble, Ms. Summers. We'll handle him from here."

Frustrated, angry, and shocked at losing a chance (perhaps her only chance) to get some answers, Del closed her eyes and leaned against the wall. *"What a lunatic,"* she groused. She wanted to fight and change what had happened more than anyone else, but fighting alone, being discovered, and then getting surgically altered wasn't her idea of the right way.

"Maybe if enough people fought together it would make a difference," she wondered. Of course, this man at least tried where she hadn't even done that. Maybe she was just a coward for blending in. Maybe she was accepting events too easily and in the end wouldn't end up any different from the VC or SA.

Even as such thoughts came into consideration, Del instinctively knew the course she had chosen was the best one for her. She had to know more and buy time and circumstances weren't throwing any great choices her way.

For now, she was neither VC nor SA and would do what she could until a chance came for one person, Adelle Summers, to make a difference, either changing things back to the way they were or at least preserving her mind as her own.

"Such noble and brave thoughts," she mused. Nothing she had seen so far offered any remote hope of changing things back to the way they were, and it appeared it was going to be a constant struggle to maintain her independence. Or sanity, for that matter. But at least she had some control; better than what Mr. Rollins would have in a few short hours.

Around 8:30 p.m., things finally quieted down as the last of the day's patient load was reduced to a couple recent arrivals. She surprised herself that recent events could boil in the background, yet she could just keep working along, one thing at a time. It gave her limited confidence in her chosen course of action.

While completing some paperwork, she felt a sudden rise in tension around her and heard an increase in the urgency of the voice commands. *"Emergency. Help these patients. They are important friends. Do your duty well."* Plus, there was something else: A feeling... Getting closer... A presence... Nothing she'd ever felt before but she was certain of its nearness nonetheless. Looking around, she noticed other staff members were obviously sensing the same thing and were moving towards the emergency room entrance. Del was closest to the door. Something was coming; she could sense it.

The door burst open and three stretchers rushed by her in quick succession. Each patient was a man in black, and incredibly, they could have been brothers they looked so similar, despite the covering respirator masks each wore. Of more importance, however, were the obvious and serious wounds. The first man had a broken arm and leg with chest bleeding. The second had an amputated leg with multiple lacerations on the other leg. The third had multiple chest and abdominal wounds; apparently gunshots. None were moving. Vital signs were in the toilet. These three were circling the drain; they all had to act very fast.

Leaping into motion, everyone filled his or her assigned roles. Del moved to Trauma Room E with the third man. It didn't look good. Removing his clothes showed a shotgun at close range had peppered this fantastically muscled man. The doctors were desperately trying to stem the flow of blood from his upper abdomen. Del matched the stream of orders for drugs and equipment, but this appeared to be a lost cause.

In the initial heat of saving a life, she had forgotten about the presence she had felt approaching, but could ignore it no longer when it came into the hospital and then inside the room to stand right next to her. The voice inside her had never been as loud or compelling, telling everyone in the room, she assumed, to, *"Relax. Do your duty well. Stay calm. Save this man's life."* She couldn't help but stop and stare at this alien being in shock, wonder, and awe, ignoring for a moment where she was and what needed to be done.

It was unequivocally, absolutely, 100% true. For years, people had reported seeing alien life forms. Believers speculated to the nth degree that there must be intelligent life and that visitations were occurring. Unbelievers scoffed and jeered accordingly, offering up their own evidence, as well as the government's evidence, that such a thing just couldn't be. Humanity had generally throughout the ages relegated the whole thing to science fiction nonsense and a trivial matter when compared to the urgent woes needing to be addressed here on Earth.

Everyone had seen or heard about the movies, the stories, and the vivid pictures drawn by abductees. This was exactly the being next to her. Large slanting eyes, long flat face, large head, small thin lips, pointed chin, muscular, no clothes, and bluish smooth yet leathery skin. It wasn't a costume. This was absolutely real and it was happening right beside her. There was nothing that could be said or done in the face of such startling reality thrust fully into the here and now. *"The kooks were right after all,"* was the only coherent thought that came to her. *"What else were they right about?"* came a more lucid and frightening thought.

Ignoring her presence physically and mentally, it brushed past, giving her a cold, tingling sensation. She stepped back to watch what would happen next, fixing her gaze on the large alien head in front of her. Other staff people paused momentarily from their life saving efforts to give the being clearance.

"Continue working while I stop the bleeding," she heard it say, then realized what she had heard was inside her head; nothing had been spoken directly by the alien. What she did hear was a slight chittering noise coming from barely parting lips. The words she heard were directly piped into her brain.

"They are telepaths!" she exclaimed to herself. *"They must be behind the voice messages I've been hearing since the invasion."* How they could broadcast it to everyone was an intriguing mystery.

"I am Quan," interrupted her thoughts, again words just as clear as if she was talking to herself. Holding his five-digited, long-fingered hand over the chest wound, the bleeding stopped immediately and numerous buck shot pellets floated upward to the grasping alien hand. *"Work fast now. I will hold the bleeding while you repair the damage to his body,"* Quan telepathed. *"Soon we will show you improved ways to heal your wounded,"* he went on, or at least she thought it was a he judging by what little she had seen of his front when he passed.

Quan's mental voice was paternal, not necessarily male if that made any sense. The voice she'd been hearing for days was neutral, neither male/female nor paternal/maternal. Quan's voice just felt different: male-like and very calming. She guessed she'd just have to wait to receive thoughts from a female so she could be sure. Anyway, it didn't matter male or female, but it was a curious thought and one she couldn't avoid doing during this first incredible, and mind-numbing, encounter.

The doctors worked quickly: amazingly so. With blood flow stopped and the patient in a form of stasis, judging by the low yet stable vital signs, they could see what they were doing and the patient stabilized in rapid order. Del was in an awkward spot to assist with instruments because Quan was in the way.

She said, *"Excuse me, Quan. Could you move over a little?"* in her mind, but was totally ignored. Saying the same thing out loud got instant results. *"So, they can't read our thoughts!"* she exclaimed internally. With a shudder of relief, Del realized this incredible stroke of luck was vital if she was to keep her little secret among humans and Quazzga.

Quan finally removed his hand; taking the shot pellets with him and releasing his mental hold on the patient's hastily repaired blood vessels. His vital signs remained weak, but it was clear to everyone this man was going to live now, something that would not have been possible without the alien's help. And then Quan left, his mental presence or aura moving away with him as he went to attend the next patient.

Minutes later as they were about to move the stabilized patient to surgery for final suturing and treatment of other minor injuries, the room lights dimmed and electrical instruments fluttered. Then everything went dark, followed almost instantly by a flash of blinding light.

Del raised her hand to shield her tightly closed eyes. She could feel the presence of many aliens around her although she couldn't see them. The intense light gradually dimmed, the presence of all aliens faded, and they were left in the dark again. Seconds later, the lights went back on. Trying to focus with the alternating darkness and blinding light was difficult. When she could again, the first thing that struck her was the patient that had been here moments before was missing.

"Hey, what's going on? Where'd he go?" barked the resident. She could hear shouts down the hall, probably indicating the two other patients were also missing. All those stories of alien abduction that Del and others had laughed at for years as total fantasy reared their ugly heads in her memory. Reality was no laughing matter now.

Those sci-fi nerds and so-called UFO wackos had been right all along. The voice was now saying, *"Thank you for your help until we could get here. Go back to work. Do your duty. Relax. We will take care of these special patients now."*

It dawned on Del that perhaps more people could have been saved if the aliens had such technology to help these dark men. *"Why the miracle work for these guys?"* she wondered. Perhaps they were spread too thin. Perhaps regular humans didn't count. She suspected the latter.

With such amazing theatrics at the end of a grueling day, Del was certain nothing could top what she'd seen so far, and she was right. Everyone was dismissed and Dan Bryers stopped by to say the shuttle van was leaving in five minutes. Incredibly, no one commented further on the encounter with the aliens. It was almost as if nothing had happened just a few minutes after the fact. Del was too wary to bring up the matter. Exhausted and dazed by the day's experiences, it would be a relief to get home.

"Wonder if we'll ever get a day off?" she said to an empty locker room as she tiredly changed her clothes and closed her locker door. Looking in the mirror, she saw a fit, young, woman who looked fatigued and stressed: all true. Sticking out her tongue in defiance, she left the locker.

The ride home was quiet. The van's passengers were a pretty sober group, all being VC. Heck, even a jerk like Dan had been fairly fun to be around in the past. He and Del shared a good sense of humor and a wide repertoire of colorful jokes.

Looking out over the Atlantic, Del could see several groups of bright lights moving in formation and dropping lower as they drew closer. She counted three sets, with about five lighted objects per set. Seeing the speed and acrobatics of the lights, it dawned on her the Quazzga were out and about. *"Busy folks,"* she concluded. The lights split off as they hit the coast just ahead of them, maneuvering northwest towards Kennedy Space Center, west towards Orlando, and southeast towards Miami.

The streetlights flickered with the passing of the sleek craft, and then steadied. It was nothing like the total blackout she remembered from the first night or like what happened at the hospital just a while before.

The group heading towards them was a rainbow of colors that brightened to orange as they got closer and passed overhead. Even the VC were watching and Dan had pulled over for a good view himself. The voice continued its soothing litany although saying nothing about ignoring the sight like it had done the other day. *"Must be getting lax,"* hypothesized Del.

All the craft were the same saucer shape, not too different from the drawings she'd seen or what had been shown on encounter type movies. It was so ironic. What had been false was now true; what had been reality was now just a memory.

The ships were close, although it was hard to judge their proximity not knowing their size. The speed had to be incredible at any rate.

Without a sound, they streaked overhead, changing from orange to silver. Then they were gone.

"Wow!" Del said, then, worried she would bring suspicion, stopped herself from saying anything else. Still, it was exciting to see such a sight, just as it had been the other day.

Surprisingly, the stiff next to her ventured a comment, although it was just the party line as she said, "Yes, our new friends; aren't they wonderful?"

"Uh-huh. Incredible," answered Del slowly, seeing nods of agreement from the others, looking just like the springed dog heads you saw in cars, going slowly up and down.

Leaving the van and entering Sandpiper East, Del could only think, *"Poor devils. They don't even know what they've lost. God, please don't let me end up a VC or SA zombie."* She hadn't gone to Church in years so the spontaneous silent prayer surprised her a little. Then she was reminded of the saying; *"There are no atheists in foxholes."*

Amazing how adversity or even disaster brings religious beliefs to the forefront. With belated regret Del wished she'd kept stronger in her faith. She would need all the help she could get. On the spot, she made a vow to go to church on Sunday. That is, if it was allowed by martial law.

Greg Burke

Fatigue

The next two weeks at work were essentially a hellish repetition of the initial three days. That meant shuttles between home and the NMC every day without a day off, at least 12- to 14-hour, fast-paced shifts, a continued, 'though slightly dwindling stream of trauma patients, keeping up her VC appearance, and a sense she individually and humanity as a whole were losing identity. It also meant surviving more encounters with Quazzga in the emergency room, although thankfully they left these patients in the hospital, all of which were severely wounded SA or VC types. No other men in black were admitted. Apparently, the men in black must be closely linked to the aliens, 'though how and for what purpose Del did not know.

Thinking back to old UFO reports, there had been rumors of men who identified themselves as government agents and generally showed up after UFO sightings, badgering people to keep the stories quiet and collecting pictures or artifacts from witnesses. There was even a movie about them, although she remembered it was a comedy. Her life right now was far from funny.

It just added to the whole mystery and Del could not make heads or tails of it all anyway. She had always been a science fiction buff, but wished she'd paid more attention to the details of UFO encounters. Maybe some detail would help her. Probably it wouldn't.

On her off hours, such as they were, Del found sleeping increasingly difficult, with recurring nightmares about aliens surrounding her and manipulating her life, being discovered as normal by Rachel, and surgical alterations against her will, some so graphic she woke drenched in sweat and couldn't stop shaking for hours. This didn't help her sleep deficit.

There were also the usual nightmares about running away from some unidentified danger in the dark, which kept a hot relentless pursuit while she ran herself to death. Her daytime work made her tired enough, and her dreams, which reflected her daymare world, left her even more exhausted. Unable to sleep, she tried to be productive and figure out some plan of action that would get her through another day, week, month, and hopefully for years to come. It proved frustrating and exhausting as she couldn't come up with any great answers besides getting through each day and hoping things might get better.

So, while work was repetitive and sleep unfriendly, it was her nonworking hours the next couple of weeks that proved to have more surprises. On the fifth day after the invasion, Del was awakened by a heightened voice command around 7a.m. to watch a presidential message. Not wanting to miss out on any news she could use, Del keyed the TV and recorder, propped her pillow against the back of the bed, and with bleary eyes listened to what President Griffith had to say this time.

"My dear friends, thank you again for enduring the hardships that have necessarily been imposed on all of us and thank you for your patience and cooperation during these past five days," began the president. The voice urged Del to, *"Listen to your president. Relax. You have new friends. Change is for the better."* Shrugging off the alien words like a bad dream, she leaned forward and tried to be as alert as possible despite the fatigue imposed by what she'd recently done and seen.

"There is good news today," continued Griffith. "Martial law will be relaxed so you can purchase the necessities of food and toiletries many of you have certainly run low on. Please keep this travel distance to a minimum. You may do this between 6:30 a.m. and 5:30 p.m.: basically sunrise to sunset. Please do not use this opportunity for travel outside of your towns. Commercial traffic has been restored so stores are stocked. Storeowners have been notified to be ready for heavy business. Manufacturing plants were recently reopened and are producing the goods you will need."

The more Del listened, the more questions came to mind. How are they doing this? How can they control so many people so specifically to get all of this done? Why the need to keep us confined at all?

She was glad for the relaxed travel restrictions, although she had been getting most of her food at the NMC during very short breaks with co-workers and wasn't in need of anything in particular aside from fresh vegetables and some milk, both of which she'd needed before the invasion and had thrown out what she had since. Still, it would be good to get out, that is if things were open when she wasn't working. Heck, she lived on one of the most beautiful beaches around and hadn't even been able to take a stroll lately. She stopped her questioning and listened as the Griffith went on.

"You will find most stores opening today and just about everything you have been used to buying will be available. Bars, liquor stores, tobacco shops, candy stores, and entertainment facilities will remain closed nor will related products be available for sale. As most of you will realize, these are no longer necessary for us to be productive world citizens."

Del was not amused. Like the proverbial other shoe dropping, first it was the Quazzga coming and throwing a giant monkey wrench into the whole planet, now things were really hitting home. While she enjoyed a good cigar occasionally and a beer or cocktail on the beach regularly, she knew they were destructive habits, deadly for some. What really bothered her was having these things yanked away, probably forever, without her consent. *"How could we let this happen to us, and what is the ultimate purpose?"* she wondered.

Disgustedly, she realized the VC/SA zombies wouldn't care and would adjust as the voice commanded, but she wasn't fully under that spell. Life was getting more difficult with each passing day. "I suppose we'll all be wearing the same clothes and eating the same food pretty soon," she said sarcastically to Griffith, a person she once admired greatly but had grown to despise in just a few short days. "Will the word fun be removed from the dictionaries soon?" she added in frustration, realizing it already had been.

Griffith continued to speak, of course, oblivious to Del's concerns or questions. "...cooperation. We have unfortunately had to deal with subversive citizens who have disobeyed martial law, damaged property, hurt other citizens, and even caused harm to the Quazzga. This is the main reason martial law has continued. So, in the interest of all of us who want our lives to resume, your help is needed. If you see anyone acting suspicious or not obeying martial law restrictions, please call 911 and notify the authorities of your concern. The sooner all of you good people are safe, the sooner we can lift martial law permanently and get on with making this wonderful new world the best it can be. In the meantime, thank you again for your patience and cooperation."

The thumbscrews on her act were getting tighter. Besides having to maintain appearances at work, she'd have to do it in public. Panic quickly rose to the surface and made her almost feel like giving up and submitting herself for judgment. That wasn't the daughter her parents raised, though, and if things kept getting tough, Adelle Summers would just have to get tougher. An internal battle of hope and fear, strength and weakness, panic and resolve continued. So far, hope was ahead, but not the favorite to win.

Luckily, being sort of a recluse would make people less suspicious of her private life actions. She greeted neighbors and people on the street in kind, even extolling the virtues of all that was happening if pressed. It almost made her vomit. At home alone, she continued to press for answers, 'though none came and she often cried her sleepy self into a restless nightmare filled sleep.

Aside from numbing fatigue, Del hadn't suffered physically. Unlike her friends who had died in the World Trade Center bombing and subsequent terrorist attacks at several nuclear power plants and the random bombings that still occurred in the U.S. and around the world, Del had escaped those disasters intact, physically. But like those early days of the War on Terror, emotionally she was a wreck. Her dogged determination to live her life as fully as possible then, gave her strength now as well. Still, she was running on batteries and didn't feel especially capable.

Just before work the next couple days, there were more presidential addresses discussing the new world economy. Hating President Griffith more and more with each speech, Del paid attention nonetheless so as not to miss anything that might prove useful in continuing her charade.

She had re-listened to the tapes of previous broadcasts, and found with each address there was less mention of America and more about the world as a whole. Del cherished individuality for herself and the uniqueness of her country in particular. Both were being wiped away, nearly as quickly as the delete command on a keyboard. A permanent and insidious lack of freedom was becoming evident.

There was not much mention of how citizens would be governed except by a benevolent VC (or even SA!) president and Congress. What was most apparent when all the speeches were taken together was that the president was becoming someone else. Whether through her own volition or not, she was becoming an automaton.

Very little of President Griffith's usual empathy and caring was apparent anymore. She might as well have been the local news anchor, the ones who can switch from a heart warming human-interest story to an execution to the weather with a smile and act as if nothing has happened of any real importance. Worst of all, in the past such speeches would have been ripped to shreds by the media. Now there was no analysis or commentary, and Griffith could recite nursery rhymes or order everyone to stand on their heads for all it mattered.

Griffith's news about the new world bank and how people would handle their finances turned out to be a lot more complex than even a math brain like Del would have expected. Numerous graphs and short explanations by economic gurus didn't really help. In the end, Griffith simply said, "You will continue to be paid on a regular basis on essentially the same pay scale as you are now. You now have access to all your bank funds and assets."

"Yeah, sure, you make me warm all over," Del groused. "What a crock!" she exclaimed for the hundredth time to a living room that never replied. Well, at least none of her checks had bounced, but then again she hadn't spent much. The bank was a couple miles away and that was too far to risk checking up on funds. The bank wasn't answering phone calls yet and a computer search wasn't available either. One more thing she couldn't do anything about for the time being. E-mail was up and running, 'though no one had sent her messages and she wasn't about to open up her life on circuits that could be monitored, so she avoided that avenue.

Yesterday, she got up from another restless sleep and decided to sit on the beach and watch a sunrise, even though she needed the sleep and actually didn't have to leave for work until 9:40 a.m. The voice gave no indication of a presidential address that morning and simply continued with its sedating and compliant messages, *"Sleep well. Relax. Obey your leaders."* Besides, it was nearly 6:30 a.m. so she wouldn't be breaking curfew. She could have watched from the safety of her balcony, but tired as she was Del felt the need for a closer experience.

Slipping on sweatpants, an oversized T-shirt, and sandals, she filled her thermos with fresh, hot coffee and made her way to the beach, not seeing or hearing a soul in the entire complex. It was just she and the petulant seagulls this morning, judging by the shrill squawks emanating from the beach as she approached the rear entrance.

The chill, fresh salty air hit her as soon as she stepped into the open corridor leading to the back of the building. Passing the heated pool, she made her way to the steps that led down to the beach, noticing the sky starting to lighten as sunrise approached. Looking up and down the beach, she could see no one. It heightened her senses, making her feel more alive, and more isolated than ever.

Such total solitude had never been experienced by Del on this or any beach for that matter. She had always fantasized about having her own private island with a white sandy beach to frolic on as she wished, and for a moment she imagined it had come true. Cocoa Beach was rarely empty, at any hour of the day. And even though it wasn't a white sandy beach, it would do for her fantasizing purpose.

She walked down the steep dry part of the beach all the way to the low tide shoreline. The tiny coquina shell fragments and sand which made up this beach crunched beneath her sandals, quieting as she reached the harder packed wet area close to the waves. The sky continued to lighten as she removed her sandals and tiptoed into the frigid inches of water that rushed shoreward from broken waves.

It was always a marvelous sensation to stand still and feel the water first rush over her feet shoreward, then pull back toward the ocean as the sand under her feet was dredged away and she sank slightly. Stepping back towards dry sand, Del sat down to watch the fast approaching sunrise.

The beach was cold where she sat but felt good to the touch as handfuls were grabbed and lazily allowed to sift through her fingers back to the ground. The wind was relatively calm and aside from a slight fishy smell, the air was crisp and clean.

Del never tired of the colors that came with each sunrise. It was like a renewal that cleansed away the past and ushered in a new beginning. She could only hope. It was cloudless this morning so the blue lightened to a red hue, which turned to bright orange then golden yellow as the sun peeked over the horizon. She smiled inwardly, and then managed a fatigued smile outwardly. It was hard to be a pessimist in the face of such grandeur. And no matter where she had traveled, sunrises from a beach were beyond compare. Her reverie deepened.

"Don't move or talk or you're dead, lady," came a deep throaty voice with warm fetid breath from behind her. Del froze instantly and tensed as something hard and cold poked her shoulder. It had to be a gun barrel judging by the dullness of the feel and given how hard he was pushing it into her.

A jumble of thoughts coursed through her all at once: *"Why me? Why didn't I hear him? What does he want?"*

Cold hands lifted her hair and felt at the back of her neck as she felt him kneel close in behind her. "Good, you ain't been fixed. Chippies give me the creeps."

Instantly she realized he'd been checking to see if she was an SA. "Wh... what do you want?" she asked shakily in reply.

"I'll do the talking, if you don't mind. What are you doing out here and where do you live?" he asked in a demanding and urgent tone.

"I... I... was just watching the sunrise and I live nearby," she responded fearfully.

The gun barrel jammed harder and his anger was tangible as the voice rose to say, "You've got five seconds to tell me exactly where, so stop screwing around!"

"4201 behind us," was her terse reply.

"That's better now. Let's go there quickly, you and me, just like good friends. No fast moves, no tricks, no talking, no alarms, no running, and relax or you'll be dead in a heartbeat. It matters little to me at this point."

There was no mistaking his seriousness, and despite nerves frazzled to the point of breaking, she braced herself and turned around slowly saying, "OK. I'll...do as you say."

Years of karate lessons and self-defense courses had taught her to know when she was beaten. It's more important to survive a few more minutes than to pull a stupid move that might get you killed. Waiting for an opportunity to overcome your opponent was far better than a rash action.

She could feel him relax, and upon seeing his face, was shocked to see how haggard he looked. Heavyset, about 6'0, he had the look and smell of a person who had slept little and seen a lot of no-good. He was unshaven, with torn and dirty clothes, and the dark, wild-eyed look of someone on the run from trouble.

She looked directly at him for a few seconds, trying to figure out what had happened to him or what was going on behind those dark eyes, then averted her eyes towards the sand, afraid of what he might do, especially to someone with a little fight or impertinence in her. He was clearly a frustrated and dangerous person. Immediately she sensed suspicion and she could feel him staring at her more closely.

"Hey, you ain't like the rest, are you?" he said, and then added before she could answer, "You can resist can't you? I can see it in your eyes."

Looking back at him, she could see hope rise in him even as a glimmer of it occurred in her as well. "We'd better go inside. This is no place to talk," she offered hesitantly.

They got up as one, leaving her coffee thermos behind. He put his right arm with the gun high on the center of her back and grabbed her left hand firmly in his left hand and they walked close together slowly towards the condominium as if they were friends.

Her knees weak with fear and eyes tearing slightly due to the sea breeze and the craziness of one thing being heaped on top of her after another, they reached the steps where she ventured a hesitant whisper, "What's going on out there? What's happening to everyone?"

She glanced his way and he was already staring at her, a small crooked smile forming on his war-torn and disheveled face as he said, "I knew you weren't one of them. No one like them watches things like sunrises any more."

He continued, "My wife, my kids, my best friends are robots or have been taken away to return as robots. It's God awful, lady. It's God-awful. Hell, they reported me in for asking questions and actin' suspicious, so I split two days before. Damn robots are everywhere. Haven't slept a wink. Didn't much sleep since they came. Crazy aliens. Stupid of me to think I could help. Damn voices..."

His voice faded and he stopped walking. He appeared to be studying the foot wash shower, but was just staring at nothing, in a trance-like state, obviously replaying private memories like she had been doing so often. He suddenly held her tighter, snapped back to the present, and added, "None of your business anyway. Nothin' against you. I'm on my own now, so let's keep walking. Help me and you'll live a while longer," he went on.

"I.... need your help too, sir. Perhaps we can help each other," replied Del.

The rising sun was warming her back as they reached the corridor leading to the open lobby door. He turned his head towards her with a questioning look on his face, which seemed to ask, "Are you for real?" and grasped her tighter. She could feel the tenseness of his arm in her back as the pressure of the gun muzzle increased. He shifted his gaze forward to secure their way into the lobby just as the back of his head exploded followed an instant later by a gunshot sound.

Del recoiled instinctively and shut her eyes from the horror, but it was like moving in slow motion, watching him fall away from her in a spurting heap as her eyes tried to close and she threw herself away and onto the concrete corridor. Too late to do anything about it and impossible to erase the memory.

She jumped to her feet in panic and pressed back against the wall as several uniformed men rushed through the lobby door (it was usually closed, but now she knew why it had been propped open) and from around the corner on the beach side of the hallway.

"Stay right there ma'am!" shouted the lead man who quickly realized her captor was dead and added, "It's OK, now. Relax. He's a goner." He got between her and the dead man and asked "You OK? Are you hurt anywhere?"

Anger welled up inside her and she wanted to slap him hard. But so did frustration, fear, agony, and pity, so she slumped down on her haunches, noting she was splattered with blood and said, "Yeah.... uh.... fine."

Other officers gathered and she could hear sirens closing in. The lead man said, "You were lucky ma'am. This man was dangerous and has killed several people the past couple days."

She looked down at the mutilated and lifeless body wishing someone would cover it up and replied, "Th.. Thanks.... I was scared."

The officer continued, "Good thing one of your neighbors spotted him on the beach or no telling what would have happened. He's dead, now, so calm down. You're safe."

"Yeah, no telling what would have happened," she replied and turned away. Del closed her eyes and took a couple stabilizing breaths. Opening them slowly, she asked, "Can I go now? I'm a mess."

"Just one question," a man to her left said and she jerked her head up to see the face that belonged to the solemn but commanding voice. A man in black, someone she hadn't seen yet, asked, "What did he tell you?" His eyes and voice probed her for the truth, a truth she dared not disclose about herself, but it wouldn't matter what she told about the person they had snuffed out.

Wondering just how many of these men in black existed, she took another deep breath and told him what happened, looking him in the eye in as calm and convincing a manner as she could muster, saying this stranger with a gun had caught her alone on the beach and wanted her to take him inside, but it didn't get that far, and no, he didn't tell her anything except he was tired and needed her to help him or he would kill her.

The MIB listened intently, and then asked in a suspicious tone, "Why were you on the beach?"

Her heart skipped a beat, eyes flickered momentarily, and a couple seconds passed before she could gather her wits and answer. "I couldn't sleep and wandered out on the beach to get some fresh air and relax. Work has been hard lately," she replied as evenly as possible.

Then she quickly added, "I know I should have stayed inside although curfew was over. It was wrong to do such a thing and put myself in any danger. It won't happen again. I thought we were safe from such people with all the great new things that have occurred." The last comment appeared to ice it for him and he backed away physically and psychologically.

After what felt like forever but was just a few seconds, he said, "You can go now."

The next thing she recalled was taking a long hot shower, practically to remove the blood and mentally to wash away her anguish. The former was easy, the latter didn't happen. She just stood facing the spray with her head down, letting the near scalding water run through her hair and on the back of her neck. She stared at the black and white tiled floor, watching the water splash from her hair to the floor in an endless stream.

Only when the water finally started to turn tepid did she move. It had become so foggy she could hardly see the floor. The air was warm and the humidity comforting so she just sat down on the heated shower floor, wiping water droplets away like tears off her face, arms, chest, and thighs, resting her head back against the wall, breathing in the hot, moist, air, thinking again about her situation and the lack of any resolution. The only feeling she had was the tingling of her scalp and shoulders from the water barrage.

"That was a close one," echoed over and over in her head, *"Too close!"* It felt like a living hell was being thrown her way. The usual, *"Why me? What did I do to deserve this?"* junk was always the first thing to pop into her head. She knew that was "stinkin-thinkin" and those were the first thoughts that would lead a person down a murky path to despair and eventual mental breakdown.

Why the worst thing always came into one's head was a mystery to her, just as this new world was a mystery. As the saying went, shit does just happen, and that certainly fit her recent life. She knew there was no cosmic force doing this just to make her specific life miserable; it was the hand of cards being dealt at this time in human existence. She also knew it wasn't just her. Everyone was having to cope and many were worse off than her, even if they didn't know it due to their newfound allegiance to the voice.

That poor man she didn't even know, whose brains got splattered on the back steps of Sandpiper East, certainly had it worse, even if he didn't care anymore. Mulling it all over, she came back to the same conclusions: Fighting alone and probably even in groups wasn't the answer, she didn't want to kill herself, she didn't want to turn herself in and become a zombie, she'd have to keep biding her time and play along.

"Yeah...just play along...," she mulled. Del hated people who faked their way through life, doing whatever it took to make everyone they met happy, which, of course, made them brown-nosers and actually had the opposite effect to what they intended. Compromise to make the best of a situation was often necessary, but forsaking principles was another matter.

"Is that what I am? A faker, a brown-noser? Compromising my principles?" She held her breath for what felt like minutes, repeating the question slowly, over and over, willing her neurons to produce a credible answer. With a long overdue exhaling breath came the answer: *"No."* Explanations were not forthcoming, just a simple no. It would have to do. She would have to trust her unsteady actions so far.

She shivered and goose bumps popped up all over her body, both at the gradual cooling of the shower air and the gravity of what she'd have to face if things got worse for her, which was almost a certainty. *"What would Dad do?"* Del mused. In an instant, she knew he'd fight and lose his life or mind. "Glad you're not here, Dad," she said as she calmly rose and grabbed a towel.

She would not have wanted to be around to see her father fail, 'though admittedly, if push came to shove, fighting would be better than surrender. Her mother hadn't called since they last spoke. That was for the better because she couldn't stomach the conversation. At least Mom was alive and perhaps there was a dim hope that perhaps they could someday have a normal conversation again.

She needed someone. Someone to talk to. Someone like herself. She was feeling very alone and lonely. Her need for someone to talk to and commiserate with was going unfulfilled. The physical and psychological void was growing.

Drained mentally from her ordeal and physically from lack of sleep and the hot shower, Del's only choice was to drag her heavy feet slowly to the bedroom and crawl under the covers. Her eyes had barely closed when immediate REM sleep engaged and she dreamed of being locked in her condo with the man from the beach, unable to get help or answer the phone which kept ringing over and over, uncertain help just out of reach.

It was like pulling herself out of quicksand to shake off this cloying dream as her consciousness realized the ringing was not a dream. She pried open one eye to check the time, hoping to get a few extra winks. The clock was reading 9:40 a.m; the alarm had been ringing for 30 minutes! *"Damn, I'm going to be late for my ride!"*

Getting out of the very warm and comfortable bed proved difficult and she found her movements woefully sluggish and her brain in a dense fog. She shook off the fatigue like throwing off a wet wool overcoat, stumbled out of her bed and hastily dressed, expecting the doorbell to chime any second. It did, just as she was fastening her bra. She quickly yelled from her room, "Just a minute! I'll be right there! I overslept!"

Passing by bloody clothes strewn on the floor brought back a flood of emotion that only her will and haste to answer the door managed to stem. That man had been murdered just over two hours before. This day was not starting as she had planned. Her resolve to co-exist in her new world was challenged each and every minute without respite.

Dan was waiting patiently outside as Del exited the condo. "I heard some guy was killed here a little bit ago. Is that true?" he asked.

"Yeah, it happened," she answered flatly. "Let's go."

His further queries were answered with a shrug or shake of her head, so he finally quit. Del just stared blankly out the window during the trip to work, feeling numb and cold.

* * * * *

That was yesterday's child, 'though, as fresh tears formed on her face, adding to the salty white streaks from earlier, blurring her view of the dark and deserted beach below. She had been sitting on the cool and windy balcony for over an hour, musing about the past two weeks. It wasn't a senseless act, but a catharsis, 'though each review didn't come up with any great new decisions, just verified the ones she'd already made. She wrapped her robe even tighter and continued to stare at wave after wave approaching and cresting on the beach with the rising tide.

Yes, she had made it through the long yesterday, completing her 12-hour shift not too long ago, somehow remaining stoic and efficient through it all, despite a fatigue she could not quench with any meaningful sleep. Blood stained clothes had been thrown away, events put into their deep mental cubicle.

Brain dead would better describe how she was making it mentally, going through the motions of her well practiced profession. Physically, her body was living off reserves she didn't know existed. Del knew her weight was down, something she ordinarily wouldn't mind, but felt she had better correct that and keep up her strength if her uncertain future as one of the girls was going to work.

So she went into the pleasantly warm kitchen, whipped up a three-egg ham and cheese omelet with some toast and a tall glass of warm milk she'd grabbed at the NMC. Recent events hung like a dark cloud over her head. She was beginning to feel like the Edgar Allen Poe victim who was sealed into a tomb, brick by brick, watching her old world being sealed away from her, vanishing bit by bit.

The more she thought about it, though, in actuality the brick wall had been placed up in one piece. Her old world was gone, and if she was going to escape the tomb, she'd better find some answers or end up a goner anyway. Still, she couldn't displace the dark cloud, 'though the good food helped one aspect of her needs and the cloud kept her sharp and thinking even if there was a twinge of insanity tugging at her as well.

The late night breakfast tasted exquisite. Del left the dishes for morning and trudged to the couch, gave a little jump and flopped face down just for the fun of it. The soft cushions easily took her weight and wrapped her in. She pulled the pillow closer to snuggle and closed her eyes to enjoy the moment. An instant later her alarm went off in the bedroom.

"What the?" cried her brain as she awoke from a dreamless and seemingly non-existent sleep. Her eyes opened quickly and she was able to rise without the bone weary fatigue of days past. While gazing at the closest clock, which read 9:10 a.m., she realized some much-needed nightmare free sleep had finally been achieved. And it did feel good!

Light was streaming in from a brilliant sun climbing warmly up a cloudless sky. Nothing new from the voice Del realized. She set the coffee brewing and went through her 30-minute morning routine that had her ready to leave from the time she woke until the chime at the door.

The knock came in 20 minutes though while she was drying her hair, sipping coffee, and eating a bagel, interrupting her carefully orchestrated schedule. Wondering why he didn't chime today she yelled from the bathroom, "Dan, you're early! Give me another five minutes!"

The knock came again, louder and more insistent.

Becoming irritated, she shouted, "What is it Dan? Give me five will you?"

Del froze when the answer came not from Dan, but from another male voice that was vaguely familiar, "Open up Ms. Summers. We need to talk to you!"

Kid Stuff

Sacramento, California was a great place to live if you didn't mind flatland living. The air was relatively clean. Crime was relatively low, especially in the burbs. Donner Pass in the Sierras and beautiful Lake Tahoe were only a few hours away to the northeast. San Francisco was only a couple hours to the southwest. The wine and fruit country was all around north and south; Yosemite National Park was several hours southeast. While dry and unproductive itself, the capital of California had some great sport teams on the outskirts and lots of neat tourist stops in the Old Town section like the National Train Museum.

Sacramento was also the home of one very scared and alone little 12-year-old boy named Eric Gomez. He didn't have friends or parents, and didn't care to meet anyone else as he stared into his small fire, 60 miles northwest of Sacramento in the woods near Gold Run, not too far off I-80. The sound of traffic was minimal, mostly occasional trucks. He'd normally be like thousands of others clogging roads this time of year to go skiing at Squaw Valley or Tahoe if it hadn't been for those stupid aliens.

Thankfully, those men dressed in black, his teachers, his parents, and the ETs couldn't reach him here, or find him. He hoped they couldn't, at least. Maybe he was nothing to them.

He couldn't figure out what he'd done wrong to deserve the past few weeks. He worked hard to do well at school and please his mother and father so they'd let him play the latest vid games, even those with thousands of players on the Web. They would let him stay up a little late sometimes, and keep on playing with his soccer friends.

He knew what had happened, he just didn't know why it had to have happened. It really messed up his life. He didn't want to be out here alone, but he had no choice. His thoughts recalled recent events as he stared into the low fire.

* * * *

He woke up and his head hurt. A lot. It was weeks before. The alarm went off, but he had to shield his eyes from the light instead of stumble around in the darkness. The multiplayer-alarm flashed 3:20 a.m., but Eric knew that couldn't be right. Dressing slowly and then heading down towards the kitchen, he couldn't believe his eyes when he saw his parents watching TV, bug eyes glued to the 7'x7'screen, neither one moving.

He wasn't close enough to make out what program they were watching, but he was distantly aware of someone speaking to him, though he didn't know from where. He kept hearing, *"Relax. You have new friends,"* and stuff like that, but he was hearing it in his head, not his ears. The words were as clear as his own thoughts, just not as loud-a mere whisper.

In trying to concentrate on his parents and what they were watching, Eric found the words in his head all but disappeared. *"Cool,"* he thought, *"They were dumb words anyway."* "Mom, Dad, what new friends?" he asked from behind the couch.

Both of them turned and stared at him as if they didn't know him. Then his mom said slowly and as if she was in a daze, "Oh son, the president is telling us about new friends, ...from outer space, ...The Quazzga."

Eric's parents were moody, so he knew when to lay low. He was skilled at getting along with everyone from school bullies to adults of all ages. This situation was very creepy and made him pause before asking anything else. It was one of those times when he needed to observe rather than discuss.

He just nodded his head, dark brown eyes watching the TV from behind the couch. Even his urge to change channels or put up four or five smaller pictures of other channels was curbed severely by the strangeness of his parents.

He watched, listened, studied his parents, and then watched some more. Eric didn't like what he saw and heard. He hated the next few days of hanging around the house, hearing police sirens, being trapped, nothing showing on TV or the Web, and his parents just going through household motions like nothing had happened. He threw his ETII toy under the bed, after tearing it to pieces.

He figured it would be great to meet people from space, figured they'd show us their ships, give us some neat technology, share some stories, and we'd share our planet, just like they showed on TV. Most kids thought it would never happen, or that it would be a *Star Wars*-type adventure with all kinds of crazy aliens showing up. Instead, the Quazzga were boring and had taken a lot of fun out of his life.

It was also very boring being cooped up in the neighborhood. His friends didn't want to play much, and even rowdy Brian acted like he was drugged. When they talked, it was about nothing in particular or about the aliens; Eric might as well have been talking to himself. And if that wasn't bad enough, at one point, Brian suggested Eric was acting weird. This made him quiet, cautious, and suspicious of everyone.

Sure, the near-silent words in his head kept repeating things like, *"Be calm. Relax. You have new friends,"* and maybe that was affecting everyone but him. He actually had to concentrate to catch the words. It made no sense. This whole situation creeped him out.

Then came the day to go to school and things got worse. He quickly realized just about everyone was acting like a robot, especially the teachers. It made him even quieter and more reluctant to bring attention to himself. He wanted to lay low and see what developed.

When an alien showed up at their school, everyone went crazy with admiration and interest. It was like show and tell. The Quazzga didn't wear any (or at least very few) clothes, in stark contrast to the guy wearing all black clothes, acting like a bodyguard. The alien even talked to them, like the faint words in his head, but this time clearer and louder. Eric felt insignificant in the eyes of the newcomer, and even more wary.

Recesses had been canceled so they could spend more time learning. They were told that with their new friends here, children needed to learn even more so they could help the Quazzga. When one kid complained, he was pulled out of the classroom for the day. Fewer kids complained in his class after that.

Lisa, for example just started to cry during that first week. She got pulled out also. In a couple days, each of those students returned as if nothing had happened. Eric could tell, though, they suddenly were even more restrained than ever, more like the teachers, his parents, and the rest of the robots. He had heard of drugs used to control unruly kids, but those never worked like what he was seeing here. School was no fun at all.

What really freaked him out was seeing his normally active Web-pal and close friend Marshall return after a couple days acting like he was sleepwalking. Eric cornered him quietly and asked what had happened to him.

Marshall just said, "I dunno what you mean," and turned away.

Then Eric saw the small mark on the back of Marshall's neck.

"Marsh, what happened to your neck?" he exclaimed, knowing it wasn't there before because Marshall sat in front of him most classes.

He touched the rough area, which felt like something was underneath, and it made him shiver with disgust.

"I dunno, Eric," he said absently, and reached back to feel himself, then stared at nothing, dropped his hands, and walked off.

Eric sneaked up on the other kids who had been gone for a day or two and saw the same mark. Five out of a class of 24. No one appeared to care, least of all the teacher. He suddenly got scared, very scared. For all he knew, he could end up being number six because he felt a lot more like the five kids who had complained than the remaining 18.

It took a couple days to get what he needed from the garage up to his room in careful increments so as not to arouse suspicion. Being an only child, he'd had it pretty good. One of the many activities they enjoyed as a family was backcountry camping. He pulled together as much gear as he felt he could carry, and shortly after midnight he made his getaway, heading northeast to the mountains. There was nothing for him here at home.

Eric slept by day, hidden not too far from the highway in whatever cover he could find, preferably wooded areas or parks no one was using any more. He hiked after dark, again staying away from, but paralleling, Interstate 80. There was no great hurry, but his plan was to get to the mountains, find an abandoned cabin, and hide out. He'd heard stories of some houses that stayed vacant for years, their owners traveling or staying in warmer climates. The more remote the better. He knew if he stayed with his parents, former classmates, and near that school, he'd end up a robot. This 12 year old didn't know everything, and his plan was far from complete, but he knew he had to get away as far and as long as he could. Maybe he'd find someone who could help him, 'though probably not.

Now and then, he saw fast bursts of light across the sky and even once saw a huge dome-shaped ship land near the abandoned military base not too far from his house. It was absolutely huge! Eric moved away a little faster that night.

He'd taken over $400 with him, which was all he had from Christmas, birthday, and good grades money. The rest of his summer work money was in the bank and couldn't be touched. It allowed him to buy food at the small gas stations along the way he dared approach in the evening, his backpack and supplies hidden nearby. He entered each one as if he knew what he was doing; although he was surprised each was out of candy and sodas. He liked Power Bars and the sport drinks anyway, which was good since there wasn't much of a choice. Still, a good Reese's Cup once in a while would have been nice.

His uncertain journey continued with his slow march to the mountains. It got colder each night and a couple times it snowed so he had to risk fires to stay warm. He missed his family, but knew he couldn't go back. No one looked for him from what he could tell. There was no sign of pursuit or searches. He had hung around some stores to watch for TV broadcasts about him. There was nothing. It appeared no one cared about a kid who showed up missing these days.

Now and then, he cried for reasons he didn't quite understand. He knew he was very lonely and hurt by what had happened, but it was more than that. The tears just came, unbidden, and like a rain shower would just continue until the clouds were empty. He felt emptied, but better each time. These were not happy days.

Eric was determined to keep going. There had to be a place he could stay and never be discovered. One small source of strength was his journey reminded him of the Hardy Boys books he read and how resourceful they could be in rough circumstances. Although he was small for his age, his thoughts were big. He fancied himself in a dozen roles, including a hunter, an Army Ranger, Indiana Jones, Tarzan, and a secret agent.

When food got scarce, as the gas stations grew further apart he resorted to raiding houses. With people acting like robots, it was easy to slip into a house, get what he needed, and head out before anyone was wiser. He'd have left money to pay, but didn't want to draw attention to himself too much; it was risky enough entering homes to snatch food.

* * * * *

Thinking about the prior weeks made him sad, but helped him make sense of why he was out here and gave him strength to keep going. Staring at the now dying fire, glowing just enough to warm his face, he wished he had a friend he could trust, just one person at least. He doused the fire and curled up for another night's cold and lonely sleep.

Greg Burke

That's Entertainment!

Fifty miles west of the Kennedy Space Center, Jackson Leigh was deep in the tunnels of a tourist-free but far from empty Walt Disney World. His electric cart hummed along, the back filled with an awesomely expensive array of specialized electronic equipment and top of the line power/hand tools that could fix/alter just about anything in the park.

The theme park designers had done a wonderful job of making even the most complex part of the operation from animatronic robots to food processors so simple that an expert like Jax, as he preferred being called, could work wonders on each and every piece of equipment in the park.

He was part of a highly skilled maintenance team they called the plumbers who went to work when anything got a glitch and handled over a hundred ongoing design improvement projects. It had been an exciting and educational 12 years. His 6'3" wide shouldered frame filled the cart seat. Muscular arms and wide hands held the steering frame lightly but deftly.

The fluorescent tunnel lights made his short red hair even redder. His fish-belly white skin looked paler than normal. Freckles stood out on all of his exposed flesh like measles. Of course, tanned skin was out of the question for Jax anyway because he just burned and peeled in unending cycles when exposed to the intense Florida sun. Besides he didn't have time for sun in this job where he worked underground most of his days or nights.

Lately it had been a lot of both. He knew these tunnels well and drove them automatically as he passed a maze of side routes, so he did his thinking and planning en-route. And there was a lot of thinking and planning to do. The past couple weeks had been incredible to put it mildly. He'd seen the impossible over and over again and it had just about fried his brain to take it all in. He gunned the accelerator as recent memories played out.

* * * * *

He had been working overtime, quietly and alone, on a new communications link from Snow White's Castle central command post to the Epcot World Center when the power had failed. As expected, the backup system kicked on in seconds, but then failed a few moments after that.

"*What in the Sam Hill?*" wondered Jax in utter surprise at the impossible. There were so many redundancies in the Disney power system that it made NASA products appear simple by comparison. The surprise was replaced with relief, as the emergency lights flicked on, just as they should although it was hard to believe it would ever be necessary. Relief slipped away when they quickly faded to total darkness. "*This is crazy! What's going on?*" he wondered. Luckily there was enough time to get his bearing and grab a nearby flashlight from his tool belt.

Things got real dicey when his brand new expensive halogen flashlight didn't work either. The only source of light was the barest afterglow of the emergency light filament in front of him as it dimmed to nothingness. His walkie-talkie was dead too. Not even a squelch. He groped for the desk phone only to find the line completely dead. All the monitors were silent. Jax was in total darkness and absolute quiet 50 feet underground. There wasn't a buzz, a whir, or a hum.

Only the sound of his breathing and the deafening beat of his heart convinced him he was still alive. Plus, there was a voice in his head, definitely not his conscience, telling him to, "*Relax. Calm down. Everything will be OK,*" in a very compelling manner which did in fact cause him to settle down a bit. Still sitting at the command console, his body started to feel very heavy and numb, and his head started hurting, worse than any migraine he'd ever had.

The sexless voice suggested he, "*Go to sleep. Everything will be all right.*" He did feel *very* sleepy come to think of it, but through the drowsiness came a mental warning, "*This doesn't make sense. Do something Jax.*"

"*But do what?*" was the faint reply. The numbness in his body spread quickly, causing him to slump forward on the console desk, his heavy lidded eyes staring uselessly in the darkness. As he tried to focus on doing something besides falling asleep, he felt consciousness slip away and a greater darkness wash over him.

When he woke up, the power was back on and the clocks read 6:08 a.m. "*Oh man, what the hell am I doing sleeping on the job?*" came his first thoughts. "*I slept right through my shift!*" came his second thoughts. Then he remembered about the power outage, the voice, and his passing out. He shook his head to clear the cobwebs and was immediately rewarded with nausea and a throbbing headache. He had to place both arms straight out on the smooth, gray console to steady himself.

Jax recovered quickly; after all, waking up with some cobwebs was normal. He flexed his strong but stiff arms, rolled his neck around slowly, and hunched his shoulders to work out the kinks. Feeling his wits return a little, he glanced at the indoor and outdoor monitors, quickly flashing through over 100 camera views of the vast complex. Two things immediately caught his attention. It was much too bright outside to be 6 in the morning and there weren't any other employees showing up on the monitors. Heck, he should have been relieved hours ago.

"What the hell's going on?" he complained. Then he quickly added, "This is nuts!" His Southern drawl as a native Georgian came through thickly and a mix of fear and anger was evident as well. The echo of his voice in the solitude added to his internal disquiet.

The complex should have been crawling with support personnel at this hour, even down below. Plus, judging by the time of day, which appeared closer to noon, the tourists should have been above ground in droves. *It couldn't be some kind of joke, not with millions of dollars on the line. Something bad had to have happened. Something major,"* he concluded.

The pesky and compelling voice in his head kept repeating, "Stay calm. Relax. Everything will be all right. You have new friends." Like getting a buzz on for the weekend, he was tempted to sink easily into its influence, just enjoying the mellow ride.

Instead, this voice became unnerving. It confused him as to its source and 'though it was calming, he forced himself not trust it for an instant, or trust anything else for that matter. Willing it to disappear by mentally shoving the voice away from him and closing it in a mental box he found it actually did diminish in volume to a bare whisper that had no effect on him. It was as if he had sent someone with an obnoxious radio down the hall and into one of the offices. He could just hear the noise, but it no longer bothered him and he could concentrate at the events facing him.

He keyed his walkie-talkie to contact the shift leader, only to get static. A minute of trying to contact anyone across the active channels proved futile.

He suddenly got a faint voice message from the far-away room he had sent that voice telling him to turn on the TV. He had complete access to a host of local cable and international satellite channels from here but only public relation types were allowed to use them. Of course, Jax had figured a way past their security locks long ago. Looking around to make sure no one was looking, then feeling stupid for the caution, he keyed six of the monitors for the major news channels. *"Let's see what's up,"* came a hopeful notion.

There was an identical "Standby for an important presidential address." message on all channels, so he keyed up a number of other channels locally and around the world, trying to see if he could get any information at all. A glance at the constantly changing Disney World camera views showed nothing had changed up top. The local channels all showed the same standby message. Strangely, the satellite feeds for international channels carried nothing but static.

Concern starting to mount, he wondered just how alone he might be in this mess. "C'mon, Griffith, let's get on with this!" he shouted. Griffith-the very thought brought contempt from his entire being. He hadn't voted for her, not because she wasn't talented or that she was a woman (well, maybe that was part of the reason), but there was something he didn't like, something he just didn't trust.

His candidate never stood a chance, but supported a few core ideas that Jax admired, even though, on balance Griffith had more mainstream ideas, and good ones too. Well, his vote had spoken, and that's what mattered, even if he hadn't voted for a winning candidate yet. Still, he wished just once he'd be on the winning side or more to the point, that candidates with his viewpoint would win.

He didn't have long to wait before President Griffith came on. Jax almost threw up listening to her, from a mix of contempt, then shock, then disbelief, then anger. Little green men? Could it really be true? Heck, who hadn't heard of all the stories that had been analyzed, confirmed, and unconfirmed?

He had watched reruns of *The X-files* until he practically had the whole series memorized, loving every encounter, but surely that was just Hollywood hype. Yet, if what this sorry piece of a president said was true, it was both an incredible and very sobering revelation. Jax didn't much care for the idea of sharing this overcrowded planet with aliens. He didn't like sharing the planet with a lot of the people already here.

"This is pure craziness! Gotta be a joke!" he shouted at the monitor. Glancing at the other monitors, still showing no one around, he instantly knew, to the depth of his being, this wasn't funny and life as he had known it was O-V-E-R.

"What a trip," he muttered in a low tone, as if anyone could hear, even if he had screamed or laughed 'til he was blue in the face. Still, deep down he was frightened beyond anything that had ever happened to him. Even worse than when his older sister had dumped a bucket of cockroaches onto his sleeping bag during his first camp out. Even worse than when she had hid under his bed until he was sleeping, then jumped out like the bogey man just as he had fallen asleep. No, this was real. And it was really bad.

So, now he had the facts. "What the hell do I do now?" dribbled from his lips slowly, his drawl deepening. Mentally he was as sharp as any, genius level, in fact, and what he surmised was that he was screwed. OK, if this were true, and there was little doubt it was, then he'd been dealt an awful hand of cards. He guessed that the voice was really supposed to control him, but for some strange reason it didn't. He also guessed he was probably quite alone, cut off from friends and family. It was a sure bet that Mickey and Donald weren't going to help. Now, sitting alone and reaching these conclusions, the sum total of what had occurred hit home. This time he vomited for real.

Jax stayed put for several hours, getting his bearings, gathering his wits, settling his stomach, mulling over these incredible events, laying low as President Griffith had asked. He knew he was safe and would never starve in this complex. He could hold out for years without outside help. Eventually, he had to talk to someone though, find out who was in charge now, and see what others had to say about what happened.

There were roughly 4,500 support personnel within a one-mile radius and there should be about 800 in the theme park alone if his memory of the night shift payroll served him well. His walkie-talkie and the phone still weren't working. *"Wonder where they all went? Guess I'll hafta visit folks in person,"* he reasoned.

Hoping some action would make him feel better, he grabbed his toolkit in case he had to explain being off-station, exited the control room, and took the stairs topside where he'd walk to Space Mountain, a usual beehive of maintenance activity. It would have been quicker to take a tunnel cart, but he needed fresh air and sunshine. Warm humid air, even on this February day, greeted him, but what he saw outside stopped him cold.

The cameras had shown no activity, but seeing it with his own squinting eyes was something different. Never had there been a day or night in his 12 years on the job when he could look out from the castle entryway towards Main Street and not see or hear a soul. In a place that comfortably held hundreds of thousands of people, the silence and emptiness was striking, and bizarre. In fact, it was hard not to visualize kids and adults laughing, people gathering at the curb for the next parade, vendors selling frozen bananas and popcorn, and various Disney characters entertaining cheering groups.

A few birds swooped to a landing close by, hoping Jax would feed them some morsel to make up for what thousands of people would normally provide. "Sorry little fellas," he said, "Guess it's gonna be a rough day for everyone. They hopped closer, then pecked the ground uselessly as Jax turned to make his way towards the Tomorrowland bridge.

He had expected to at least see someone walking about between errands, then realized they had been told to stay put, so perhaps people were holed up. The voice was urging him to continue to his work and relax. Well, his assignments mattered little at this point. Besides, his job could be anywhere he wanted in case someone asked, which didn't appear likely at this moment.

It felt bizarre walking in broad daylight in such emptiness. Scary actually. He reached Space Mountain in just a couple minutes' walk, entering the service door off the main entrance where usually hundreds waited in line at any hour the park was open for the ride of their lives.

It suddenly dawned on him he should take advantage of the emptiness and help himself to some rides. A devilish grin started, then faded as he realized the enormity of what had really happened. *"No time for fun and games, pal,"* he admonished himself. His footsteps echoed solemnly as he went down the stairs.

The normal musty smell of damp concrete assaulted his nostrils as he reached the main service corridor in short order. The usually packed maintenance/engineering control room was empty, so he headed for the break room. Thankfully, he heard the sound of humans in conversation as he neared the entrance. He recognized gorgeous Alyssa, the chief tool pusher for all of Space Mountain, and diminutive playful Matt, her partner in keeping this massive monolith running smoothly. They were standing together with three other people. Strangely, a woman he didn't recognize was standing guardedly off to the side, watching the five in conversation with concern.

Talked stopped when he entered. Alyssa and Matt said a curt, "Hi," then they restarted their conversation. Jax paused. Alarms and red flags were going off in his head warning him to take caution here and assess the situation before jumping in. They were talking about the other woman's behavior and trying to figure out what to do. He decided to talk to the group, especially since his friends were there, even though they at present didn't appear to want to give him the time of day.

"What's up? Can I help?" he ventured carefully.

Alyssa pointed at the other woman and said slowly in a serious tone, "She's up, and she's up to no good."

Jax stared blankly, hoping for more info before committing himself. Alyssa then impatiently blurted out in deadpan, "Jax, she isn't listening to them. She's calling this all a big mistake, the president a liar, and saying that we don't have new friends. She thinks we're nuts!"

Jax couldn't assess anyone's mental state by a glance so he didn't try. This whole situation was dicey for everyone. Considering the world had just been exposed to a phenomenal event, strange behavior of all sorts would be understandable. What was bothering him was that Alyssa wouldn't normally care what anyone thought. She was quite a fun loving and care-free radical, which had made for some fantastic technical pranks on staff and guests alike: highly against regulations. She also didn't care for government of any type, let alone the president.

"So why the dadburn stupid statement?" his brain queried, gears working in overdrive trying to figure it out.

Then it hit him like a wet towel. The voice! Alyssa was doing as the voice was instructing, and its compelling, calming, tone must be affecting her normally emotional and charismatic manner. In fact, she was looking and acting a bit like a zombie or a stern faced animatronic figure from the Hall of Presidents. The meaning to Jax was clear, 'though. This group of friends were all likely under voice influence, which meant he had be *real* careful here.

"Thank Lord Almighty for those mental red flags," he praised.

Alyssa was still staring at him, expecting an answer obviously, when he sensed strong suspicion growing in her. His high school buddies hadn't called him Smoothie for nothing. Echoing the voice he said, "Relax, Alyssa." Then he quickly added, "Everything will be all right. We have new friends."

She calmed down in a heartbeat, as did everyone nearby, except the woman across the room who suddenly became more agitated and a notch more wary, like a cornered animal.

Jax was about to deal with that when two security guards entered the room. He recognized Rob and Hasan from his night shift. Good men and a good team. Instantly, 'though, he realized they weren't their normal, cheery, good-natured selves. Their serious looks were mirrors of each other and their whole demeanor was that of men on a combat mission.

Those looks quickly focused on Jax as Hasan asked dourly, "What are you doing here, Jax? Weren't you in the castle last evening?"

"*Jeez!*" Jax thought, "*This is getting weirder by the minute!*" What he said was, "Everything was OK there, so I wanted to make sure people were fine and that my hardware around here was still working A-OK. Just doing my duty Hasan. Gotta make sure stuff is working for our new friends." He held up his toolkit for emphasis. A twinge of guilt rose up with such gawdawful lies, but he had to admit he was good.

Rob and Hasan appeared a bit confused at that response, but slowly acquiesced and turned their attention to the rest of the group as a way of regaining the advantage they obviously desired.

"Everyone else fine?" asked Rob. There were quick, curt nods individually, then the main body cast their eyes knowingly towards the woman off by herself. Rob and Hasan followed their gaze. The woman's cornered animal look became even more evident as she backed towards the far wall. Alyssa whispered into Hasan's ear. Jax just stared at the unfolding drama as if he was watching a movie, unable to affect the outcome.

The security guards started instantly towards the woman. "Come with us, Miss," said Rob.

"We can help you get through this," added Hasan.

"Forget it!" she piped up. "I just want to be left alone and get back to my job!"

"We insist," replied Hasan and reached for her arm.

She ripped her arm free of his tentative grasp and started to mouth a protest when Rob whipped out his nightstick. With lightning speed he clubbed her head, knocking her out before she could utter another word.

Jax nearly dropped his tool kit in shock. His jaw dropped as low as it could. He'd never seen or heard of a Disney World security officer using force. It was unthinkable, impossible, something that just never happened. His eyes blinked in disbelief. The others standing between him and the altercation just nodded approval. The voice was echoing, "*Everything will be all right. Let them do their duty. Relax.*"

He snapped his mouth closed, ground his teeth, clenched his massive fists, and let anger rise as they started to haul the unconscious woman out of the room. "*Do something!*" his brain screamed. "*You can't let this happen without a fight!*" Even as those thoughts came up, self-preservation took over and he let his anger steam away with a long sigh. This was not the place or time to make a stand. It was too soon and he knew too little. Still, he vowed he would figure a way to make things right though *how* was pure speculation at this point. He for damn sure didn't like what he was seeing of this new world and if it was in his power, he'd see it changed back.

Greg Burke

Soldier of Misfortune

Senses honed by years of hard training and experience, Navy Commander Don Drury used all he had at his disposal, plus maybe an extra sense he'd earned for living this long. Absently he silently and slowly shaved a branch he'd cut, just to make it sharp, like his senses.

The Sierra mountains were still now, snow falling straight down on his uncovered arms, melting instantly, providing chilling signals to his nerves, increasing the heightened awareness he was enjoying, sniffing out the enemy. If a coyote had breathed within a mile, he would have known it. A mountain lion had approached him an hour before. He'd known it was coming the entire time. Finally, sensing him rather than seeing him, it bolted like a forest fire had erupted, tail tucked and ears flat, knowing it was in danger. Indeed, had Don cared, he'd have been eating mountain lion for dinner right now.

As fate would have it, he was sating his hunger with a different meal called hatred and the fury of knowing that something horrible had occurred to mankind, something he was working to change, but yet didn't have the strategy and resources to accomplish. No, this was going to take some planning, some time, some cunning, and he was just the man to make it happen.

Of course, it had been different a couple weeks before. Luckily he'd been on secret maneuvers out of China Lake in the El Dorado National Forest east of Sacramento; rugged and unforgiving high Sierra country that was perfect training for the many scenarios future commandos might face. Out of about 200 soldiers, he was the only one unaffected by the brainwashing from the aliens. His entire training unit had marched on to Sacramento like sheep to slaughter, picked up or herded on the way. He'd had to shoot a couple soldiers who asked too many questions, a damn shame, but a necessity, probably saving them from a life of hell, maybe even doing them a favor, but more importantly giving him cover to escape.

The news channels, radio, military frequencies, every form of communication had been dead at first, then clearly co-opted by the enemy with the stupid orders he'd heard. The results were clear. He was on his own, and not for the first time; but of all the battles he'd survived, this one was going to be the toughest.

What made him most angry in those early days was remembering all the lies he'd been told. He should have known better, questioned some incongruities, but he trusted his leaders, trusted his country, trusted them all with his own life, following their orders blindly like a good soldier. That had been a mistake, he now realized.

Everyone knew and joked about black projects, the old Area 51, the new base in Utah, reverse engineering, lights at night. He'd heard whispers from fellow officers, pilots, even NASA astronauts that something was up, but no one could elaborate, so he put it down to the rumor mill, and overactive imaginations. He now wished he'd done some checking himself.

Not that it would have made any difference, but instead of the ragtag bunch he had now, perhaps he could have mounted some defense, personal or otherwise, to improve the safety of his troops. He missed his family, especially his wife of 23 years. Going to San Diego to find out their status had been ruled out from the start. He'd had to forget any sentimental desires and concentrate on survival. This was war.

Then there were the crazy words in his head, the ones that had sent his soldiers acting like mindless numskulls to Sacramento, words that appeared to have no effect on him. Perhaps it was his hatred of what had happened, his overactive emotions, or just plain stubbornness. No matter, the words in his head had no effect, and he knew the source, hating it more and more with each passing day.

He rounded up as much equipment, food, weaponry, and ammunition as he could find, which was just about everything his men had dropped when they left, found an abandoned cave, and made it his base of operation. As only a veteran decorated SEAL could do, the area was reconnoitered and he found some willing assistance in survivalists and civilians who had had the presence of mind to head for the hills when things went south. In a 60 mile radius, he'd managed to find over three dozen people eager for survival, eager for his leadership, even eager for a little payback if possible.

Some of them had been lost, though, as civilians under alien control turned them in when they strayed too close to populous areas getting supplies. Some had been picked up by alien craft scouring the countryside. Some had gone off on their own, recklessly, stupidly. But the two dozen left were all he knew of humanity and they would have to do.

Surely there were pockets all over the globe, too few to be certain, but better than none. Here at least they were still truly human, and that meant at least a chance for them, maybe others as well.

They bided their time, pooled resources, trained as needed, and planned. It hadn't been brain surgery to track the recent flight patterns of the alien craft to know they were doing something at McMillan AFB, only 20 kilometers from their base camp and that aroused his curiosity and fear. As the person most familiar with the area, he'd been keeping an eye on things. He didn't like what his steel blue eyes were seeing. Something would have to be done, and soon.

Shaking the snow from his short, light brown hair, he stiffened and rose silently, mimicking the serenity of the landscape around him. The snowfall would end soon and there was work to do; hard work, serious work. He sensed a juncture approaching that would demand his talent and action. Death had knocked at his door many times, but Don Drury accepted whatever fate laid before him as a challenge, an opportunity, never a problem.

Greetings, Earthlings!

The cart careened wildly around a sharp turn in the tunnel, rear wheels skidding slightly as Jax tightened the turn even more. The well secured equipment shifted a little. It felt good to be a bit reckless, and mulling over the past couple weeks was a catharsis that didn't offer answers to his predicament, but added perspective. He'd have to slow down soon anyway, as he was approaching the Magic Kingdom perimeter. Things down here were a lot busier than the designers had ever planned. Walt Disney himself would roll over in his grave if he knew what was happening to his dream.

* * * * *

He remembered going back to the Space Mountain control room after seeing that woman knocked out. A few systems were given a cursory check, then he dismissed himself and walked the tunnel route slowly back to the castle. It didn't make sense to stir the pot too much by visiting other areas. That would have to wait. He didn't feel mentally strong enough to face more of what he had just seen.

So he decided to busy himself with his long list of projects for a few days. It would be nice to actually get ahead, since it was clear the park would be closed for a while. A few people stopped by, including other security personnel and his shift boss. It only took him seconds to realize that all of them were acting zombie-like, clearly under the influence of the voice in their heads, and thus untrustworthy.

He gathered no one was coming to replace him since he would see the same people day after day. His boss would drop off maintenance checklists, but others left him alone, not requiring anything, seemingly busy on errands of their own. He didn't offer conversation either.

He wondered if there was anyone else like himself, then wondered what would happen if there wasn't. This line of thought only brought up more feelings of isolation and despair on top of the heavy layers already present so he quit wondering.

"Best to keep up some hope, stay busy with work, and bide your time," he kept reminding himself. He was sure he couldn't be the only one able to resist the voice. He was also sure he didn't want to share that little secret with anyone right now.

He ate when he wanted to, slept when he needed to, which wasn't much of either. It was actually cozy enough down here away from the topside heat. The employee facilities were adequate, especially the showers which never ran out of hot water. It would have been nice, however, if someone had offered him a spot in one of Disney's famous, posh hotels but that didn't happen and he didn't ask. Best to be alone and close to work instead of mingling with the zombies.

He wondered what had happened to all the guests. He supposed they were here at Disney World in the thousands of hotel rooms available. Millions would be within miles of this complex. Had they disappeared, or been moved? Were they just sitting quietly in their rooms? Since it would only be conjecture on his part and not likely anyone would explain it to him, he didn't waste much time on it. He supposed he'd find out when the time was right.

The monitors got quite boring though, continuing to show a lack of activity topside. Also, none of the domestic and foreign channels were available for entertainment. Technical manuals couldn't replace a good sci-fi novel, although he chuckled inwardly at that idea. *"Hell, I'm livin' in a sci-fi novel!"* he told himself.

There wasn't even a good radio station available. So, he played his one Garth Brooks CD 'till he had every word memorized and could lip-synch the entire album. This caused a little consternation to the few who stopped by, as no one else carried *Walkmans* anymore or played music, but he kept the sound low and spouted the party line whenever he met someone.

He wanted to go home, but didn't feel it was safe to ask. A terse dialogue with one of the security guards indicated the outside world was of no concern. Nor could he call outside for some unexplained reason. He wanted to check with some of his friends and family on the outside. Restricted from doing that, he felt like he was under house arrest.

Griffith's pronouncements the next few days were chilling and added to his sense of isolation. Thinking about what must be going on around the world made his head hurt, so he stopped. There wasn't anything to be done about it at any rate. Everything appeared so unreal.

There were a few calls for his service (the walkie-talkies were up and working again) but nothing serious. His list of projects was dwindling as the days dragged on. He was patching together a redundant power system for the tunnel power grid when he got the call, "Jackson, topside at main entrance, 10 minutes, copy," from his boss Karl.

"Sure. Copy that," he replied quickly. "What's up?"

"Visitors on their way. That's all I know," was Karl's stoic reply.

The beautifully manicured gardens at the main gate and surrounding topiaries always got his attention, though he was panting as he appreciated the sight because he had to hustle his big frame to get there on time. Karl and about 500 people were gathered loosely at the entrance area, the most he'd seen in a week. More folks were coming from the monorail walkways and others were gathered around the docks nearby.

Before he could start a conversation with Karl, he heard helicopters coming closer, a lot of them. Minutes later he was concerned by what he saw though clearly everyone else didn't care. A fleet of about 30 helicopters, mostly the big troop carriers, was landing on every available space around the Magic Kingdom. No sooner had they landed when soldiers and civilians came pouring out. The voice was asking them to relax and help as needed. Following the voice in general had helped immensely these past days so he prodded himself forward. Boxes, crates, and baggage were being off loaded in a flurry. He pitched in as best he could.

A man in a grounds keeping uniform started to back away and yell something Jax couldn't make out over the noise of 30+ sets of rotors. Several soldiers pointed towards the man in alarm. While everyone else engrossed themselves in unloading the choppers, not noticing the commotion, Jax paused to check out the situation.

Perhaps the man was upset at having some of his work utterly trampled. At any rate, three men dressed in all black clothing with sunglasses converged on the man with incredible speed. In seconds, the man was unconscious and slumped in their arms. Jax didn't even see them hit the man, he just went limp. The three ninja, as Jax dubbed them, carried their charge right into the train station. No one appeared to notice what had happened or care.

The ninja bothered him. No badges, markings, or whatever. He'd never seen any personnel like this, except maybe on TV. Besides, who in their right mind would dress in black in Florida, even if it was winter? Oh well, another mystery that paled in comparison to having aliens come to the planet. Even the choppers were unmarked, black, not typical military or civilian issue.

He resumed his work, but clumsily bumped his package into someone else causing her to drop several boxes. Jax blurted, "Sorry, ma'am," and stooped to help her out.

As he picked up one of the packages and faced her, he recognized her as the woman from Space Mountain who had been knocked out by

Rob and Hasan. "Say, you OK? I mean, is your head fine...where they hit you?" he asked.

Her brown eyes looked toward him, but not at him, almost as if she couldn't focus. The dazed look revealed little of the emotion she had shown the other day. "I don't know what you are talking about," she stated blandly and bent to pick up the other packages.

"You know...in the control room .... under Space Mountain...the other day," he explained, his hands pointing and gesturing toward the mountain as if she was deaf.

She just shook her head slowly and said, "No, you must be mistaken. We have new friends. Isn't it wonderful?"

Jax felt sorry for her. He suspected she must have been brain damaged from the blow. As she bent to pick up the remaining packages, he noticed a small scar and bump on the back of her neck as her hair fell away. It looked fresh. *"God, maybe they had to operate on her! Poor soul."*

None of what was happening made much sense, so he quit wondering and got back to work. It was over six hours of work that didn't end until well after dark. Three more convoys of choppers came and went, leaving hordes of crates everywhere. Jax's back felt very tight and sore. He was no weakling, but this backbreaking work was not his kind of activity. He much preferred to keep his lifting to the light stuff like a tool pack or 12oz curls at the local bar. Still, he felt good for the exercise. With bars now closed, the 12oz curls were a thing of the past.

Most of the civilians who arrived were apparently staying as they busied themselves hauling belongings toward the hotels or equipment down below into the tunnels. He knew he'd sleep well tonight for a change.

There were several days of quiet, if you call unpacking and setting up thousands of crates quiet, but at least nothing new happened like someone getting beaten or a bunch of choppers landing and taking off. It was real neat stuff they were unpacking: definitely top of the line.

As much as he worked with and trained on Disney's advanced technology, this equipment was quite a bit more sophisticated than anything he'd every heard of or seen, certainly nothing he'd read about in trade magazines, *Popular Science*, or *Popular Mechanics*. He didn't have a clue what this hardware did let alone how to work it. Most of the crates had armed services logos, 'though some of the equipment had markings in Russian and another language he didn't recognize.

No one was taking any time to explain the equipment to him other than to tell him what went where and what power requirements were needed. Besides working with a bunch of zombies, they were a very uncommunicative group. He was starting to miss his Garth Brooks CD. The few ninja who stopped by never said a word or even changed expression. Their stern faces were blank slates. They just stared like it was possible to see through you and then moved on.

A few nonchalant questions to the people he was assisting about setting something up or what a particular piece might do were answered with "No," and, "You will find out when it's time." Jax decided it was wise not to press. The voice just kept up a drone of *"Do your job. Everything will work out. You have new friends."* He was bored and on his own.

It would be nice to have someone to talk to, Anyone. He couldn't be the only one with some ability to act independently. Yet, no one presented him- or herself in a manner that gave him the slightest hint he or she might be normal. Only the woman under Space Mountain that first day and the man the other day who was sacked by the ninja acted different. The reminder of what that had cost them kept him acting like the majority, and alone.

He laughed to himself, fearing that when he found that one person, he or she would probably be some total geek, a former enemy, or would have any number of characteristics he couldn't stand. Still, thinking further, it would be better than never meeting someone like himself again. He shuddered thinking about the never as he opened another crate.

His musings about finding a normal person brought up a good question: How would he know? Were people affected to varying degrees or was it all or nothing? So far, it was all or nothing from what he could tell. If true, there would be clear differences between zombies and what used to be normal folks.

Too, they would be searching for someone like himself and maybe he would be able to tell by their mannerisms. On the other hand, they would also be concealing their situation like he was, so maybe they would act like the rest of the zombies. Plus, the longer this went on, the better the acting. He could sense that in himself, blending in just like one of the gang so gradually his own mannerisms were being suppressed.

As for physical differences, everyone he knew still looked the same with one, no two, exceptions. Jax spied the groundskeeper who'd been sacked by the ninja one morning. Curiosity got the better of him so he detoured over to the where the man was fixing a work-cart. He stopped cold, 5 feet away, when he saw the mark on the man's neck, just like the woman from Space Mountain!

The blank look he got when he said, "Hi," confirmed his suspicion that someone had operated on the man so now he was a zombie too. It was too much of a coincidence not to be true. He almost couldn't work the rest of the day after realizing the implications of that. A new very penetrating fear was added to his already long list of fears. *"Don't let that happen to me,"* he kept repeating to himself.

He wasn't a doctor, but he watched prime time doctor shows. He knew surgery when he saw it though he couldn't imagine what exactly had been done to change a person so dramatically. He wondered why the back of the neck instead of other parts of the brain. At any rate, it was clear the powers in charge wanted everyone compliant and would accomplish that through the voice or physical means. It was also clear he should do checkups from the neck up when looking for normal people.

Then it suddenly hit him how he might know: the eyes! Zombies and people who had been cut in the neck appeared dead in the eyes. He looked in the mirror and practiced his most glazed look, but just couldn't quite match what he was seeing. Fortunately, as long as he acted like everyone else, no one appeared suspicious. Only the ninja gave him the heebie-jeebies with their all seeing stare from behind mirrored glasses, but even they didn't appear to care as long as the work was getting done. Yes, he'd have to look in people's eyes. Perhaps that would work best.

It would be quite a crapshoot though. He'd have to be very, *very* sure before he'd reveal himself. It made him shudder just thinking about exposing himself and the consequences if he was wrong. *"Damned if you do, damned if you don't, Jax,"* he concluded. It would be a real leap of faith when the moment came, if it ever came.

In just a few days, the tunnels near the center of the park, some of the rides topside, and the shops on Main Street USA were starting to look like research laboratories with shiny equipment and busy computer terminals on newly installed cabinets and counters. Jax was kept very busy rerouting the Disney World's ample power supplies from overhead busses or theme park terminals to the new equipment. The setup greatly reduced the starkness of the tunnels even if it did make them a bit more cramped. What didn't mesh aesthetically was seeing a particular array of equipment surrounded by toys, books, and T-shirts, or even wilder, watching people install their labs in the heart of the Haunted Mansion.

More people kept arriving, because whenever he glanced at his monitors in the castle control room, people could be seen coming and going. He estimated some 5,000 to 10,000 in the Magic Kingdom alone. As far as he could judge, they were all technical types, even more geeky than he was. None of them registered as normal.

It was looking less and less like a theme park every day. He knew a similar makeover was happening at EPCOT judging by the massive antenna array being attached to the "big golf ball" as tourists called it. He had few details, however, as no one was briefing him on the purpose of all this activity.

Jax had assumed this mobilization for Iwo Jima had to do with their new friends, but couldn't figure out what. President Griffith had made it clear places like Disney World would not have a purpose in the new world order. He guessed the government couldn't wait to get their hands on such prime property. Still, something big was going to happen, and happen right here. At least he had a front row seat.

Over a week later, he got an eyeful for an answer.

He had just plugged in a mother board for new circuitry at It's a Small World when monitors, overhead lights, and nearby lab equipment flickered and died. He swore inwardly, certain he had just overloaded the local grid. "Way to go, Jax! You shouldn't have tried to put this much juice on line," he muttered out loud. When his flashlight didn't work either, he knew something was up, just like when they were invaded nearly two weeks before.

What was really weird though, he also *felt* something was up. He could sense something coming closer, a mental pressure building. Then the voice started saying, *"We are here. Come greet and help your new friends."*

He stumbled out of this work area in pitch blackness towards where he thought was the entrance. Smacking his head into a conduit helped him get his bearings but added to his already growing headache. Sliding his hands along the conduit got him to the doorway at the same time the lights came back on.

"Thanks a lot," he grumbled to no one in particular.

Stepping outside into the cool Florida night, he noticed the clear starry sky was now very cloudy, as if a storm had suddenly come up in the 15 minutes he had been inside. He could see other people coming out of buildings, working like himself at this late hour. They were headed towards the main entrance, so he followed along, a mental picture of the main entrance appearing in his mind along with the voice.

As he cleared the castle entrance, looking straight down Main Street USA, he froze in disbelief. He had to blink his eyes several times to make sure he wasn't seeing things. Coming through the train station tunnel he could see the Seven Seas Lagoon was covered by an alien craft of awesome proportion.

It looked like a giant, shiny, black baseball cap with a tiny bill facing him. The dome of the hat had to be over 60 stories high and sloped smoothly to a flat bottom. It was easily a mile wide. Lights of all colors flashed in a rotating pattern around the bottom. White lights studded the rest of the dome in no particular pattern. Other craft were flying nearby and landing. They were smaller, about the size of basketball courts, saucer shaped, again with multicolored lights. A glance towards EPCOT showed another giant ship over that lagoon. None of the ships made a sound. It was deathly quiet outside, eerily quiet.

Anger, excitement, and fear washed over him. He was going to be able to meet the beings who had just turned the human race on its ear and taken over an entire planet without a moment's notice and apparently without a care. He hadn't realized it before, but seeing this ship here brought everything to a head and took events from fairy tail imaginings to hard cold reality. He was angry that the Quazzga were here. They had put a wrench into his life big time. As is true for so much in life, he hadn't asked for this; act of God was one thing, act of Quazzga was another.

Still, it was exciting at the same time to be so close to a part of history that had only been speculated and fantasized about up until a few weeks ago. Seeing and possibly meeting life from another star system would be a thrill, even if they were unwelcome guests. Mainly though, he was fearful of the whole situation and the unknowns he would have to face in dealing with these creatures and his own very uncertain future, hiding amongst foes, human and alien.

Anger was pointless at the moment and fear was an enemy he had to control if he was going to get through this. Excitement would have to take the lead.

Jax closed his eyes to steady himself, then opened them to the same picture of seconds earlier. He steeled his nerves and sturdy frame to handle the worst, and started moving towards the main entrance again.

The entrance was packed with onlookers who had been summoned to be here so he was at least 200 feet from the edge of the huge ship. Being tall was an asset he was glad to possess.

Short ramps had been extended around the base and he could see aliens departing from at least three wide openings. This was a place where the ferries had deposited hundreds of millions of tourists over the years. It was a sure bet Disney never expected these types of visitors.

A closer look at the base of the ship showed it was hovering a couple feet above the lagoon. The water underneath was calm and smooth as glass. Despite the stormy looking sky and the movement of the ships above, there was no wind.

Like so many times in recent days, Jax's jaw just dropped. He probably looked like the village idiot taking in the sights. Whatever power was noiselessly holding a ship of this size in place had to be awesome! He could not even fathom the technology which made all this possible. Sure enough, these folks were light years ahead of Earthlings.

He closed his mouth, gained some modicum of composure, and focused now on the approaching aliens. Uncontrollably, his jaw dropped again with the shock of their appearance. Not that he could have guessed in a million years what form alien life might take, but this was too much of a coincidence. They looked exactly like what had been the popular conception of UFO occupants for years now, *exactly*. Smooth hairless bulbous heads, big slanting eyes, diminutive mouth, ears and chin, light bluish or gray skin, no clothing or particular sexual features, long arms and fingers. This was truly incredible! *"The crackpots were right all along! What a trip!"* Jax exclaimed inwardly.

What their appearance confirmed was this wasn't their first visit to Earth. *"Who knows how long they've been coming here?"* he wondered. He shook his red haired head in amazement at this spectacle and the twist of the truth now coming to light.

There were hundreds coming towards them and streaming out the other exits as well, looking a lot like tourists offloading the ferry. Judging by the size of the ship, this was still only a fraction of what must be inside. Most of the aliens looked about the same facially though there was the normal variation in height, head shape, and eye size one would see among humans. It did appear the creatures with gray skin were shorter and stronger looking compared to bluer colored beings who were as tall as Jax yet more delicate in build. A few of the aliens had necklaces; whether decoration, insignia, or something entirely different was anyone's guess.

He could see no aliens who looked small enough to classify as children though how he would know either way was pure speculation. Applying any human-based concepts might be totally useless. It would serve him well to remember that until he had more direct information.

There were a dozen or so ninja gathered in a line across the bottom of the ramp closest to Jax. They stood at attention and formed a barrier between the aliens and humans, their backs to the humans, facing the aliens. They raised their right hands in unison, chest high, fingers loosely splayed.

The closest group of aliens then halted their descent, one of them raising its right hand in a similar fashion as the ninja. *"Greetings,"* Jax heard in his head, just as loud and clear as if the man next to him had said it. *"Thank you for meeting us,"* was what he heard next.

Jax glanced quickly around and concluded there weren't any ventriloquists in the crowd. The alien's mouth never moved from what he could see at this distance, but his hand dropped at the end of the last statement meaning that what he had heard in his head had no doubt come from that particular alien.

He pondered this voice for a second, then concluded, *"Telepaths!"* It was the only explanation and it was amazing, because again popular culture had said they were telepaths, communicating with people in their native tongue, no matter what it was. So far, the abductees and UFO buffs were batting a thousand.

Thinking of other alien qualities that had been written about and played out on the networks, the Web, and in print, Jax wondered if other things were also true. Events such as sexual experiments, operations, cattle mutilations, hybrid breeding, abduction, and flat out disappearances had been presented in convincing fashion for years. Unfortunately, that information was often picked up and presented by questionable sources so that generally such tales were ignored.

The problem now though was many of those tall tales were probably true. And if they were true, such stories damn sure didn't jive with a completely benevolent species because often aliens had been represented as nasty little varmints. In fact, he'd heard some pretty ghoulish stuff if his sci-fi memory served him well. He wasn't an expert on this like some of his friends, but he didn't think he was mistaken.

Hell, if he'd been visited out of the blue, abducted, and probed, he'd probably be scared to death and wouldn't have a whole lot of nice things to say. Only time and first hand experience would confirm or deny the stories. Either way, he felt pretty certain he was screwed with little to no chance of changing things regardless of how true or false the stories turned out to be.

Worse yet, the cover-ups and denials by governments the world over rang very hollow now. Those deceptions suggested collusion with their new friends. His stomach twisted and bile rose. *"Did that mean they were all pawns? Had this been planned all along? How much had been hidden?"* he wondered.

One could always hope for the best, right? After all, some of the UFO stories did mention attempts at benevolent contact with offers of help. Perhaps it was too early to tell whether they were friend or foe. Still, the whole way their coming had occurred didn't lend itself to a friendly visit, no matter what President Griffith might say. Jax would have to be wary, vigilant, and secretive.

Despite his growing worries, it was amazing to watch these beings (from God knew how far away) amble down the ramps. Their gaits were halting and jerky as they moved downward, but smoother on flat ground as their long legs moved steadily towards the crowd. *"Perhaps they didn't have their "Earth legs" yet,"* he mused. Jax had seen astronauts come back to Earth walking much worse.

None of the aliens were carrying anything of any substance, like luggage, or backpacks. He also didn't see any personal electronic devices. That was one difference from the normal airport disembarkments. Still, they appeared like tourists, many of them looking around slowly with interest, taking in their new surroundings, as if they were recording everything.

He could hear no further mental messages, though there was pressure in his head and a slight buzzing like static as the throng of aliens got closer. He suspected they had to be communicating amongst themselves at a level he couldn't understand and that was causing the pressure, similar to the voice. He'd be happier when the buzz quieted down.

The ninja guided them past the crowd and into the larger service tunnel doors by the main entrance train station. The aliens never stopped surveying their surroundings as they passed through the doorways. Now Jax finally understood the tunnel and upper building modifications. They were going to be living quarters for the Quazzga. That would explain the sealed and expanded areas, the specialized equipment, the sprucing up of larger areas. *"Well, there goes the neighborhood,"* he complained.

After an hour of proceeding out of the ship, the alien crowd thinned a little. Floating covered pallets 8' to 10' high and 6' wide escorted by one or two aliens each came out next. They too headed down the service entrances to the tunnels. It was hard to take it all in, but estimating by Disney standards some 50,000 Quazzga must have exited along with about 200 of these pallets. It appeared they traveled light, meaning what they needed for food, water, and accessories would be found here or brought later. The image of aliens wearing Mickey Mouse hats and riding the Tea Cups made him chuckle inwardly, then frown as he realized humans would probably never again enjoy this wonderful park.

Finally, he heard the voice say *"Get some rest. Everything will be OK. There will be lot's of work to do tomorrow."* Jax did feel tired, though overwhelmed was more like it. People started easing away from the main entrance. For him, it was hard to leave such an awesome event so soon. So, he stepped to the side and watched the giant ship as the last of the Quazzga and their pallets departed, watched until the ramps slid away, doors closed, and the huge bulk rose noiselessly up and disappeared into the clouds.

He watched a while longer, stifling numerous yawns as he looked skyward, searching for any further activity. In quick order, the stormy sky cleared and brightened with stars and a crescent moon. Jax lowered his head and looked around at a deserted main entrance. He hoped his solitary presence wouldn't cause any suspicion, but no one was left to notice and he'd have a good story if questioned. He was getting good at it.

He'd have *never* believed this past hour if he hadn't seen it with his own eyes. Now it was like sensory overload. Still, it was better to see this first hand than doubt the tales of others. Of course, no one really told him anything anymore so he had to get his info first hand. He caught a shadow standing by one of the nearby entrances and realized with trepidation it was one of the ninja. The cold placid face turned his way. Jax fumbled with his tool kit at the lamp post he was leaning against and pretended to be finishing fixing something. Then he turned away towards Main Street and the Castle, hoping his staying behind hadn't made him stand out too much, jeopardizing his precious secret. He didn't risk looking back until he was at the castle. A quick glance calmed him; there were no ninja in sight.

Success

Large smooth black mirrored eyes looked out the view port as his fellow Quazzga entered their new homes and work areas below. 318 of them were from his collective, or family, as humans would call it, and it was with very little effort he conversed with each of them along their own unique mental wavelength. In seconds he relayed his instructions, encouragement, and assurances he would join them soon. He was proud of recent events because it would at long last provide a future for the Quazzga.

Satisfaction registered in every part of his being, darkening his slightly blue color. Yes, Ramsees was very satisfied with his work and the work of his people. Long, nimble fingers danced smoothly over the console with thousands of command nodes in front of him as he finished up the last of his duties prior to takeoff. Finally, delicate fingertips touched together lightly, eyes lidded shut, tiny nostrils flared, other minds tuned down, and his head dropped, long narrow chin touching his barrel chest as if he was falling asleep. Flickering blue and green lights from the console cast an eerie yet soothing glow around him. He could now take time to savor this victory and reminisce as he conserved energy for what lay ahead.

* * * * *

It had not been easy or certain when they had started this venture some 15,000 years before. There had been an impending need on his doomed home world of over a 100 billion inhabitants to come to this planet. Resources on his larger planet and in neighboring systems were dwindling beyond their ability to replace them. A million Earth years of Quazzga habitation was finally taking its toll. His solar system, in one of the oldest parts of the Milky Way would not last another 200,000 Earth years with its current population and finite resources. Despite zero population change in the last 500,000 years and incredible conservation efforts, their extinction was inevitable.

Thus it was decided that colonization would be necessary, something not easily arrived at for proud beings entrenched and content with being in one place for so long. But the Quazzga had achieved too many great things to disappear quietly from the galaxy. They should be growing as a species and achieving even more for themselves and future Quazzga.

Space travel had been possible for millennia as they filled up the habitable worlds in their star system. They had learned how to fold space and time in a manner beyond Ramsees understanding so intra solar system distances could be traveled in less than a day. Twenty-three Earth years was all it had taken to bring them here, although they hadn't stretched their technology to such limits until this crisis imposed itself upon them. When they began their exploration, such a journey to Earth took about 100 years. In a Quazzga lifespan of over 700 years, though, it was not an impossibly long journey.

The problem with space travel outside their stellar system, though, was their one weakness, the separation from other minds. Most Quazzga could not handle being limited to under 100 minds of conversation, even those of exemplary mental stature. Only a very few could travel with less than five minds. None could go it alone. Even with mechanical communication enhancements, mind speech beyond a solar system wasn't possible. Thus they had to construct larger ships for what would clearly be an expensive phase of exploration. Selecting the most capable Quazzga proved tedious and required a lot of testing.

Next, the Quazzga had felt it would be simple to look at their detailed astronomical data and find a myriad of suitable solar systems. Early hope dimmed to frustration as one by one, the closer targets were found uninhabitable when analyzed first hand. They enhanced their space travel capabilities and sent out thousands of explorers in an ever-widening sphere to check out every possible prospect. Frustration gave way to despair as ship after ship returned without finding a new home for the Quazzga and nearly 3,000 years passed by without an acceptable result.

Despite thousands of systems which ought to have suitable worlds to colonize, the reality was the diversity of planets was also great and one thing or another made so many planets incompatible with their needs, the needs of a trillion highly developed Quazzga.

Many planets could serve as a space station, and resources could be gathered to make them inhabitable, but they were not that desperate, not yet. They wanted to survive, but more than that, they wanted to thrive. Occupying just any group of planets with a sun was not the goal. It had to be a system or systems which would support at least five times their number for future expansion. It was becoming a daunting task to find the right combination of size, climate, geography, and resources.

They had even found various forms of life, though nothing near as complex as themselves or useful for anything besides food sources or simple pets. The Quazzga searches for intelligent life in their region and during all the initial missions had always been a fruitless effort. The question of whether they were alone in the universe could not be answered in the affirmative.

Then, one ship returned from the edge of the galaxy to report success. They had found and surveyed a solar system of incredible potential. In fact, it was more than they had hoped for after so many failed attempts. Two of the planets were easily habitable along with several of the moons. The small sun had eons of life left. The mineral and chemical resources of the solar system were vast, even by Quazzga needs and standards. The most exciting find, though, was the third planet and its contents.

Unbelievably, the third planet was a near copy of their own home planet of a million years before, although slightly smaller. It was fairly stable, subject to normal fluctuations in temperature and geology like their own world. Atmosphere, gravity, and temperatures were nearly perfect for their needs. Even water was abundant, a true luxury compared to their nearly dried up husk of a world.

Almost every aspect of the planet they analyzed gave positive results. The only minor cause for concern was the possibility of collision with other celestial bodies. In fact, it was clear that this planet had suffered several large impacts. This had not been a problem on their home world, but nonetheless, Quazzga technology had long ago addressed this problem and so they could easily protect this solar system. Mental waves of excitement spread rapidly through the Quazzga who were quickly referring to this blue-green planet as their future home.

Another amazing find was the diversity of life forms, from very small bacteria to huge water dwelling creatures. There were millions of different types of life forms all over the planet. It would take years to study them and decide which would stay and which would have to be eliminated to conserve resources. Still, the sheer number of choices would make what survived a thousands times greater than what the Quazzga planet had in its grasp even a million years before.

Then came the bonus find: primitive bipedal creatures, who eventually called themselves humans, were identified that resembled the Quazzga in terms of height, weight, and abilities to use their hands. In fact, it was clear a culture of sorts was being formed by these widely scattered beings around the planet. Similar creatures were found clinging to vegetative areas of the major land masses. These hairy versions were quickly found to have far less promise than the more advanced humans. Likewise, several waterborne species were identified as intelligent and worthy of keeping later on, but would not be useful to the Quazzga like the humans.

They continued to probe the planet, but of the myriad of creatures they studied in those early years of exploration, the humans continued to be the most intriguing. They had highly advanced brain function and evolving mental capabilities, more so by hundreds of magnitudes than any life forms they had ever found in all their journeys. They were the closest thing the Quazzga had found to themselves.

It might even be possible to train these creatures, then use them to assist the Quazzga in the necessary menial activities of life. This would free up valuable Quazzga brain and body function for more useful pursuits. They had learned long before that mechanical models of themselves or other constructs could never respond and serve them as they needed. Nothing like these humans had ever presented themselves to the Quazzga. It was a discovery almost too good and unique to be true.

Being a patient civilization, though, the Quazzga explored hundreds of other planetary prospects over the next thousand years and found five others that could work if needed. None, though, held the promise of this solar system and the hope of the humans. Repeated visits to the third planet continued to confirm this as their best choice. Rather than split the Quazzga and secure several far ranging, systems, it was decided to put all efforts forth to colonize the one system with the wonderful third planet. Other planets and moons would follow later, but this planet was the prize.

With a burst of excitement on all the Quazzga worlds, plans were made to colonize this distant planet. Traveling in five- to 80-occupant ships was one thing, preparing ships to carry tens of billions would take time. The daunting work was divided and efforts focused. It would take thousands of years and many generations before they would be ready. In the end, it had taken even longer than they had planned.

Preparations were divided into four areas: providing for those who would be left behind so they could eventually follow over the next hundred thousand years, building transport ships in the quantity and size they would need, readying the colonists for the journey and arrival at a new home world, and preparing Earth and the humans for their arrival.

While the entire undertaking was monumental beyond the scope of anything the Quazzga had ever even contemplated attempting, it was only the last item which proved difficult in retrospect.

Yet they had done it, accomplished the greatest feat in the history of their civilization, and now they were here among these creatures, in full control and ownership of this entire region of space, resources beyond belief and anticipated luxury. Ramsees' high cheekbones crinkled and darkened as his satisfaction peaked, then crested leaving him on a plateau of peacefulness. He opened his mind, then his ebony eyes, and looked ahead to view his ship's approach to the twenty mile long mother ship above their long established and nearly invisible Martian base, the one near the face as the humans called it. *"What a strange species,"* he mused. Thousands of messages conveying victory were shared while he nimbly assisted in the docking procedure, pale digits moving in a blur over the console.

He relaxed again, or tried to, tuning down his fellow voyager's thoughts of victory. Tiny wrinkles then formed on his taught forehead and his slit like mouth turned down at the corners in an ever so slight frown. Inwardly, fear, anger, and frustration mixed in a dark emotional whirlpool which drowned his well deserved peacefulness. Ramsees knew all too well how close they had come to near disaster with their colonization. How close they had come to losing their new home. It had been too close and it could have been disaster for the Quazzga.

All the more reason for him and a select trusted few of his collective to get to work on the next phase of a very private venture back on Earth. He could brook no delay in this very un-Quazzga like action. He felt strongly on this matter, following his elder (and now dead) collective member's instructions, orders, that he would have carried out anyway. It made sense, not for the short term, but for the long term of his civilization. Still, many delicate months and years of secret action remained and if truth be known, there would be violent opposition from many Quazzga.

Ramsees only hoped it was not too late. Much of the groundwork had been laid in the past century years and he hoped his instructions had been followed these past few weeks. The future of the Quazzga, more than just simple colonization, was at stake.

Greg Burke

New Beginning

Gritting her teeth 'til they hurt, Del looked through the peephole, surprised and then shaken to the bone to see that it wasn't Dan from the center as she had expected, but good old Officer Roy and the first MIB (or at least it looked like him). She backed slowly away from the door, panic rising into numbing fear. "Open up Ms. Summers, we need to talk to you." said Officer Roy again.

"Ms. Summers, open the door!" she heard forcefully from Mr. Black, impatience at her lack of a nanosecond response evident. Del braced herself and in a flash had the door open with her most practiced apologetic face on.

"Hello, I wasn't expecting to see you. Is there something I can do to help?" she stammered. Del could feel all four eyes and perhaps something more probing her appearance and response for the truth. Neither man registered any overt emotion that gave her a clue as to what would happen next. Neither man said anything for what felt like a minute but was only a few seconds.

"We heard about yesterday. Glad you are OK," stated Officer Roy with so little feeling it made her shudder a little and wrap her arms around her chest for comfort. Then he extended one of several envelopes he was holding towards her adding, "Change of plans. New assignment for you. Bus leaves in an hour. Be out front then."

With that, both men turned around and went on with their errands. Del paused just inside the door, saw no other activity, then closed the door slowly, dropping her head in resignation. Her stomach flip-flopped and she felt weak so she just sat down unc, eremoniously near the door on the soft carpet. Ideas tumbled out of her muddled brain: *"Is this some kind of joke? How long can I survive this emotional roller coaster? I thought I was a goner for sure when they showed up."* Looking at the nondescript envelope, she realized she'd better open it and pull herself together.

Her shaking hands fumbled but managed to get out the one page memo. It took effort to focus on the small type and brief contents of the message. Her duties at the NMC emergency room were over. She was to join a staff of nurses and doctors at Walt Disney World and would be briefed when she got there. And she was to pack for an extended stay.

"That's just great. What the hell do they need me for at Disney World?" she ranted. "Let's see, Mickey has burns, Minnie is pregnant, Pluto has the runs, and Dumbo has an ear infection. This is too bizarre. Does that sum it up?" she blurted to the closed door. Not getting a splinters worth of an answer, she resigned herself to her fate.

The hour passed swiftly because of all the things Del had to pack and prepare around the condo, but mostly because she moved like she was in quicksand. There was quite an internal debate about whether or not to notify her mom. In the end, she just couldn't bring herself to do it. Indecision about what to bring and how best to continue her charade weighed heavily on her. All she could come up with was to carry on, go with the flow, and hope some opportunity to change things would occur. Hope was a bitter pill at this point, though.

Wearing loose-fitting plain clothes, Del grabbed up her light suitcases and secured the door, lingering briefly, not wanting to leave her only solid form of refuge just yet. Then, with little choice, she hastily turned away, ready as she'd ever be to face new challenges.

The drive to Disney World was uneventful, but the view was shocking. The Bee Line from Cocoa Beach to Orlando was nearly deserted, except for a few buses and trucks. Even with the cool weather, this road should normally have been crammed with cars and tourists. It was an eerie feeling to see things so quiet and, of course, another reminder of how much things had changed. They even breezed right through Orlando and into the Disney World without slowing, something that had become unimaginable in recent years with the continuous growth in resorts, entertainment complexes, the native population, and tourists. What would have taken hours was reduced to 50 minutes.

There was no discussion on the bus even though Del knew many of the passengers. Everyone sat like the living dead and Del mimicked the stance as best she could, staring blankly out the window on what was actually a gorgeous clear day. The voice droned on its platitudes. It was a lucky thing she could tune it out or else she would have been driven insane or into a total submission through sheer repetition. She knew in her heart it was all crap now, a manipulation of her species, and a damn shame.

For brief moments, very brief, she almost wished she weren't different so the nightmare would end. "Better Red than dead", was the phrase she repeated to herself in recent days. It was a slogan her father had told her about when people felt it was better to join the Communist revolution, even though they disagreed with the system, than to die fighting it. *"How ironic,"* she mused, *"That people would actually appear to go along with new leadership, even though they might be revolutionaries themselves or totally disagree with what was happening."* It fit her situation perfectly, even though she didn't think of herself as a revolutionary, especially with the taste of bile so near to her lips. She wasn't that tough yet.

It was pointless to speculate on what her next job would be so she didn't. Del just hoped that whatever was planned for her would be something she could do without having to interact with a lot of SA, VC, or Quazzga. *"Brace yourself,"* and *"Be a VC,"* were other phrases she kept telling herself.

What surprised and disappointed her, though, was how busy it was at Disney World. As they neared the main parking, she saw it was nearly full of school buses, tour buses, and cars. "There goes peace and quiet," she mumbled to the cold bus window. It was odd to see things so busy when everything else associated with the word "fun" had been banned as unnecessary.

The reason for this hub of activity became clear a moment later when they passed the main entrance and a host of military vehicles and personnel, plus several smaller Quazzga craft came into view. These Quazzga craft had become even more openly visible in recent days at Cocoa Beach. There was more of the same as they drove up to the Contemporary Hotel. This was not some medical emergency for humans. Alien intentions slimed all over this latest development.

"That ices it!" she complained. Not only do they have to take over the world, but they're taking over a world treasure and perverting it to whatever possible use they could make of this place. She closed her eyes and lowered her head. *"It just doesn't get easier, Del."* Her anger now all but blacked out the voice which chimed on with, *"You have new friends. Relax. Greetings. Help make this a better world."*

Del had to take offense. This was a place she had visited dozens of times, baring her youthful spirit, even in adulthood, to thoroughly enjoy some relaxation and fun. Like desecrating a church, making this place a military and alien bastion rubbed her raw. It was wrong.

At the lobby entrance, non-Disney types offloaded luggage, took their names down, and gave each passenger their room assignment. Hers was 8104. She guessed the keycards would come later. There were dozens of better accommodations on the premises, this one being the oldest, but it would do. She'd stayed here and in the other theme hotels many times before and everything, even older accommodations were always first class. This was no vacation, though, and it became clear they weren't tourists when a very sober sounding head honcho poked her head in the bus and barked, "Remain on the bus! Work assignments at the next stop!"

Shrugging her shoulders with the futility of asking to go to the bathroom, she sat quietly, taking in her surroundings. Magnificent and lushly green topiaries of all types of animals and Disney characters in gay poses dotted the short ride to the main entrance. "At least you can stay oblivious to this change," she whispered to the sculptured animals and tried to drink in each one so she could hold the memory of better times past.

Once at the main entrance, there was clearly a lot of activity. People were very busy coming and going through the now removed turnstiles and gates, many carrying packages. At least she wouldn't have to pay for this trip; in fact, they'd be paying her she hoped. It was small consolation for visiting such a wonderful place under these circumstances.

The bus stopped smoothly and an Army type came on board, telling everyone to get out. The clipboard in his hand indicated assignments. Squinting as she stepped into the bright sunlight, she looked at the paper she'd been handed after showing her ID.

Adelle Summers: Meet Sergeant Ogato in the Magic Kingdom, at the Adventureland tunnel entrance by the public restrooms, just beyond the Swiss Family Robinson Tree house. Take the monorail ahead.

"Gee, no pleasant orientation, no cheerful explanation, nothing. Just get to work," she groused.

The monorail ride to the Magic Kingdom was ghostly quiet. Despite being full, no one said a thing. The few eyes she made contact with were all lifeless, void of any humanity. She should be thankful for the lack of kids and strollers, but she could have tolerated those better.

Del would have preferred to take the paddle boats. She loved the smell of the fresh inland lagoon and the sound of water rushing past the hull. Even the jocular captains were memorable. The longer ride made the slow approach to the Magic Kingdom even more exciting as adults and children crowded the rails expectantly.

The colorful Mickey Mouse flowerbed grinned at her for no reason in particular as she came down the cobblestone ramp from the monorail station to the main entrance of the Magic Kingdom. Gates and turnstiles had been removed here as well to make room she guessed for all this heavy traffic.

It was clear she'd be left to get to her assigned destination on her own. Knowing the Magic Kingdom very well, there wasn't even a need to ask for directions or consult the map she'd been handed. Amazingly, she'd been handed the same brochure every tourist received with times for all the shows and hours of operation. *"Surely the Diamond Horseshoe Review won't be kicking up their heels for this crowd,"* she quibbled inwardly. *"Bet Disney never expected this kind of adventure."*

With just her fanny pack, paperwork, and light jacket, she headed through the main gate and down Main Street, trying to mimic everyone else's bland expressions and mannerisms as best she could. That meant not staring at anything in particular and no happy expression. Still, it was hard not to smile in a place which held so many fond memories.

What sobered her was the lack of bands, gay chatter, children, and the sight of closed shops. In fact, the deathly quiet was almost unnerving. No parades, the smell of popcorn, street music, or ice cream vendor wagons. Even the gulls and smaller birds cleaning up popcorn were absent. Likely almost three weeks without the usual tourist handouts were enough to send them on to better pickings. "Gosh, I'd hoped to buy a frozen banana today," she whispered.

Del felt cynical amusement as she passed the brightly colored and immaculately landscaped flower beds thinking about the irony of the Quazzga being here. Names such as Adventureland, Tomorrowland, Frontierland, and Fantasyland took on a whole new meaning now. She even felt kinship with the Swiss Family Robinson as she glanced up at the huge tree house in the distance, given her current situation. Perhaps this was the perfect place for her after all.

Rounding the corner at the end of Main Street, she slowed to admire what she felt was the best landscaping in the Park, the beds near the Crystal Palace restaurant. Sadly, in just a couple weeks, she could see the lack of regular maintenance was taking its toll. While still prettier than anything she or her mom could ever put together, the beginning blight of wilting flowers and dead leaves was telltale. Moving her view towards the castle, it was clear the landscaping was looking less fresh. In a month or two, things would probably look downright ugly. This didn't help her dark disposition.

Adventureland was quieter than Main Street, but not by much. Still, it was nothing like it should be. This was one of her favorite areas of the Magic Kingdom, especially the Pirates of the Caribbean further up ahead. It was difficult to see so many people not having any fun in a place that normally oozed amusement. Rounding the corner to the public restrooms and tunnel entrance, she immediately picked out the military type who must be Sergeant Ogato and froze.

He was facing away from her, bent in conversation. Only partly hidden though were the unmistakable forms of three Quazzga. She gasped for air, suddenly realizing her breath had been held and she must have been frozen in place for 20 seconds. *"Oh great, Del. You wanted peace and quiet and no Quazzga. Today is not your lucky day."*

"You OK, lady?", broke her out of her stillness. Startled, she looked at the stocky young redhead, then blurted, "Uh...yeah. Just a little lost...I guess." For a moment, they both looked at each other intently and then their eyes averted simultaneously. Del saw something different in this young man in the brief instant their eyes locked. By his quickly doused expression of curiosity, it was obvious he saw the same thing in hers. She wanted to gaze into them again but dared not lest it reveal her secret.

She added, "Is that the Adventureland main tunnel entrance?" her eyes now back on the human/Quazzga foursome.

"Yep, right by that soldier," he responded in a Southern drawl. She could feel his stare on her and knew she was getting a thorough going over.

Things were getting too uncomfortable so she muttered, "Thanks," and walked away from this strange man before he could say anything else. She could still feel his eyes on her, but didn't want to glance back and check. If she was exposed here, it would be all over in minutes. This was definitely the enemy camp.

She decided to dodge the sergeant and aliens temporarily and use the restrooms, both for relief and composure. A few minutes later she had accomplished both.

Exiting the restrooms in the archway by the tunnel entrance, she made a beeline for the foursome, mustering as much calmness as she could. The Quazzga raised their heads to Del and the sergeant immediately stopped talking to look at this interruption. The Quazzga hadn't said anything which was puzzling until her mind was filled with a clear, *"Welcome."* Just like when the Quazzga had helped in the ER at the NMC, it was as clear as her own thoughts, sexless, but assuring. She couldn't tell which one had greeted her, but caught a flicker of motion in the slit-like mouth and the whisper of a chittering sound from the largest of the three.

Trying to mimic her fellow VC or SA, Del just raised her paper to the sergeant and said flatly, "Adelle Summers reporting sir," hoping to have the right combination of civilian and military tone. He didn't appear to notice or care one way or the other. She gazed at the hulking Sergeant to avoid staring at the Quazzga. Their black mirrored eyes were like aviator glasses. You just couldn't tell what part of your body they were looking at and it was always unnerving. It was apparent they wore little to no clothes which added to her uneasiness. Like the one time she'd been to a nudist camp a year before, it just wasn't her cup of tea.

The sergeant gave her another slip of paper and said, "Go through here, down the stairs to the second lower level. You'll be working in section A-10. Here's a map. Stay in the green zone for now."

Leaving them was a relief, though leaving for what was the question. She had never been to the guts of Disney World, the vast rumored underground city that supported the fun above. That countered some of her trepidation. Del didn't mind a little adventure. Danger, of course, was another thing.

Heading through the door to the underworld, it was a relief to be alone in a damp dark concrete jungle. The further she could get from Quazzga and VC, the better. Although she would certainly have liked to know more about the redhead with the strange look in his eyes, the moment had passed. It wasn't clear to her whether she'd met a friend or foe.

At the bottom of the stairs, she opened the tunnel door and couldn't believe how busy it was. Del had expected to see a few people, but this was Grand Central Station. It made the activity above ground appear tame by comparison and made her wonder just how many humans and Quazzga were here.

It was also quite bright, almost daylight. Numerous odors assaulted her, a mix of concrete, body odor, tire rubber, and outside air being pumped in. There was even a slight breeze though all the movement could have accounted for that. The temperature was very comfortable and the air lacked the above ground humidity.

"Lookout!" accompanied by a loud horn made her press reflexively against the door she'd just opened. A service cart swerving to avoid other groups of people nearly ran her over. The driver said nothing more and just continued. Several other carts also whizzed by. Between the vehicles and the pedestrians, it was down right claustrophobic. People were carrying packages and pushing carts full of equipment. Every cart was overflowing with crates or covered loads.

She took notice of the hectic and green-walled surroundings, glanced at the map, saw green arrows pointing off to her left, and headed for what she hoped was A-10.

Sure enough, 5 minutes of jostling in a crowd got her to A-10, indicated by huge letters on double doors. Traffic had lessened somewhat as people headed into other directions and moved off into other intersecting tunnels. Good thing the floor had green arrows. Plus, she had entered at A-2 and the numbers had risen from there. Now she stood alone and couldn't help but wonder what might await her now.

The doors slid open as she approached, disappearing into the walls like the old *Star Trek* shows, 'though not with the "swish" she remembered. A short unremarkable corridor faced her, with guarded windowless doors at the end. MIBs were standing there at attention.

"Saints preserve us," mentally echoed her grandmother's favorite phrase. She walked as steadily as possible and held out her papers, figuring that's what they'd want to see. "ID please," was all the MIB on the left said. She fumbled in her fanny pack and handed her NMC badge to him. The MIB took it and her other paperwork, glanced at them, attached a clip and holographic sticker to her badge, and passed it back. "Wear it at all times," he said evenly.

Clipping the badge to her collar, she couldn't help but think of a dozen witty things to say such as *"How're the suits today boys?"*, or *"Seen any aliens lately?"*, or *"If you keep that look up your face will freeze that way."* She knew it was really nerves when one line digs came to the forefront. In fact her palms felt clammy despite the comfortable air temperature.

The other MIB keyed a gadget in his hand the size of a pager, and the doors swung away from her silently. "First room to the right. Change and scrub up there. Then enter the clean area."

The extra security was eerie. She approached the 1st unmarked door with trepidation. It slid silently open to let her in.

It was nothing other than a locker room, though a very new and clean looking one. Del started to look for an empty locker when a 40-ish string bean of a man stepped around the corner leading presumably to the sink area. He simply said, "Here's the next open locker. Scrubs are behind me facing the sinks."

Pausing only a few moments, she said "OK," trying to look nonplussed.

"So, this is going to be a unisex facility," she concluded irritably.

He stayed put for what felt like an eternity and she wondered if he was going to stare at her undress, but it was clear he was just in a fog, and soon enough turned around, going the same way he came. She felt a little more comfortable getting undressed then.

While dressing and sanitizing her hands, as if prepping for an operation, she had to wonder why she was here and what she would be doing. The room was deathly quiet, no windows, no schedules on the wall, no instructions, and not even background music. Only the sound of water and a slight hum reached her ears.

Like everything else, she'd find out when someone wanted her to find out. On a deeper note, what was Disney doing with a facility like this? Was this their underground hospital? What would involve the Quazzga and MIBs?

A blonde woman in her 20s followed by a dark-skinned, mustached man in his 30s entered the locker area and were greeted similarly by the string bean who appeared to be the caretaker of the room. No one was big on conversation other than a, "Hi," or, excuse me," so Del, gloved, masked, gowned, and booted figured it was time to move to the next area, marked by a door marked Clean Room - Enter. Perhaps now she'd find out what she was supposed to do here.

The answer, or at least part of an answer, was right in front of her as this door too slid open automatically to reveal the cavern ahead. The room was huge and round, 10-foot-tall walls like the rest of the tunnels, at least 200 feet in diameter, and filled with equipment she had never seen in her life. It was like a clean room, everything brightly lit, white and silver, sterile looking, immaculate. Unlike the tunnels she'd just left, Quazzga were everywhere, at least a hundred, busy in a calm way, working panels, clearly getting this room setup for something.

There was a central circular core of panels and the rest of the room was laid out in three concentric rings from there. A path ahead of her led directly to the center, and there were two other paths heading out equidistantly from the edges. Some of the equipment ran from floor to ceiling, especially in the outermost ring. *"No way this is a Disney original,"* she marveled.

Del gawked shamelessly. It was hard not to. What boiled up in her brain was awe, and despair. *"Girl, you should ask to be surrounded by aliens. Maybe then you'd be left alone. Why do I keep getting the opposite of what I want?"* she thought.

An MIB appeared to her right, seemingly out of the wall from nowhere, and stood in stark contrast to the bright room. His face pointed towards Del, glasses mirrored like the eyes of the aliens he served. Not that she'd seen many of these MIB, but it made her wonder why no women had this role. Even the staunchest of male professions weren't 100% men any more. His continued gaze made her realize he must be watching her in particular and it chilled her blood.

Collecting herself, she returned her gaze to the room, studying the occupants as well as the surroundings. *"Just protective of their bosses and distrustful of any newcomer,"* she conjectured, trying to dismiss his presence, hoping she was right.

The few humans present stood out like a tree in the Kansas plains in their green hospital garments. From what she could quickly gather of their smooth interactions with surrounding Quazzga, they must be familiar with the aliens or had at least been here a while.

Ignoring the stare of the MIB, she continued to look over her surroundings. The voice kept chanting the same old stuff, but there was a mental pressure or buzzing making the voice harder to ignore. There also appeared to be numerous conversations going on just out of her comprehension, like when she used to play with her father's ham radio. Other than that and a few brief words by other humans, it was quiet. The equipment made little to no noise, which was unusual as all labs had a background electrical hum.

"Hello!" and, *"Welcome!"* in her head pulled her away from the observation, but she couldn't tell who had addressed her.

Thirty feet away, two Quazzga were looking directly at her from what she could tell, on the outer ring near a row of tall vertical tubes. One had a metallic blue necklace and started to move her way. *"You can begin your training now."* It wasn't exactly an order, but it wasn't a request either. Mentally she said, *"Yes, I am ready,"* though outwardly she just stared back. Their response was lightning quick as one of them asked, *"Are you OK? Can you begin?"* There was even a hint of irritation in the question.

With relief, confirming her earlier test that the Quazzga could not read human thoughts, she answered, "Yes, tell me what to do," and moved as steadily as possible towards the duo.

She'd have to get used to those eyes which only mirrored her face and were impenetrable as far as emotion went. This was only her second close encounter, so being calm was no easy feat. Judging by the slightly rougher skin texture, the alien with the necklace was older than the completely naked Quazzga. How they regulated body temperature was a mystery. It was definitely on the cool side down here. Maybe they had rhinoceros-like hides, although neither had any indication of an ounce of fat.

Not that there was anything sexual or sensual about these aliens. Quite the opposite. The lack of sexual features on unclothed bodies was actually repugnant, not unlike seeing old folks on the beach wearing very little, except there wasn't a wrinkle on these two.

"I'm Adelle Summers. How may I be of assistance?" She had a thousand other questions to ask, but as an acting zombie, she felt brevity was better. Answers would have to be found out by her astute observations alone.

The necklaced alien telepathed almost before her last word *"I am S'curoo and this is Dionee. You need to learn how* this *works and quickly,"* its right arm swinging smoothly away from Del.

"This" was a bank of controls at waist level with hundreds of multi-colored and illuminated dots, squares, and triangles organized in several sections over a 10-foot area. The tall tubes in front of her were glowing slightly, a faint whiteness like a dim fluorescent tube. Each was about a foot wide. It was totally foreign. She felt like a 2-year-old who was being handed a scanning electron microscope.

"Relax, we are your friends. Open your mind to S'curoo." The mental words were so strong and close, that Del found herself relaxing and opening her mind unconsciously.

S'curoo raised its right hand to touch Del's left temple with the lightest of pressure. Without waiting for any action from Del, S'curoo started to transmit instructions on how to operate this station. And transmit was the right word for it was a stream of information at high speed; like listening to someone speed-read a page per second, it was seemingly gibberish but the comprehension was there.

There was no time to pull away nor amazingly, any desire to do so. What to do, when, how often, which combination, when to report a problem, who to contact, and so on. In minutes, by her guesstimate, she had it all. Looking down at the panel, she understood what each button and combination of buttons would do. There were some symbols, a combination of Chinese and Sanskrit at first blush, but it didn't matter what they said because she knew what to do. *"Incredible!"* was all her awestruck mind would say.

A long slender finger from Dionee pointed to a center grouping of triangles. *"The purpose of these is?"*

Del quickly answered, "Solution temperature, barometric pressure, turbidity, and humidity."

"And these?" pointed S'curoo to the and upper array of dots.

"Solution composition specifically pH, electrolytes, nutrient, and amino acids," Del replied, amazed at her answers which she knew to be right.

"What potassium level is needed?" chimed in Dionee.

"0.03% to 0.05% for six equally spaced two hour increments, and 0.08% the remaining hours, all preprogrammed."

The questions went on for another half hour, covering every aspect of the station. It was clear they were not going to let an amateur work here. What baffled Del was she knew *everything* with total clarity. Neither alien corrected her so she assumed the answers were right.

A sixth sense told her the MIB was still boring his eyes into her back not too far away and a quick glance around confirmed it. Dionee and S'curoo angled their heads slightly in his direction and the MIB suddenly stood to attention and headed out of the room. Apparently, Del was no longer a threat or question mark which greatly relieved her but did not explain fully the MIB presence in the first place.

It was interesting the Quazzga could so finely tune their speech to a specific human, not like a broad band transmission the whole room could hear. Del swore she could hear snippets of mental conversations, but how they conversed so clearly with her alone, she could not fathom.

Finally, S'curoo, (she had started to pick up the difference in their mental voices, even detecting femininity if that was possible) said, *"Good. You learn fast. Any questions?"*

Without thinking, Del blurted "You've taught me how to use this equipment, but not why it is here. What will I be doing? I am able to work even better if I know the whole job, not just the mechanics."

The two aliens paused and Del felt her stomach sink. *"You idiot Del. Zombies don't ask questions. You're going to blow it!"*

For what appeared to be forever, the two conversed. Like the shortwave radio, Del couldn't quite pick it up. *"You are a curious species."* S'curoo finally replied. *"We were told there would be variations in your reactions to our teaching and presence. You act different from other humans we have worked with, but you also appear to learn better than others. Perhaps that is the difference."*

Dionee added smoothly, *"You will be in charge of this entire section."* Her slender index finger touched the visual grid controls and the translucent tubes cleared before her. *"You will oversee the growth of our offspring."*

And Del did see with startling clarity. 10 infant Quazzga, suspended one per tube in this small section. It was hard to listen to the rest of the lesson and not stare at the infants. *"You had to ask didn't you?"* she chastened herself.

Greg Burke

Hideaway

Eric Gomez was very cold, tired, and hungry as he started his evening trek. The deep snow forced him to stay far too close the highway, but traffic had become almost non-existent at night. A couple of times he had to duck behind a roadside snow bank and once he had nowhere to go when a truck passed by. Either the driver didn't notice or didn't care, but the unmarked double-trailer vehicle kept on moving.

At least the moonlight was helping. He found a few small, empty cabins, but they were just that: empty inside. They provided some measure of protection, but he was cold nonetheless. He needed to find a vacation home like his family had used on a few outings, guessing correctly that no one would come back this time of year and possibly never the way the world had changed.

The ornate padlocked gate ahead of him had to mean a big house at the end of the driveway. He hoped so. It was nothing to climb over the short fence beside the gate. The snow was only a foot deep leading up the house. He noticed rabbit tracks crossing the drive as he approached the house.

It wasn't a big house, it was gigantic! It was a mansion, all wood timbers and stone, at least four levels. The snow outside made the wood tones inside look especially warm and inviting. Antennae and satellite dishes were on the roof. There were lots of big windows. It was classy and expensive, much more than he could have hoped to find, but then there were a lot of rich folks up in these mountains.

His excitement was extinguished, though, when he saw a few lights on inside. He needed an empty house, not one with robots in it or worse. He rested a while, trying to catch a glimpse of the occupants, if any. Maybe they were just lights left on like his parents did when they went out. But then there was some movement inside to answer that question with sad finality. Between curtains and blinds, he couldn't tell how many people there were, but at least one person was inside. Disappointed and now even colder, he lowered his head in defeat. He'd have to move on.

Turning, he heard a noise and looked back. The side door opened and a bundled figure stepped out heading purposely towards the nearby woodpile. It looked like a lady. And she was singing! He hadn't heard that in weeks. After gathering an armful of logs, she stopped, then turned to look right at his hiding place. "You coming in or not?" he heard from a sweet voice with an accent, like he heard when his family visited Canada.

"How'd she know I was here?" he wondered.

As if she could read his mind she added, "I knew you were coming. It's OK. Come in before you freeze."

Eric got up slowly and hesitated. What if this was a trap? She could have called the police or worse. What he really wanted was to be alone, warm and fed yes, but alone, warm, and fed. She looked nice enough though, and the house was more than inviting.

"You can trust me, young man. I'm like you. This invasion hasn't affected my mind like all the others. We need to talk. It will be good to have a normal person to talk to. I'm assuming you aren't affected either or you wouldn't be out here by yourself in the dark and cold."

He hesitated so she continued, "Tell you what. Stay outside if you wish, the door is unlocked. Come on in when you're ready." The door closed slowly, then thudded shut.

Given his current situation with food, water, and this very cold night he needed to do something besides standing in the snow. The evidence was overwhelming. This was a safe place to be. Remembering the story of the gingerbread house where a nice place turned out to be a witch's home, he shrugged and decided to check it out anyway.

Once inside, the warmth melted away his doubts. It felt great! He stomped his feet to remove the snow and worked off his gloves. His hands tingled painfully as they warmed. Frostbite would have been a danger tonight. It was warm enough to remove his shoes, backpack, and coat and he did so as the house warmed both his body and spirit.

He worked his way through several storage rooms and an immense kitchen to the main room that was bigger than most people's entire home. There were couches everywhere in sections around a central fireplace that was burning brightly, though it was a gas fireplace. He wondered why she had needed wood. The furniture had a lot of cushions and matched the exterior with lots of wood armrests and backs. An old piano was in one section. Tall plants were everywhere, allowed by the ceiling which must have been 20 feet high.

Still carrying his shoes, gloves, and coat, he looked around for his mystery host.

"I'm in here, young man!" he heard from the left, the voice sweet and welcoming. Following the wide hallway, he saw her stoking a wood fire in the room at the end. It was a huge room also, full of books in dark wooden cases against every wall. Two chairs were pulled up close to the fireplace. A desk and an awesome array of computer equipment filled out the rest of the room.

"Make yourself at home, little one. You need to warm up," she said, helping him set down his snow wet articles, pointing to one of the chairs. "Can I make you something to eat?"

"How did you know I was coming?" he had to ask first, being both suspicious and cautious.

Reaching into her pocket, she pulled out a palm-sized computer. "The alarm went off a while before, probably when you hopped the fence. Then I saw you on the camera here," she went on, showing him a clear live picture of the area where she had found him, snow still falling lightly. "There are about 40 cameras around so I was able to follow your walk up the drive."

He gazed at her more closely now that she was unbundled. Long gray-black hair, but smooth, light-colored skin, thin overall, hazel eyes. Not as old as his grandma, but definitely older than his parents.

Satisfied with her explanation, he spoke up, "I'm hungry and I can pay you for food, ma'am."

"Call me Lady Henri or Jennifer, whichever suits you. Would soup be acceptable?"

He nodded, and 10 minutes later, they were friends. He told her what had happened to him, and his family. Lady Henri said he could stay as long as he wanted. She told Eric her wealthy husband was overseas and hadn't been heard from since the invasion. They always prepared for at least two winters, so the house was self sufficient for at least that long. She painted and critiqued theatrical manuscripts on the Internet to fill her time. She hadn't moved off her property in weeks, nor did she think it was safe to do so.

While Eric didn't understand the reason for the invasion, Lady Henri appeared unconcerned. The soup and the fire made him sleepy and he settled into the soft, high-backed chair. Sleep was tugging at him, making it hard to stay alert. It was good to be inside a real home and to talk to someone who wasn't a robot.

He was staring into the hypnotic flames of the fire when she added another log. As she bent forward, her hair fell to one side, revealing a scar on the back of her neck just like those he'd seen on changed kids at school.

Hide and Seek

Jax paused as he watched the attractive newcomer walk away from him towards the tunnel entrance. In the weeks since the invasion, he'd seen a lot of folks come and go and all of them were mindless freaks, or had been changed to mindless freaks. This lady was different, though. Those deep brown eyes and the expression inside them told him so. *"Ya gotta be sure, ol' boy,"* he told himself as a warning, but every ounce of his being, what little instinct or gut feeling he had, was telling him, though, that it had to be true. "She's like me!" he whispered louder than he should, willing it to be so, hoping beyond hope it was so.

When you're alone without people, it's one thing. Being alone with people who don't give a damn is another. Jax had always felt that stroke victims like Gerry Peyton, his neighbor, weren't just unthinking prisoners inside poorly functioning shells, unlike the zombies. He'd seen the frustration and anger Gerry had exhibited during his rehabilitation, and knew it had to be a living hell. Gerry wasn't just a vegetable who didn't care what had happened, he was a thinking, lucid person.

Jax guessed if he became a zombie too, none of what was going on would matter. But that was the rub. Life, his life, did matter. And like his buddy Gerry, he felt like he was trapped in a prison not of his making. Seeing this woman today was like the few times he felt Gerry and he had actually connected, beyond the slurred words and paralysis, and it was suddenly just like the old days when they played softball, fished, and watched the Miami Dolphins kick butt.

So this discovery couldn't be left alone. The one ray of hope in weeks needed attention right now. He had graduated from the Montgomery Scott school of engineering of the old Star Trek series fame, so he padded all his work with plenty of room to perform miracles, or in his more practical way of thinking, allow more time to goof off. Thus, the hour-long task he needed to complete at the Adventureland substation would only take twenty minutes, which left him forty minutes to get some answers. There was probably cushion on top of that if he needed it. Luckily, he'd been given a ton of latitude, as long as the jobs got done.

He overheard the sergeant bark "A-10!" as he surreptitiously ambled closer to the human/Quazzga group. A-10 was the modified area, heavily modified. In fact, he couldn't believe how much they'd changed that section in so little time and suspected it wasn't the only area affected within Disney World.

Not being a spy or commando, he simply took the easiest approach to following her, blending in with others, staying far enough back so he could see her, knowing at a leisurely pace he'd end up at A-10 about the same time. He'd have to see what developed from there.

He waited a minute, looking busy doing nothing near the tunnel entrance, then headed down after her. As soon as he hit the main tunnel, he wished he'd had his cart. "Jeez it's crowded!" he grumbled. He could just spot her unmistakable figure up ahead, edging nervously along the wall of the tunnel.

When things thinned out near A-10, he was sure he'd have his chance to do something, but suddenly it was just him and her rounding the bend to the newest section and he slowed to a stop, unsure how to proceed. He didn't want to scare her, and deep down he was scared to death that it might turn out he was wrong.

That hesitation cost him as she slipped through the door ahead. Approaching the A-10 entryway, he called it quits and chickened out. He was not authorized to be here and no doubt there were surveillance cameras that would watch his actions.

Looking around as if he knew what he was doing, Jax checked the markings on some nearby utility closets, glanced at his watch, checked his toolkit, then headed away. In retrospect, meeting her in this hallway near the new section might have tipped them both off to the ninja or worse. Still, he mentally kicked himself for the lost opportunity. Hanging around to wait for her to come out would be crazy. Maybe he'd see her again, but with so many people and random schedules, it was not a sure bet.

As he walked back to his original task in Adventureland, something else struck him. *"What 'ya gonna say to her when you do get her alone?"* That was a million dollar question. Hell, billion dollar. He didn't have a clear answer and figured he'd wing it as he had been for weeks, play a hunch, smooth-talk his way to finding out the truth, then figure out what to do from there. *"You ain't no genius, boy, just a man trying to get by the best way he knows how and the best way will show itself when the time is right,"* was the best internal encouragement he could wring out of this disappointing encounter that never was.

Then it hit him, *"Hey, I've got full access to the Disney network here!"* That meant not just maintenance schedules and operating hours for every sector, but also employee schedules and duty rosters as well as guest lists. He didn't have official access to the info, but had hacked his way into that area years before with the help of his techie colleague Joshua in Personnel, who had since gone on to greener pastures, but left Jax with a lot of secrets.

There hadn't been any great use for the employee info and it was more of a curiosity to see if it could be done. He'd even found personnel records of the top brass as well as his coworkers, some of it very juicy indeed. Still, it was the thrill of victory, not the agony of others that drove him to do it so nothing ever came of the revelations he uncovered. He wasn't even into scorched earth politics should, God forbid, they ever decide to fire him.

With any luck, though, he should be able to find out who this mystery lady was and where he could find her. That hope kept him satisfied as he completed his duties for the day.

It was difficult to stay on task and finish the work on his duty list, especially when things kept being added at the last minute. It appeared there was no end to the re-routing of power couplings from one area to another and he wondered if there was a conspiracy to keep him away from what he really wanted to do.

Clearly, though, as the day wore on, priorities remained down below on what his bosses wanted him to do, not up above on his private investigation. The work orders just kept flying at him. The rate at which attractions were being stripped made the demise of this world-class playground all the more painful for him.

Finally, he had the chance to get back to his station and access what he hoped would be useful information. "Keystrokes don't fail me now!" he said to the four walls, grateful that everyone had gone home for the evening. He was even more grateful they hadn't assigned him to the hotels like many of the staff. Since he'd been staying down below the castle for weeks, guess it made sense to leave him there. And he'd been a model citizen, as much as it galled him.

Josh had designed much of the software and thus its safeguards. It was a game he and Jax played, trying to figure out the delicate balance of access and security. Josh was a master, but Jax his equal. Truth be known, they'd both have been canned if anyone had ever got wind of the point-counterpoint games they played openly on live systems. Luckily, or perhaps a tribute to their skills, nothing ever crashed.

Remembering his lessons well, he entered the guest records through the back door of cyber space, weaving surreptitiously through a host of security zones 'til he had full and unrestricted access. "Bless you Josh," he whispered. "Hope to God you're safe in all this mess."

The records of new guests were massive and locating his target lady would be like finding the high school ring he'd lost in the 10,000 gallon orange juice vat during his job one summer in college. So he dug deeper, careful to not set off automatic cyber alarms, and categorized the guests by arrival date, figuring she must have arrived today or yesterday by the way she looked disoriented. Dead end. No cross references available and still too many names.

A few more subfile queries got him into interesting territory, listing people by work area. Ten minutes of reading boring lists, then cross-referencing with new arrivals clarified the picture. "Gotcha lady from A-10. Your knight in shining armor is ready to defend your honor," he spoke with confidence, as he prepared a little surprise of his own, taking his time to be prepare carefully. Jax then deleted all evidence of his ever accessing information from this terminal, just as Josh had taught him. Mission accomplished.

* * * * *

Del stared out her Contemporary Hotel porch window at the evening sky, parting expensive drapery, not willing to open the curtains fully, wanting as much privacy as possible. It was too cool to sit on the deck. Quazzga ships replaced the night sky lights of what had once been a busy Orlando traffic pattern of jets and STOL craft.

It always surprised her to find a twinkling star with a reddish color, only to realize after watching it for a few seconds it was just a jet passing through. No one would mistake the Quazzga ships for stars. They generally moved too fast with too many light colors and in quickly shifting patterns. They were almost hypnotic in the graceful way they moved.

Stars were better seen in the Keys or when camping in the Everglades. They were best yet when viewed during the new moon in Rocky Mountain National Park at 8000 feet above sea level. Vivid memories of every constellation came back to her, remembering her glorious family vacations to Estes Park, Colorado northwest of Denver. Those were stars you could almost touch and scoop out of the sky. Those wonderful days of hiking and fun in that slice of heaven were memories even the Quazzga couldn't ruin, as long as she kept her act working.

Staring at nothing in particular now, she reviewed some of today's events, the beautiful view failing to improve her mood.

Her day had ended badly, all on top of the underlying shock when she realized she had to care for the enemy, innocent as they were. Turning herself in, getting it over with, almost felt preferable to what appeared to be a continued tightening of the noose, ever so slow, but certain. *"How long can my luck at this charade hold out?"* she wondered. *"Hell, a quick lynching would be preferable to this torture."* she thought, then instantly regretted it.

Remembering what her grandparents had told her about life for blacks or even people that looked black in the South decades before brought a wince of regret. No, she'd been over this almost daily and despite the torture, she'd go on. At least she was herself. She had to keep reminding herself she was lucky, even if her situation wasn't.

Still, something or someone upstairs had a real mean streak, putting her in situations that could only end up badly in the long run. She wanted to be as far from Quazzga, VC, and SA as possible, yet here she was living, eating, and breathing with what must be the world's greatest concentration of all three.

Dinner itself was interesting. The fourth floor restaurant was an open buffet of bland food, cooked by people who didn't care and eaten by people who didn't have a care. Conversation was out of the question for Del, but people did talk about their assignments and how exciting it was to have new friends. There was little feeling to the conversations, though, as if people were just repeating the platitudes from the voice, no original ideas of their own. It was too bad the bars were closed. This group could use a little loosening up. So she ate what little was needed and excused herself. No one appeared to notice or care.

The lack of MIBs or Quazzga relaxed her and the atmosphere in the hotel was luxurious with colorful carpets, beautiful murals, and expensive artwork, although it was grandeur and talent wasted on this crowd.

The instructions they'd received when arriving back at the hotel had good news and bad. It looked like they'd all be cared for very well in terms of food and laundry. *"Like a pet, no doubt,"* she suspected. That was the good news. The bad news was it was one to a bed and Del had been assigned a double. *"Super. A VC roommate. Just what I needed,"* she lamented. Now she'd have to keep up the charade 24 hours a day.

What no one at the front desk mentioned and none of the other arrivals asked for or received as she waited in the registration line though was a room key. Since everyone just headed off for their room, she did likewise. The answer was simple when she arrived at 8104, the room wasn't locked.

"Oh for crying out loud, no privacy for me and anyone who wants to can come in here anytime," she complained, entering the room. Her suitcases were just inside the door, this latest twist of unlocked doors still puzzled her as she moved them to the bed, removed her belongings, and settled in.

Why no locked rooms? Guess in this brave new world it just doesn't matter was all she could deduce. Breaking the problem down into parts to analyze each danger, Del realized she could relax. Everyone, SA, or VC acted politely. There had been no storm trooper activity since the invasion, at least not towards her. Crime probably didn't exist anymore so there was no fear from that quarter. Finally, no guy or girl had made so much as a pass at her in weeks meaning rape was probably out of the question. In fact, with what little she knew about VC or SA people, she'd doubted they even had sexual thoughts any longer.

That would mean zero population growth in a hurry, something which would certainly make the ZPG folks very happy indeed. *"Would the Quazzga do something about that or was that the Quazzga plan?"* she had to wonder.

Her head slumped down in weariness, anger, and frustration. *"My God, what is going on? What will happen to us?"*

Her view of the mirror-still lakes around this grand hotel and the unused pools below clouded with the beginning of tears. It was too much for one person. Too much to have to consider all that could happen, while living the nightmare that was happening. A deep breath, then another, helped her gain composure. Then there was a knock at the door.

"Who is it?" she asked, doubting it was room service, more likely it was her roommate. When there was no answer, she sat down calmly on the bed and said, "OK, come on in."

The door opened slowly and the face and body that popped in quickly, almost nervously, was not what she'd expected. It was the big redhead she'd encountered in Adventureland!

He closed the door quickly, obviously pleased to see it was her also, and then just stood, back to the door acting nervous and shy, staring, clearly not sure what to say.

Del had a thousand questions to ask, but the top of the list came out first. "Who are you and what do you want?" she queried in as level a VC manner as she could. She could tell that put him off and he acted like he suddenly wanted to leave, as if he'd made a huge mistake coming here.

So they just stared for what seemed like minutes, each of them alternately getting more tense, then relaxed, each probing and gauging the situation with every sense he or she possessed.

He finally broke the ice, answering her question "I'm Jackson Leigh, and I just came here to talk....to you....ma'am. I'm sorry if I worried you."

Was this a trick, an illusion, or a trap? Her fear rose exponentially as she remembered the man at the beach. Her mind raced with all the possibilities, eyes locked on his, which continued to remain locked on hers.

He moved tentatively forward, extending his hand and added, "I hope you are what I think you are, or I'm in a world of hurt."

Whatever the consequences, there was no turning back now. If it was a trap, it had been sprung. If it wasn't, and every ounce of her intuition said it wasn't, then finally a prayer had been answered. She extended her hand to grab his, an electricity of emotions exchanging with that firm touch, "Adelle Summers, and you may not really want to know me, Mr. Leigh."

"B..beg Pardon?" he stammered as they each took a step back.

"Relax, Mr. Leigh," she continued, lowering her guard, dropping all reservations as this was obviously a normal and sweet person who stood in front of her. "I guess we're in the same boat, even if it is the Titanic."

He let out a breath of air, visibly relieved. "You don't know how fine it is to hear humor again. Guess I won't be needing this to knock you senseless," as he pulled a short club from under his jacket.

Surprised, but then again not, Del responded, "Who said I was joking?" The club was suddenly in her hand, the distance between them gone, his arm wrenched painfully behind him, her arm around his throat. "Karate lessons, you wouldn't have stood a chance," she whispered behind him. She released him almost as quick as she'd taken him, but not before checking the back of his neck.

She could still read pages of surprise on his face as she swung back in front of him, club in one hand, tapping the palm of her other hand. He held his hands up in surrender. "OK, I give up, ma'am. Guess I surprised you wrongly."

"First thing, Mr. Leigh, stop calling me ma'am. I'm hardly your mother. Just call me Del. Second thing, I owe you this," and she turned around, lifted her dark brown hair, exposing her neck.

Jax was taken aback by her boldness, opening herself to him completely, revealing herself for what she was. He could see for sure what he'd sensed personally and no longer had any doubts. "You sure 'nuf ain't like the others ma'... I mean Del," he breathed, more an affirmation of total relief than just a statement of fact. "Oh, and you can call me Jax." he added.

She turned around slowly, dropping her hair, the club and her arms. They locked eyes, then they rushed together and locked arms. It was a hug of mutual reassurance, kinship, and bonding of prisoners in the same living hell. They held on as tight as they dared, savoring a moment neither expected but were both overwhelmed to experience. Each took and gave comfort at the same time.

In silence, they finally let each other go. Jax could see moisture in her eyes, but hope and happiness as well. He was flushed with emotion also.

"How did you....?" they spoke simultaneously, then stopped and laughed. Weeks of questions needed to be answered after the initial shock of finding another normal human being.

"You first, Jax," offered Del. "Ask me anything, but we don't have all night. This is a double, so my roommate might come at any time and these rooms aren't locked."

"Aw, don't worry 'bout that. It's all taken care of," he responded casually.

Alarms suddenly went off in her head and seriousness replaced her recent happiness. Perhaps this was a trap. "What do you mean by that?"

He looked at the floor, then sheepishly volunteered, "'Cause I'm your roommate."

Seeing her jaw drop, he quickly added, "I hacked into the computers to locate you, and thanks to an old friend who taught me some awesome tricks, I set it up so we could be together."

Still seeing doubt in her eyes, he continued, "Look, most of my cohorts were being moved from temp quarters in the tunnel to the resorts and my turn was soon. No one will suspect a thing with all that's going on. I had to take this chance 'cause I was going nuts anyway. Plus, better us together, then stuck with zombies for roommates separately."

He still detected a trace of suspicion. "If 'ya want me to undo it, consider it done. It's your call. I didn't mean to intrude without your permission."

She couldn't argue with anything he said except it was bold and reckless, possibly leading them both into trouble. She also felt a bit conned. Looking at him squarely, he appeared honest enough and her fears melted. With a wry smile, she said, "All right big guy, you, me, and the four walls. Outside of here, though, we're strangers, got it? Inside here, we'll see."

"You betcha!" he beamed and they shook hands, one firm up and down motion. "I'll go get my stuff."

Grabbing his arm, she said, "Wait a minute. You can go later. We need to talk now while we've got a chance. I need some answers."

He decided his possessions could be sent over or he could get them in the morning. Shoulders drooping, energy draining off his body, he made for the closest chair and slumped down like a giant rag doll, not a bad analogy with all his freckles and red hair. "Yeah, me too. This is all so crazy. You don't know how good it is to see a real human being again."

The ensuing hours were like a debriefing. Both shared their stories, recent and past, finding common ground in their experiences, agreeing on the desperateness of their predicament, filling in gaps about events, speculating where gaps still existed. Their discussions were intense, two sharp minds in action. Mostly their brains were in overdrive as each had a chance to actually discuss, talk, commiserate, and unburden words and feelings to someone, someone real, unloading weeks of pent up questions and conversation.

Del liked Jax's zombie terms better than SA. Jax like the MIB designation better than ninja. In exploring why they weren't affected, they figured there must be more people like them, but not very many. Like the bell curve, some people were highly susceptible and others less. They obviously fell at the edge of the curve labeled "least susceptible". Why them, they couldn't fathom. There could be a genetic reason, but more likely it was just the luck of the draw. Whoever was in hiding like them, those numbers were bound to drop over time as fate caught up with them.

He was saddened by what Del had been through. His experiences were tame by comparison. Neither could come up with any suggestions for a way out. There were still too many unanswered questions and their jobs were a trap they couldn't evade. Escape was out of the question.

Both concurred they didn't want to be exposed and become surgically altered, nor did they want to completely capitulate, forever being unwilling zombies. The also agreed two against the Quazzga was better than one. Hope had more than doubled with their meeting.

The revelation that Del was taking care of Quazzga young brought some finality to the invasion. The Quazzga were here to stay and they were making inroads as quickly as possible. And what would happen to humans if they stopped reproducing? What was the full human role? They agreed the answers would be troubling. Humans were getting the shaft in this deal, and the magnitude of the Quazzga influence was overwhelming.

Jax filled up every inch of the armchair but sat in every position imaginable, getting up occasionally to pace the floor or get some water. Del talked from the bed and alternately sat on the edge or middle, laid back, or rolled over on her stomach, head propped in her hands. As the hours wore on, they formed a bond of trust, respect, and friendship. He was more than just a big mechanic, she was more than just a pretty face.

Several times they had to shush each other as their conversation became animated. By mutual consent, they agreed to keep their jokes and laughter to a minimum lest neighbors began to wonder. The rooms were fairly well soundproofed, but one couldn't be too careful.

Finally, exhaustion took over and neither could stay awake. It was past 3 a.m. and both had their normal busy schedules ahead with little sleep to boot. They handled bodily functions and Del let him use her toothbrush. His boxers would double as pajama bottoms. It was too warm in the room for heavier clothing since they had closed the windows and sliding door for privacy. She wore an oversized shirt, but didn't act comfortable with that much on. They smiled nervously, set the alarm console between them for less than three hours later, cut the lights and went to their separate beds.

Twenty seconds later, Jax heard his name in the dark. "Yeah?"

Her voice was a low whisper, "Could you hold me?"

His covers lifted as he said, "Sure." Her warm compact body slid neatly next to his, the double bed holding them with little room to spare. He was on his back, and she nestled into his shoulder, her right arm draping tightly across his barrel chest. He patted her shoulder lightly. Before he could get any wild ideas, he could feel she was dead asleep. The last thing he remembered was thinking about their uncertain future together.

* * * * *

He woke to the resonant sound of the shower, the constant dripping of water on the shower floor and thrum of water moving through pipes. He must have slept like a rock, unusual for him, but then last night was out of the ordinary.

Waking up fully, Jax smiled with satisfaction. He wasn't alone! And if there was him and Del, perhaps there were more. And if there were more, perhaps they could form some sort of underground. The more they could find and work with, the better their chance of not only survival, but a way to beat this problem.

He glanced at the clock, then exclaimed, "Oh man! You're gonna be late!" He usually popped out of bed before his alarm and he had set the clock for the last possible second. Jumping out of bed, he dressed so fast he almost fell on his face pulling on his pants. He knocked at the door to the bathroom and shouted, "Del, gotta go, I'm way late, see ya tonight!" Without waiting for an answer, he bolted out the door, then moved in as calm and unhurried a fashion as he could to the castle control room for the start of another day. His unique night though would make this day a good one. It was hard to control the excitement of having found a normal human being, but he smirked a little as he realized his incredible fortune in finding such a wonderful gem of a person. He also remembered how the night had ended with her awesome body next to his, even if she didn't care about him...yet. Things were really looking up in more ways than one. It was hard to think about the many tasks on his job list and concentrate on his job as the day started.

* * * * *

Hot showers always helped Del think. Meeting Jax had been incredible, a gift, an answer to her prayers, and a relief. She stood directly under the hot spray and let the water cascade over as much of her body as possible, warming her thoroughly. For the first time in weeks, she felt happy. She felt hope.

It was great to have someone to hold her. Male or female, she needed the closeness of another human being. Jax was something else, though, and they clearly needed each other. She was very lucky to have found someone of his capabilities, compassion, and understanding. Not to mention she was mildly attracted to him. *"Careful, careful, Del!"* she admonished herself. *"Don't fall for the first normal person you see, even if it's the only one."* Still, waking up near him this morning, refreshed and surprisingly alert despite the short night, made all her fears appear small, made her feel human again for the first time in a long time.

She heard him shout something about being late through the door, and smiled mischievously, knowing she'd been the cause. It was great to have some real fun, even at someone else's expense. The temperature was bumped a notch warmer. She had a little more time and wanted to enjoy every second. Life may have dealt her a winning hand finally.

Greg Burke

Double Jeopardy

Neither Jax nor Del could concentrate much on their assignments that day or the next. They had talked so much the previous night and yet had so much more to talk about. Calling each other was out of the question. Jax worked well into the night and she had to get up nearly as soon as he got in. They agreed quickly to eat separately, and when their schedules allowed, they'd talk some more. Neither wanted to wait, but both knew it was prudent to do so.

Del was astonished at how fast the Quazzga young were growing. Doing some estimates on start to finish curves, extrapolated from her heightened knowledge of the equipment, the tube gestation would only be three months. The idea of true test tube babies had been in sci-fi for years, but nothing had come close other than fertilizing eggs, then growing them inside a human host. Even cloning techniques hadn't progressed much beyond that step. What had been cloned hadn't survived or had limitations which made human cloning unlikely. Funny how duplicate sheep might look and act the same, but cloned monkeys had proven that identical genetic codes did not produce the same functioning being.

She studied the 10 tubes closely with more than just robotic efficiency. Sure she logged their progress into the console, carefully indicating any adjustments made as required, but from what she could tell, it was all on autopilot. There were alarms and automatic countermeasures for every parameter. So far, she was just marking time and could do this job in a chair reading the Wall Street Journal off the Internet if there had been a chair or computer console, and if the Wall Street Journal was still being produced.

Thus, she tried to understand more about the fetuses, and by extrapolation, the Quazzga. Del had obviously missed the opening steps of the process and it was estimated they had been growing for about three weeks. *"Hmmm. Just like when there's a blackout in cities and a resultant baby boom nine months later, the Quazzga couldn't help but celebrate the invasion."* How it started she couldn't guess, but judging by the tiny, nearly vestigial fetal sex organs and the apparent lack of adult sex organs, it was probably a very clinical and unemotional process.

Their development was actually very human-like, though fetal Quazzga brain size was enormous. The surrounding fluid in the tube was crystal clear and their bodies were transparent to translucent allowing her to visualize most organs and the bone/muscle structure. There was a silvery/bluish glistening to their skin color.

How could something from so far away with not even the slightest chance of connection to humans be so similar? That debate had raged in the scientific community, and despite the movies showing all manner of alien life, the first contact that shows up proves not to be too much different. Coming from such distant primordial soups, the result had been nearly the same. If geneticists and anthropologists had cared any more, it would be fascinating study and debate.

She couldn't get DNA samples, nor would she likely be allowed to find a lab and study them if she could, but it would be very curious to know their DNA structure. There were organs she couldn't figure out at this stage, but one heart, two lungs, digestive tract, cardiovascular system, all similar to humans and near perfect bilateral symmetry. There were more bones in the hands, neck, spine, ribcage and feet. Amazingly, each fetus also had an umbilical cord attached mid body like most Earth mammals. So many similarities, so dissimilar the end result. "Maybe God did create people in his own image and worked in different sections of the galaxy," she concluded.

The passive six inch long fetuses floated safely in the carefully controlled, oxygen aerated solution. There was ample room for growth upward as the umbilical cord trailed downward to the placenta, which occupied the entire base of the tube.

The placenta was a biomechanical wonder. There was a mass of tissue for sure, but it was interspersed with tiny lights and filaments of wire so it was not just tissue and not just hardwiring. That had to be where all the sensors on her panels got their readings, and they provided nourishment, chemicals, and hormones, as well as maintained temperature.

Del was highly impressed, from a professional standpoint. This arrangement virtually guaranteed safe and stable growth for the infant. The Quazzga probably weeded out genetically deficient donor materials so only viable babies would be tubed. Quazzga parents could just go on with their lives, leaving it to the baby sitters, in this case Del and her round the clock group of companions. She didn't agree with the whole thing in the least, but appreciated the efficiency. She knew nothing of Quazzga society, so imposing terrestrial standards was pointless and possibly wrong.

Two more banks of tubes had been added to the nursery since yesterday. That brought the total to 140. 250 was probably the max, for this room anyway. *"Wonder what's going on in other parts of the world?"* she mused. *"Is this it or are there more here in Central Florida and elsewhere?"*

None of the other workers said much at shift change, on breaks, or otherwise. She hadn't met any of them before and no one went out of their way for introductions aside from a quick, "Hello, I'm so and so." It was almost like people were becoming more zombie like. Perhaps the constant psycho-babble in their heads acted like dose after dose of sedatives. Everyone acted proficiently and you could get a detailed answer to any technical question, just like asking a medical-terminal, but the who, what, when, where, and why questions got short or non-committal answers. She kept her involvement with others to a bare minimum. Her hopes lay elsewhere, in another person altogether.

The Quazzga popped in and out with regularity in what appeared to be almost mother-like interest in the "tubers", as Del nicknamed them. MIBs were rarely seen except when she reported to the A-10 entrance. S'curoo and Dionee showed up occasionally to teach other human attendants, stopping by only briefly at her station to quiz her about their offspring's progress. With satisfaction, Del noticed that other humans took many training sessions before they were left alone, unlike her very short and perfect indoctrination. *"See you idiots, you take the fight out of us and you take a whole lot more,"* she thought scornfully.

The background buzz of unintelligible mind speech was strong in this room, even stronger near the tubers. That puzzled Del until she bent her head over the panel and concentrated her thoughts to hear better. This was dumb since she wasn't really hearing anything. *"Hey gal, it's in your head!"* she finally concluded. Amazingly, the buzz became clearer and more intense as she moved her head closer. Like getting near high voltage, she felt a tingle on her skin, but mostly inside her head. It was very unusual and highly unsettling. Not being able to catch the gist of the information, she could tell it was a steady stream of information, not too different than when she'd been taught how to work the console.

Dizziness started to overcome her and her natural reaction was to pull back and gain her balance. Stepping away, she was left with a growing headache. Suddenly, it became clear. *"They're teaching them while they grow!"* she realized with astonishment. The general tone of the information stream was instructional, laced with some comfort and even singing. So, these kids weren't on their own. They probably came out of the tubes knowing everything they needed to start being productive. *"Wow, this was better than the nuns. These kids will be ripe from the get-go!"* she concluded, feeling insignificant in comparison.

It was a relief when the shift ended and she could get back to her roommate. They had a lot to discuss and she missed his company dearly.

Jax was sitting in one of the two armchairs when she got in, flipping through some tech-manual as if that occupied all his interest. There was nothing good on TV she knew, but he kept his nose in the manual with only a non-committal, "Hi, Del," from behind the pages. That miffed her since they'd seen so little of each other and she expected a warmer greeting.

His belongings had evidently been put away because of the additional clutter on the dresser and suitcase on the floor. "Is that all you have to say?" she asked peevishly.

The pages fell down on his lap and she knew she'd been had. The boyish and mischievous grin was a mile wide. He got up smartly, and hugged her tight saying, "I missed you Del." The bear hug was warmly returned.

Still smiling, he stepped to the bathroom and removed two items. One was a cup filled with beautiful but on the dead side bouquet of flowers and the other was a bottle of chilled Champagne. "Surprise!" he beamed. "The flowers are compliments of Snow White's Castle. I had to sneak them here in my jacket. The champagne is complements of my director for finishing the Cleopatra section, something you and I will likely never see unless the aliens develop a love of the arts and entertainment. I had been saving it for when the director and I had a quiet moment, but I don't think his addled brain will mind now."

Del had to indulge herself. A carnation was swept from the cup and tucked in her left ear. The bottle was snatched from his hands, foil peeled unceremoniously from the top and like a pro, the cork was eased out in a low, satisfying pop that didn't hurt the ceiling or put out an eye despite the warnings. Studying the label, sure it was a cheap bottle of something local, she had to raise her eyebrows in surprise, "Dom Perignon, 1986. I'm impressed."

"Yeah, well, I did a helluva job on that ride, it should have been something a lot fresher than that," he answered deadpan.

She wondered for a few seconds if "Mr. Wholesome" didn't understand the concept of vintage years, but he winked conspiratorially and they both giggled.

"What are we celebrating?"

Jax had a ready answer, "Hope and us."

Her eyebrows raised in disbelief. "I like the us part, not too sure about the hope."

"It's been a rotten month for me. Much worse for you," he continued, heading back to the bathroom for some drinking glasses. Then he turned around, looked her square in the eyes and said with a deep seriousness that warmed her, "Finding you Ms. Summers has been the answer to a prayer. I'm so glad we found each other."

"Don't get all mushy on me now Mr. Leigh. It was pure luck and you know it," she said wagging her free index finger at him. She grabbed a glass, poured for both of them, then also looked him squarely in the eye, "To hope, to us, and I'm glad we found each other too."

Glasses were clinked, their bond strengthened, and they sat in the armchairs, sipping slowly in the silence. With nothing to watch on the TV and the radio equally bad, each other's company would have to do. Which was fine by Jax. It reminded him of those times when there'd be a blackout and everyone would sit around a fire, or light candles, and just sit to discuss things. At those times, families were the closest and the times the most memorable.

Del couldn't wait to tell him about her wild day and a half. It was fantastic to finally have a chance to unload her thoughts to someone who not only cared, but understood her frustrations.

He was amazed to hear about the tubers but not surprised either. "I helped set up that room several days before you arrived. Very secretive, lots of neat equipment. I'd wondered what they were up to."

His day had been the same old same old, fixing things and setting up new equipment. The Quazzga were definitely settling in. Although he didn't work with any of them directly, just about all the equipment deliveries and setup were in newly renovated areas that were living quarters, labs of some sort, and general Quazzga accouterments.

No alien had trained him on anything yet, but he'd seen their training process and agreed most zombies took a while to learn. It appeared to him that only former Ph. D. types were being taught. "Guess you must be special for them to bring you in and teach you," he quipped.

She smirked at him saying, "Trade you any day. I'm way too close to them for comfort. I have to walk on eggshells all the time."

Their conversation, like the other night, continued into the wee hours, long after the bottle had been finished. There was just so much catching up they needed to do.

Eventually, there was silence between them. The few minutes pause felt good, each other's company being enough for the moment. She was staring at the ceiling, her head resting on his shoulder when his warm hand clasped hers.

"Thanks for listening and talking. I needed it," he said quietly. Jax stood up, still holding her hand and pulled her to him, hugging her tight. She hugged back and they lingered in the embrace. Something clicked in those seconds that neither had expected, a change in their relationship, a warming of souls, a mutual need.

Minutes later, fatigue of the late hour forgotten in heated passion, clothes strewn around the room, they were embraced again. Sweat glistened on their bodies, tenderness giving way to urgent desire.

Neither heard the snick of their room door as they edged towards mutual crescendo. They shuddered together briefly and stopped as if frozen. In fact, they were paralyzed, stuck together at the moment of bliss, eyes open wide, wondering with utter dismay what was happening.

"Human mating is fascinating," came a clear, unemotional, and male-like alien voice in their heads, *"But it takes too much time and energy in your lives."*

Del could see the alien approaching them out of the corner of her eye. Jax looking down at her propped slightly on his elbows, cradling her in his arms, could not; but his eyes spoke volumes of questions, fear, anger, and even resignation at being caught, literally, with his pants down.

"I am Ramsees," he stated blandly, hand outstretched, clearly controlling and maintaining their paralysis. *"You two have been too careless,"* he continued. He moved around the bed slowly, taking his time to study them from all angles as if he was looking at specimens in a jar. Cocking his head now and then, bending as necessary for a clearer view. Del followed him as best as possible. Even Jax could see a little of Ramsees' actions.

Helpless minutes went by. The sweat on their bodies had cooled rapidly. Any passion had been doused by fear as cold as ice water. Slowly, the paralysis was lifted and Ramsees stepped back towards the door. *"I have something better for you to do than this,"* he telepathed and waved carelessly over their naked bodies.

Regaining free movement, they collected themselves in front of Ramsees as best they could, covering themselves up, trying to maintain some composure under his black, mirrored, watchful gaze.

They were caught. Their brief life together was over. Jax let out a sigh of resignation but gave Del his best supportive look. She looked angry at the intrusion, making Jax proud.

"Why hadn't I sensed him?" Del wondered in frustration. *"What will happen now?"*

They had just shared something very intimate and private, and it had been ripped away from them like a parent stripping a warm blanket from a sleeping baby, or the Gestapo bursting into a home in the middle of the night. It was outrageous, frightening, numbing.

"What do you want from us?" Del asked softly though pleading and anger were evident. "Can't you just leave us alone?"

Part of the answer came with movement behind Ramsees. Fear escalated in an instant to absolute, blind terror as two MIBs stepped inside. *"You have a new directive,"* their minds heard. Before either of them could react Ramsees raised his hand slightly, their paralysis returned, and the MIBs blurred forward. With a sharp pinprick, consciousness slipped away.

Del could see the regret in Jax's eyes.

Jax read hopelessness in Del's eyes.

Big Boys Don't Cry

Eric got up abruptly from his chair and backed towards a book case. *"What now?"* his mind screamed. *"Get out of here now! Don't walk, run!"* The thoughts came like lightning. He'd made it this far and this long and he could make it farther. She had appeared OK and he would never have expected this .... this .... trap. It must be a trap. Maybe she heard about him missing and was waiting for him. She did say she was waiting. Maybe it was more than just the cameras.

Blue eyes he had recently admired suddenly glared at him directly, probing him thoroughly, freezing him in his tracks, paralyzing him as he pressed against one of the darkly stained bookshelves. He felt those eyes were now malevolent.

"What's wrong, young man?" she asked, concern registering in those hypnotic eyes.

"I...gotta...go," was all he could get out as he unconsciously rubbed the back of his neck.

Puzzled, Lady Henri studied the clearly agitated and scared to death boy. She mimicked his hand motions in an effort to figure things out. He had that caged animal look and was going to run, she could feel it, and didn't know why. Then she did feel it, the tiny scar on her neck that had changed her life 28 years before. Her hand stopped and realization dawned on her.

"You saw my scar. And you've seen something like this before. And the people who had it acted strangely?" she surmised, eyebrows raised in question.

His dark brown eyes were wide with astonishment and not much belief. Eric nodded affirmatively but slowly.

"You poor dear. You've been through so much and now I've given you a fright." Waving her hand in casual dismissal she added with a comforting smile, "Well, you can see I'm as normal as you, can't you?"

After a pause and no answer from Eric she went on, "Make up your own mind. It's something I don't care to talk about that happened a long time before, but you're in no danger. Leave if you want, but get warm, eat your fill, then decide."

Eric didn't move, didn't flinch. He wanted to believe, but every fiber of his being said *run!* Remaining frozen with fear, confusion, and indecision, watching her return to tending the fire, then taking their dishes away, he finally relaxed and sat slowly back down by the fire.

When Lady Henri returned, he was staring deeply into the fire, brilliant random flashes filling his entire sight, eyes unfocused. "What happened to your neck?" he asked her directly, eyes still buried in the fire.

"It's a long and painful story I'm afraid," she answered, sitting tensely in the empty chair near him, "But we have the time and you deserve an answer. I also want to hear what you've been up to."

The fire continued to consume his gaze, but his ears burned with interest as she poured out her unbelievable tale.

Duty Calls

Consciousness came slowly to Jackson Leigh, like a dense fog slowly burning off at sunrise. Unconnected images came and went. His mind was a jumble of thoughts and sounds. There was a pervasive feeling of peace. He could go on like this forever...drifting in the fog...drinking in the blissfulness.

As the haze cleared, thoughts took on form and meaning. He was being reassured: Everything was fine. He was fine. He had new friends. He needed to help them. His eyes opened slowly and the ceiling came into focus. Rising up groggily, he tossed back the bedcovers and sat on the edge of the bed, the last tendrils of sleep vanishing quickly. He felt rested and calm.

Taking in the surroundings and absently acknowledging his ill-fitting, open-backed gown, he decided this had to be some sort of hospital room, 'though why was unknown. The stenciled "MAFB" on the sheets, pillow, and gown meant nothing to him. It was daytime, probably morning judging by the light.

He arched his back, stretched his arms, rubbed his eyes with both hands, and rolled his neck around to clear the last of the cobwebs. Easing off the bed, he used the bathroom, and wandered around the small room trying to figure out his situation. Looking absently out the window at unfamiliar desert surroundings, it was as if he had just shown up here, no past and an uncertain future. He rubbed his stubbled chin, and scratched a few itches on his body, especially the back of his neck.

He felt the slightly raised area. Acne: Leave it alone. A droning mental voice kept reassuring him and he felt calm despite the little information his mind possessed. Puzzled, but not really caring, he walked around the room for lack of anything better to do. Reluctantly, his mind was clearing bit by bit. The peacefulness slipping away, causing twinges of regret and fear.

Gossamer threads of answers started to work their way into his consciousness, slowly, teasingly. His non-existent past of a few minutes before started to gel into cohesiveness. His name was Jackson Leigh ....an electrical specialist... employed at Walt Disney World... a master plumber... now helping friends from far away... special friends... to help... and to serve. There was more than that he was certain, but it wouldn't come into focus, reveal itself completely. He felt there were truths that for now wanted to stay hidden in the shadows of his mind. Other sounds besides the commanding voice flitted into being, but disappeared too fast to comprehend.

Absently, he continued to pace the small area of the room, noticing with more interest the unfamiliar territory outside, not really caring that more answers did not come, waves of mental reassurance continuing to bombard him. He should get back to work and help his new friends.

A curtain hid the rest of the room, the type of curtain that separated patients, the curtains used to for patient privacy or when doctors didn't want the public to see what they were doing. Vaguely curious, he peeked behind it to see if anyone was there. To his surprise there was a woman. That didn't strike him as normal for a hospital. The resting patient was relaxed, peaceful, and beautiful. She looked familiar, but like minutes before he still couldn't piece together the memories that would provide certainty, and it didn't appear to matter anyway.

She appeared to be comatose, with very shallow breathing and no other discernible movement, hands crossed on her chest. With a lily in her grasp, the pose would have been that of a corpse. Her dark complexion was pale. He stood and watched, staring at her face and other features barely hidden by the bedcovers. He could have studied that face for hours 'though he didn't know why. There was a strange attraction that wouldn't allow him to simply close the curtain and walk away. After all, he didn't know her. Or did he?

Her breathing suddenly quickened, and her unfocusing eyes blinked. She was waking up. Watching her regain consciousness, he again rubbed his stubbled chin and scratched his neck.

Like the old switches that clicked audibly, the truth suddenly flooded in, and with it the memory of who he was, who she was, and what he last remembered. He flung himself to the bathroom, now fully alert.

Using the vanity mirror and the mirror on the back of the bathroom door, he took a closer look at his neck. He'd been operated on for sure, full consciousness informing him he'd been changed like all the others.

"No!" he yelled and the mirror broke violently under his ham fisted swing, shards as sharp as the pain in his hand fell all around him. He stared at his bleeding knuckles and realized something was wrong, and right if that made any sense. Blood was flowing freely from the dozen cuts and it hurt like hell, but he flexed his hand anyway, adding to the red splotches filling the sink, letting the pain clear his head further.

He turned on the cold water, washing the wound as best he could, making sure no glass was embedded and grabbed a towel to apply pressure. He used another towel to clear a path through the broken mirror fragments and gingerly made his way out of the bathroom. She was propped up on the bed looking at him.

"You OK?" she inquired in a calm manner.

He decided a little caution was prudent. "Yeah, sure. You?" he replied evenly, hiding his towel wrapped hand as if nothing was wrong. "Do you know who you and I are?"

With a puzzled look at the question she replied as evenly, "Yes, I'm Adelle Summers and you are Jackson Leigh." After a pause, she added, "We met at Disney World. We have new friends. Everything will be all right."

He couldn't hide the shock on his face and started to back away until she smiled warmly, then laughed, "Come here big guy. Give me a hug and let me look at that hand. What's the matter anyway? Did you think I'd been turned into a zombie?"

"I...I..didn't...know for sure," he stammered. "I've got some bad news for you Del. I've been operated on."

Her mouth dropped open and dark eyes widened in shock. Then, her hand flashed to the back of her neck and her concerned look changed in an instant to anger. "Shit!"

"Yeah, I feel the same way," he answered in resignation. "What I don't understand, is why it isn't working on me, or you for that matter. At first when I woke up, I was thinking about all that voice crap like it was true and I couldn't remember much of nothin'. Then everything hit me and I got angry, busted up that mirror real good."

"Maybe it hasn't kicked in yet," was her only reply, watching him while rubbing the back of her neck thoughtfully.

"Perhaps there's surgery, then something else is done to make it work. Damn it anyway! Things were actually looking up 'til we got caught," she groused.

They looked at each other meaningfully, both obviously remembering their last minutes of consciousness, unbelievable joy turned to embarrassment, anger, and hopelessness.

"Maybe we should start where we left off?" she suggested lightly, patting the tiny bed.

Jax smiled warmly and grabbed her hand with his undamaged one and kissed it gently. "We should, but we also should make sure we won't be disturbed, figure out what's going on, figure out where we are."

"You could be a zombie in ten minutes. Last offer, Mr. Leigh," Del proffered, her arms stretching his way.

In response he joined her in the bed and hugged her fiercely, his meager hospital gown not hiding his intention. They kissed passionately and a fire burned between them, any worldly cares about their safety momentarily forgotten.

Many long joyous minutes passed. Then they relaxed their embrace, slowly, not wanting the closeness to end. The flames of passion retreated with reluctance.

Del finally spoke up, "That was better wasn't it? And no intrusion this time. Amazing. Now let's take a look at your hand shall we?"

Both wanted to remain embraced but it would have to wait for a better moment. While they still had a shred of normal human mentality, they would have to put their faculties to the best use for their survival, if not for others like them. Their sense of duty or priorities would have to put some pleasures on hold.

While cleaning his wound, they assayed their situation. They'd been abducted. They were SAs now. They were unchanged behaviorally for the time being. They were no longer in Florida, but out west apparently, probably in an Air Force hospital if the "AFB" in "MAFB" had any meaning. They'd been treated reasonably well except for the implant. There were no guards or nurses. Someone wanted them alive and functioning. They didn't know what to do next or how much time they had left

"That looks much better," Del quipped, admiring her handiwork as he sat on his bed being treated. A first aid kit and other medical equipment had been found and worked much better than the towel. "Can't do anything for pain, though. You'll have to suffer," she pouted.

"This is the least of our worries," he replied, shaking his bandaged hand at her. "Let's do some scoutin' and see if we can figure out where we are, then come up with a plan. We're still trapped like at Disney World, but maybe they figure we won't do anything because of the implant except sit still like a couple zombies. We might be able to walk right outta here."

"Do you think that's wise? If they catch us again, maybe they'll double the implant, or worse."

"Del, we can't stay here and act the role anymore. That one alien's smart. He found us the first time and he'll know if we're actin'. We gotta move, and soon!"

"OK, OK, you're right. Let's just be careful Jax."

"Sure 'nuff, lady." he smiled. "Maybe we can find some real clothes.

Your rear bumper is showing."

Scolding him with a quick glance, she tied the gown tighter and they went to the door. The wire-meshed glass window showed the coast was clear. Slowly they opened the door, Del looking left, Jax looking right.

The hallway was clear on the right, but the tense body in front of him made him glance left.

"I decided it was best to give you a little more privacy this time. You two are a bundle of emotions. Are you finished with the mating ritual?" the Quazzga named Ramsees intoned, the abrupt clear mental voice always startling. He was standing, alone, just to the left of their door.

One Quazzga, two of them, perhaps they could take him Jax surmised. The MIB suddenly stepping into the hallway behind the alien killed that hope. Those guys were dynamite.

The MIB was carrying a bundle of clothes and stepped around, handing it to the couple. *"We gathered these from your room last night. Get dressed now if you need to and come with me,"* the alien telepathed.

Grabbing the clothes, they backed into the room and started to dress. "Great, no socks or underwear," Del commented and then in a whisper continued, "What the hell is going on?"

"I dunno, this is nuts. Why don't they just get it over with? Why the games and niceness? Sumpin' ain't right," he drawled back in a whisper, worry creasing his face.

"Let's go now," they heard.

Looking every bit like caged and frightened animals, they followed the alien/MIB duo down a long, empty, cold corridor, and out into the bright sunlight. On the way, Jax noticed a wall plaque. They were at McMillan Air Force Base, near Sacramento, California, and if memory had served him right, it was one of the biggest bases in the country and one of the largest employers in central California.

He wondered where all the tens of thousands of people employed here had gone and guessed they were probably off on some Quazzga project. It troubled him that aliens now controlled such a bastion of American defense, and brought their bleak situation home to him again.

Once outside, the dry heat and bright light pained them both and they shielded their eyes as best they could. At least it was warmer out here. The Quazzga/MIB pair appeared unaffected as they made their way towards a huge group of hangers nearby. Silently they strode ahead on the walkways, no one offering further explanation, just one foot in front of another until the bizarre group entered the largest of the buildings, which was completely empty.

Del and Jax exchanged puzzled looks. Big whoops. What was this all about?

"We can talk more in here," they heard from Ramsees. *"Your species is fond of stories and this one is...a whopper,"* they heard, Ramsees obviously searching for an appropriate phrase. Without warning, the massive eight story hanger that would hold 10 football fields shimmered to reveal countless Quazzga vessels, the biggest now closest to them would dwarf the largest plane on Earth. Ramsees gestured towards the huge hat shaped ship in front of them, *"It's a long story and we have little time. Enter and have your questions answered."*

Building Blocks

Eric woke from a fitful sleep, full of contrasting nightmares and wishmares. The nightmares were a mirror of recent experiences: cold, fatigue, fear, hunger; the wishmares were fleeting hopes of parents that listened to his ideas, gold bullion that he found underwater and only needed to bring to the surface, endless days of school being closed for no apparent reason.

Vividly clear and intertwined with his dreams was the incredible tale Lady Henri had told him the previous night. The sun shown brightly as usual through unshaded huge windows, washing away all doubt, cleansing his thoughts so he knew the truth. She had revealed to him, a kid, an awesome conspiracy. It explained a lot...and nothing. He knew more than he cared, and less than he needed to fill the void of questions.

Still, he trusted her and her words. No one could make up such nonsense and when connected to recent events, it all made more sense than he cared to realize. He smelled bacon cooking, could hear the sizzle distantly. The large bed was very soft, the thick covers warm and comforting. He hadn't slept so soundly or comfortably in weeks. His small campfire replaced by a fireplace. Sleeping bag forgotten with the enveloping magic of a real bed.

Her humming drifted along the same tendrils as her cooking, his senses somehow more sharp this morning. He was very hungry, again. Rousing himself reluctantly, wondering if he could eat and sleep at the same time, he noticed cleaned and folded clothes on the dresser by the bed. *"Does she ever sleep?"* he wondered, not remembering enough of last night to answer the question. He must have been very tired indeed. Judging by the sunlight, it was nearly noon.

"Will scrambled eggs with bacon be OK?" she asked as he ambled into the kitchen.

"Mhmmm," he answered affirmatively, "Smells great," and sat in one of the six chairs at the table.

She continued beating the eggs and mixing ingredients, silently studying the young man who still looked a bit dead on his feet.

He stared at nothing in particular, just enjoying the security of a safe place to stay, some real company, and the very real promise of a decent breakfast. As much as he hated to admit it, home cooking beat store bought donuts and Twinkies hands down. It made him miss his mother in particular, parents in general, knowing they didn't care for him any more, but hurting inside because of what had happened to them that they couldn't control.

Pulling himself back to the present, he asked, "Was all that stuff you told me last night really true?" trying once again to be sure of his guest, testing her reactions.

"Yes," was her quick and deep reply as she threw ingredients together on the skillet. She knew her story of the past night had been incomplete and it had pained her greatly to tell it at all. She hoped Eric had understood the abbreviated version.

"Well, why would aliens take you away for a while and operate on you? Why?" he pressed. "And why aren't you like all the kids and parents that act like robots?" He'd been too tired and spellbound to ask these sensible questions previously.

"I don't know, young man," she said, stopping her cooking to look him in the eye. "But as I said last night, I really think they mean us well and want what is best for us. I really do. As for why their operation didn't change me, especially when so many people are affected, and as you say, most people you knew in Sacramento, it may just be a mistake. I remember other people with me on the alien spaceships and some acted normal, others acted very much like robots. All of us could hear the aliens. Some of them are quite friendly, you know."

Eric wondered about that. He felt sure she was telling the truth by the way her voice sounded scared, and by the furrows that creased her brow when she talked about the scary details. She said she had been abducted about 10 times in the past 25 years, most recently a couple of years before right from this home.

It had driven people away from her, especially her wealthy husband, who had basically left her to her madness in the isolation of the Sierras. No one believed her, though she did little to publicize the matter because she couldn't tolerate the few who wanted to use her beliefs for their own ends. Plus, there were many who simply scoffed, including her psychiatrist. "What would they say now?" she had repeated many times in the past few weeks, clearly upset that no one had taken her seriously.

It had nearly driven her insane, trying to reconcile what her doctor said was just random alpha wave fluctuations that induced a common abductee experience, especially the very popular alien abductee scenario, with what appeared more than real to her, terrifyingly real, particularly given the physical evidence of her neck (which the doctor judged was self-inflicted) and other parts of her body which she dared not talk about.

"Are we safe?" he asked breaking her dark thoughts.

There was a long, long pause as the finished eggs were dished up. Approaching the table, she answered, "I don't know the answer to that either. For now, out here, I'd say yes. But what the future holds, I don't know."

It was honest if not fully comforting. At least he wouldn't go hungry and be alone he decided as he dove into the delicious brunch.

She smiled, enjoying his company and their mutual satisfaction in the face of the unknown.

Later, they sat quietly again in the study, enjoying the never ending warmth of the fire. Lady Henri explained it was a gas fire and they had enough fuel for two winters. The wood fires she kept going were just for aroma, the permanent ceramic logs never quite gave the look and smell of a real fire. Her husband had been a stickler for living in comfort amidst the wilderness and spared no expense.

This huge house had the latest in solar and wind power, security systems (as Eric had discovered), water filtration and storage, communications, and home energy management. The home was as self sufficient as one could get. It even delivered power to the utility company now and then.

Neither of them wanted to talk much more. It was as if they both needed to sort things out. Eric explored the house some, enjoying the numerous games reserved for younger visitors (nieces and nephews, she had said). She was reading each time he peeked in on her. He loved the pool table and was lost for several hours with computer games he hadn't tried before.

The house was cavernous, and even bigger inside than it had looked from the outside. There were four levels and many side rooms off small stairways in between levels. There was even an exercise room in the lowest floor with a swimming pool, sauna, hot tub, and the latest in fitness equipment. Even the new high school near his house didn't have anything like this.

It was dusk when he wandered back to the study and found it empty. The smell of food, *good* food, reached his senses from the kitchen area. Pizza! Out here in the mountains, it couldn't be delivery, though this smelled even better, even better than the stromboli his aunt made. He followed his senses to the source. It was nearly done.

"Can I help with anything?" he offered, hoping for a taste of some left over ingredients. She must have known about young boys as there were some pieces of dough and several slices of pepperoni for taste testing.

Suddenly, flickering lights in the kitchen and nearly every device within eyesight caught him off guard and he wondered what could be happening now. Lady Henri was suddenly a statue, mouthing, "No, not now!" over and over, abject fear written all over her face, panic starting to rise inside Eric.

The wash of bright lights outside the house reminded him of the police dealing with criminals, helicopters descending on local scum. The lack of sound here was curious, and even more curious was the fact that his feet no longer touched the ground. Lady Henri was also floating, the look of fear on her face even more exaggerated than before if that was possible. Together, her first, they floated through now open sliding doors and outside, no hint of near-zero temperatures registering on his skin. In fact, warmth and peace overcame him as the two approached the bright lights above.

A moment before, he'd been ready to enjoy pizza. Now, he was headed into a brilliant abyss, and for some reason didn't care. It was like falling asleep on the beach, awash in warmth and light. There was a lingering moment that made him desire the warm fire and promise of his favorite food, but this new experience pulled him more strongly and pleasantly. It just felt right, and the words in his head assured him it was so. His last thought was that he'd heard of people dying and seeing bright lights. Was that happening now?

The Truth

Ramsees was straight with them, and "them" was about 200 awestruck people from all walks of life, shapes, ages, sizes, and races. Apparently the Quazzga had no biases or preferences. The old prejudiced statement, "They all look alike to me," came to Del's mind. More than likely, to the Quazzga, a human was a human.

They were gathered inside the largest of the numerous ships that had shimmered into existence right before their eyes. Earlier Jax and Del had been ushered inside and were enjoined not to touch anything. *"The important controls take mental as well as physical cues so there is no way for you to affect any vital systems, but it's wise to keep your hands to yourselves, something you two are fond of doing,"* an amused tone accompanying Ramsees' last statement. There were no sharp angles or turns anywhere inside, just smooth curves blending throughout the wide corridor and intersecting corridors. It was beautiful, the blue and iridescent colors pleasing and rainbow-like, the colors shifting perceptively yet not changing the overall color scheme. The walls appeared to be the only source of light.

The hallway suddenly widened as they entered a huge amphitheater, or so it appeared to them. They emptied out into the lowest level, forty yards across. From there rose a tower of recesses in the walls above them, about 30 levels high, each of the recesses occupied for the most part by reclining humans, at least what could be seen from the lower four or five tiers.

Jax was still upset about the neck surgery, and his now throbbing hand was a constant reminder. *"When do we get an explanation?"* he wondered impatiently as he scanned the cavernous area.

"Take a place and relax," intoned Ramsees. *"We can communicate with each other here."* In answer to an unasked question, each human rose involuntarily, to empty recesses away from each other nearly at the top, and glided softly to rest, eyes able to see that most of the cubicles were indeed full, their silent human occupants unmoving. Several gasps and a few cries were heard as people struggled with this unnatural way of being moved about.

It was eerily quiet as the levitation took place, their bodies moving without volition, entering a dully glowing and foreign cubicle, yet strangely at peace as they reposed therein, a feeling they were in good hands. Stranger yet, the cubicles grasped their bodies, held them in place so movement of any type was out of the question.

As soon as they were settled, mental images of Ramsees, and a host of others they could not see were thrust gently into their minds. They heard a mental narrative of Quazzga history; how they came to find Earth from such a great distance away, how it was the salvation of their people, how plans were made to colonize the planet over 15,000 years before.

Del was stunned by the revelations. Her head was unable to shake but her brows furrowed in pain and disbelief despite the calming effect of the cubicle. Curiosity had long faded. She didn't want to know this! Even after absorbing the thoughts, she had no idea this could really have been happening for such a long time. Still she had no choice but to continue listening.

"The Quazzga are peaceful and there has never been a war among us, but we do not always agree on what must be done even though we bow to the collective good of our race, unlike what we've seen among humans," Ramsees continued in what only could have been perceived as a melancholy tone, now telling the story exclusive of other mental voices.

"Please relax: hold your questions until I have finished. It's for the best. I can feel the incredible pressure of your many concerns and understand your desire for answers and truth. Patience please and don't fight the knowledge. Let me convey this story. You will all have the chance to get your questions answered, but let me finish what I have to say first.

"I must caution you I will be as blunt and direct as possible so you will fully understand us, and then understand me and those who stand with me. Please do not interpret my story harshly until you have heard it all. It is a credit to the inner strength of you few in particular that you can exert such strength of will in the face of what has happened to you and what we are telling you. You have made it this far; let us go further together.

"First, you are nothing to us. Again, please wait, calm down, listen carefully. You are nothing to the Quazzga collective. You are very special to me. My forebears were thrilled to find such versatile and useful creatures as your ancestors. Immediately, work was begun to cultivate your maximum usefulness for later colonization. Unfortunately, there were disagreements on the best way to prepare for our coming.

"Some Quazzga preferred direct intervention and there was plenty of that. Whole human populations disappeared in several parts of the planet as we experimented openly and casually with your ancestors. Several in the African region showed exceptional capabilities, but our minor interference's doomed them. Similar disasters occurred to recent civilizations including the Incas, Mayas, the people of Easter Island, the Anasazi of the southwest United States... the list goes on. Understand, my forebears were alone, unsupervised, out of communication for centuries at a time, with only the directive to prepare the way for colonization and prepare you for our arrival."

Del wanted to scream out loud and found she couldn't. She wanted to jump from her high cubicle to smash Ramsees face, despite the unsafe distance, and found she couldn't. She shouted all forms of mental profanity his way on him and his race, to no effect she could fathom, except emotional release. *"How dare they!? How could they!?"* The rage built up to the point she felt her heart wanting to tear apart, her veins standing out as she strained in her prison-like bedchamber. Whatever peacefulness had gotten her into this chamber had exploded away with the force of her fury.

Ramsees continued, seemingly oblivious to her pointless thrashing and rage, *"You are all under great stress because of our arrival and subsequent events. Again, relax. You are among friends and not the ones that have been broadcasting into your minds. I personally, and my pod in particular, understand you humans are special, and worthy of better treatment. Please try to relax. We do feel the pain and sorrow our presence has had on you personally and your fellow humans, and regret the treatment of your talented kind. What has happened is truly regrettable, but we must also move forward now as we cannot change events which have occurred."*

Whether drained from her efforts or just numb, Del started to rein in her anger and calm down. Her analytical self took over. Aside from the surgery, Ramsees had not personally harmed her, or anyone else here that she could tell. He wouldn't take the time to relay all the gruesome details just to cause emotional distress: It just didn't fit from what little she could sense of these beings. There must be a purpose, and clouding her judgment with anger wouldn't help her understand. Perhaps, though unbelievable, Ramsees was offering this group a way out or at least through their current predicament. She hardened herself as best as she could, all of these thoughts occurring in a span of seconds, and continued to listen.

Several cubicles away, and a little lower, Jax could only chuckle inwardly at the folly of humans, and now the almighty Quazzga, as well. What Ramsees revealed was amazing, but it hadn't shocked him. At long last perhaps there were reasonable explanations for some of the greatest mysteries in human origins and development. It was hard to believe creatures from so far away could have such influence, even a few visitors. But it made sense.

Humans had been guinea pigs for quite a while. It was sadly humorous. All the time the human race had felt in control of its destiny, squabbling over this blue-green rock, they were really being setup. Only instead of the caretakers being omnipotent, it sounded like they had a few wrinkles of their own. Perhaps there are common traits to any sentient creature. Perhaps just being able to think screws everything up. It was ironic.

Jax settled into the monologue, wondering what else might be revealed and wondering how Del was handling things. He suspected she was over thinking the whole matter, mad as hell, but probably coming up with the perfect solution to get herself, and him he hoped, "moving forward" as Ramsees had just said.

"I sense you are beginning to believe and accept what I have told you. We know it is not easy to hear and you have no reason to trust us after what we've collectively, but not individually, done. You need to know more, though, before we can proceed with a course of action.

"Our colonization preparation, despite unfortunate and large scale consequences to your ancestors, was actually going along as planned on this planet. Preparation on our home planet was proceeding apace. Prudent measures were taken to avoid further mistakes. My forebears and others were given more specific direction. In particular, it was felt that less direct contact and more passive observation was needed. My forebears, and other Quazzga groups acted upon those instructions differently.

"To be blunt, humans were going to be our slaves, a biological alternative to machines that could make our new world more comfortable than we were used to, perhaps a salve to make us forget what we left behind. Even as used up a husk as our home world had become, and as rich, promising, and comfortable as your planet appeared, it would never be home. But this planet would have to suffice. And make no mistake, we felt this planet to be ours by right of occupation, and feel so now, 'though we had no idea of what we were really doing to humans like yourself.

"Similar to how your populations spread around the planet, not caring who previously owned the land, just that you could take it and that meant it was yours, my race makes no apologies for taking what it feels is ours to take. But, you humans complicated matters and made our colonization efforts of almost 15,000 years a near failure."

At hearing the near apology for their desecration, Del cheered at possible Quazzga defeat! *"Go away!"* she screamed mentally. *"Leave us alone!"* Then she was humbled by what she heard next, sorry she had been so harsh, not with the Quazzga in general, but with Ramsees, who she now felt understood her, and was on her side. It embarrassed her to find out he must have heard her tirade, or at least felt her strong emotions.

"Yes, Adelle Summers in particular, we understand your grief, anger, and pain. Many of you feel the same as this special human, though you have not heard her mental anguish. Perhaps we should go away and leave you alone, or more appropriately, we never should have treated you so casually or assumed what we did. Let me continue.

"Our colonization was intended to occur in another 200 years and would have been so peaceful you would not have cared. Our preparations for this planet included making sure the environment remained stable and that humans became suitable tools. After earlier direct attempts which ended in failure, more subtle engineering of your species occurred.

"We experimented with telepathic modifications which would make you hear our thoughts in our language without the surgical manipulation required of your distant ancestors and other now extinct human groups. That was imminently successful although it took nearly a thousand years to genetically alter the auditory centers of the major human groups, and nearly 10,000 years for all humans to contain the correct and now dominant DNA codes without exception.

"The next step was more delicate and it involved making sure you were susceptible and pliant to our commands without exception. We wanted you to work for us in as peaceful and cooperative manner as possible, and not have to worry about any chance of our wishes not being fulfilled. Again, surgery would work, but the resources and time would be enormous, exceeding all allowable timetables.

"Further genetic modifications were tested and proved promising, though we did not have the 20,000 years it was estimated it would take to duplicate prior efforts. The human population had increased dramatically, despite your overwhelmingly self-destructive nature and your sheer numbers made direct efforts too great a task.

"Our scientists also worked on ways of using telepathic messages, wavelengths, and patterns which would work with existing acoustic center modifications. This, too, was promising and is the technology that is allowing us to live on this planet with near complete control."

Ramsees paused, again sensing frustration, anger, even hatred, but he permitted it to flourish and then settle down, allowed his charges to absorb. The resiliency of this species was remarkable and they proved it again as emotions toned down even faster than before.

"What happened next surprised us, as humans began to populate the this planet in staggering numbers, again despite natural diseases and your propensity for unending wars. Our travel technology, advanced as it was, still required a journey of a hundred years when we first visited your planet. Six centuries ago, it was clear we needed to speed our efforts. There was panic in the Quazzga home system when those closest to the colonization project realized from Earth scouts that humans were rapidly evolving technology that was beginning to have an adverse affect on our future home."

Ramsees felt a collective squirm from his Audience. Uncomfortable truths were being revealed. Layers of ignorance were being peeled back, a vegetable called an onion was the favorite human analogy, and the core was near. He continued, tempering his projections, pacing the information, seeking the optimal thoughts that would accomplish his goal.

"Let me remind you not all Quazzga had agreed on the best way to accomplish colonization, and it was less clear as human civilization rapidly advanced both in numbers and in science. The updated directive made it clear we could not overtly reduce your numbers, even seemingly dangerous elements of it, since we expected all of your population to be available for our needs.

"However, certain scouts and their pods took it upon themselves to affect events in a manner that would appear favorable to colonization and preserve the planetary resources. Not that we expected the planet to end up a wasteland through your inauspicious existence, but the Quazzga treasure every drop of water, every mineral, every source of life-giving energy, so it was very disconcerting to see even the smallest of resources squandered by such a minute percentage of this planet's biological mass.

"Thus, certain diseases were assisted which controlled populations, such as the plague, smallpox, malaria, tuberculosis, Ebola, AIDS and most recently a variety of flu strains. It was a foolish gesture. My forbears and even current pod members did not see this as the proper way

for preparation though they reluctantly went along with some of these measures.

"What we could not control, though, was the technological and emotional forces you humans bring to bear on your world. Yes, we studied you in so many ways, physically, psychically, anatomically, and genetically, but in the long run, underestimated you. At least that is my conclusion and the conclusion of my pod. It is the reason we communicate with you special humans now. We hope it is not too late."

Del sensed victory. Even stuck in this cubicle, the joy of having bested a superior, at having some measure of worth, made her feel strong. Even as the mosquito draws blood from the giant host, facing a possible swat to extinction, she felt more like the virus that brings down the mightiest of animals. It was a feeling she felt like savoring. She wanted to hear more when minutes earlier she had wanted the opposite.

"Human achievement continued at an incredible rate, a rate we could not control with the numbers of scouts and ships available. The difficulty of deciding courses of action multiplied with the permutations in your behavior that were manifested into actions. The details are too numerous to go into here, but when your so called Industrial Age occurred, followed by planetary conflagrations, the Nuclear Age, and finally the Information Age to use your terms, we were at a loss to manage the outcomes that would lead to effective colonization. Our entire efforts of 15,000 years were in jeopardy.

"The nuclear era was the most devastating blow to the Quazzga, as it appeared our supposed servants were on a course which would destroy the planet entirely, and raise the dust several times. Scouts were in abject panic. In addition, even if the planet was not annihilated by nuclear weapons or what you call conventional weapons, there was ample evidence that precious resources were being expended at an intolerable rate. We had clearly underestimated the effects of non-interference and your ability to both reproduce and soil your nest, as some would say.

"Action, direct action was called for. Timetables had to be moved up. In the late 1940s, we began to implement the more distasteful elements of our colonization strategy in what to us would be considered very haphazard, even reckless fashion, reminiscent of failed efforts thousands of years earlier. It occurred on two fronts, biological and political.

"Surely many of you are familiar with reports of abductions, experiments on humans, lost time experiences, even direct communication

with so called aliens. If not, understand this: They are true for the most part, even the wildest of stories. It was us, the scouts, attempting whatever was necessary to achieve our goal. I had arrived to assist my senior pod progenitor, "father" you would say. The situation was not in our favor.

"With the panic of scouts in place, confusion of newly arriving scouts, and lack of direct contact with our collective, there was great disagreement among Quazzga in this solar system on the best course of action to ensure smooth colonization, including what to do with a deteriorating situation regarding humans.

"The biological interference included trying to create hybrid Quazzga/humans for our use, implant surgery for monitoring purposes, implant surgery to effect direct control, stepped up methods of direct mental control, and in-depth studies on the best means of eradicating humans entirely without undue harm to our colonization efforts.

"Political methods of control involved direct contact and control of world leaders and events using whatever technology and controlled human resources available. My progenitor and I urged caution and restraint in going too fast to implement more drastic measures, but we were not fully heeded, to our great regret, because hundreds of thousands of people like yourself are now lost to further study and usefulness due to implant surgery. Worse yet, the loss of unique specimens (that is you) continues at a high rate. Thus, we come to our present situation and the reason you are here. We, I, want to save your uniqueness, the part which makes you immune to our control, you few who have adapted somehow. And we need your cooperation to accomplish this. We've made some grave errors that I hope to fix.

"Most of you are aware of the surgery you have undergone. It is only for monitoring purposes and the reason some of you were found and saved. It also helps you to communicate with me telepathically when you are in this vessel. Your best interest is involved and it is a necessary evil to protect you. Now, what else do you need to know?"

Q&A

Eric listened with his mind as the alien sent his thoughts to every one. He didn't understand a lot of what he heard, but for some reason he trusted Ramsees and felt assured by his thoughts. It seemed the Quazzga were a bit like humans: fighting over things, making mistakes, changing things, making more mistakes. Ramsees appeared more human than any of them, actually caring about people, especially this group, instead of using them. But, then again, he knew Ramsees better than most in this huge room.

His journey from Lady Henri's house had been awesome. After being lifted into the spacecraft, he had met Ramsees. Lady Henri's initial fear melted away when Ramsees showed himself. It turned out he and Lady Henri were old friends. Several times in the past 20 years they had met. Neither of them went into details, but it was clear they were working together to save humans and make room for Quazzga to live with humans, not just have them as slaves.

It was also clear that Ramsees was, in a way, like himself and lady Henri, separate from the rest of each other's kind. If Ramsees had been running things, the arrival of the aliens would have been a lot different. Eric wondered if that meant Ramsees could fix things, make his parents and friends back into the way they were.

Ramsees patted his shoulder, *"Sorry, but no."*

During their short trip Eric was told that all the changes in his life were permanent and nothing could make things as they were. It was the meeting they were going to, though, the one he was now a part of, with kids and adults of all types, that would help set a course of action that might make things better for everyone.

So with the long speech over, Eric listened in his strange cubicle to questions, arguments, hateful words, and answers. He tried to pay attention, but his thoughts drifted to recent events and the dizzying amount of information now being bantered about.

He was glad to be involved, and very glad not to have been like his family and friends who were nothing more than simple robots and slaves. Eric felt insignificant, though, amongst all these strangers. Thus he clung to words Ramsees had spoken in the spaceship: "You, young human, are perhaps the most special of all humans and will have to be as clever and strong as you have shown yourself to be these past few weeks."

He wanted to talk more with Ramsees and Lady Henri, but not like this, with everyone hearing everyone else's thoughts. He felt too fragile to jump in with a question, so he just kept listening absently, not really paying attention to anything in particular.

Suddenly he felt a mental nudge, not unlike having a teacher tap him on the shoulder in a silent cue to get back to work. Before he could question the source, a tight focused message said, *"Listen and learn,"* unmistakably from Ramsees, and seemingly meant as a rebuke only for him. Eric was fully attentive in a heart beat and vowed to stay that way. It must be important he guessed.

What he mentally heard was an ongoing stream of questions, and answers. He had caught the gist of what had already been asked and answered. Parents, and apparently Ramsees too, don't realize how much kids pick up when it seems they aren't listening. Eric prided himself on often being able to repeat details of conversations going on around him while playing a computer game that everyone assumed had him totally absorbed.

Nearly everyone was concerned about the incredible story Ramsees had told and was dissecting every detail, testing the validity of each revelation. Ramsees was patient and answered every question as directly as possible. In fact, the questions and answers overlapped so much at times that Eric wondered if everyone could keep up.

The host of voices indicated nearly everyone was participating. One woman sounded especially hurt and angry, Adelle was the mental name he picked up. It appeared he could pick up names and even a little insight into the character, sex, and age of a person, but could not actually read their minds. "That's good," he mumbled. He didn't think he'd want to do that or to have others read his mind. It was bad enough having Ramsees being able to sense his emotions and directly talk to him mentally.

One band wave he recognized with joy, asking about how this small group could help, was Lady Henri. Funny, but her mental voice was the same as hearing her in person. Probably, others heard his voice as that of a kid.

One question that intrigued him greatly had to do with the implants they had received. He was reassured when Ramsees answered that in addition to enhancing communication and serving as a locator, they blocked further control, especially direct control by close proximity voice machines. On the down side, they could be removed and new implants put in which would render them helpless.

Another question that made him listen closely was about the dark suited men. He shuddered as he remembered the body guard types at his school. Memories of a childhood, parents, and friends ripped away from him increased his anxiety. Ramsees explained that the dark men were a secret and fiercely loyal army of abducted and long co-opted humans. Many of them had been altered beyond just implants and obedience.

Most had biological enhancements including increased strength, heightened senses, and improved mental abilities as well as Quazzga longevity. A few were even hybrids, abominations better able to serve the purposes of subduing humans and preparing Earth for conquest. They were everywhere on the planet and had Quazzga technology at their disposal for use as directed by their mentors. In many ways, they were more frightening than the Quazzga.

That chilled Eric and he sensed a collective shudder among everyone else. For seconds, maybe minutes, there was mental silence, the first since Ramsees had finished his narrative. When the mental dialogue resumed, it sounded less argumentative. The woman Adelle, chimed in early with a question that appeared to be on everyone's mind as well, judging by the collective mental nodding he sensed.

"What do you want us to do now?"

Ramsees replied, *"It seems you have accepted my story as truth, which it is. That is good, for by accepting the hard truth, we can now move ahead with some actions. It is my intent, agreed upon by my pod, to protect you from further harm: first by isolating you under our protection as we have already done; next, by explaining to the Quazzga that you exist, need protection, and must be cherished as a resource to the Quazzga, and legitimate co-inhabitants on this planet. Both of these will be very difficult, and the likelihood of acceptance is questionable but it's a step we must take."*

"What if you fail?" asked the impatient but strong-willed Adelle.

"We may have to protect you in other ways," answered Ramsees, *"Ways that haven't been fully thought out, some passive, some less passive."*

"But why are we important to you," asked Eric, his mental voice joining in for the first time.

Ramsees replied with a mental smile, and all of a sudden telepathic pathways cleared, everyone tuning in to listen closely: *"Welcome to the conversation young man. The answer is very complex. Our frantic research is ongoing, even this discussion being a part of that research. So, we have not yet formulated a complete answer to that question. I'm sorry to have to be so vague."*

"We do know this," he continued *"You have evolved quickly for such a young species. You have evolved technologically and mentally at an incredible rate in recent centuries, exceeding our wildest expectations of what any species should have been able to accomplish, especially in the realm of psychic abilities. You individuals here have proven yourselves unique and resourceful in escaping our mental conditioning and physical colonization, something you should not have been able to do at all. Your ability to interact mentally is more advanced than that of your fellow humans who are under absolute Quazzga domination.*

"We don't know why, however. Studies on people like Jennifer Henri with us today have not conclusively shown any genetic or other explanation for your uniqueness. It appears to be a random occurrence, but one we do not care to see eliminated. I sense it is important to preserve your uniqueness and many Quazzga agree with me. Unfortunately, we cannot be more specific in our sense."

Another hush descended on the alien amphitheater. It appeared to Eric that at least for now, most questions had been answered. He still did not understand fully why they were special, but he trusted Ramsees.

Not far away, Jax mulled over his thoughts during the ensuing silence. He was proud of Del for her tough questions and insight. He could only listen because all his questions were being asked before he could form them as complete thoughts. It was an amazing mental dialogue. Surprisingly, it didn't give him a headache. It was a lot to absorb and much of it hard to swallow at all. They'd been given the straight scoop though; that much he believed.

The seething volcano that had been Del's anger was nearly extinguished as the last of her doubts cooled. Still, actions spoke louder than words, and what was proposed would put them all in a lot of hot water if they couldn't convince the rest of the Quazzga to save them. But remembering the daily fears she faced working with the Quazzga at Disney World, she'd take her chances here because at least there was hope, even if only for a few more hours or days.

What was better yet was the whole charade had been dropped. She could be herself, without fear of discovery, without having to watch every step. In a big way, Ramsees had saved her from what would likely have been a far worse fate. *"Guess I owe this creep an apology."* she concluded.

The silence stretched as each individual was lost in thought. A few stray phrases or starts to questions were mentally voiced, but they all trailed off.

Finally, Ramsees addressed them. *"I need to leave for a time to confer with my pod members and implement the first steps to save you. Feel free to wander around this ship or the hanger area, but stay indoors until it is safer for you to be in the open."*

Without warning, the humans felt themselves being released from their beds, gently pulled from the cubicle, and rested on the ground. Jax marveled that any mental or technological source could do this. Still, he couldn't help flailing his arms during the descent, not quite trusting whatever power was pushing him around.

He looked sheepishly at Del who settled next to him, nearly in the same spot they had been picked up. Her look was serious as she landed easily, not seeming to notice she was being handled by remote control. Clapping her arm smartly on his shoulder, leading him along, she spoke in a whisper, "We need to talk... now... outside this ship."

Greg Burke

Counterpoint

Heat waves rolled off the flat, sandy surface. The breeze was just a whisper. Few animals stirred in this desolate area. Even in early spring, the landscape was torrid, inhospitable, and dry. A formidable fence secured the miles of terrain. Signs on the fence warned off trespassers with dire consequences.

What was usually a boringly empty landscape of low hills, desert, and scrub brush, was now dotted with Quazzga ships of all shapes and sizes, especially on the runway areas. It had the look of a convention with the parking lots full. Never had the runways been this full in broad daylight.

Area 51 had long been suspected of being a secret base for reverse technology development of new aircraft from crashed UFOs. In truth, that was only a minor function of a facility that showed a few buildings above ground, but contained mammoth caverns and tunnels below ground housing thousands of military scientists and technicians who had been brought secretly to this facility over a 50-year period from all over the world.

When the Quazzga invaded, the defenders of Area 51 went swiftly into action as protectors of the free world, and welcomed the aliens with open arms.

This had been, after all, a Quazzga brain child. Development of the F-117A stealth fighter had only been a cover, grudgingly admitted, a bone for the masses not yet under Quazzga control. It was not something the aliens would have wanted developed anyway considering the destruction the planes had wreaked, but the cover story had worked.

Aside from the base on Mars, this was a place where Quazzga could work in relative secrecy, preparing the planet for conquest. They could have picked a more hospitable location, but the remoteness from prying eyes and proximity to power centers worked well. It met their needs and even gave them one of many places to service their ships.

Far below, in a specially prepared cavern the size of the Houston Astrodome, several thousand Quazzga gathered in an environment sculpted especially for their proportions and comfort, every inch a recreation of the best their home world had offered in relaxation and enjoyment: a special place they could commune with each other away from space vehicles and the distractions of their conquest and especially away from the creatures they had conquered.

Their ships were models of transport efficiency. This was the opposite. Spacious, gracefully lined, comfortable, comforting, familiar. The walls and sloped ceiling featured strikingly colorful artwork, including scenes from their beautiful planet. Above the excited chittering of the hundreds of pod leaders, soothing Quazzga music could be heard emanating seemingly from everywhere. It was a haven, a place where sweet victory could be savored, where they could commune in peace, a refuge. It was Quazzga heaven, or at least the next best thing.

As the aliens found suitable places of repose throughout the cavern, long arms and hands folded on chests, it appeared as if they were going to sleep. Then the random conversations began to focus on the matter at hand. Hardly a debate or organized discussion of any sort, it was an overlapping of many minds at a speed which conveyed thoughts in seconds what would take humans minutes to say. The thoughts flowed together like a river into an ocean, primary thoughts breaking like waves on the shore where there was general consensus. In part, the non-linear gestalt conversation went:

"...*glorious... victory... so fast... better than hoped... grateful for the preparers... few complications... all being dealt with... operations in nearly every land mass... pods settling in... most adapting... humans proving useful... hybrids especially hard working... young ones growing already... joy... resources under our control... much has been saved... almost too late... just in time... word sent to home world... room for more... explore nearby planets... complete control of this planet... and system... no other obstacles... some humans resist control... no consequence... curious though... insignificant... being dealt with... must maintain control... wise... necessary... wasteful... insignificant... this is home now... the humans help us... serve us... we must complete colonization... ships continue to unload... there is no hurry... must be patient... work to be done... in progress... enjoy this victory... the Quazzga have a second home... we can grow and expand from here... many great steps ahead... rest... enjoy... savor... plan... make this planet like home... better...*"

After a time, the thoughts muted and the chittering noises quieted. Only the soothing music could be heard and those gathered appeared truly at rest in this Quazzga sanctuary.

Ramsees patiently waited for the end of the rest cycle in his place near the floor of the huge amphitheater, cloaking his own thoughts both not to disturb the blissful peace of his fellow Quazzga and because it was critical to present his ideas in the right way at the right time This might or might not be the right place, but he felt it was the right time and hoped his idea was the right way.

He marveled at the soft beauty of this place, the clean smell, the rainbow colors, the peace. It made him both homesick and glad to be on this planet, knowing they were safe on a new world and could remake the best of their old home world. It soothed him almost as much as the victory of their conquest. While waiting, he closed his ebony eyes and joined in the silent reverie.

Like waking from a drugged sleep, the Quazzga slowly returned to consciousness, all clearly refreshed from their rest, flexing long arms and fingers as if awaking from hibernation. Chittering noises grew louder as the entire group came fully alert. It was time to socialize, then discuss business.

Ramsees mentally located his pod members and they tuned to their unique frequency for a group discussion. In minutes, they had updated each other on their multitude of activities around the planet. Then, Ramsees updated them on the humans and his plans. *"...bold... rash... unwise... too soon... too late... possibilities... must be careful... a risk... necessary... interesting... valuable creatures... unique... they are willing?... apparently... can they be controlled?... certainly... what is the benefit?... we need to study further... possible genetic superiority... more usefulness for us?... yes... not highest priority... will be hard to convince others... you risk us Ramsees... you have our support... it will be done... now?... soon... take care... opposition will be intense... we cannot be too tolerant..."*

Other pods were in similar group dialogues about other issues. Once these discussions ended, there was a general communing, coordinating the work of all pods for the betterment of the Quazzga. *"...growth cycles acceptable on young ones... food is being made/grown... human infrastructure stabilized... conversion to Quazzga food will occur as existing human foods are depleted... Plenty in storage until then... Mars colony expanding for those who are choosing that environment... Moon colony starts soon... many new Earth areas being explored... weather and seismic controls are being implemented... resource management plans are being implemented on schedule... no Quazzga health concerns... a few have been injured and killed through accidents... new planet... new challenges... human population stabilized... will be reduced/increased as needed... some not proving worthwhile to train/maintain... will be relocated as needed... hybrids continuing their work..."*

Hours later, and now in total darkness and utter silence, the ships rose like fireflies from the desert floor, transporting their alien occupants to resume their new lives and activities. There would be more meetings. Ramsees felt uneasy about not revealing his plans to everyone in attendance, but he also felt a better time would present itself soon. He needed to plan more. He didn't want opposition turning into disaster.

Greg Burke

Harbinger

"Do you see what I mean?" Del demanded in a low but urgent tone of about twenty interested fellow abductees. "We've *got* to look out for ourselves!" Blank sets of eyes that stared back at her as if she was speaking a foreign language.

Almost pleading, she added, "Look, Ramsees seems OK, but we all know what his kind has done to our planet, to your families, to your friends, to us for cryin' out loud!" she said raising her hair and stabbing a finger at the back of her neck.

This brought people out of their stupor a little. One grizzled old man who looked liked he'd been in the mountains forever piped up, "You've got a point, young lady."

A middle-aged woman who looked a little like Del's mother added, "This has been a day for revelations. My head is still spinning. What do you suggest we do?"

Before Del could answer, Eric spoke up, "We should talk somewhere else, where we aren't being watched. I don't want to get into trouble."

At that, everyone noticeably winced at the truth of his words, several eyes scanning the area for alien spies; though since leaving the ship they'd seen no Quazzga.

Jax broke the tension with his answer, "How about let's get some grub and discuss this further in private if we get a chance? I'm starved!"

Del's first reaction was to scowl at Jax for interrupting this dreadfully needed conversation, but she calmed, conceding he was right and the young boy had wisdom beyond his years. Plus, she recognized her own hunger now that she was past the anger and frustration. Looking around, she noticed that a large part of the group was over by the far wall in what looked like a food line and makeshift cafeteria. It appeared to be self-service as there was no evidence of cooks or their alien hosts.

It was typical post invasion food, similar to what she had eaten at Disney World: healthy and bland. She ate what she needed quickly, then elbowed Jax who nearly spit out the heaping mouthful of food he was inhaling. "I'm serious, we need to develop a plan of our own and we need to do it soon!"

He lowered his shoulders in resignation, but took control of himself by slowly setting down his utensils and wiping his mouth. "Of course you're serious. Aren't you always?"

Seeing the you-know-what-I-mean-look on her face he added in a more serious tone, "Yes, yes, you're right, but we'd better approach this cautiously. We've been given a reprieve of sorts and a lot of answers from the aliens that we shouldn't throw away by rash action. Look how easy we got snagged by Ramsees. Let's not underestimate their abilities. We gotta be careful, OK?"

She nodded, blushing with embarrassment at how they were caught. There were a lot of nods around the table of eight people and nods from people at nearby tables who were listening.

The old man who had agreed with her earlier said in a low voice from behind her, "We're with you lady, but your fella's right about us being careful. I've seen some awful sights and lost a lot of good friends. I don't trust anyone much, but I trust humans over the aliens, you over most folks, but myself over anyone. I want freedom too, but don't go lousing it up by some crazy headstrong reaction. You have a good head. Just slow down and use it. All of us are dependent on each other now."

Stunned by the rebuke, she looked over at the young boy, Eric. His eyes were fixed on hers. She read trust and saw him nod slowly in agreement with what the old man had said.

Straightening her back and looking at Jax for support, she replied calmly, "Very well. Thank you for your....bluntness. You are right. I want something good to come out of all this, not that I have a specific plan. Guess we should figure out what most people are thinking, see if anyone has any suggestions. Ramsees may be the only one who can save us, but we should figure out a backup plan in case his friends don't care for his ideas. Anyone else have a suggestion?"

Secretly, though, Del did have a plan of her own for escape, but didn't dare share it with anyone else. Not yet. Not even with Jax. It was reckless and unlikely to succeed. A lot of details still needed to be worked out or too many of these precious few remaining humans would be at great risk.

Unaware of her silent reverie, Jax spoke up, "How 'bout we split up, each of us talking to about 20 other folks and see what they're thinkin'. Then we meet again at lunch tomorrow and formulate our actions from there. What d'ya say?"

There were affirmative nods all around and it was agreed they would start right away. Several in the group stopped eating, gratefully it appeared, and went to sit down at nearby tables.

Getting up to head for a group near the far corner of the hanger, Jax noticed the worried and detached look on Del's face. "What's up good lookin'?"

Her eyes met his directly but appeared to be looking at nothing, "I'm worried," she replied tonelessly, "I don't think we have much time." Grabbing his hand and squeezing it she added more reassuringly and with a slight smile, "Let's get going. The sooner we talk to people the sooner we can move if we need to."

* * * * *

A day later, the group had swelled to over a hundred co-conspirators. Del looked appreciatively around the tables they had pulled together, glad that Lady Henri had joined them, satisfied they had some real leaders here, amazed there was actually general agreement to band together in saving their own skins.

It had not all gone smoothly. In fact, many had been opposed to any action independent of Ramsees. For the first time, some felt safe. Others were unwilling to go up against such awesomely powerful beings or hazard losing the Quazzga's protection. Still others just didn't care.

Del understood their anxiety. They were numbed by their individual experiences, overwhelmed by the futility of any action on their part in light of Ramsees' story. It took all the restraint Del could muster not to shake people and yell at them to make them understand. She actually surprised herself by presenting rational arguments that they were more than just pawns, pets, or guinea pigs, yet it appeared to be falling mostly on deaf ears.

Their small group appeared to be on the brink of defeat when talks continued to with no productive solutions around dinner tables. When a Quazzga named Turooz showed them quarters nearby, Del and Jax went wearily together, wondering why Ramsees had not reappeared, more apprehensive of their situation than ever. As they held each other for comfort and security that night, both agreed that something had to be done and went to sleep vowing to do so even if no one else went along.

Morning brought a surprise, though, when person after person gave her a nod, wink, or murmur of support at breakfast. A few explained that upon further deliberation, her group was right. It lifted her spirits immensely to see the change, though she chafed at the idea of this being "her group", not happy with leadership being foisted upon her, especially when she secretly harbored other plans than what she suspected could be carried out.

For the most part, they had been left unsupervised and there was curiously no sign of Ramsees. With nothing to do except lounge around the hanger among the Quazzga ships, Del was anxious to meet with everyone when mid day arrived.

"I do hope you'll agree to be our leader, Ms. Summers." Lady Henri said softly to those gathered closely. A chorus of affirmations followed before Del could open her mouth in answer.

Del felt hooked and cooked.

Her response was measured as she looked everyone in the eye and placed both hands on the table in front of her for emphasis, "Look, I'll do it, but we're all in this together and there must be consensus about what we do or we do nothing. And if I screw something up, or don't agree with what we plan, then I'm out. Can you live with that?" Again, there were nods of agreement and even a few thumbs up.

They spent the next 40 minutes reviewing the reactions of those they had talked to, listing the actions some had suggested, trying to distill the wide variety of emotions and suggestions into something meaningful. An hour and a half and a lot of paper scraps later, they had consensus on a loose framework for action.

Perhaps they had more in common than being able to resist Quazzga mind control, because as diverse as the group was, they worked extremely well together. Simple ideas were built upon and enhanced until they made perfect sense. No one dug their heels in and no ideas were criticized unjustly. It was a blending of thoughts working in unison for a common goal. Del had never been in a meeting that went so smoothly. It gave her hope that maybe they would make it.

"So, plan A is to work with the Quazzga as much as possible, learn all we can, and as soon as we can, look for a way to gain our independence or find a way to protect ourselves," Del summarized. "I like it. It's a bit devious, may take a while, but would appear to be our best chance outside of leaving our fate entirely up to the Quazzga. The devil will certainly be in the details which we'll work out later today. Any questions?"

No one raised an objection, so she went on, "Plan B is to try to secure our own place out of the way and live out our lives as best we can, hopefully undisturbed. Not bad, probably less of a possibility given that the Quazzga own the whole show now, but definitely worth a try if plan A fails. Did I get this right?" As if they had all picked up on some collective joke, she was answered with silent smiles, and unanimous enthusiastic thumbs up.

Smiling broadly, she wagged a finger at them all and added in a low conspiratorial tone, "Now, let's figure out how to accomplish plan A."

Hours later, still amazingly undisturbed and approaching dark, they had things worked out. Del was heartened by their efforts, especially when some of what they planned dovetailed well with her secret plan C. She had a twinge of guilt, knowing she was keeping this from the others, but when the time came, if it came, she would have to act as her conscience dictated. The only hitch in plan A for her was that, by group consensus, she was the best person to break the news to Ramsees and get his approval.

"You have a lot more confidence in me than I do," was her response as she reluctantly accepted the role. "Anyone mind if Jax comes along for moral support?"

Jax looked stunned at first, but then warmed to the idea, glad to be of some help. No one raised an objection so Del responded, "Come on big guy, let's see if we can round up an alien."

That proved harder than she would have figured. It had puzzled her why they hadn't been under constant supervision. Perhaps they didn't care what the humans did or felt no need to watch over them like prisoners. Maybe they trusted the humans, at least this group. At any rate, there were no Quazzga in the hanger or visible on the grounds around the hanger. When they went to the big ship where they had their "meeting" and knocked on the side of the opening, even yelled, "Hello!" a few times. No one showed up. They felt silly standing there like Jehovah Witnesses waiting for someone to come to the door.

Finally, Jax suggested, "Let's just go on in and look around for one of 'em."

Shrugging her shoulders, she pushed him ahead with a smile saying, "You first."

Twenty feet into the corridor, a side panel opened up and four aliens strode out pointing small palm sized discs at them. The intent was clear as they blocked the way. Before either Del or Jax could stop or raise their arms in surrender one of the Quazzga queried, *"Why are you here?"*

"Whoa. Easy boys, we don't want any trouble," Jax answered. "We're just looking for Ramsees. Can you help us find him?" Jax and Del had their hands way up in the air, stiff as sticks. They felt stupid and awkward, hoping the aliens would recognize their gesture as surrender.

"This area is private and you are not to approach unless asked," the aliens countered almost as one. Suddenly they paused, then added, *"Ramsees is being contacted and will see you when he can. Return now to your living area."*

Backing slowly away with hands still raised and heads nodding agreement, they removed themselves from the ship.

"Jeez, what grumps!" Jax sighed, glad the aliens hadn't been trigger happy. He'd never seen what they had in their hands before, but had no doubt he wouldn't like the result.

Del was miffed as well. "It'd be nice to have a look around these ships, but we better play nice or they'll get suspicious." Biting her lip and rubbing her neck, she added, "Damn, Jax, they know right where we are probably, each of us a blip on some screen. We can't go to the bathroom without them knowing. Probably have us coded as well so they know exactly who is with whom. We'll have to be more than careful, even in meeting."

"Aw, I don't know if they care all that much, but you make sense, as usual," he agreed, smiling in a loving way. "Ya know, we make a good team. Let's say we get married, then we can be together a lot more and they won't suspect a thing!"

The look he got was obviously not what he expected because his playful smile turned to alarm, then fear, as she swung a roundhouse punch at him, missing his body as he ducked, then stopping cold as he caught her arm with his unbandaged hand and spun her around to face him squarely.

"Hey, easy there, lady! Ya coulda' hurt me good!"

With eyes burning through him she blurted out, "That's... that's the best proposal you could come up with? And just to... to... throw some aliens off? I'm insulted!"

He relaxed his grip and spun her neatly away, then looked at her directly.

"I'm sorry Del. I didn't mean it like that. You know what a goof I am and I can't help feeling so much in love with you. It was bad timing, but I meant the part about us gettin' hitched."

Her glare softened a little, 'though her arms were still crossed. Jax stepped closer.

Bending down on both knees, he gazed deeply into her dark brown eyes and put his arms out to her. "Del, would you marry me and make me the happiest man left alive? I don't give a damn what kind of world we live in, but I love you and want to spend my life with you. I haven't known you long, but I feel like I've known you forever." He cocked his head, eyes pleading, eyebrows lifted a little, ears waiting for an answer.

Still shocked at what she was hearing and not quite certain about this wonderful man she had grown so fond of in such a short time, she uncrossed her arms, allowed a smirk on her face, and grabbed his hands.

"Get up you big lummox. I'm not sure of a whole lot either and not sure I can trust myself to make the best decisions right now, but yes, why don't we get married?"

Hugging each other tightly, their joy was evident and the feeling was mutual.

Del broke away first and wagged her finger at him, "But remember: This is strictly business, so we can spend more time plotting strategy."

As always, she was way ahead of him and this statement disturbed him. When she broke into a big smile, he knew the joke was on him. Jax tapped her smartly on the side of the head in acknowledgment, shaking his head at his gullibility.

"You two are funny," came a voice nearby which startled them both. Eric's face showed puzzlement yet curiosity. "Well, do you two like each other or not? It's hard to tell, not like it was with my parents." At that his face clouded and he started to turn away.

"Wait, Eric," Jax and Del blurted out simultaneously. "What's the matter?" Del added, reaching for Eric.

"Nothing much. Was just wonderin' what you were doing out here by the ship and why you were fighting. My Mom and Dad used to fight a lot until they got changed. That scared me a lot, 'though I'd rather have things the way they were," Eric revealed. "Then Mr. Leigh got down on his knees to ask you something and I got curious."

Del couldn't help but smile and looking at Jax he was grinning widely also. "You're lonely, Eric, aren't you?"

He started to shake his head no, then said, "Yeah, but a little scared too. I was just hoping you weren't fighting because it only seems to cause problems.... for everyone."

Squeezing his hand in warm reassurance, she said, "We're fine, it was play fighting, a joke. In fact, we're going to get married!"

That cheered the boy considerably and he let out his breath as if he had expected something bad. "That's great news! Can I tell everyone?"

"Leave that to us, my boy. We want the honors, right Del?" asked Jax.

"Sure. In the meantime, we were out trying to see if we could find Ramsees and get our plan into high gear. Instead, the goon squad inside sent us packing. There's always tomorrow."

"You called....I am here," rushed into their minds, and all three nearly lept out of their skins.

Spinning about to locate the alien and not having success, Del shouted into the darkness, "Ramsees, don't do that!"

The trio was still looking all around when they spied a saucer dropping briskly to the ground. *"My apologies. You caused some concern. I came as fast as I could and contacted you this way as we approached. What is it we can do for you...three?"*

Struggling to compose herself and glancing nervously at her companions, Ramsees' ship came to rest and he smoothly exited facing the trio, Del stammered, "Well...we...Jax and I,...and now Eric, and really many of us, were wondering if we could help you in any way, as a way of thanking you for saving us and treating us as, well,...humans, which is leaving us as we are. We're really grateful and know we could be of some help if you'll give us a chance."

She felt stupid. All of her practiced thoughts had fallen apart and her ideas were being conveyed in a half-baked manner. This scene wasn't following her script.

The mirror-black eyes and the rest of his motionless body revealed nothing. Del knew her impromptu speech hadn't worked and she wanted to blurt out any number of sentences to further explain herself. Her father had taught her one key to winning negotiations was to make your case, as best as you can, then shut up; whoever speaks next loses. Still, this was killing her. Jax and Eric looked equally unnerved as the silence stretched out for what felt like minutes.

Standing it no longer, she started to speak, when, *"How magnificently special you are,"* came into her head.

Ramsees continued, *"You do your people justice, offering help to your conquerors... and saviors. Such strong will. Such unique philosophies. Yet I sense... conflict... doubt... fear...from you, Adelle Summers. Please explain."*

Feeling her goose was cooked if most of the truth was not revealed quickly, she answered, "You're right, and you know, I don't feel all that great about your people coming to our planet. But we talked about what to do next and we came to the consensus that we should help you as best we can. What's worse, they named me a leader of sorts to break the news to you. So here I am and I'm passing on the groups feelings, even though I have some personal reservations about helping the Quazzga in any way, or that we can even be of help to you, or even that it's in our best interest."

"That's very forthcoming. The explanation is appreciated. I am getting to know more about all of you and am pleasantly surprised. It bolsters my convictions about saving you and as many others as possible."

As his chittering died away, the foursome were left standing silently under a clear starry sky, no one speaking further, everyone apparently lost in thought.

"There may be a way...," Ramsees offered.

The Frying Pan

Jax awoke to a horrible mix of emotions, churning in his head like it was a blender, giving him a migraine. Actually, he'd gone to sleep with them, not able or wanting to sleep at first, but finally giving in to his body's demands. *"What a mess. And it gets worse every day,"* he grumbled.

He'd been overjoyed by the plan everyone'd developed the day before, unsure about telling it to Ramsees, and afraid for his life when the Quazzga kicked them out of the ship. Then there was the stomach-knotting nervousness of formally proposing to Del followed by elation at her acceptance. Finally, the meeting with Ramsees and his later discussions with Del and other people still awake. Those events added hope, fear, certainty, uncertainty, joy, and even terror to his already-aching skull.

As much as their world had changed, one thing had not: his mind. Sacrificing that would be too much. He'd watched his friend Gerry Peyton waste away in a nursing home, a vegetable after several strokes. He'd read and talked to Gerry many times, but there was never an ounce of recognition or change in brainwaves. *"What an awful prison!"* ran through his thoughts every visit.

And what was going through Gerry's mind? No one would ever know, as those thoughts, if there were any, went to his grave. And that's what bothered Jax. He'd seen many other stroke victims, and from what he could tell, they wanted to talk and do things, but their minds couldn't control their bodies, mouths couldn't form the words they wanted to say, hands couldn't write messages. Like the rage of late-term Alzheimer's patients, it was hell on Earth.

Which brought him to his dilemma. He'd work for the Quazzga in any capacity they asked as long as they'd leave him *as is*. If it came down to it, he'd rather escape or die trying than become a zombie. To him, it was like the stroke patients. Maybe people in comas, or folks with mental defects, and now the zombies, just didn't know better and were happy as larks, but he didn't think so. That blank look in the eyes told him the change was permanent and not for the better for thinking individuals. He would rather stay plain old vanilla Jax.

This would have to play out he knew, but he didn't like it one bit. Like the old spy shows, where you had to consider the possibility of swallowing a cyanide pill rather than be taken by the enemy, he'd have to think of a backup plan that would save his skin, and now Del's, if things went south.

"You think too much," broke him out of his brooding as Del came back into the room in a perkier mood than he was in. "You're gonna pop a blood vessel."

"Thanks for the advice," he answered somberly. "Del, this is serious business! We could risk everything!"

"Seems to me we have already," she quipped sitting down next to him on the couch.

"What d'ya mean by that?"

With a sigh, Del went on, "I'm worried too, but aren't we just along for this grand ride already? We're weathering the storm as best we can, but we can't change what's happened... happening to us. I'm not real keen on Ramsees' plan either, but we risked everything getting this far and every day is a risk for all of us. If we don't go along with it, it might be worse for us yet, especially since we offered our help."

"Yeah, but in many ways, it doesn't appear to be so brilliant an idea now," he offered solemnly. "Plus, I sure hate being first hog at the trough on this one. We're going to be like guinea pigs y'know."

In silence, they hugged for mutual reassurance.

"I'm scared Del, that's all."

Massaging her hands, lifting her beautiful face upward, and looking into her soulful eyes for many long seconds, he spoke again, "I don't want to lose you, lady, not after what we've been through separately and together, not after how I feel about you. I don't want to be captured or altered either."

Flushing with feelings of love, she kissed him, then patted his cheek. "I don't want to lose you either and I'm damned scared of this whole business too. Tell you what. Let's keep our options open as long as we can. We've made it this far. We'll have to trust our instincts to get us farther. Anyway, I like our odds better when we're together."

In a mangled Southern version of an Australian accent, Jax said, "Like no worries, mate?"

Laughing, she replied, "Yeah, something like that, only it'll be us on the barbecue instead of shrimp if this doesn't work out. Come on now, it's time to go."

Six members of the group met at the hanger near the shuttle Ramsees had arrived in the previous night. It was shortly before noon on a dry, warm, and cloudless California day. When Del and Jax arrived, Lady

Henri and Eric were there. Neither acted particularly worried and smiled quickly and amiably at their approach.

"Eric tells me you are getting married," Lady Henri said in greeting. "How magnificent!"

Eric's faced purely beamed as Jax and Del said, "Yep." and "Yes." at the same time.

"Does everyone know?" Jax asked Eric.

"All I could tell since last night," Eric answered, his smile now full of boyish mischief.

Two more people approached the conversation: The old mountain man named Ben Johnson, and a teenager named Shandra Miles.

Actually, Ben wasn't a mountain man, he just looked like it. He was a retired gas station owner from North Carolina who had set up a small antique shop in the Smoky Mountains for the previous 20-odd years. His wife had passed on and his five kids had grown and moved away. He looked 70 but was 88, and pretty spry for his years.

His white flowing hair, mustache, and beard hid a few wrinkles, but didn't hide sparkling blue eyes full of vigor. His casual clothes were all "part of the act" he said, which helped him sell a ton of antiques to the tourists. He'd made a bundle on Web investments so he didn't need the money. He liked visiting with customers, and his mountain man look plus an easy smile opened folks up to talk about themselves.

Shandra looked like she could take on the world, and probably had. The tall, thin 14-year-old had long beaded corn rows, piercing dark eyes, a pierced eyebrow, and wore a confident yet serious expression. She was living near Chicago when the invasion occurred. Like Eric, she had escaped her family, friends, and neighborhood. By her wits and perseverance, she had managed to survive in Southern Illinois farm country until being picked up by the Quazzga and taken to the base. She played the violin and was an honor student. Basketball was a hobby though her Junior Varsity coach and her stats would tell you she was a rising star.

Jax wasn't surprised to see Eric or Lady Henri waiting here for Ramsees, but the other two were a welcome surprise.

"Did Ramsees ask you to come along?" Del queried the two newcomers.

"Well, ask is a might weak," answered Ben.

"We were ordered point of fact," added Shandra.

"Some group this is," chimed in Del. "Young, middle aged, and old, male and female. Is this a coincidence?" When no one answered, she went on, "I didn't think so either."

As they were exchanging pleasantries, Ramsees eased out of the hanger area towards the shuttle. Jax still found it hard to believe they were assisting an alien in this matter. As hard as it was for ordinary humans to work together and get along, dealing with a totally new life form was taking some real getting used to.

"Thank you for coming. Let's go," Ramsees intoned. *"I trust you will leave things alone in this smaller ship and behave yourselves when we get to Mars."*

Eric jumped at that. "Mars! How cool!"

The other five registered surprise in various eye-popping and eyebrow-raising gestures.

Del flashed a warning look at Jax. "Did you know about this?"

He shrugged his shoulders and answered, "It's news to me."

Ramsees had mentioned coming with him on a trip to meet his ruling council. He hadn't mentioned Mars. Things just kept getting more interesting.

Gesturing his guests into the sleek, saucer-shaped shuttle, they started to file in when Jax piped up, "Ramsees, what do you hope to accomplish by this meeting really? You act like there's no concern, but I'm worried about your friends and my friends. How 'bout lettin' us in on what's going to happen?"

Ramsees paused for longer than normal and they all heard, *"I sense you are worried and there is some reason for concern, but I can and will protect you from any direct attack on your persons if that will help. We must be going. There will be time on our trip to answer more questions."*

"I'm not sure I feel better," Jax answered, "But what the heck, in for a dime, in for a dollar," he said as he proceeded into the ship with the rest of this motley group of humans.

This was only his second trip in a Quazzga vessel that he knew of. This particular craft was as sleek and smooth as all the other myriad vehicles, but it was only about 40 feet around and ten feet high. Despite its small relative size, the inside was spacious: he could see just about the entire interior from any point inside. There was little light, but enough to get around. Most of the illumination came from what appeared to be control consoles around the walls as well as the entire ceiling, which glowed dimly.

Ramsees guided them to a dozen slightly reclined sofa chairs in the center of the vessel. These were similar to the cubicles they'd been floated into when they first arrived at the base in that as soon as they positioned themselves onto them, the soft and comfortable couches sucked in their bodies and held them fast. Also, Ramsees' calming thoughts drifted into his mind almost as soon as he had settled down, telling them to relax; that the restraining couches were for their protection in flight. Like before, they would be able to send thoughts as well as receive them in these couches.

There were two other Quazzga in the ship, who were busy at their consoles. Jax wondered where the view ports were when panels ahead of these two irised open to reveal the clear California daylight. Like looking through strong sunglasses, the view added little light to the cabin. Other view ports irised open above and below the centerline of the vessel so there was nearly a 360 degree view of the outside, both ground and sky.

A much smaller Quazzga swung out of a couch opposite the entrance and approached them, clearly studying each human like it had never seen one before, finally settling upon Eric. In fact, they were about the same size. It twittered at Eric, who appeared none too worried about the attention, even though he was pinned down in his couch and was being subjected to careful prodding.

Ramsees' thoughts intruded, *"This is Isees. He is one of the youngest members of my pod, born just before our trip here. He is barely skilled enough to talk with you, but when he is positioned over there, you may pick up more of his thoughts. He is very curious about all of you and asked to be along on our visit."*

"Pleased to meet you, Isees," Eric both said and thought.

"Hello," was Isees' simple reply.

Isees chittered even more and there was a hint of muscle movement around the mouth, perhaps even the barest smile. He touched Eric's hair, nose, ears, eyebrows and chin, even looking closely at his fingernails. Isees then walked around and studied the other humans, pausing again at Shandra, apparently interested in humans more his size or age.

Del didn't care for the scrutiny and when Isees touched her breast, she hollered, "Watch it buster!" causing Isees to jerk away and rush back to his couch, casting fearful glances back at Del.

"Please. Relax. He means no harm. He is young and you are new to him." Ramsees explained, as he settled into a console area and worked with incredible agility on the panel in front of him, lights changing color as his nimble fingers danced over the controls. *"We are leaving now."*

Jax could feel his body sink into the couch slightly as they rose silently and pulled away from the ground with incredible acceleration. In seconds, they had risen miles above the ground in an oblique maneuver, the former air base a mere speck, and the California coast and mountains retreating rapidly. In less than a minute, they had slipped through the atmosphere and were silently watching Earth shrink below them.

The feeling was awesome to Jax. How many times had he wondered what it was like to be out here, and now he was. His heart raced with exhilaration. He dared not close his eyes lest he miss anything. His companions were equally enthralled. He stole a glance at Del beside him and winked at her excited face, as she smiled back. Even skeptical old Del was enjoying this.

A look of wonder was evident on every human face, a realization more important than their first space flight. "No voice in my head!" he mouthed with delight to Del.

Her nod was one of relief. Like taking the tension out of a rubber band, he felt he finally could relax against the nagging assault that had been like a sliver in his head since the invasion. He suspected once away from Earth, the projections disappeared altogether. He stole a conspiratorial glance at Del. Could she be wondering the same thing? It would have to wait for later private discussion.

"We have several hours before we arrive," Ramsees interrupted. *"All of you appear to be relaxing. Let me take some time to answer your questions."*

Del couldn't wait and pounced so quickly it broke whatever reverie they had briefly enjoyed. "Like Jax said, what's going to happen exactly? You've been a little vague on details."

"As always, you are direct and I must caution you that your tone will not be acceptable to my leaders. Now is the time to use the resourcefulness that allowed you to evade capture by those who would have changed you into a .... person less than you are. You, Adelle Summers, in particular must act more... calmly and without malice. Yes, you are upset and rightfully so, but that will not help your/our cause. I brought you along for your leadership despite your emotional flaws, but you must control those emotions if we are to succeed. I would ask if you cannot do that, please stay behind in the ship and the rest of us will proceed without you."

That took her aback, and banked the fires of her fear and impatience. "Fine. I'm...sorry. This is very frustrating. I'll cool my jets. Just tell us what's going on."

"It is as we discussed yesterday. A personal appearance on your part is needed to convince my leaders and the elder council that it is important we save you, intact, and allow your existence for further

study by me and my pod, and to preserve your uniqueness. We will meet with the leadership, and ask for their forbearance, to secure a promise of your security from other Quazzga who might fear your existence and do something about it."

"Sounds like you want some zoo animals, mister," snorted Ben.

"You are more than that to me: much more. My race may see you as pets or even slaves to be used as they desire. I believe you...and I, can change that opinion."

"Just how do you propose doing that?" asked Jax.

"We will present you for their questioning and also show them data we've collected: brain and genetic scans showing you are special, worthy of our notice, perhaps even treatment as near equals, as another sentient species, the first we've ever encountered."

"What are our chances of succeeding? Is this a sure bet?" Del asked, more calmly than earlier.

"I have learned much about your race over the years, and one interesting activity pervading your race is gambling. We don't understand the value to you, but we do understand probability mathematics. On a scale with success at one end and failure at the other, we are closer to success if that helps. I have some influence in this matter, despite the reservations of many Quazzga who are troubled about this entire venture of ours, mine in particular, and want total success at any cost and do not want colonization efforts...complicated. Even a rejection of our idea won't necessarily spell doom. As I've heard some humans say, let's look on the bright side."

For a while, there was silence while everyone pondered their own mostly gloomy thoughts. Then Shandra spoke up. "With humans to help you, kinda like slaves, what will you do to animals and Earth's resources?"

Ramsees transmitted a wordless wave of amusement at the unexpected turn in the conversation. He continued *"I am continually amazed by your thought patterns. Thank you, young human. To answer as directly as possible, this is a very rich planet in resources and living beings.*

"We were most fortunate to have found such a treasure and will not squander this opportunity. Humans have tried, but by our understanding have not grown adequately into the role of caretakers of this planet; you merely existed and ran amok doing human things. Recently you were learning from past mistakes and the damage you caused had not been significant or irreparable by any means, but we were greatly concerned that you would destroy yourselves and greatly damage this planet

through a nuclear holocaust that would occur beyond our control, making this planet unlivable in the short term.

"The numerous species of animals, plants, and insects on this planet will be maintained as we deem prudent, better utilized for food and supplies than you had been doing. There is a lot to do in the meantime dealing with loose and uncared for pets around the world and cataloguing species in zoos and in the wild to determine the best course of their use, extinction, or conservation. We have experts in this area who are working diligently on this matter. Unlike our home world, this planet is far richer and with our resource conservation technologies should be able to sustain our race here in any numbers for tens of millions of years.

"Indeed, this entire solar system is a treasure far beyond our expectations. We are dehydrating massive quantities of food supplies and will be sending specific needed resources to our home world, but it is an insignificant amount of your renewable resources. Other than that, we will keep things as they are. Did you control any species in your domicile, Shandra?"

"Uh, if you mean house, yeah, we had a pug and a ferret. I don't know what's happened to them," she answered solemnly.

Not waiting for a pause, Jax asked, "When Del and I were in Florida, she was assisting in the incubation of baby Quazzga. How many do you plan to have on this planet? Do you control your populations?"

"We did not maintain breeding facilities in our ships for our journey here and some Quazzga perished during the trip for a variety of reasons, so we are breeding replacements to be sure. In addition, though, now that we are settling in on this planet, we plan to breed as many new Quazzga as we can so we can propagate our race and explore and utilize the resources of this solar system and beyond. There should be tens of millions of Earth-born Quazzga on this planet within 20 years. There will be tens of millions more coming soon. We have controlled our population for too long. That will change in an exponential fashion."

Alarmed, Del said, "Well just make yourself at home why don't you. Is there room enough for the two of us?"

There was an uncomfortable silence for what felt like an eternity, humans again struck by the unpleasantness of their fate, Ramsees seeming to mull over Del's most recent biting commentary.

Ramsees broke the silence, his mental voice somewhat deeper and measured. *"That...was part of...the original plan. It's...hard to explain. Much...has changed...is changing...will have to change...if there is to be coexistence. You...are part of the new plan...my plan. There is much that is...uncertain."*

"Fella, you are worrying me," Del answered nervously. Everyone else was watching the two of them intently. Eric's eyes were almost bugging out with a mix of fear and interest.

"Ramsees...I've never seen you so solemn," added Lady Henri trying to probe him more deeply. "What are you thinking?"

"My apologies if I have alarmed anyone. You all continue to amaze me with your depth of emotion and understanding of your situation. I hadn't expected you to be so probing in your questions. I have much to learn. My race thinks you still the savage brutes they encountered millennia ago. It is truly remarkable how much you have evolved in the past thousand years. And are still evolving. There is much they do not know and much we need to show them."

"Damn straight, pardon my French," added Jax. Smiles broke out all around, somewhat forced, but smiles nonetheless. The tension that had built so quickly ebbed away.

Shandra spoke up too adding, "Yeah, let's do as Ramsees suggests and look on the bright side. Let's make this a good situation rather than assuming it will turn out bad."

"You are wise, young one. Thank you."

"So, are we there yet?" asked Eric. Hearing chuckles from the adults, he went on, "Hey, I'm a kid and kids always get to ask that question!"

Their conversation with Ramsees had run the table from peanuts to dirigibles. Everyone, even Ramsees, was subdued with the breadth and scope of their conversation. There were more questions than answers, but Ramsees was patient, even if Del was not.

Like during the initial debriefing on Earth, everyone, all secure in the massive amphitheater, a silence, a brooding silence, took hold as humans and Quazzga alike took their own council, fleeting knowing looks communicating volumes. This was no walk in the park for anyone.

"Ramsees?" asked Jax, "Is it too late to turn around?" The curve of his lips indicated he was just kidding, testing. There were nervous smiles in response; a part of everyone wishing they didn't have to go through with this.

Ramsees' silence indicated he understood their feelings. It also meant there was no turning back.

Greg Burke

The Fire

Thoughts of what they were inexorably fated to do diminished as they approached Mars. All eyes moved towards the view ports and the beautiful red/orange scenery steadily approaching them. No human, that they knew of had ever been this close to Mars. Even most of the unmanned missions had gone awry, which made Jax wonder how much of an accident that was. Still, what an incredible sight to see, not from net pictures of satellite flybys or artist renditions, but up close with his own two eyes.

You could see a thousand pictures of Mount Rushmore, the Taj Mahal, or the Eiffel Tower, but until you actually went there and saw them first hand, you really wouldn't know what is was like. No picture could adequately describe the feeling, the grandeur, the magnitude of these sights like being there. The same could be said of Mars.

From crisp polar icecaps, to huge craters, to mountains that would dwarf anything on Earth, to erosive canyons that made the Grand Canyon seem insignificant, Mars was a geological wonderland.

"Damn, what a sight!" exclaimed Ben. He remembered the close-ups from various probes and none of them had fully revealed what he was seeing first hand.

"This is the coolest!" shouted Eric, as he gazed at a world expanding before his eyes, a world he could have never imagined visiting.

"We're the first women here, right?" asked Shandra, intrigued with the history-making visit.

"No, I've been here before," answered Lady Henri, in a matter-of-fact tone that brooked no question.

"Jax, are you believing this?" whispered Del.

The pristine surface did not surprise Jax. As long as these boys had been around, they had maintained secrecy pretty well. There was no indication the planet was inhabited in any way. Sure, there were Quazzga ships in orbit as they made their approach, but nothing showed on the surface. *"It must be hidden very well indeed,"* he mused.

"Why Mars and not the moon?" Del asked.

"An easy one even you will understand," responded Ramsees. *"Your moon is cold and inhospitable, and with our ships there is not much time difference between your moon and this planet. In addition, this planet has habitable qualities, resources, and a stronger gravity."*

Del, as usual, found it hard to forget why they were here, even in the face of such an eye-popping personal experience. Trepidation started to build, and it took a constant force of will to calm herself. She'd seen too much in the past few months to trust anything and let her guard down, even in the face of the most awesome and inspiring beauty she'd ever seen.

But looking at the others, especially the kids, it was hard not to smile a little and relax. Eric and Shandra were constantly pointing out things as they got closer, in the excited way only kids could do, and with wide-eyed delight. Ramsees was a poor tour guide, offering nothing in explanation. That, of course didn't deter the youngsters.

"Look at that moon, did you see that asteroid hit? It must be miles wide!" shouted Eric. "Which one is that, Deimos or Phobos? Can we get closer and check it out?"

"No way, boy, the planet is so much cooler," countered Shandra. "Look at those canals! We've got to see that. What about the face on the surface people used to talk about? That's a huge mountain! Is there any life Ramsees?"

There was a constant stream of curious questions no human or Quazzga could answer and it continued until Mars filled the view screen. Even young Isees was quiet, or at least he didn't intrude upon thoughts. The way he leaned forward in his seat, though, mimicked the young humans in their excitement. This was probably all new to him as well.

Jax broke the mood as they neared the surface. "So, where are we going? I don't see any base or place to land."

In response, Ramsees' fingers buzzed over his control panel and he waved his hand towards the view screen. Nothing happened until they curved toward a mountain shadow. In the shadow, an opening was forming with a faint light visible inside. The graceful ship angled sharply, like a fighter plane coming in for a strafing run. Thankful for the sticky couches as the lightning-fast maneuver pulled him severely, Jax had his answer.

The ship was suddenly in the opening and stopped in almost an instant, leaving the humans feeling like they'd been in the wildest roller coaster ride ever, with the ever-familiar rapid deceleration at the end. The faint lights outside the ship shut off, there were numerous muffled sounds around them, and even some hull noises, then the lights came on again, though much brighter, more like daylight.

As if in response to their arrival, the chairs relaxed their grip and the Quazzga stood up. The humans, from both abruptness of the landing and uncertainty of being on another planet, got up much slower, not quite having their Mars legs yet. Lady Henri was surprisingly agile, being one of the first to move towards the door, even if it was a slow motion gait. The lighter gravity seemed to agree with her.

At only a third of earth's gravity, 215 pound Jax felt light indeed, by his calculations only 81 pounds. A slight step would take you three times further and it was all he could do to control his bulk, arms flailing to catch himself, trying to adjust to this drastic change.

"Well, that was some landing, Ramsees. Remind me to check your license next time," Del quipped as she too struggled with the gravity. The deceleration and low gravity left her a bit nauseous. She hated roller coasters. This was worse.

In response, Ramsees only deadpanned, *"We will meet the elders soon. Mind your manners."*

Shandra and Eric jumped up and down to see how high they could go. Both could touch the ceiling of the ship easily. They laughed uncontrollably, enjoying the trampoline-like experience. Ben just took things slowly and edged his way towards the door, smiling as he watched the kids.

Everyone filed out into a small tunnel connected to the ship. The ground suddenly took on a sticky quality that held their bodies more like Earth gravity. It made walking easier, but it disappointed the kids.

The air was a bit musty, but not bad, certainly breathable. *"At least Quazzga didn't stink and they kept things pretty neat,"* Del complimented.

"Jesus!" she thrilled, "I'm on Mars!"

The smooth bluish tunnel was wide enough for two and Jax quickly sauntered up from behind Del and grabbed her soft hand with a strength he hoped would comfort her. His warmth spread through her, a welcome relief from the tension she wasn't aware had been building again.

"Some ride, eh? And here we are without fanfare, no first man or woman on Mars hype. What an awful shame. They just don't allow for proper celebration of a such a momentous occasion, do they?" he offered.

Her smile at his jesting was all the encouragement he needed to lean forward and give her a big, wet kiss, which she returned with gusto. Then he exclaimed, "Aha, now that, the first kiss on Mars, shall go down in history!"

Pushing him away teasingly, she added, "What else do you have in mind for firsts? Oh, let me guess. How about the first knuckle sandwich? And may I remind you, Lady Henri was here first."

Feigning hurt, he curled his arm in hers and grinning they continued following the others, working their way deeper into the mountain. Before long, they were escorted into a small chamber. The complex they had seen so far didn't appear big at all, 'though they hadn't had access to several corridors they passed. The 50-foot-wide, circular cavern turned meeting area had a half-dozen Quazzga resting in couches, including a couple of what Del now understood to be females, judging by the collar decorations she'd seen in Florida.

Disappointed and surprised, she blurted out, "This is it? This is the big meeting? This is what I got all worked up about?"

"Quiet please. I must confer with members of my pod before we assemble," cautioned Ramsees. *"Now is the time for those manners I mentioned."*

Jax tugged hard on her arm to distract Del just as she was about to release a pithy remark. He lovingly pushed up on her chin to close her open mouth, then pantomimed zipping his mouth and locking it.

Never one to totally submit, she let out a noisy sigh and sulked. He hugged her silently, recognizing she was trying.

Everyone else stood silently. Like visiting a girl friend's parents for the first time, it was awkward being here. They were definitely fish out of water. The only sound now was the Quazzga chittering. Del wished there were some other noises, especially some good music. *"Stairway to Heaven would fit nicely,"* she mused.

Instead, the silence was deafening. A slight shuffling by a bored Eric made so much relative noise he stopped immediately. Either the room was well-insulated or Mars was a pretty dull place. Come to think of it, everything the Quazzga did had a quietness to it. Other than their chatter and internal thoughts, the ship had been remarkably quiet.

Judging by hand signals and posture, Del surmised Ramsees was getting support. Of course, he could have been ordering a pizza for all she knew about these aliens. She certainly couldn't tell by their faces what was going on. Even with pets you could tell something by their eyes, their tails, their body language, but not these folks.

The seemingly endless chittering stopped suddenly, adding to the absence of sound. Then all of the Quazzga headed towards the humans.

"My fellow pod members welcome you and want to know more about you before making any decisions," voiced Ramsees.

Hackles raised on Del's neck, but Jax's steadying yet gentle rubbing on her neck instantly calmed them. He again put a finger on his lips in a hushing gesture, knowing she was ready to react as usual. *"Hmm....give this guy a gold star,"* she thought warmly as she leaned into him.

The Quazzga group ambled over and began a silent study of each human. They were very thorough and painstakingly slow. In no time, the humans felt like animals on display. Thankfully for Del no one felt the need for touching as she probably would have lost it. It was nerve-wracking, but everyone held their ground and let the obviously curious Quazzga have their way.

The lack of mental speech was surprising, as Del had assumed they were going to fire a bunch of questions at the humans. There was a slight pricking feeling in her head like the voice, but it was different and she couldn't be certain it wasn't just her imagination.

Eventually, the Quazzga broke off and stood apart with Ramsees. The chittering was even faster than before. Eric suddenly tugged on her sleeve and he motioned her to come closer to his mouth. When she bent over, he whispered, "I can hear what they are saying. Not all of it, but I can make out the general meaning. They like us, a lot, but they're worried. Also, there's more happening than we're being told."

"How are you able to do that? Why can't we...? Never mind, thank you," she whispered back. Thinking a second, she added, "Let me know if we're getting into trouble. You are quite an amazing young man!"

Del could only wonder at this extraordinary development, trying to quickly assess what this development could mean for them.

Smiling from the encouragement, Eric listened again more intently.

Shandra must have overheard their whispers as she added quietly, "I can hear a little also, but they go so fast, like those people who do auctions."

The other humans appeared to be catching the drift of what was being said about the kids. Jax could only shake his head in amazement, guessing that the whole mental speech thing had a lot of angles: for example, Ramsees not being able to read their thoughts but able to project his own. Then there was the one Quazzga who instantly taught Del how to run the nursery, yet she was the only one who had done that to any human he knew so far.

Perhaps their special resistance to the voice made mental transmission more possible, both ways. It was all a lot of questions and not many answers. It was also unlikely they'd get much chance to find the answers. Still, here was a new wrinkle. Maybe kids had better brains or special neural connections that gave them this talent. Maybe they were more special than he thought. Who knew?

Ramsees straightened and voiced, *"We need to study you further, just one of you, we have to be sure of our....actions."*

The humans looked at each other in confusion, Del's mind and face filled with horror, when Ramsees added, *"Adelle, please come with us."*

Her name sounded so distant as her mind closed down. She could also hear herself whisper, "No. Not me. I don't trust you!" but it all felt like a dream. Her mouth went dry and her stomach churned. Her legs weakened. *"Why me? When will this bad dream end?"* she wondered.

Jax patted her cheeks which had lost all color, "Del, hey, it's OK, what's going on?! Talk to me honey!" Others gathered around in concern.

That cleared her a bit and she steadied herself, looking at her friends for support. Eric reached up and put a hand on her shoulder. "It's OK Miss, I think. I don't sense anything bad."

Shandra nodded her head also. Jax and Ben looked on with concern and terse nods indicating support. Lady Henri added, "Trust them. I would if it was me."

Shaking off the last of another one her spells, she gathered herself and replied, "Fine, let's do it, and quickly," with as much confidence as she could muster. She felt stupid for acting so scared, and didn't fully know why she had reacted so adversely. It had to be the cumulative effects of what she'd experienced since the invasion. Plus, she didn't fully trust these folks.

"The rest of you relax here. We will not be gone too long," added Ramsees.

With that, Del was escorted out of the room through a door near the back, down deeper into the complex through a narrow corridor into a smaller room, bright with light and brimming with equipment.

She stiffened, but Ramsees said, *"Relax. You are with friends. You must trust us."*

"Just tell me what you are going to do and why first, then I'll let you do whatever you want," she answered.

"Very well. We are wasting valuable time, but if you must know. We need to examine you physiologically and mentally. This...lab...has the necessary equipment for that. You, and your friends, are special as I've said. We need more information to know how special. We will be taking all manner of samples, but we need the data to support saving you. We detect that your young friends appear to have strong mental abilities, as do you. The older humans, less so. You being average and of a strong enough mental strength were chosen for our study. This would work best with your cooperation. Please, Adelle, play along. This is important... to you...and to me."

Remembering the stories she had heard about abductees and the sordid, painful experiments, she really did not want to go through with this. Fearful they might harvest her ovaries, and dreadful of any experimentation which would leave her as a vegetable, or worse, she mulled over his explanation. Thinking of Jax and their uncertain future and how Ramsees had treated them so far, she decided to trust a little and said, "Just knock me out or something, OK? I don't want to feel what you're doing. Can you promise me there will be no permanent damage?"

"There will be no permanent damage, but there may be a little discomfort," Ramsees answered in as calming a fashion as he could.

"Gee, never any black or white possibilities," Del muttered. *"Always a compromise."* "Let's get on with it," she said directly to the observing Ramsees and the others waiting to start the examination. "I'm as ready as I'll ever be."

Seeing the reclined chair like they had used in the spaceship, she laid down in it in as commanding and dignified a fashion as she could, the couch holding her tight as soon as she settled in. The other Quazzga started moving a dozen consoles around her, nameless gizmos and lighted instruments being prepared in seconds. It was a lot like being in a dentist's chair, except there were six hygienists, and they weren't just here to check her teeth like some horse at an auction.

Something was placed against her temples and instantly she felt her body go numb with paralysis. She could see more instruments being placed against her head though she couldn't move, couldn't protest. It made her understand with frightening clarity what Jax had said about his friend. There was some pressure in her eyes, building to a headache and there was the vague feeling of things happening to other parts of her body. Then she blanked out.

Truth or Consequences

When Del woke up, only Ramsees was there looking silently at her, a patient sentinel without expression. She felt alert and rested, like waking up fresh without an alarm. Easing herself carefully out of the couch, she could see the lab was all back to normal, neat and clean. She stood up steadily and did a systems check. Everything felt good: no pain, clothing unruffled, nothing out of the ordinary. She felt great, in fact.

"Well, gotta hand it to you, Ramsees, I expected to be naked, implanted, impregnated, disemboweled, beaten black and blue, lobotomized, in a heck of a lot of pain...something," she quipped.

"We....have not always been this gentle. Though you are mistaken: you still have the implant which did make data collection easier. We have learned a lot in our dealings with humans and you have helped us even more. Thank you."

How could she forget she wondered, as she fingered the healed spot at the back of her head. "So now what?"

"My pod members are assembling a larger meeting...so we can make a decision about you. Let's get back to your friends."

There were bright smiles and hearty greetings as they stepped back into the small meeting room. Jax was overjoyed and hugged her tightly. "I'm so glad you're all right. I was worried. We all were. What did they do the past hour and a half?"

Peeling back his strong arms, she said, "Easy big guy. Save it for later. I'm fine, really, better than I hoped as well. And frankly, I don't know what they did. I asked them to knock me out."

Twirling steadily in front of everyone, she reassured them, "See? Same old Del." She patted Eric's shoulder as well who hugged her in return.

Ben had remained so silent through the trip and this early meeting, it was almost a surprise to hear him speak. Perhaps, he carried more weight when he asked directly, "So, what did you find out, mister? Is it good news or bad?"

Ramsees could sense similar feelings from the others and gave it to them straight. *"It is both. Let me explain. You are all very special, even more special than we had thought. Your ability to avoid our control is genetically based, but its actual workings are a mystery. You are still evolving your abilities. That may worry some of our kind, amaze many, anger a few, and confuse still others.*

"The good news is we have more evidence to support your special status. The bad news is a positive outcome is not guaranteed. We will have to present our plan and be as convincing as possible. I personally feel better about this next step. Not all of my pod agrees, 'though they are supportive."

The ensuing silence could have been cut with a knife. Lips were being chewed on. Anxiety and mental gyrations filled the air. It was Lady Henri who finally spoke up. "I've lived a long and good life, but I think it is far from over. At least I hope so. Ramsees has a tendency to be pessimistic I've found from past dealings. Yes, I'm worried too. Who wouldn't be? We need to see this through, and the best way to do that is to face it headlong, give it our best shot.

"Let's trust Ramsees to manage this event in our interest, and let's all do our finest to represent the human race embodied in each of us to the best of our abilities. No regrets' is something I've lived by and it has suited me well. We made a choice to be here. Let's go do this thing and get back home," she finished.

Eyebrows raised and Shandra let out a, "You got that right."

Jax sliced his hands in the air over Lady Henri's head, then smiled at Del. "See? No marionette strings! I'm with her."

That brought a guffaw from Ben and relaxed Del. "Ramsees, after you," she gestured to the door.

"Very well, follow me. If it will help, I am nervous also. Thank you, Lady Henri, for your kind words. Let's hope my prognosis is pessimistic. Just follow me, do as you are told, answer when asked questions, and behave yourselves."

They were back in the wide corridor, but now descended further into the planet. Several groups of Quazzga were headed in the same direction. There was some surprise at the presence of humans judging by those who stood back and let them pass, otherwise they stayed together and kept moving. Within a short distance, they arrived at an area with several large oval doors.

Behind those doors was an amphitheater of immense proportions, filled with the ubiquitous Quazzga couches, or at least some variant on the floor level. Instead of holding maybe hundreds of Quazzga, this room clearly could hold thousands, and indeed was nearing capacity even though more aliens continued to file in. The sides were higher than the center. It appeared to once have been a huge natural cavern that had been converted. Quazzga engineers were indeed impressive.

They entered at the lowest level and approached a center area with consoles and a dais of sorts and a handful of slightly larger couches. Looking up, Jax saw concentric row upon row of couches, not too dissimilar from the room at the airbase where Ramsees had broken the good (read: bad) news to his fellow humans. Only in this case, the scale was a hundred fold larger.

Jax held Del's soft hand for comfort as well as loving support. He whistled softly, an engineer's admiration of the monumental efforts it took to build and maintain such a place. The amount of fresh air needed for this room alone was phenomenal. Then there'd be filters, vents, and humidifiers. It was truly amazing, and as impressive as some man made monuments on Earth, if not more. He sure would like to see the technology that made this possible. It far outdid the amazing work he'd seen at Disney World. *"What could they accomplish on Earth if they can do this here?"* he wondered.

Aliens: thousands upon thousands of them were floating up into couches. It made Del's head spin and she felt insignificant and greatly outnumbered. Of course, the real aliens here were the humans. This was Quazzga territory for sure. *"Lord, get us through this,"* she prayed.

"This is awesome!" concluded Shandra. She knew the adults couldn't really handle this type of input. Despite natural fears that kids dealt with every day at home and school, this was a cakewalk compared to the cyberspace world she often navigated. Still, this was *real*, but she felt like she'd trained for it. Eric acted pretty cool about the situation and she wished she could talk to him alone. They both appeared to be hearing more of the alien language than the adults, which had to be important. The real old folks with them just acted numb. Jax and Del looked distracted, confused, in love. Oh well. She'd have to be tough and get along as best she could.

As they approached the central area, the voices Shandra heard stilled, like something was about to happen. Sure enough, a dozen Quazzga popped up through the ground near the center to stand before them. Not knowing what to do personally, she stopped, as did her friends. The silence became total, mental and physical.

Then the chittering could be heard again, but the shouting in her brain became like listening to a hundred rock bands play at once. The debate had begun in earnest. She looked around at her companions and saw mostly confusion, except for Eric. He squared his eyes with hers and mouthed, "I know!" giving her the thumbs up for emphasis. Why he could hear as well as she did was a mystery, but they both were catching glimpses of what was being discussed that the adults couldn't.

What she heard was a wild and lightning fast mix of thoughts: *"...animals ...not worth any effort ...laudable ...highly intelligent ...must be exterminated ...clear the way ...precious resource ...unpredictable ...must be studied ...worthless ...grave threat ...no control ...higher mission ...look to Quazzga needs ...unique ...evolving...coexistence ...not possible ...dangerous ...risk to plans ...our future ...could help ...advantage..."*

There was an ebb and flow to the conversation that clearly was a struggle of thoughts, more like an open debate between thousands of minds at once. The sheer magnitude of ideas and projected thoughts was hard to fathom, or for Eric to keep up with completely. In minutes, he had heard volumes. It made him appreciate the Quazzga intelligence in a way, but made him fearful of their superiority. *"How significant could he be to them? Maybe they were right about how lowly humans were,"* he wondered.

Del and the other adults stood in silent frustration. They could sense that waves of mental energy were being deployed around them and there was the faintest plucking in their minds of the thoughts, but nothing would gel other than faint emotions from a war of thoughts. Like hearing a foreign language underwater, any guesses as to meaning would be futile but you might make out a feeling or sound here and there. Looking at Eric and Shandra, they were clearly intent on what was going on. *"Could they be catching all of this?"* she wondered, *"And if so, how?"*

As the Quazzga continued the debate, Eric sensed things were going nowhere and these aliens were not going to agree on anything. Finally, the mental conversation began to die off, as if everyone had spoken their minds and the debate was winding down. Ramsees had stood stone silent the entire time. Eric hadn't recognized his voice in the debate, so his pod members must have been carrying the cause.

One of the aliens nearby stood up. It was hard to say, but Eric guessed this was someone of importance, perhaps the leader, even Ramsees' boss of sorts. *"We are not of one mind on this, clearly. It is difficult to decide such matters when other issues of importance face our race. This effort of yours seems insignificant, yet we must deal with it since you have made an issue of it. Do you have anything to add?"* he questioned before reclining, a direct challenge to Ramsees.

There was a long pause before Ramsees responded, turning once towards the humans, then to the Quazzga assembled, and finally towards the leader. *"These humans are unique and worthy of saving. You have seen the data. Regardless of our race's needs, these people must* be preserved. They have offered to help us, contribute, coexist, but as equals, not as slaves. I must agree. This was not something we have ever encountered. It is a new but controllable variable in our mission. Let us give them a chance to prove themselves. Other actions can be taken later if needed."

Eric gasped aloud. Del looked at him quickly, sensing trouble, but not sure what it was because she couldn't hear the mental conversation. Shandra's eyes were wide as well so Del knew something was amiss. Unable and unwilling to interrupt the group meeting, she could only stand there in frustration as seconds passed and fear rose. So far from Earth and totally alone with these aliens, there was no hope for them if things turned south.

Eric unexpectedly broke the silence. "I can hear you, Ramsees."

Shandra added, "Me too."

The aliens stopped conversing immediately and Ramsees turned to look at the youngsters. *"You can hear me now? On this frequency?"*

Eric and Shandra both nodded silently.

"And now?" Ramsees asked patiently.

Again the kids nodded.

Then there was silence in the kids' heads. Eric suspected Ramsees was switching channels or something and now they couldn't hear him. What little they could glean from other Quazzga communications was shutting down fast. Only chittering, and a growing amount of it filled their ears.

"Jax, hold me. Something is up and we're either saved or in big trouble. I can feel it!" Del whispered.

"How 'bout you hold me? I'm as worried as you," he answered, cradling her body next to his.

Ben and Lady Henri silently shook their heads in confusion. Ben added, "Trouble's brewin."

"You know what I know," intoned Ramsees solemnly and abruptly aloud in the human heads as he spread his arms toward his fellow Quazzga *"Give me a moment to speak to them."* Adults and adolescents alike were hanging on every word.

"Well, you are full of...surprises, and are more interesting than even I had imagined. This is an amazing development... that helps I hope. Let us finish without interruptions. I will project my thoughts so all of you can hear. It had been meant to be a private conversation more for your protection and freedom from stray thoughts, but you will at least hear my part of the discussion. Some of you may hear even more," he said, turning meaningfully towards Eric and Shandra.

Eric gave Shandra the thumbs up. She replied with an unfamiliar gesture, but the meaning of support was clear.

Del whispered to Jax, "This might work out OK after all. Thank goodness for their talent," as she looked at the now confidently poised kids.

The ensuing discussion lasted only a couple minutes. Ramsees made his case again more forcefully. Eric and Shandra could catch only a bit of the overall conversation. While Ramsees was being open, not many of the Quazzga now were.

Finally, the nearby alien who had stood up before rose again and there was utter silence, both mental and to the human ear.

In a frequency every person could hear he started, *"This has been educational. What you ask, Ramsees, will be done with our support. The burden of responsibility, as it has been for years on this mission, rests again with you concerning these humans. Do with them as you will. We will not interfere as long as they do not affect our plans. Let us continue with other affairs."*

At that, Ramsees turned and ushered them out of the room. The entire meeting, while seeming to be an eternity, had probably lasted only 15 minutes. Watch worked only intermittently, basically not at all when around Quazzga equipment, but that was his best guess.

"We goin' home or what?" asked old Ben to Ramsees.

"Yes," was all Ramsees had to say, as they thankfully worked their way back towards the ship along empty corridors.

Mind Games

Several more Quazzga Del hadn't seen before met them at the ship. After meeting so many aliens, it was getting easy to spot the subtle differences in appearance.

"Some of my pod members are coming with us. We have lots of work to do on the way to Earth," explained Ramsees.

Eric groaned, "I thought we were gonna have some fun and I'm hungry."

"Some other time for fun, perhaps, and nourishment will be provided soon. We were fortunate to have accomplished all we did. You could call it a major victory, thanks to you two young ones. You have a phrase... Yes, I owe you one. Lets try to arrange for some ...fun ...later," responded Ramsees.

"You got it," interrupted Shandra, "We're going to hold you to it. Let's go home."

All the humans in one fashion or another echoed that sentiment. Del felt particularly grateful to be leaving Mars. This whole trip had been incredible, and stressful. Like someone who journeys to extremely remote areas or who travels a lot by air, she felt that there's no place like the good old Earth and home, even though they hadn't been gone that long.

As soon as they were seated and doors were sealed, the graceful ship started moving smoothly under Ramsees control. He explained where nourishment could be found along the couches. The food, if you could call it that, was like bland rice cakes, but brown in color. Ramsees assured them it would meet their requirements.

"Yeah, but what about our requirement for taste?" asked Shandra as she nibbled her cake. There was no answer.

Isees, seated near Eric started a mental conversation with him and Shandra. The adults could not pick it up except for the spoken replies of the kids.

This excited Eric, and he could tell Shandra enjoyed this attention and activity as well. Forgotten was the spectacular view of a shrinking Mars, and its tiny moons, and distant growing Earth and its large one. Forgotten were the adults around them. This alien kid was talking to him!

"*Can you hear me now? ..... Now? ..... Now? .... Now?*" Isees kept asking, explaining he could communicate across many frequencies and wondered which ones the humans could use. From their answers, it was quite a broad spectrum, including many of the ones used for normal Quazzga communication. Isees explained Ramsees had been exclusively using the most common mental frequency when speaking to humans, one that had been used over the thousands of years of preparation for colonization.

Isees kept firing questions, but the answers in English were hard for him to grasp. He kept asking them to slow down and simplify their words. He did not understand human speech very well yet, but was learning from our databases. He knew the basics of six human languages, but he found English one of the more difficult because it had so many rules to both remember and break at the same time.

"*It would be more efficient if we could just exchange thoughts,*" voiced Isees.

Shandra stated bluntly, "Maybe we can, if you'll teach us how."

"Yeah!" echoed Eric.

If Ramsees had eyebrows, one of them surely would have been raised as he turned to face the youngsters. "*We thought we knew a lot about human mental capacity, but you two have showed us differently. Isees, proceed if you can.*"

Del listened to the mental voice of Ramsees and spoken words of Eric and Shandra, but it was like trying to read a book when you only had every other page. Nonetheless, it appeared the kids were trying to learn how to project thoughts. It was something Del wasn't sure she wanted to learn, because it might mean opening her mind to the Quazzga thoughts in a two-way manner, something she wasn't ready to do yet or maybe ever. She liked the status quo.

Now, just partway into their journey home, these kids were braving new territory, again. The humans aboard ship and the entire human race by association, were being raised up a notch in Quazzga thinking.

While the kids were busy, Del wished she could have a private conversation with Jax, but it would surely have to wait. Just as she was about to reach over and seek comfort in his touch, his chair released him and his eyes bugged wide open. They had been held secure on the trip to Mars. This sudden release surprised him. The ship had a weak indoor gravity, about like being in water, so he didn't float away, but the feeling was not secure. Ramsees voiced, "*Please come lay near me. It's time you learned something that can help us.*"

Her seat also lost its grip, and at the same time she heard, *"You too, Adelle."*

With uneasy steps, like treading through water, they eased themselves over to Ramsees. There were two unoccupied couches near the main console and they welcomed the 'grip' of the couches as they settled in. "Some warning would be nice next time, Ramsees," she commented.

"Forgive me, I was having a little fun as you say. Quazzga are seldom known for being whimsical. You are teaching me about exceptions. Now pay attention."

Del realized both species could be full of surprises for each other. Perhaps they could coexist, even learn from each other. There was always hope, and more so with this latest turn of events.

"You should learn how to operate this craft and other of our ships. Your physiology and mental slowness might make it difficult to actually do, but there are other activities my people and I need to engage in that would make it helpful if you could handle some of the more mundane functions. S'teer and Rishnoo are specially trained and will assist in your learning," Ramsees explained.

Two of the Quazzga passengers eased over to Jax and Del. Ramsees words were both a compliment and an insult. It was difficult to be reminded these aliens were vastly superior in many ways. It made her mad enough she promised to do her best and surprise them back.

At Disney World, Del had been shown how to run the incubation equipment in mere seconds, 'though it was not a very complex job. Like at Disney World, the Quazzga who voiced her name as Rishnoo bent forward and touched Del's temple with her long, slick-feeling fingers. Immediately, a stream of information started pouring into her head. She was learning how this ship worked, the general principles of other ships, navigation, maintenance, star charts, gravity wells, speed controls, atmospheric maneuvers, landing, the whole nine yards. It was so much information coming so fast that, like a balloon filling with water, she felt pressure building, slowly but steadily. And then there was nothing.

When she awoke, it was like a five-alarm hangover, and she needed more sleep! An alien other than Rishnoo was near her, touching her head lightly in several places. Weakly she tried to wave the hands off. She didn't even have the energy to speak. All she could think through her mental fog was *"What .. the .. heck? What...happened? The training! What went wrong?"*

"You will be fine. Relax," Ramsees told her. *"That was more information than you could process. We are sorry. Just when we think we understand you, your minds surprise us. Let S'teer minister to you. She is adept at mental healing."*

Hardly able to fight losing consciousness again let alone argue, she acquiesced to the alien's soothing touch, and shortly thereafter slept.

When she woke again, Del felt better, much better, but not 100%. S'teer was still there, still rubbing her temples and touching her forehead. The five alarm hangover was now down to a one alarm, and she felt more rested. "How long have I been out?" she croaked dryly.

"You missed half the ride home, lady," quipped Jax from a nearby couch. "You OK?"

"Yeah. Other than feeling like my head has been a punching bag, I'm peachy."

"You gave us quite a start. I passed out too, but for just a little while and I'm fine now. You really took a turn for the worse. Guess cramming all that stuff in us was a bit much. Do you remember anything?"

Pausing and racking her overwrought brain for several seconds, she answered weakly, "Yeah, everything. Wow, what a rush."

"Ain't it though? Wish we could have learned this way sooner. Would've saved me a ton on tuition. I know I burned a few brain cells at the bars, but this would have been worth it."

Ramsees interjected, *"We have not burned any brain cells, 'though we did push the limits of your capacity to receive information. This is how we teach each other what we know. It is highly efficient. Other means, like learning through your human databases or by direct individual experience are inefficient and much slower. Still, Isees has taught much to other Quazzga about your languages. It is his...specialty. Mr. Leigh, are you ready to put into practice what you've learned?"*

Dumbfounded, he blurted, "Are you serious? Now?"

"I am quite serious. Will you do it?"

Rubbing clammy hands on his pants, he whooshed out a held breath and said, "Sure... I guess so."

"Then take my position and guide us in. Adelle, if you are able, watch and follow. I'm going to rest." Ramsees then stood and moved to another area. It didn't even appear he was going to watch!

Talk about being handed the wheels, this was far beyond anything he'd ever thought of attempting. Sure, everyone had played the flight simulator net games, but this, this was for real. The word nervous was a total understatement. *"Boy, if my maintenance friends could see this!"* he thought excitedly, then darkly, knowing that day would never come.

Sitting in front of the controls, he scanned them to get his bearings. Only a few things made sense and all of a sudden, he realized he didn't have the faintest clue what to do next. Panic set in.

"Close your eyes and remember. You can do this," encouraged Ramsees from somewhere behind him.

He did as Ramsees suggested, willing himself to calm down, trying to let the information rise to the surface. Like cramming for a test, it sometimes didn't help to try to rip the information from your brain. You actually had to let go and trust your brain to find the answer. In a rush, all the telepathically-fed information came to the forefront. He did know. He could do this.

Smiling over at Del, he winked with a confidence he now actually felt, "Piece of cake, my dear."

Rolling her eyes, she responded, "Well, let's do it, flyboy!"

His hands moved over the console, a blend of actions like playing a keyboard and the ship moved from automatic to manual and there were sudden shifts in their movements, appropriate maneuvers he felt, as they approached home. Lights and elaborate displays assured him they were on course and the ship was functioning well.

What a craft, he marveled. *"Gotta hand it to these Quazzga; this is one smooth piece of machinery."*

She watched his efforts, proudly amazed at his skill. Even more amazing, she knew what he was doing and followed his movements critically, gauging her own knowledge against his. She was glad he was the pilot.

"Jax, Del," she suddenly heard in her head and turned in surprise to Jax. He shrugged his shoulders quickly returned his attention to his piloting. The mental voice was faint, but sounded like it was from... Eric. *"Jax, Del, can you hear me?"*

Turning around, Del saw a wildly grinning Eric. "What do you think?" he said out loud. "Did you hear me clear enough?"

Del sputtered for several seconds, then exclaimed, "Eric, you are doing it!"

Jax was too nervous to take his attention away from the console during this critical entry maneuver, but added, "Yeah, we heard ya kid. Way to go! How the heck are ya doing that?"

"It's not hard, but it's hard to explain, and it hurts a little, kinda like studying too long."

"Assuming I don't crash this thing, you'll have to show me. Is this what you three have been doing back there?"

"Yup. Shandra is close too, I can feel it, uh hear it, I guess. Isees was a big help."

"I'm proud of you, Eric, and Shandra. That's amazing." Inwardly she wondered if this was a good development at all. Would this open Eric up to two-way transmission? Could his mind be probed for information they hadn't shared with Ramsees? Could this lead to exposing them, her? She wanted to urge caution, but didn't want to alarm anyone in public. She'd have to let it wait. The list of conversations for later was growing exponentially.

"What a marvel that these children could learn such a thing. Was it their special resistance to the alien voice control or something else entirely. Was it a characteristic of youth, like being able to learn a foreign language or anything else for that matter?" It was a mystery, an awesome mystery.

To her knowledge, no human had ever been able to project thoughts despite numerous charlatans and even million dollar rewards for those who could prove it. When she was much younger, she tried and tried to be a telepath in church and in school with her best friend, but nothing ever happened. Eric may have just scored another first for humans, what few of them were left.

She turned her attention back to Jax, who pulled his eyes off the console to stare at her briefly but deeply. Besides unconditional love, she read that he too might be wary of what Eric could now do. "Can I give you a hand, captain?" she offered.

"Sure. How 'bout you take the wheel?"

"Not a chance, pal, but it looks like I could assist you with deceleration and landing preps from this side while you handle navigation over there. I'm surprised how well you've done with only your two hands."

"Thanks, my lady," he drawled. "You're right about needing a little help. My fingers can't quite move like Ramsees' and these folks made the controls very precise yet complex. Plus, there are a number of shortcuts I can't access without psychic skills. Wonder if they can pass that power along? Anyway, glad you asked," he continued with a wink, followed by a quick pat on her leg which was cut short as he really had to concentrate on the console.

Time passed quickly as they worked in tandem mastering the controls and getting this technological wonder home. Earth loomed very large now in the view screen, North America's west coast ahead as they zoomed towards the California base and their friends.

Del enjoyed working with Jax. They were an excellent team, seeming to read each other thoughts as they coordinated their actions. Very few words were needed. Except for the near-death experience of learning how to fly, she really got a kick out of this. *"Wow, first man and women to pilot alien craft,"* she mused. *"Like the wonderful kids around them, they were breaking new ground as well. Guess that came with facing an alien invasion head on, and surprisingly on their own terms."*

Several times during the approach, Ramsees telepathed them encouragement. Like a good teacher, he was nearby in case he had to intervene, but didn't stand over their shoulders expecting disaster. Jax was like a kid in a candy store, grinning at how well the craft handled from space to the atmosphere. Del could sense he enjoyed the speed also.

"You know you're breaking the speed limit," she quipped.

He just grinned and nodded. "Feels good doesn't it?" For good measure he threw in a few sideways maneuvers, getting the hang of atmospheric flying.

"Show off," deadpanned Del.

Jax's kid-in-a-candy-store smile widened.

"Just set us down more gently than what Ramsees did on Mars. OK?" she requested.

"You've got it, captain!" he replied with a military flair.

Greg Burke

Cool down

Once landed, the humans were overjoyed to be back on Earth, hale and whole, and with a little more hope than when they had left, which had only been that same morning. It was good to stare at the clear late afternoon sky, and then see friends who came out of the nearby hanger and ops buildings to greet them.

Minutes later, Ramsees said he had other things to attend to and took off in the craft Jax had just landed, heading eastward. Jax and Del watched him go, wondering what he was up to now.

"How 'bout some real dinner and conversation," Jax offered as soon as everyone had been properly welcomed and well-wished. The questions had been flying fast and furious. It had probably been a stressful day for those left behind.

Once fed, they gathered in what used to be the officer's fitness center. This place had it all: heated pool, hot-tubs, saunas, racquetball courts, weight rooms, meeting rooms, movie theater, virtual reality game room, and a full bar, complete with dart boards, even a small bowling alley.

It was explained to Del that their Quazzga guards had pretty much told those left behind they could roam around and explore the base. So while she and the others were gone, they'd found this place. The pool was a little skuzzy from recent neglect, but the autochem, water supply, and heating equipment were still working so it should be warm and clear in no time. With nothing better to do, they had spent most of the day getting the place in order. On the sly, a few people were mixing drinks, hoping the Quazzga wouldn't take notice or action.

There was way too much to tell about their incredible journey, so Del simply summarized the important details, mainly that they had been given a reprieve and were under Ramsees' protection in return for helping the Quazzga and learning to coexist peacefully. There were a few vocal skeptics about alien intentions as expected. Everyone was enthralled upon hearing that Jax and Del could fly a spacecraft and that Eric and Shandra could transmit their thoughts. Plus, there was excitement just realizing that humans had been to Mars! Those were the best of the highlights.

As for the lowlights, no one appeared to see a downside, especially as the bar opened for business. Pretty soon, everyone was just glad to be safe and alive, and was enjoying the reunion and asking related questions of the travelers as the unofficial meeting ended. It was probably the lightest moment any of them had experienced since the invasion. Considering no one had brought their bathing suits, a few brave souls decided to swim with their clothes on or in their underwear. A few braver souls decided that was far too much clothing and in the buff was the way to go. One thing led to another and it was chicken fights in the shallow end, dunk contests, Marco Polo: you name it. A life guard, had there been one, would have been blowing his whistle constantly.

It was a time to let off pressure, and well-deserved. Jax and Del headed off to one of the saunas. Alone, they could have talked as they needed to, but it was other desires which took over first.

"Jax, you know I'm safe: no worries about kids just yet. Are you cool with that?"

"I figured, 'though we probably should have talked about it before. I'm with you either way. You are one fine lady, and I love you," he answered.

Her warm toes rubbed against his, both sated and comfortable in each other's embrace. "I love you too," was her answer, as she kissed him deeply.

The heady evening snowballed into an enjoyable party. Kids bored with the limited VR rooms, dart boards, and a few tired adults headed to their beds responsibly as the night dragged on. The remaining adults kept the celebration going in their own particular ways, 'though a few had fallen asleep already in lounge chairs by the pool or in smoking rooms.

After several rounds of the pool, hot tub, and sauna, Jax and Del finally had a poolside seat in barely covering towels they had found along with some wild concoction from the bar.

"Cheers," he offered, feeling totally refreshed, exhilarated, and smitten.

She nodded and they clinked glasses as she took her first sip. "Not bad. What is it?"

"It's called a "Lala Paluza" or something like that. It has milk, coconut, and a little of everything else. Be careful, these finished the night for many a spring break pal in Fort Lauderdale."

"Good advice. Wow, hasn't this been a wonderful evening? I haven't had this much fun in months, maybe years."

He smiled warmly, said nothing, but just gazed into her eyes and then leaned over to give her a hug. She rested her head on his shoulder, nuzzling him warmly.

"This may be as good as it gets." he answered. "Of course, once we're married it will be even better!" he quickly added.

Skeptically, she raised an eyebrow. "Yeah, how's that?"

"Well, you know. We'll make it good, right?"

"That's so lame, but I love you. Yes, we'll make the best of it. Do you think the worst is over for us?"

"I hope so, but I really don't know," he answered more solemnly. "It's been a helluva ride so far. Like you said before, this telepathy stuff worries me a little. I don't want these aliens reading us like books. On the other hand, it seems like we've started to take control of what little we can. That's got to work for us in the long run. And, the longer they keep us around, the longer we have a chance to make a life for ourselves. Still, I can't help but think we're like pets, and expendable pets at that."

"Oh, I thought I was the worry wart. That's pretty heavy thinking, mister," she replied lightly, but didn't refute what he said. They both understood their situation.

Quiet for several minutes, sipping their drinks and staring into the quieting evening, just enjoying each other's company, he broke the silence, "Sorry, didn't mean to sound so depressing. I love you too."

Their strong drinks finally gone, they decided to call it a night. Rising a bit unsteadily from their chairs, they noticed Ramsees standing by the door like a statue, black eyes piercing them, hands crossed at his midsection.

"How long have you been there?" asked Del.

"Only a short time. I did not want to disturb you as I have in the past, and I was not sure if you were engaging in some mating ritual again. What has happened here? And what is that odor?"

Gazing around the pool, things were a bit of a mess. Ramsees appeared unsettled or nervous if that was even possible. Usually he was a rock when it came to telling his emotional state.

"Just letting off a little steam. Taking a break. Having some fun. Nothing to worry about. We're fine," she slurred as they walked his way.

"Yeah, you missed a good time. You are smelling pool chemicals and what we call a party. Not the cleanest of air and a bit humid, but necessary. Do you ever have parties?" asked Jax, his normal drawl was even thicker with the alcohol he'd consumed.

"We do...recreate, but it takes a less chaotic, smelly, and noisy approach"

"Boring!" laughed Del.

"Never mind her; just a little tipsy is all. Been a long day," Jax explained, helping her along right up to Ramsees who remained close by the door.

"I see," he replied. *"I was hoping to..."*

Ramsees was cut short as the next few seconds appeared to last forever as time switched to slow motion. Del slipped on the wet floor. Jax lost his light grip on her arm. Del grabbed Ramsees' slightly outstretched hand. Ramsees lost his footing. Del hit the floor, arms flailing wildly, losing her towel in the process. Jax tried to catch them both and his towel flew off. Ramsees flipped like a rag doll head over heels into the pool: the deep end, of course.

Then normal time was returned in a flash.

"Holy shit!" screamed Del as she lept to her feet.

Ramsees let out a horrible wail from his slit of a mouth and his mental waves of fear hit them like a battering ram, a mental scream, that made it hard to concentrate on helping him. He flailed uncontrollably. Clearly he was going to drown, as his efforts only made him sink inevitably and splashed his mouth and eyes with water.

Jax acted quickly, instinctively. Being an excellent swimmer and former lifeguard, he knew entering the water would mean a drowning for him. Ramsees was far too panicked to get in the water and help him out. He'd have to find another way or wait for him to pass out so he could get him to safety. He quickly grabbed a safety pole which was hanging on the near wall and shoved it towards Ramsees.

The pole suddenly flew back towards him like a missile, nearly knocking him over and wrenching his arm out of its socket. Ramsees was fighting him psychically!

With renewed determination, he shouted, "Ramsees, grab the pole! We will pull you out! Listen! We are trying to help!"

Ramsees was only a couple feet from the wall, but his flailing wasn't getting him any closer to getting out of the pool and would sink him shortly. This time, when the pole was offered, one of the alien's arms lunged for it, firmly. Jax quickly pulled him to the edge and they both extended arms to help him out. He was as light as a feather; it was like pulling a 10-year-old out of the water.

The whole incident had probably lasted about 30 seconds, but it was the worst kind of excitement for all of them. Jax and Del had sobered instantly, all relaxation of the past few hours and any inebriation dashed in an instant. Losing Ramsees would be a disaster! Worse, it might not be looked upon as an accident. That would doom them all. They pulled his light frame away from the edge of the pool. He was gasping for air, dark eyes blinking out chlorinated water. Del grabbed her towel and tried to dry him off, feeling the sheer terror of near drowning running through his slick body.

"Ramsees. Steady. It's OK. You're safe now. Relax. Easy does it. OK? Relax. We're taking care of you," she soothed.

The mental screams died down and he started to catch his breath. He was still trembling. still breathing fast, still clearly panicked.

Other humans came out of the bar and rec rooms in response to the commotion. At the same time, about a half-dozen aliens rushed through the door Ramsees had been standing near a few minutes earlier.

Del froze, literally, hard, couldn't move a muscle. Jax stopped moving also. *"Why can't this happen when I've got clothes on?"* she wondered, having offered up her modesty to save Ramsees.

Several disk-like weapons were pointed their way. The aliens moved quickly to Ramsees' side, pushing the paralyzed humans roughly away. Del at least fell on her back, still in a kneeling position. Jax wasn't so lucky, falling on his head with a smack on the wet floor.

The aliens lifted Ramsees to a standing position. His body shook like a dog, and several towels were offered to quickly remove the water from his skin. After shuddering from cold or fear, Ramsees steadied visibly. He was gradually getting over his near-fatal experience.

Moments later the paralysis was gone as Ramsees chittered something to the other aliens. Del snatched a nearby towel for cover. Jax ran a hand over the growing bump on his head, wincing all the while. Del threw a towel at him. The aliens withdrew from the pool area, leaving Ramsees standing over them, now a little more composed from what could have been certain drowning.

"I am sorry... I panicked... Thank you for helping me," he voiced a little shakily.

"Look, I'm sorry for slipping. It was my fault. I'm so glad you're OK. Are you?" Del asked seriously.

"I'm... better. That... was a... terrifying.. event.. that I don't want to repeat. Quazzga don't use such bodies of water."

"You mean you can't swim, don't swim, or won't swim?" asked Jax.

"We could I suppose... but we don't...choose to use water for this purpose. It's too precious a resource."

"Don't you take showers?" inquired Del.

"Not...as you do. Again, water is precious...sparingly used."

"Whatever. Let's just not do this again. OK?" Jax said with grateful finality.

"Agreed," said Del.

"Agreed," 'pathed Ramsees.

With that, Del and Jax found their clothes, dressed quickly, and the trio left the rec building in a hurry. Ramsees couldn't get away from the building fast enough. It appeared he was looking forward to a much drier and less dangerous location.

Trailing behind Ramsees, not sure where they were going, Del whispered to Jax, "Guess we won't expect many Quazzga at our pool parties. Man, that was a close one!"

"Maybe I can help teach them to swim as one of our ways to help out?" suggested Jax sarcastically. "On second thought, table that motion."

Del nodded, but then added. "I don't think it's natural for them. Could you imagine how hard it would be to teach them? Even one at a time could be a nightmare. Still, it's not really so bad an idea."

Arm in arm, they followed an unsteady Ramsees who was clearly heading towards his ship. Brushing off the bad moments she commented sarcastically, "Jax, this has been a hoot tonight. Let's do it again sometime!"

"You bet. How 'bout tomorrow?" he responded. They chuckled all the way towards Ramsees' ship.

Greg Burke

What Now?

Under the clear, cool California night sky, the three approached Ramsees' craft, the same one they had piloted from Mars. It was certainly quieter and safer and they could talk without the risk of further accidents. Ramsees was still rattled, as his telepathic voice sounded shaky.

"I am glad to be away from that liquid danger. This is much more...comforting. Do you use water like that often?" asked Ramsees.

"Yes, some of us do. It's actually a lot of fun, Ramsees. Perhaps I could give you lessons?" quipped Jax, poking mild fun at the nervous alien.

"Perhaps some other time, well into the future," he answered. *"Now we need to continue securing your existence."*

Like a bucket of cold water or a slap in the face, reality hit them hard. Drying her hair with an extra towel, Del asked directly, "What do you have in mind?"

Settling into one of the couches and getting more relaxed by the second, Ramsees laid out his plans over the next hour. It was hours after that before they finished.

* * * * *

When they woke up the next morning, despite sleeping in, neither Del nor Jax felt very rested. They had spent most of the night discussing Ramsees' plans and trying to find the best way to make them work. Now they had to tell the others and meet some deadlines.

"No rest for the weary, my dear," prodded Jax, as he threw off his covers and headed towards the bathroom.

"All work and no play makes Jax a dull boy," she replied after the door closed. Del was worried, even more than usual. A lot was being laid on their shoulders. Ramsees had gone off on some other task, a "pod concern" he said, and wouldn't even be around to offer encouragement. Maybe she'd just have to trust people would follow their lead and get involved. It wouldn't be easy. Nothing ever really is.

So, after a late breakfast gathering, where the main topic revolved around Ramsees' near drowning, and the great party of the past night, there was an expectation of something more as conversations wound down. Del suggested they break and head for the nearby auditorium, making sure any stragglers not at breakfast were notified. "We have to talk," was all she said for the time being.

Half an hour later, everyone was present.

"Good morning!" Del shouted to break the small talk, speaking from the stage podium "We have some announcements... er, actually, Jax does."

He spit out the water he'd been sipping, almost choking as he bolted upright.

"Just kidding, dear," she smiled, enjoying watching his face turn even more red than usual.

The acoustics were great and it appeared everyone had comfortable seats. Del wondered how many meetings and what manner of meetings had occurred in this very room. She was glad to have such a fine facility this morning. Heck, her taxes probably helped pay for it. It was better than gathering around the hanger by the Quazzga vessels. There were no aliens in attendance. Maybe they were being given a longer leash.

Her joking with Jax lightened the group a lot so she continued, "The good news is that humans will have exclusive use of the pool. The bad news is the Quazzga have confiscated the booze, what little was left anyway." A few mixed cheers and hisses could be heard.

"Anyway, we need to determine exactly how we are going to co-exist with the Quazzga and get acting on that plan. There's a lot to be decided, but I suggest we just take things one step at a time and try not to get bogged down in details. Our government is gone as we know it and there's no denying who runs the show now. But, we are alive, intact, and actually have some sort of status that appears to have a future. You selected me as spokesperson, but I think we should have a longer range view of things now and discuss it as a group.

"So unless anyone has any great objections, I want to show you an outline of some possibilities Jax and I worked on after meeting with a certain wet alien last night." Again, some chuckles went up and it looked like she had everyone's attention. Even Eric and Shandra could be seen towards the back listening. She wondered what private conversations they could have now.

"Let me reiterate, none of this is carved in stone. It's just some ideas to start us off."

She went to the paper flip chart they had found earlier and flipped the page. "First, democracy seems to have served us well so let's start off with elections," as she pointed to the first page which read:

-Election of Officers
    -Determine what type
    -Nominate and vote

-Rules of Conduct

"Personally, I don't mind winging it and you all have been pretty easy to get along with, but it's unlikely that will continue if even the best of our human history shows itself. We need some sort of organization, though as small as we are we should be able to keep it simple. Are we agreed on that point?"

There were lots of nods, many yea's, and even some clapping. "OK, you're either an agreeable bunch or had an even better time than I had thought last night." Again, a few snickers and chuckles. Jax was smiling with approval at her from his front row seat, and his support and love made her feel confident.

"Good, I would guess we need at least a spokesperson to represent us to the Quazzga and an assistant. Beyond committee chairpersons, we probably don't need any other officers. Does this make sense?"

Again, lots of positive responses. One young woman Del did not recognize raised her hand and stood up. "How about you as our spokesperson! You've done good so far!"

"That's very kind of you," blushed Del. "But we should take nominations so we don't leave anyone out who wants to do this. I'd really rather not have the position. This has been hard enough. Are we agreed on the two positions?"

Everyone nodded or said, "Yes."

"OK, any nominations or volunteers for these positions?" asked Del.

There was silence for several seconds, then about a dozen hands went up, some tentatively.

Del called on the first person, a man she'd met the previous night, Paul McNair. "I liked the first suggestion. Why not you?"

"Really, I'd really rather..." she stammered as other hands went down and people started applauding. When that died down, she asked again "Anyone else? Please?"

Then Jax shouted, "All in favor say "aye"!"

"Aye!" was the loud response.

"All opposed?" he asked next.

When there was no answer, he put his arms out to Del. "Congratulations!" and he started an applause which was taken up by everyone assembled. Jax loved her dearly, and so did everyone else. Why they felt she should lead them wasn't clear, but among the people gathered, she just seemed to be the natural choice. He knew it would grate and embarrass her, but a quote came to mind: "Mine is not to question why, mine is just to do or die." It was a bit morbid, but the gist of the quote was accurate for his lovely fiancée.

Sighing loudly, she went on. "Thanks, I guess, for your confidence. I'll do my best to represent you, but I'll need your help and council in a lot of areas. I'll deal with you later, Mr. Leigh."

There were a few guffaws and Jax feigned innocence, his mouth open wide, pointing at his chest, smiling conspiratorially.

"We're behind you all the way!" someone shouted from the back, bringing on more laughter.

Narrowing her eyes, she looked directly at Jax who squirmed uncomfortably under her gaze. "As for an assistant, how about Jackson Leigh?"

His expression grew serious as a number of people said "Sure.", "Good idea.", "Yeah.", and "Makes sense.".

"What's good for the goose...," she figured, then saw Lady Henri raise her hand.

"Yes, are there other suggestions?" acknowledged Del.

"Mr. Leigh would make a fine assistant," she responded standing a little gingerly. "But I recommend someone who can already communicate readily with the Quazzga .... namely Eric over here. He's young, but he seems to have a good head. Young man, what do you think?"

Eric shifted nervously, then stood up. "Shandra can talk to them also and she's older, so maybe you should... 'Ow Shandra!' OK, never mind. I'll do it!"

Apparently Shandra had given him a mental barb, because she hadn't touched Eric that Del could see.

Jax, clearly glad to be off the hot seat, shouted again, "All in favor?"

"Aye!"

"All opposed?" he asked again.

Silence.

"OK, mister, anyone else you want to railroad," Del said softly. That brought chuckles. Jax just crossed his arms and smiled smugly.

"Well, any objections?" she asked?

Silence.

"OK, let's continue with rules of conduct. Jax and I felt we should have some guidelines to our group, but nothing so fancy as a constitution or thick book of rules. Any suggestions?"

An older man near the front spoke up, "How about the Golden Rule or the 10 Commandments? They're simple. No offense to other religions, but it's just an idea."

This made Del squirm mentally. She didn't want things to break into a religious discussion, 'though she was Catholic herself. But his point was valid. "That is a good idea though I was hoping for specific guidelines which would ensure we listen, get everyone's opinion, and operate as much like a true democracy as possible. Let's write his idea down."

Other hands went up and ideas flowed with general agreement on how they would simply conduct themselves. The brainstorming session was going well and in an hour they had a pretty good outline.

"This is great folks!" Del said admiringly. Was it being thrown together under such difficult circumstances or was this an unusually special group that could work together so well? "I'll have Jax polish this up into a coherent statement and then we'll vote on it at our next meeting: sound OK?"

There were lots of nods. "Let's move on then," she said, exposing the next page of the flip chart.

-Brainstorm Activities
    -Basic necessities
    -What we can offer Quazzga
    -Interactions with Quazzga

-Review Quazzga needs/timeline

-Assign Committees and Chairpersons

Three hours later, they had finished their work and adjourned to get going on what they'd established. She'd wanted as much detail as possible and contingencies in case some things didn't work out. It was the most energized she'd people, including herself. Del was impressed. This was going well. Best of all, no one had blinked at the Quazzga requirement they show immediate action in helping Quazzga in any way they can. It appeared everyone wanted to get on with their lives in some fashion. None acted like they wanted to run and hide, though secretly Del wished she could find a remote island with Jax, somewhere far from here without aliens or the responsibility of having to represent this wonderful group of friends.

This was the world now foisted upon her and she had to get used to it, but it was hard. All of her old friends and relatives were gone, or at least changed beyond recognition. She wondered what they would think now if they saw old Del being put in charge like this and actually helping their conquerors. She felt a little guilty, but just as one step begins a journey, she had taken the logical steps available as options were placed in front of her and now she was here. It had to be the best way. No other alternatives had popped up.

At least she had Jax, someone she could never have imagined meeting any other way, someone so special, like it was meant to be, her soon-to-be husband. *"Speaking of which,"* she realized, *"I owe him one for putting me up to this."*

Everyone had proved more resourceful than she had imagined. They brainstormed all kinds of ways they could co-exist and help. The list was extensive and included maintaining human/Quazzga equipment, agriculture, teaching Quazzga about humans, procurement, and a whole range of services which would make Quazzga life easier and hopefully, keep them useful to the aliens. In jest, someone even added swimming lessons.

The brainstorming went on for another day; and no aliens showed up to interrupt them. She couldn't wait to show Ramsees their ideas, which ended up conforming to his requests very neatly. In the meantime, she wanted to talk with Eric.

Jax was waiting for her outside the auditorium, finishing a conversation with several other chair people. Del had made sure he didn't get passed by for some responsibility, but he gladly accepted the maintenance chair. He really wanted to figure out Quazzga technology, as well as help them maintain the more useful human technology that would still be needed.

"Join me for lunch?" she asked.

"You bet, lovely lady," he responded with a beaming smile, taking her arm into his and escorting her to the mess hall.

The Quazzga had agreed to let them do a little cooking of their own, which pleased her taste buds immensely. That tasteless alien slop wouldn't help morale long term and the humans had some fine cooks among them. Until they could grow their own greens, the base stores of packaged goods (which appeared sufficient enough for many years to come) would have to do.

At the cafeteria, they found Eric, who was now inseparable from Shandra. "Penny for your thoughts," offered Del.

"Actually, I'd pay a fortune for what you two can do," added Jax.

The kids stared at each other for several seconds, then giggled.

"Jax, my ears are burning. Yours too?"

"Yes'm. They certainly are. How about you two showing some respect for your elders?"

"We're just having some fun Mr. Leigh," offered Shandra. "It's pretty cool having a conversation that no one else can hear. We'll have to show you how if you want to try."

"You think you could?" gasped Del.

"We do!" answered Eric confidently. "But not here. Later maybe where we can have some privacy and quiet. You'll see."

"That's fantastic! Count us in!" replied Jax.

"What kind of a conversation can you two carry on? I mean, is it simple messages or a whole range of feelings and ideas?" Del asked.

"It's hard to explain," they both answered at once, then giggled again.

Eric continued, "We're getting better all the time as we practice. At first it was simple stupid stuff, but now it's like talking inside your head and it's fast, real fast. Also, we can send feelings. It makes what we say in our heads to each other more easy to understand than when we say it out loud if that makes sense."

"Can you always hear each other's thoughts?" asked Del. This was the one big question for her, crucial, in fact, for her even attempting this type of communication.

"No thank goodness!" answered Shandra, "That would be creepy."

"Well, how do you keep it all separate?" countered Del.

"Like I said," Eric replied in an exasperated manner, clearly having difficulty slowing all this down for the adults. "It's hard to explain. Think of a...radio with different stations...or better yet, you know,...a cell phone. We can talk if we want, but we have to make the call. We can hang up anytime we want, but call anytime we want on a channel we leave open for messages. Also, when we're thinking, it's one-way thoughts, 'though we can both project at the same time if we want."

Del and Jax thought they understood, but neither could fully grasp the concept.

"He's right," added Shandra. "It's really neat and a lot of fun."

"So let me get this right. You can hide your thoughts if you want. Neither you nor the aliens have to know what you are really thinking. Right?" pressed Del.

"Mostly," answered Eric. "It's easier to tell if someone is fibbing, though, so you'd have to be careful. I can tell if Shandra is hiding something. We've played some games and, you know, girls always have some secrets."

"Does it give you a headache?" piped in Jax. He was very interested. This was an incredible breakthrough for all humans, those few like them anyway.

"Naw, but it does take effort. Kinda like taking those tests in school every year," replied Eric, then added, "It's a little uncomfortable, like someone pushing on your skull or just a funny feeling inside your head, but it's not bad really."

Remembering back to her few Quazzga training sessions, Del could well imagine the similarity. She winced a little thinking about the last session which had knocked her cold. It made her head hurt just thinking about it.

"It's like he says," said Shandra, "But it's getting to be less of a problem the more we practice. Still, it's simple, but not easy, if that makes any sense."

"Just like flying a space ship, eh, Del?" chided Jax.

"Yeah, piece of cake," she replied with eyes narrowed to mock him. "Let's find some time later and give it a try. You've made me feel a lot more comfortable about this whole mind speech thing. Maybe it's our ace in the hole."

By mid-afternoon Ramsees' ship touched down gracefully and soundlessly near the hanger. With the implants, none of the humans had any privacy, as they could be found anywhere, anytime. This bugged Del ("Excuse the pun," she would say when she and Jax discussed it), but it was a condition of their freedom that they were tagged, for their own good. At any rate, Ramsees found them quickly and summoned them to his ship.

"How did your meetings go?" he asked.

"Better than I expected and pretty much as you desired," she answered before she filled him in on the details.

"Excellent. I too have good news that will allow us autonomy and acceptance, although many from other pods are still skeptical. However, with other more important tasks at hand, we should be left alone. I thank you for your help in managing this group."

"It's nothing. We're glad to be of some help and we definitely want to stay as we are, unaltered. You know what I mean?"

"I concur and I understand. I've had some time to reflect on your...situation. Were things reversed, I would feel and act somewhat

like you, Adelle Summers, although with much less emotion. There are others who agree as well."

Del was stunned by this admission, and the look on Jax's face showed he couldn't believe it either. "My God," she thought, "Maybe there is hope for us after all!"

Reaching to Ramsees slight shoulder to give him a pat, she quipped "You're OK, Ramsees, you know that?"

Jax just smiled. "Hot damn. We've got a chance, thanks to you. We won't let you down."

Unfazed by her touch, actually seeming to welcome it, Ramsees answered, *"I'm proud of you. All of you."*

Heat

Hatred burns as hot as the desert, crisping the soul rather than skin. Don Drury knew hate, and love, and a hundred other emotions, but hate was what he felt as he watched the activity at McMillan airbase from his secure hiding place in the rolling grassy hills near the main building area. Getting here had been easy since the base was abandoned just after the invasion. He knew every inch of this base blindfolded anyway. He'd trained here and elsewhere for years on hundreds of secret missions.

Too bad all of the planes and ammo had been removed or disabled. He'd have liked some of that hardware. He could care less about the soldiers and civilians who'd been here. They left or were carted off west towards the city. He didn't get one recruit from the soldiers stationed here as he'd watched them leave like sheep, no one putting up a fight.

Rough, thick, and tanned fingers gripped the latest in binocular technology so hard with seething anger it was a surprise the lenses didn't break. He figured he'd seen it all in recent months, but this was the strangest yet. He'd found it, the hive, the source, or one of them at least. Several long days of reconnaissance had brought him to the unmistakable and, frankly unthinkable, conclusion. These humans were different, normal like him, and they were willingly helping the aliens.

"How could they? How dare they?" he repeated in his head, a guttural growl building in his throat. The answer could be many reasons, but his conclusion was that they were responsible for, or at least accomplices in, what had happened to humanity, his troops, good fighting men and women. He lowered his head to wipe sweat from his forehead, sweat born of hot midday sun and anger. He nearly let out a sob of frustration, but disciplined himself and let the soldier and warrior in him take hold.

Desert fatigues camouflaged his lean, conditioned presence, plus it wasn't been the aliens' modus operandi to still be hunting people down after all these weeks.

Raising his head again, he trained his eagle eyes on the buildings and hangers, memorizing every detail, cataloguing every possible strength and weakness, already formulating plans should it come to any direct action. He still couldn't believe his eyes. It didn't make sense. *"Why would anyone cooperate with these bastards? Were they really part of what happened?"* He'd have to get closer to find out. Nightfall would be his best chance. In the meantime, he patiently kept up his watch. There was gold here, he knew it. He just had to keep digging.

* * * * *

"My head hurts. I'm going to bed," Del announced as she jumped up off the floor.

"Aw, c'mon. This is just getting fun!" Jax pleaded. Shandra and Eric giggled at that.

"No way, I've had enough. We've been at this for hours and we're getting nowhere. Face it, I'm a psychic basket case."

Eric and Shandra had been patient with the adults, but it had proved more difficult to teach mind speech than they had anticipated. Isees had made it appear so easy to do. At 10:30, it was getting late. Jax and Del were eager, but their interest was definitely waning. At least they'd made a breakthrough with Jax, even if it was limited.

"OK, OK, you're right. It's gettin' late. Of course, jealousy makes me tired too," Jax drawled.

Del swiped at his shoulder, but he was already ducking for cover and guffawing at her efforts. "I'm not jealous, just tired and my head really does hurt!" she frowned, hoping for more sympathy than she needed.

It worked. Jax immediately became like putty, coming to her side to hug her. When the kids broke out laughing, she raised her head to see why and saw they were looking at Jax. His face was furrowed in concentration, staring into her eyes now. *"Can you hear me now?"*

Breaking his grip and stepping back she wagged her finger at him, "You...you .. stop it OK? I'm just not getting it. What so funny anyway?"

Eric and Shandra were rolling on the floor. Jax looked sheepish. "I've got no control directionally yet. Sorry. They were hearing me transmit, *"I love you."* over and over."

Grabbing his hand and returning his gaze with loving eyes she asked, "Can you read my thoughts now?"

"Uh, no. I mean yes, uh, you know what I mean," he stammered.

"Sure you do. Some mind reader. I'm getting ready for bed. See you soon."

With that, he dismissed the kids, thanking them profusely and agreeing to work with them more tomorrow. This was exciting. With great effort, he had learned to send and receive limited messages, mostly one-word thoughts. But it was working! What a rush, 'though his head hurt a little too. Clearly it was easier for Eric and Shandra, whatever the reason, than it was for him. Still, Del wasn't having any luck. Maybe she was trying too hard. The kids could only shrug their shoulders.

They had taken up residence along the row of one-story military houses near the main building and hangers. The former occupants sure didn't need them and it would be a shame to leave them empty. Plus, there were ample stores of food and regular household amenities, including clothes, toiletries, furniture, and privacy.

The house they picked was small and not very fancy, but certainly met their needs and all the utilities worked. Everyone else had just picked what was left and suited their needs. Shandra and Eric opted for one of the barracks with a couple other kids. Some adults who didn't feel a need for privacy agreed to chaperone the youths.

Jax headed down the short hallway from the living room where they had been conducting the training session to the bedroom, hoping to catch Del in the shower before she was done. To his surprise, the shower wasn't running and his search of the rooms showed her missing. "Del? Del! Where are you?" It was then he noted the sliding door to the porch was open and the drapes were fluttering slightly.

Wondering why she'd be outside instead of showering, he became concerned. Rushing through the drapes, he stormed outside. "Del?"

In a few steps, he saw her, standing alone, walking slowly in the back yard. "Del, what's up?" he asked.

"I just needed some fresh air. It's a beautiful night out, wouldn't you agree? I feel better already."

Smiling, his apprehension dissipated like air being let out of a balloon. He marched over and swept her up in the air. "Sure is, but not as beautiful as you. Sorry things weren't working for you in there. It might just take some time."

"Forget it. I'll try again in a couple days. It doesn't really matter anyway. It was just a lark. I'm happy for you though, and maybe a little jealous."

Smiling a little wickedly, he retorted, "There, I knew it! Just kidding. It's hard for me too. We'll probably find out that many of us can't do it at all. It's just one more tool for us. We should be thankful any of us can do it." He set her down carefully, then added shivering, "Wouldn't you rather come inside where it's warmer? I'll start the shower, OK?"

"Sure, give me a minute and I'll be right in to do your back."

Del stared at the wondrous starry sky for several minutes, reveling in the beauty of such a clear sky, at how small her universe had become, at the marvels she'd seen on her trip from Mars, at how insignificant her actions were, except for another human named Jax. She'd come so far since that night in Florida when everything had changed just about a month before. A new world. A new Del. Despair into hope.

The clapping of a hand over her mouth was so strong and abrupt her ears popped from the pressure. Her heart surged into overdrive, adrenaline flowing in microseconds where there hadn't been a need an instant earlier. She couldn't catch her breath and realized she'd be faint in no time.

"Don't move or scream or you'll be dead before the sound clears your throat!" whispered the voice from behind her left ear. There was no doubt he meant every biting word and could probably carry through on his those words without hesitation.

The arms which held her were hard like iron and had her wrapped as tight as a fly in a spider's cocoon. His hot breath stank and her mind was plunged instantly to the time at the Beach in Florida and that deadly experience. Fear and bile rising, she relaxed in his grip and nodded her head in acquiescence.

His arms relaxed yet his fingers held steady, shifting only slightly to allow her some air through her nostrils. "That's better. Good for you. We're going inside now. I have a few questions for you, traitor."

He lifted her bodily and they moved into the house in seconds, no one apparently disturbed by her brief abduction. Once inside, a chop to her neck knocked her out.

* * * * *

Like Del, Jax enjoyed his showers immensely, especially long hot ones, but he was lonely, and wondered what was taking her so long. Giving her some space which he sensed she needed and wanted, he waited. When the water turned cool, he figured something else must have grabbed her attention. Perhaps she had other plans for their evening. Drying in the steamy bathroom and wrapping his towel around his waist, he sauntered out to see what kind of mood she was in. Her limp body on the bed made him gasp with concern as he ran to her. The chop to his neck sent him to the floor in a heap.

* * * * *

Don stared at these pathetic humans, now trussed up like pigs so he could get answers without them endangering him, especially the big guy. He'd have loved some better supplies, like tranqs and a couple other choice drugs, maybe a few implements, but fear, force, and his vast experience in dealing with the enemy would have to suffice.

These were the two all right, the two he'd seen with the alien. He'd like to pop a few rounds into the lot of them, but he had to think bigger, keep his options open, and gather as much intelligence as he could. A few rounds could wait.

The first thing he'd done after subduing them was check the back of their necks. What he saw chilled and sickened him. Of course, as he suspected, they were chippies. He'd heard the stories, seen many himself, had to eliminate a few. Don just had to be sure.

It made him uncomfortable being with these alien lovers, even though the surgery confirmed they couldn't help themselves. It reminded him of his isolation and further reduced his pleasant memories of humanity. Still, something about the behavior of these two wasn't quite right, not consistent with what he'd witnessed of other chippies. They were different in some way. He'd find out soon enough, that's for damn sure.

Hearing a faint moan, he glanced at Del who was starting to wake up. Tapping her cheeks roughly, he leaned closer and said "Well, you're up first, lady. Let's see what's behind door number one."

Easing over to the bed, he place his razor-sharp SOG SEAL against her throat and pried her left eye open. "I'm going to remove your gag. You're going to answer some questions. Any commotion, and you and Red are dead meat. Got that?"

"I've got questions for you, mister!" her mind screamed through her headache, another killer one as her thoughts came into focus slowly. But his last statement finally registered and she silently nodded her head.

"Good girl," he added soothingly as he removed the gag, but not the knife. She wasn't going anywhere, but one never relaxed in any situation, especially when some civilians could be as dangerous as a trained commando. He watched her with patience, working her mouth as the gag was removed, moistening her lips and tongue so she could speak. What struck him most was the fire in her eyes rather than the blank look of a village idiot other chippies had. This might prove interesting after all, perhaps the mother load, but filled with danger all the same.

"What is it you're doing here with these creatures?" was his first question.

"You're going to think this is strange, but boy am I glad to see you," was her steady and quiet answer.

Don was taken aback, his knife pressed further into her throat, ready to rip into her lifeblood in less than a centimeter of movement. "That wasn't what I asked. What kinda game you think I'm playing here?"

"I'm sorry, really. No games. We're not who you think we are, but it will take some time to explain," she blurted out, not wanting this conversation to go south. Clearly this man would kill her and all her efforts not to be killed or modified by the aliens would be all for naught, ending at the hands of another human, perhaps a fitting twisted joke to what her life had become. She didn't want it to end this way, though.

A sliver of doubt crept into Don's mind. "C'mon now. What's going on here really? You've got two minutes."

Del rattled off as much as she could in the time allowed her. She wanted more time, and his demeanor indicated he would give it to her.

Minutes before, he'd wanted to beat these two senseless and worse, take out some of his rage and frustration on a pair who he wanted to blame for most of his misfortune, or humanity's at least. When she stopped talking, he rubbed his heavily stubbled chin, mulling over her response, dozens of questions and thoughts swimming around his brain.

"But why help the enemy at all?" he asked, finally removing the knife from her neck. A good question, one that had been asked during countless wars, hostage situations, and conflicts. He needed to know their level of sympathy or empathy, weakness or strength.

"We had to make the best choice for survival, putting that ahead of everything else, buying us time," she answered. "They'd have made us real chippies in an instant, despite how much this Ramsees likes us. I gather that most of the aliens wouldn't have wasted a second on us if it weren't for him. We still don't know what the future holds, but at least we're surviving and learning a few tricks and information from them along the way that might help us. Or you."

A groan from the floor indicated Jax was waking up. Don prepared to clock him again, not wanting the interruption to what he felt was a crucial moment in the conversation.

Del interrupted his movement, "No! Wait, please! He's OK too!"

Jax's eyes came into focus, taking in the situation, his memories finally catching up to current events. Shifting from Del to the soldier, he tried in vain to figure out the situation, but seeing Del essentially unharmed, he relaxed a bit and tried to gather his wits.

Don's hand stayed, satisfied Jax wouldn't be trouble. "She just saved your keister pal. Just stay quiet and let us talk." Looking at Del he continued, "Tell me more of what has happened. Tell me all you can."

Surmising this man wanted strategic information that could help his cause, she told him about events in Florida with breeding, her dealings with the aliens young and old, their trip to Mars, learning how to run alien equipment, and their disk weapons. Like a military briefing, he took it all in, repeating details that showed his memory was a sharp as the knife that had been ready to kill her.

This was an amazing turn of events for Don. Not at all what he had expected tonight. This group had done well with the enemy and learned a lot that might prove useful. Mind speech too. Go figure.

He had a few more questions about numbers of ships, aliens, guards, base defenses, and so on, but most of that stuff Del had never really considered. Don had gleaned much of that info from his reconnaissance of previous days, but he'd hoped for confirmation. No matter.

Standing up, he spun his knife in the air and deftly caught the hilt, cut her bonds, then shoved it smoothly into its sheath on his thigh.

"What're your names?" he asked brusquely.

"Uh... Adelle Summers and Jackson Leigh."

"I'll let you untie him after I'm gone, just out of caution. No hard feelings, mister. I'm sure we'll meet again." Don saw the blazing fury in Jax's eyes, unable to protect someone he cared about. He knew the feeling well.

Del blurted, "But when will you be back? Shouldn't we set something up, plan some joint action? What are you going to do now?"

Steely eyes regarded them both, then stared ahead into the walls. "Now... I'm going to talk to my troops, such as they are, and see what they think about this development. We might be able to help you...join you. We'll see."

Fearing an armed conflict that might jeopardize all they had worked for, Del admonished him, "Don't do anything rash like shooting the place up. Let us know what you decide. You'd probably all be welcome here and could help us out."

Walking briskly out into the night, she heard his fading answer, "Sure. Be in touch. Carry on."

She quickly bent down to Jax and untied him, giving him a strong hug for reassurance which he returned eagerly.

"Are we jinxed or something? Is there a higher power at work here? All I wanted was a warm shower and some company. Is that too much to ask without having something crazy happen?" Jax asked with exasperation.

"Maybe we're charmed instead. Can you believe it, Jax? More people like us, up in the mountains nearby. And the aliens don't know about them!"

"Jeez, Del, what are you thinking? That guy is some kind of nutcase! Who needs someone like that messing things up? We're barely in control as it is!" He was clearly upset and Del wasn't sure if it was just because of being tied up or some other macho reason. They might not be thinking along the same lines in this case.

Reaching out to hold him still, she answered softly, "Relax. Just thinking. Of course he's a nutcase. Who wouldn't be in this whole crazy situation of ours? I just hope he doesn't do anything stupid. But at least we're not just this one tiny isolated group here. Who knows? There are probably groups all over the planet. Let's just not blow him off entirely, OK?"

For moments, he regarded her darkly, probing, trying to discern her thoughts, rubbing the back of his sore neck. He held her close and she could feel him relax. "He spooked me, Del. Seriously, I was worried for you."

"That makes two of us," she shuddered now that the danger was past, "It was just like that situation in Florida I told you about. I didn't know how this would end either." Patting his back for assurance and returning his squeeze, she added, "I still need a shower. Want to join me?"

"Yeah, sure, but let's go together this time. I never know what kinda trouble you'll get into when you're out of my sight."

She swung at him playfully but he ducked deftly out of reach and ran for the bathroom, throwing his towel at her for interference, Del on his heels.

Pause

The weeks that followed were thankfully uneventful compared to experiences of the previous month. There was actually a routine people started to follow. Jax and Del explored the idea of setting a marriage date, but both agreed the time was not quite right. Still, their love blossomed as the days grew longer.

There was lots of activity to keep them busy. In a mere two weeks they had accomplished or made good headway into many of the goals they had set as a group. Everyone had a job which would benefit the Quazzga in some way and everyone had tasks, even the kids, that would ensure routine needs were handled such as trash collection, cooking, maintenance of housing. Many people had mastered the basics of maintenance and even operation of Quazzga equipment and ships. The Quazzga handled the power and water needs. A few avid gardeners had volunteered to start growing vegetables (no one was completely ready to convert to the alien gruel); and greenhouses that had previously nursed decorative plants were converted to vegetable gardens.

About a third of the group had experienced mind speech to some extent, a couple as well as Eric and Shandra. Del's brain was still a lock. She could receive any messages, but just couldn't send anything, no matter how much she tried or how much people tried to help her. She was a little depressed about this and Jax wisely didn't press the issue, but no one appeared to care one way or the other whether people could send thoughts or not.

What few refreshments they had besides water, coffee, tea, and dried milk had been quickly consumed. Requests to go off base to retrieve liquor and soda replacements had been denied so everyone was on the wagon. The few smokers among them had quit cold turkey and were doing fine.

The aliens left them alone, 'though Ramsees appeared to enjoy observing them, privately amazed at their individuality in recreation and work. Cookouts and volleyball games intrigued him the most. He didn't understand the human need to enjoy work and to play after work as a means to relax. It was as foreign to him as his deep meditation and communal mind melds were to the humans. Still, it was a cozy relationship they had settled into. The humans could keep the pool and use water as they needed to grow things, and in return they helped the aliens to the best of their ability.

Sitting in the back yard watching Del cook, Jax scanned the horizon occasionally, wondering if they were being watched by Drury or one of his gang and what they would make of developments in the past few weeks. He never paid them another visit. Maybe he'd decided to leave them alone and go elsewhere. Jax doubted it.

"See anything or anyone?", asked Del, turning steaks that sizzled on cue, the delicious aroma wafting invitingly towards Jax.

He inhaled with gusto, then turned towards her. "Makes ya wonder doesn't it? The more we don't hear from him, the more worried I get," he reflected.

"I'm with you. But my guess is he'll meet us on his terms, if he ever does come back. It would be great if he just left us alone." Unspoken to Jax, it comforted her that there were other humans like themselves nearby. Perhaps an ace in the hole if things went wrong here. But like making a pact with the Devil, it could also ruin their plans. So, unable to resolve her feelings on the matter, she refrained from discussing what might only agitate Jax who clearly didn't like the man. Perhaps it was a guy thing, macho stuff.

Other neighbors were cooking also, people pairing off or remaining separate as they chose fit. It was a warm evening with a slight breeze. Days were lengthening quickly now as they moved into spring. It was relaxing, just the sort of thing to make Del question the day and wonder what might happen next to throw a wrench into their relatively smooth running lives.

The "commune" as some dubbed their 200 plus group had numerous meetings and they were productive, serving to make sure they stayed on track. Del still hated running things, but it hadn't proved overly taxing and people for the most part contributed positively, chipping in as needed. Ramsees showed up occasionally, even set an appointment one time. Things were changing if even Ramsees was treating them more like equals.

Del sensed, though that they weren't getting the whole story and that maybe something was wrong. "What do you sense?" she asked Jax directly as they cut up their medium rare steaks and sipped sun tea.

"There's something, but I can't make it out, mentally or from his behavior. Maybe running interference for us and managing his planet-wide activities is wearing him down?"

"Could be. My female intuition senses it's something else, like a weight, burden, or distraction. I just don't know. I'll ask him next time he's here. I'd sure hate to see him get depressed or go crazy. You think that happens to them? You think they get stressed out, get homesick, get Earth fever?" she queried.

"Jeez, you look at all angles that's for sure. How do you sleep nights? Who knows anything about these guys? Guess if they went bonkers and left the planet to us, worse things could happen. Best ask Ramsees directly. He's been straight with us for the most part. I wonder about you sometimes; you going to be an alien shrink now?"

Surprised by his mini-tirade, she shot back, more sharply than she wanted, "We know more about them than anyone! And yes, I do look at all angles, because I want to stay sharp and not miss anything that can help us!"

More softly she added, "We may be cooperating with these aliens, but it's to save our bacon. That's the only reason, at least for me. And I do sleep well nights, thank you very much, because we are making a difference. And I love you even when you question me."

"All right, already, you made yer point. I like these little discussions of ours; they keep me on my toes," he grinned.

Not sure if he was complimenting her or teasing her, she only added. "I'll ask Ramsees. I have to know, for our sakes."

Later, they sat quietly together on the lawn chairs, watching the stars come out as the last of daylight faded in an orange/yellow glow. They just enjoyed being together, lost in their own thoughts, savoring their company and the peace of the evening. Birds were making their final sweep of the night for bugs before roosting. The few mosquitoes around were tolerable. The air smelled clean. It would be a great night for stargazing, a chance to look skyward and ponder nothing and everything.

Greg Burke

Child's Play

Ten houses away, Eric and Shandra were into their mind games, and having oodles of fun. Like two kids who had just received wrist communicators for Christmas, they were testing the limits of their sending and receiving skills. It appeared there weren't any significant barriers so far.

It was one thing to be able to talk without words when they were together in the same room or outside looking at each other, but when Shandra called Eric outside to see something when he was inside, his eyes popped wide and he smiled with excitement. Running outside, he saw a mirror image look on her face.

"*We gotta see how far we can communicate,*" he telepathed. "*Why hadn't we done this sooner?*"

So for the next several hours they moved in opposite directions, telepathing each other their positions. In second floor buildings, in basements, under cars, across the football fields, on either side of Quazzga ships, it mattered only slightly. Even after what they guessed was several miles of distance between them, they could still communicate clearly. There was only a slight fading of signal if things got in the way. They tried several frequencies or levels of communications, and still distance didn't matter and obstacles just a little. Either they were getting very good at mental speech, or it was simply a far superior form of communication than they had realized.

After hours of wandering all over the base, they returned home tired but happy. Lady Henri shook her head as they were such a mess, but she was glad to see them enjoying themselves so thoroughly.

The young alien Isees barged into the house not long after they arrived. "*I heard both of you calling and playing nearby. Is anything wrong?*"

"No," said Shandra, "*I mean, 'No.'*" she telepathed, switching away from verbal talk, knowing Isees' preference. "*We were seeing how far we could communicate and in how many ways. Is that OK?*"

"Yes," replied Isees, "*But I was not sure if you were in distress as I could not hear all the details of your messages. When my people are young, they sometimes put out messages like you did, indicating distress. Rather than ask you telepathically, I wanted to make sure in person.*"

Isees had visited them many times, uninvited and unannounced, but he always came as a friend to teach them some new jobs or skills. He never stayed long nor did the youngsters ever seek him out. Eric suggested Isees was just checking on them like pets, but Isees answered it was more than that. He liked being with them, as they reminded him of when he was young. Plus, they were eager to learn and much easier to communicate with than other humans.

Satisfied Eric and Shandra were in no danger physically and mentally, he admonished them to protect their thoughts or at least not scatter them so wildly. He added that their range was probably tens of miles on the ground, more in space.

Isees cautioned them that other Quazzga might interpret their thoughts as a threat and that wide-open communications might bring them unwanted attention from others outside the base. He recommended they use mind speech only when they were close together as that would keep their mental projections more tightly focused. The more distance between them, the less focused their projections would be. After that, he left. Eric shrugged. Shandra just telepathed, *"Whatever."*

So as the night came over them, the two tried something new and exciting, eavesdropping on alien and human conversations. They had no idea whether or not this might be dangerous. Like listening to parents' late night conversations from another room, it was just something neat to try. Of course, they had some idea how to start. Using themselves as guinea pigs, they had practiced trying to probe each other minds while attempting to keep their own thoughts to themselves.

Neither could read each other's minds. That hadn't worked at all. They were actually very grateful for reasons neither of them had to explain. But if Eric projected a specific thought at Lady Henri, who was telepathically deaf to all but the main frequency Ramsees used, then Shandra could often pick it up. Like switching radio channels, you just had to search for the right frequency and you'd pick up the thought.

Eric called it hide and seek. Shandra called it a shell game or find the pea. The rules were simple. One of them would telepath some idea or phrase and the other would have to find it. When the words were found, you would telepath the idea or phrase and voice, *"tag!"*, or *"found you!"* Then the other would start a new thought to be found.

Each of them, in the silence of their own rooms, had occasionally caught snippets of mental projections from humans and even some aliens, but nothing was ever sought out or tried to be actively collected. Tonight, they tried to focus on finding thoughts from anyone they could.

The agreed upon game plan was for each to seek out thoughts in a very slow and meticulous manner and if anything was found, they'd contact each other and try to draw the other's mind to the active frequency. At least that was the plan. After half an hour of open-minded searching, nothing happened. Neither perceived a glimmer of thought. Their brows were furrowed as they laid on their backs in Shandra's room.

"This isn't working," Eric said aloud in frustration. "I'm getting a headache."

"Yeah, me too. We must be doing something wrong or it isn't possible. Let's go to bed and try tomorrow."

The next day, Shandra was frustrated. She knew they might not be able to pick up random conversations, but that didn't make complete sense. After all, they'd picked up the alien conversations on Mars pretty well before they were shut out. Then it dawned on her. Maybe they should focus the location better, try to hone in on a place and listen there specifically.

Looking at the largest spacecraft in the hanger from their vantage point at the officer's club, she focused on the interior of the ship, starting at the front and working towards the back slowly, patiently.

"Voila!" she shouted to Eric both mentally and verbally.

She was picking up thoughts, albeit jumbled and singular, so they didn't make any sense. Eric telepathed forcefully, *"What is it? Tell me! C'mon, let me know what's going on!"*

"Quiet!" she answered, *"As soon as I have something I'll let you know, but give me a minute, OK?"*

Taking his silence as a yes, she got back to fine-tuning her mental eavesdropping. She focused again on the location where she'd first heard thoughts. Nothing. In frustration, she wondered, *"They couldn't have shut me out that fast could they?"* Then she wondered if the source had simply moved. A moving target would prove difficult. *"Eric, I lost it, but give me a little time to find it again. They may be walking. I'll try to find something more stable."*

After another few minutes, she found thoughts again, but they were from someone else. The speed of the thoughts were fast, so fast it was hard to make anything out, but concentrating, she could get the gist of what was being communicated. It was boring and technical; hardly good gossip.

Switching back to Eric's frequency, she apprised him of her findings and guided him to the source. Together they listened for 10 minutes.

Nothing was mentioned about humans, just technical jargon, a few aliens doing their jobs.

Anyone walking by would have wondered what these two kids were studying in silence, but they pretty much had the area to themselves with the adults off performing their various duties. Heaven only knew if the Quazzga took breaks or naps, but it was a quiet mid-afternoon for the entire base. Perfect for continuing their experiments.

Eric agreed, *"This is boring. Let's try somewhere else."* They turned toward another ship and began a methodical mental scan.

In a few short minutes, they both were picking up thoughts, much more interesting ones. These aliens were talking about the humans. Shandra heard, *"... news has been very good...resistance a thing of the past...lots of work still before others arrive...these here are special...somewhat useful...interesting...unpredictable...possibly a danger...meeting soon to decide next steps...Ramsees believes in them...not alone...not unanimous...uncertainty of purpose...Ramsees actions will affect us...caution advised...must do what is best...many decisions to be made...could affect us...and the humans...both of us for the better...or worse..."*

Then, the thoughts trailed away like reception on a radio getting bad. "Aw Jeez, this is harder than I thought." complained Eric.

Shandra looked at Eric and put her forehead to his forehead. "It might just take practice," she said aloud, "You gotta be more patient. That was some pretty neat stuff we heard. Not sure what it all means, but we should talk to Del and some of the others; let them know about this."

"Can't we just listen some more, find them again?" Eric pleaded.

"I'm still not sure we should be doing this in the first place. But anyway, I'm a little tired and thirsty. Let's do it later, OK?"

"Sure, guess the fun is over," he replied with disappointment.

It was more over than either of them realized.

Greg Burke

Second Coming

Near Mars, an armada of Quazzga colonists folded out of space in huge ships that dwarfed the largest of the vessels that had already arrived. They were predominantly cylindrical in shape, black as space itself and nearly invisible except for the stars and planets they eclipsed. Each carried several hundred thousand colonists: some 20 million in all.

In human terms, these were essentially ferries. Faster traveling than any ships that had been built before, easy to outfit, just transports for Quazzga and their belongings. It was another success in their proud history. In self imposed stasis, Quazzga could meditate for years. It was one way they had reduced stresses on their own ecology and psyche and it came in handy as a practice on this 20 year journey. A few biomechanical techniques made the stasis even deeper, so a trip three times this could easily be tolerated.

They paused in orbit around Mars for an update of the situation on Earth. Those Quazzga not currently in stasis were briefed in their particular areas of expertise, and leaders were told how colonization was proceeding. The news was exceptionally good, for the most part. Leaders were chosen, however, on their ability to see difficulties where there were few and address them before they became many. There were still minor problems to resolve before Earth would be ready for all the colonists, especially some of those to come who wouldn't tolerate disarray.

Thus it was agreed to hold in Mars orbit a few Earth days to make the necessary special preparations. After all, this group of colonists had unique skills, particularly in the advancement of colonization, either aggressively or passively.

They were anxious to finish their journey and establish themselves in the new world, but a day or two of waiting was nothing. The "human situation" as it was called, had proven more complicated than expected. Scouts were notoriously optimistic in their reports and disliked owning up to any problems. Still, it was nothing that couldn't be handled, 'though it was surprising there remained any resistance at all.

Genree, in command of the armada, was one of those leaders who was ready to finish this colonization on Quazzga terms. She was not satisfied with copious positive reports, preferring to dwell instead on the few negative details. Those qualities had served her well in her mature 680 Earth years of existence and were not qualities she would cast away this late in her life.

These humans, these mere creatures, had been given far too much attention, especially this most recent freak show which while interesting, proved nothing and was a distraction to the very grave and serious purpose of her civilization in this solar system.

It was incredible that the leadership here had given Ramsees permission to harbor and nurture these aberrations. Such a sanction galled her, rubbing raw against her mission objectives. She wondered if Ramsees hadn't suffered overexposure to the humans.

Quickly scanning all the data while communicating with hundreds of her brethren, she decided that this charade had to end. Any humans not fully cooperating and subservient to the Quazzga needed to be converted or eliminated. Now. Too much was at stake to have any distractions take place. Now was not the time to have a handful of humans cause trouble lest it spread to other areas. Taken singly, this appeared to be no threat. Genree believed otherwise. Past Quazzga epidemics had started as isolated instances of disease. This was no different.

What bothered her the most was how badly flawed their research had been with regards to the humans. Given time, and not much, they would have destroyed their own planet. *"How could the scouts have been so wrong?"*, she wondered. *"Why wasn't more known about the humans? Their resilience and resistance is striking. This latest display of mental abilities by the young humans was even more disconcerting. How much don't they know about the humans? How much could these creatures develop? Could even those under Quazzga control cause trouble?"*

There were too many unknowns and not enough time to sort them out and find the best solution. Hard action was needed so they could move on. More Quazzga were coming, and it was up to Genree to smooth the way and make this planet ready. Her course of action was decided for her by virtue of her responsibility to those here, those who would be coming.

Gathering her thoughts, she made some tight communications to her fellow leaders, who, for the most part, agreed with her plan. Several other quick communications filled in appropriate pod members and started her plan into action. This would require a personal approach for best results. She was superior to the leadership here and would do as she saw fit for the benefit of all Quazzga.

She moved from her command quarters to the launch bay and the shuttle that would take her to Mars. From there, appropriate ships would take her and a modest force to Earth, and Ramsees. She would allow her fellow colonists to remain in stasis while these details were cleaned up. A few days more wouldn't matter and a few days would be all she'd need.

* * * * *

Ramsees had not gotten to his age and place in Quazzga civilization by appointment. He had earned his place of strength through mental prowess, discipline, hard work, and a willingness to take risks. Moreover, he had a sense that allowed him to recognize danger and opportunity. That sense was sending him alarms even before he received confirmation that the second group of colonists had arrived at Mars. It had been causing him some trepidation in the past few weeks knowing a day of reckoning was coming eventually.

He understood Quazzga politics and thinking very well, another trait which had served him in the past. He knew that the details of what he had accomplished here would not go unnoticed. He knew despite his success, some would view his actions as dangerous, reckless, and possibly even an affront to Quazzga society. He knew as well that preventive actions and cautious diplomacy would be needed.

This next wave of colonists, and their leaders, would not fully understand the hard work that had gone into getting things to this point. They would not fully realize the magnitude of the tasks completed or the work yet to be done. As such, they would not appreciate this small enclave of unique humans and what they might represent to the Quazzga if allowed to live independently.

He closed all communications, silenced himself to his pod and everyone else around him. His pod and closest associates would understand the silence; it was something he rarely did, but something he found necessary at times for clarity. Just as extended fasting or sensory deprivation tanks brought visions to humans, closing off his psychic sense often gave him a fresh perspective. It would keep the swirling maelstrom of events at bay for precious seconds, even minutes, perhaps as much as an hour. Ebony eyes lidded shut and folded arms wrapped him in warmth. In seconds his self-induced trance was complete.

Three hours later he awoke from his most intense vision ever. There was trouble for sure from several fronts and only thin threads of a solution. He saw conflict and death for humans and Quazzga alike for reasons which were not clear. He even felt a death-like stab of pain at the end of his vision that snapped him out of his trance in nightmarish fashion. The vision was so real, he had to check himself and his surroundings to be sure he was OK. His body functions calming down, he realized he was well. Still dampening communications, he took the time to evaluate what he had seen to draw a clearer conclusion from his vision.

Like seeing an entire movie in seconds, he had to slow events down, piece together the fragments of his vision, and finally decide what to do about what he had seen. Several things were clear. He was in personal danger. His band of special humans were in danger. They were going to be attacked by humans and Quazzga. There would be casualties and death. It would happen soon. He did not know how or even *if* they could survive.

He stiffened, realizing time was against him. He would have to act quickly he felt, without much of a plan. His little paradise and the respite they had been granted was over. Seconds later, the effects of his trance fully shaken, he strode briskly from his ship to talk to the humans. A worried Isees sprang noiselessly to his side from an adjoining corridor and they both strode towards the exit.

* * * * *

Commander Drury had used his time wisely, as usual. His military training demanded perfection. Maximum results had to be achieved with the least amount of resources. Sleep was not necessary; only discipline of mind and body were needed to achieve his objective.

The few weeks afforded him had allowed him to pass on what he had learned from the woman he'd interrogated briefly at the base to every enclave he knew, allowing him to marshal resources. The liberation was close at hand and he was eager to begin. There was hope for the future of humans if what he planned succeeded. It had been a while since he had tasted victory. It had been a while for his troops as well- too long. He saw heartened looks as he scanned his personal army which had now swelled to 72 followers.

In just a few short weeks the knowledge that other humans were surviving and thriving independently had given everyone a renewed sense of purpose, and somehow fellow survivalists, soldiers, and other solitary figures had come out of hiding to join his cause. He had nagging doubts about the true loyalties of the humans he had met on the base, but the one called Del had a rebel attitude that struck him as true. Still, people had tried to deceive him before, and he always kept a couple backup plans in case.

He was proud of his army, and ready. He'd never been more muscled, more disciplined, more alert in his life. This was it. His soldiers might not all be up to the task, but he'd seen what these men had survived and he was satisfied they would give it their all. The alien scum wouldn't know what hit them.

A weapons inventory amazed even him. Biologics, sarin gas, anti-aircraft missiles, flame-throwers, even so-called micro-nukes headed the list. There was nothing nuclear about those last, but for a grenade-sized device, they packed the punch of a whole truckload of fertilizer. Added to that were stockpiles of conventional weapons that would make any terrorist smile. The nearing conflict heightened his senses to a level he could barely contain. These aliens had messed with the wrong damn country, and the wrong damn man. It was payback time.

Even their simple plan amazed him. Surprise the enemy, overwhelm their defenses, capture technology, destroy anything or anyone that resisted, liberate the civilians, and escape repercussions. The elements might be complex and the execution was fraught with possible failure, but observance of the enemy had shown each element could be accomplished with even half this army conventionally, even less so with the armament they would employ.

Don was pleased, but the possibility of overwhelming success always gave him pause. It was too easy. There must be something he was missing. The unexpected must be anticipated. Thus they all discussed their options and dissected each element, leaving nothing to chance, including weather, the humans they must deal with, and what the aliens might throw at them with their obvious advantage in technology. Still, it appeared like too easy a mission. So, they practiced and exercised, working out every scenario possible. Amazingly, the upper hand was still theirs, and now they were as ready as they were going to be.

There was a slight concern for human casualties, both his soldiers and the civilians on the base. Nothing could be guaranteed in any operation. He would have preferred to inform the base residents of their pending action, but he couldn't risk losing the element of surprise in case someone squealed. Then they'd have the whole alien fleet down on them and it would be a suicide mission.

No, he pondered for the last time, the civilians would be liberated, but not warned. At the time of attack, they'd have to decide where their loyalties lay. Those against him would suffer the alien fate. Those with him would be protected and maybe even allowed to help free the rest.

Every soldier had been briefed. They all knew what they were up against. Each knew this might be his last battle. Even victory might be short-lived if they couldn't successfully hold up against retaliation. But they couldn't continue to hide out passively in the hills forever, risking capture one by one. This was their best chance for freedom, and, for Commander Drury, honor.

Night was deepening. It was time to ready the attack.

* * * * *

Del loved the stars out west. They were so clear, so bright. It was humbling. The stars were even clearer in Colorado, but the California sky was OK. Florida felt so far away in time and space, and the stars never looked this good from her condo. Jax sat nearby in his lawn chair, as usual, enjoying this nightly ritual with Del.

Their day had been pretty normal, as far as normal went. Nothing out of the ordinary. The previous night, though, Eric and Shandra had gone on for hours about their little experiment. Their growing talents in telepathy were nothing short of astounding. No one could interpret what little they had gleaned from their eavesdropping. There was just not enough information to draw any conclusions. Jax reminded them all that anyone's thoughts, particularly his own, might not bear up to a lot of scrutiny. Eric and Shandra laughed a lot, emphasizing the point that Jax was right, causing him to wag his finger at the youths.

"You two need to be very careful. You have a talent that takes responsibility. You could scare people, so keep your thoughts and eavesdropping to yourself, do you understand?" Jax asked.

"I don't mean to throw water on your fun," he added as he saw their disgruntled looks. "If I were you, I'd keep what you know amongst us four. I envy you in some ways, but I'm not sure even I could handle what you can do. There are private things and it will take time for us to catch up and adjust to your talents. Does that make sense?"

Shandra spoke first. "Yeah, we were wonderin' about that. It's hard not to use somethin' that's so much fun. It's scary too, though, so we understand you. We'll be careful. One nice thing, though: If you need us, we're just a thought away. Even though you can't project fully, Del, we can sometimes pick up your calls for Jax. Does that help?"

"We want to help Jax, not hurt. We're sorry if we act...too different," added Eric.

"Of course we understand," Del sympathized, "And we're glad for your very special abilities."

That covered, the kids left for their home, gears turning in their minds which kept either from getting a lot of sleep.

For Del, it was relaxing to just sit with Jax and soak up the evening peace. Jax had a lazy smile on his face, eyes closed, not caring about stars. His nostrils flared slightly, absorbing the fresh air. She reached over to stroke his arm and halted. Ramsees was strolling up briskly, an alien on a mission. So much for a quiet evening. "What now Ramsees?" she asked.

Jax opened his eyes and said out loud, "C'mon, old boy, what ya doing at this late hour?"

"There are problems...and not much time to explain. Come with me. Now"

Simultaneously, the three of them straightened, *"Jax! Del! Something's wrong!"* Shandra and Eric shouted in mental unison.

Luck of the draw

Del had the feeling cards were being laid on the table by a higher power as Shandra and Eric shouted their warning. Would they get a full house, straight, four of a kind, or would it be junk? The problem with this game, however, was everyone had to ante up and no one could fold. You had to play, no matter what you were dealt. Whatever confluence of events occurred, you had to ride with it.

Jax and Del jumped immediately up to follow the retreating Ramsees. In front of the house, they saw Eric and Shandra running their way, worry written on their faces. *"We must hurry!"* telepathed Ramsees. *"My ship!"*

The four followed Ramsees at a trot, Del asking Shandra, "What are you sensing?"

"It's hard to explain," she answered panting. "Something bad is about to happen... to us... here... from out there and up there," pointing to the fields west and the stars above.

"Truly remarkable and accurate," Ramsees added, a note of surprise and awe in his thoughts as the young humans had matched his prescience. Their mental skills were advancing rapidly.

"Well, fill us in, kid, we're all ears!" Jax added as the group trotted along.

Eric piped up as their pace quickened, "It's not clear, Mr. Leigh, but someone is out there and we feel it coming this way. It won't be long now."

Del was scared and didn't even know why. Like horror movies, you knew something bad was going to happen as the suspenseful music indicated, but you didn't know exactly what. It made her fast moving legs unsteady. "Shouldn't we warn the others? What about our friends?"

Ramsees slowed a little, then stopped. *"Of course. I understand. You are right. Let me take the children. You go and gather everyone at the hanger and meet me at my ship."*

Jax and Del glanced at each other and headed off towards opposite ends of the housing area. They knew instinctively they had to split up. Jax waved good-bye as he jogged into the dark. "Last one to the hanger is a rotten egg!"

She waved him off and responded, "You're on!"

Del felt an urgency, but didn't want to overly alarm people. So she knocked on the first door and quickly but calmly wakened the occupants, giving them cursory instructions to alert the next house, then head towards the hanger. This saved what might be valuable time by not having to cover every house, and soon this part of their confused little community was on their way to the hanger. Few questioned her instructions. Everyone appeared to understand something major was happening and they had better act as instructed.

She hoped Jax was having an equally efficient time of getting people together. Del mentally shouted to Eric and Shandra they were on their way, hoping they could pick it up.

* * * * *

Seconds later, the base lit up in a huge explosion. The hanger, and everything nearby was toast. Don Drury smiled with satisfaction, and cheers of "Yes!" and "Oh Yeah!" rose around him. The commandos on the far side had done their job. He moved forward in unison with those around him, calling into his mic, "Phase two—go!" This was going to be their night.

The fence had been sabotaged days before so it wasn't even a barrier. They were on the base in seconds. Other units would be closing in as well. He hoped the humans were laying low, if they knew what was good for them. They'd take the aliens out, then worry about removing the humans from the housing area later. He jogged forward with confidence across the air strip, housing and logistic buildings getting closer.

Reports were coming in from the units north and south of him as they converged on their targets. All clear so far. Another 15 minutes and this would all be over. Then they could take cover before the aliens had a chance to react. He smiled again as another explosion near the hanger area lit up the sky; it was like shooting fish in a barrel.

The sudden static on his mic raised a red flag. He signaled a halt and dove for the ground. The dozen men and women with him sprawled flat following suit. In seconds they were invisible.

* * * * *

Genree was appraised of their imminent arrival. It had been an uneventful trip. Nearly a thousand Quazzga were ready to carry out her command. She dared not signal Ramsees. That was not her purpose.

He would be informed after action had been taken. The half-dozen ships with her prepared for a quiet landing.

Mental and audible alarms disrupted this plan, however, as the bright explosion in the view screen startled even the most hardened of Quazzga guards. The ships and building they were approaching were gone in an instant. Thoughts raced through her agile mind. *"What is Ramsees doing? Did someone alert him? Is this some accident? Are the humans involved?"*

Instantly every ship was put on alert for offensive or defensive actions and she risked a mental call to Ramsees. Silence. A general call to the base personnel was greeted with panic, surprise, outrage, but no answers as to the cause. There were only a few Quazzga voices replying from the ground and they were in pain or panic. There were obviously casualties, probably a lot. She was not prepared for this development. None of them were.

Genree, like her fellow Quazzga, avoided anger in any form. But she was not without the capacity for a strong response. What they had just witnessed strengthened her resolve as never before. "The humans must have revolted. We need to neutralize them now and restore order! Land immediately!" she commanded to all the ships.

The ships landed in seconds in a ring around the disaster area. Quazzga poured out to secure the area and help or fight as needed.

* * * * *

Commander Drury saw the ships coming down fast and couldn't believe it. Dumb luck, no luck, bad luck, or just fate, it was all the same. His mind raced. *"How could they possibly respond this fast? Did they detect us? Is there a traitor among my troops?"* It didn't add up, and it didn't matter at this point. Like any battle, it didn't change the objective, it just changed the duration, and perhaps the outcome.

The huge saucer-shaped ships came down around the base, one so close to him he had to jump and roll to avoid being crushed. One of the men near him wasn't so quick or fortunate. He was squashed like a grape.

"All units, incoming enemy at perimeter. Engage and destroy!" he shouted. A door opened on the ship near him and a ramp slid smoothly out, scores of aliens spilling forth before the ramp touched the ground.

They didn't have a chance. Each carried a disk like weapon and a few of his troops right in front of the ramp froze instantly. Don wasn't so encumbered and he mowed down the densely packed group in seconds. There were pitiful shrill shrieks, but they didn't last long. Seconds after that, like lemmings over the cliff, he had to mow down another exiting group. His frozen men regained their legs enough to stumble out of the door and away from the alien weapons so they could inflict damage as well. Others near him added increasing firepower. It was a slaughter of hundreds.

"This is pathetic!" he concluded. Clearly the aliens had no battle skills. He stopped shooting long enough to grab a mine and slap it against the hull but something prevented him from placing it on the hull. He was stopped mere inches from the surface and the mine wouldn't hold in mid-air. Dropping it on the ground as close as he could and adding two more, he ordered everyone back.

The stream of aliens exiting the ship had trickled to nothing. "Get something inside, *now*!" he ordered and several people started firing into the opening which was retracting the ramp and closing up. Several grenades were lobbed inside, as well as a micro-nuke for good measure just as the door shut. Don was ran at full-speed to get some much-needed distance.

When the mines outside went off, he could feel the shockwave and spared a brief glance to see only minor buckling of the hull and electric sizzling of whatever field was protecting the hull. He kept running, knowing he needed more distance. Seconds later, the ship exploded in a ball of flame and twisted wreckage, small bits of which showered around them.

Before he could even enjoy the victory, the ship just south of them exploded like the first. He had trained these people well. Two down, four to go. Looking north, he could see the firefight closing in on that ship as well. "Bravo 1, report. Victor 1 close on my position. Over," Don called to his perimeter troops.

"Alpha 1, Bravo 1, hold sec. Over." Several seconds passed. "Alpha 1, Victor 1 coming your way. Over." Don looked around to assess the battle and saw his Victor 1 troops trotting his way. He could hear fighting from the hanger, but couldn't see what was happening. He assumed his on-base commandos were engaging the enemy. They would need his help and soon.

"Alpha 1, Bravo 1, fireworks away, heading north to assist Zulu 1. Orders? Over."

Simultaneously, a third ship exploded just as it appeared to be lifting off the ground.

"Bravo 1, Victor 1, nice work. Victor 1, move west to housing rendezvous position. Bravo 1, close with Zulu 1. Report casualties! Alpha 1 over."

"Alpha 1, Victor 1, negative."

"Alpha 1, Bravo 1, two-zero percent."

"Not bad. Excellent, in fact," pondered Drury. Even these unexpected alien reinforcements were proving easy to deal with. Still, the other three ships were dumping out their scum, and they had to deal with them first before they could rescue the humans and go home. Worse yet, there might be a second wave any second. That would be a more serious situation.

Mowing down exiting aliens was one thing, defeating them spread out could be problematic, as he knew nothing about their weapons' range or full effects. "Zulu 1, report," he commed to his commando's inside the perimeter.

"Alpha 1, Zulu 1, team leader and three others incapacitated by aliens. Four dead, five of us left. Several hundred aliens gathering civilians south of hanger and spreading out towards barracks. Orders? Over."

Don pondered the report from the "Baker's Dozen", as they called themselves, then responded, "Zulu 1, move towards closest ship and neutralize, eliminate all aliens you can, mining as you go. Bravo 1 will close with you soon. We'll work southwest and meet you at the last ship. Happy hunting. Alpha 1 over."

In less than a minute, they were gazing out towards the ruined hanger area while smoldering Quazzga ships east of them lit their backs. Carefully peering around the corners of housing units, they could see clusters of aliens rounding up humans. They were in the process of penning them up in bundles of green slime for God only knew what purpose.

A hundred other aliens were circled about, facing outward and setting up in defensive positions around the remaining spaceships. Only a few aliens had spread out into the housing area, ostensibly to look for humans, and these had been quickly dispatched. The alien reflexes were amazing slow. They were clearly out of their element. One soldier was briefly paralyzed, but recovered as soon as the aliens targeting him were neutralized. The weapon from the dead alien proved useless in human hands. Too bad. It was a neat trick.

Don studied his options and hated the limitations. Too many civilians were now involved. Why hadn't they stayed low, hidden in their houses? People are supposed to be sleeping at this hour for Christ's sake.

"Victor 1, Alpha 1, swing south and take out that ship. Alpha 1 will engage and confuse center. Alpha 1 over."

Looking to his left and right, he gave hand signals which resulted in the appropriate switch in armament while snipers took up positions. One man stepped out to get a better angle and froze instantly. "Damn!" Don muttered, "Their range is greater than I thought."

His next signal produced a better result as dozens of explosives were lobbed towards the outward-facing aliens. Several were somehow suspended in air, but that didn't matter. Stun grenades were awesomely effective and the whole eastern flank of alien soldiers dropped to the ground. His paralyzed troops recovered their mobility immediately.

The aliens started to fall back, leaving their cocooned human bundles. This was it. They had their advantage. He shouted, "Alpha 1 to all units, finish this now. Commence squeeze play, over!" and moved quickly ahead, pressing the attack to a bloody conclusion, mowing down fleeing aliens before they could reach their ships.

* * * * *

Genree's synapses were nearly shot. The events unfolding before her were incomprehensible. It was hard to block the screams of so many dying Quazzga, many from her pod.

They had barely landed when the screams started, followed by the first of three ships being destroyed. Events were happening so fast it was hard to coordinate a response. Mental orders were fast, but so was mental anguish, and this tragedy was overwhelming. They had come in peace to eliminate a distraction. Now she was in the midst of a battle, and it had not gone well so far.

"Who was this unseen enemy? Where did they get these horrible weapons? Was Ramsees involved? Surely not! Where did this enemy come from?" None of these questions were productive, yet it was hard to concentrate on actions to be taken and orders that desperately needed to be given.

"Three ships! Hundreds of dead brethren!" This should have been an insignificant mission. Nothing of any danger. Nothing that would take long. They were due back to Mars in less than a day.

She had ordered the humans around the hanger to be rounded up and for guards to secure the area. They would be cocooned for later action. That appeared to be working when more attacks occurred, and close by.

It was clear her strategy wasn't working. They had greatly underestimated the base occupants. They must pull back and bring in reinforcements. She gave the order to withdraw, distressed to continue hearing screams of pain and death from closer and closer. *"Forget the humans! Get back to your ships! Take off as soon as you can!"*

"This is not over. We will return!" she warned no one in particular. It had not occurred to Genree to call for help. It shouldn't be needed! Her senses twinged, warning of danger, then she wondered, *"How is this possible?"* It was her last thought as white hot pain engulfed her.

* * * * *

Don could not believe their fortune as a fourth ship blew up, then a fifth. They had hoped to strike a blow against the base inhabitants, but were in the process of winning a major battle against a small group of ships as well. It couldn't be just dumb luck. Their planning and precision was paying off, despite this greater challenge.

A few humans had been hit by stray fire as they passed the eerie bundles, judging by blood oozing from the walls of the green goo. He couldn't do anything about it right now and would have to attend to them later. Everyone, soldiers and aliens, were converging on the remaining ship, aliens dropping in dozens under withering gunfire. A few tried to aim their paralyzing weapons, but they couldn't stop all the converging units. A cursory glance indicated well over half his force was still intact and were quickly wrapping up this battle As for the rest of his force, that too would be dealt with later.

Before the fleeing aliens reached the remaining ship, however, the ramp was retracted and the ship door closed, the craft rising rapidly out of range before they could get some ordinance inside. A barrage of heavy and light arms fire had no effect as the ship disappeared over the horizon.

The hundred or so aliens left behind looked equally confused as they slowed then stopped. Some dropped weapons, others assumed defensive positions and tried to level weapons. It didn't matter. For Don Drury, he had no choice but to eliminate this threat. There was no room in his plan for alien prisoners. Perhaps these interloper believed in an afterlife. He hoped so as his units completed their gruesome mission in a final burst of gunfire.

It was time to grab the hostages and retreat, quickly. That one ship would certainly report what had happened. Reinforcements would be legion, no doubt. Time to head for the hills. He would have liked to scour the area for parts and double-check the buildings for other civilians, but there was no time.

In retrospect, he could not believe how easily they had destroyed ships and aliens. This might go down in history as a rallying point, a single victory that would stir the remaining thinking humans to action. He felt more alive than ever. The day, or early morning at least, was theirs.

They freed the civilians from the goo with some effort. Many appeared confused. A few ingrates shouted obscenities at the soldiers for ruining things. A few others welcomed their help and pledged support, future soldiers he hoped. Don would have to sort them out later, make sure they hadn't taken any spies or jeopardizing baggage. His medics treated the injured on the fly.

Remarkably, they found working transports from the motor pool. These would save them time and a long walk. With great haste they loaded the base occupants, gathered up their dead comrades, grabbed as many supplies as they could, and headed east on a tear. It puzzled Don 20 minutes later when they hadn't seen new lights in the sky. Where's the pursuit? Those six ships came so quickly. There must be more. Did we hurt them so bad they don't know how to respond? He had a lot to think about as he savored this victory.

Aftermath

Tears crept from the corners of swollen eyes and flowed slowly down dark, silky skin. Burn marks oozed lymph and small cuts dribbled blood. The tears mattered more. Adelle Summers needed to cry. It had been one long nightmare filled with periods of great joy and hope, but linked together with fear, pain, and heartache. This was not the ending she had hoped for.

Her secret plan all along was to get cozy with the aliens, learn as much as she could, then create havoc, steal a ship, destroy the voice transmitters, and free people of the mind control. Once free, perhaps people could be rallied to fight the Quazzga and turn the tide of this invasion. That plan, while a long shot, was now down the toilet, as was the plan of mutual cooperation. The deck seemed stacked against them with no wild cards to play.

Nearby, Eric and Shandra, injured and shaken, sat quietly in their sticky lounge chairs, lost in their thoughts, or perhaps even thinking to each other. It was hard to tell and it didn't really matter to her. A dozen or so of her friends, several badly injured, were scattered about the bridge level. Ramsees was piloting the ship to God knew where and didn't look that good either. As a nurse, she should be taking care of them, but couldn't bring herself to the task, couldn't see through her own pain at the moment.

All they had worked to accomplish was ruined. The one person she had grown to care for was lost or dead. In a few minutes of lunacy, her manufactured personal peace had been blown apart. The painful memories were now indelibly etched into her memory, along with the loss she now felt.

She had no sooner woken people up and began moving towards the hanger when it blew up in their faces, the shock wave knocking people flat, injuring many who were closer. Stunned, people gathered themselves slowly, looked around, and wondered what to do next. Del's thoughts were on Jax alone. *"God, please make him safe!"* Out loud, she shouted, "Jax! Where are you! Jax! Talk to me!"

No answer came and her fear grew. Ramsees came stumbling away from the hanger area, hobbling, injured, holding the children protectively, Shandra and Eric, who appeared to have only minor injuries. She surmised that Ramsees' ship was no longer the rendezvous point.

After the hanger explosion, six Quazzga ships landed out of nowhere. She wondered why they would blow up their own ships and attack their own kind. This was not something she'd ever expected from them. She knew her own kind could be ruthless, but this was a side of the Quazzga she hadn't expected. Then there was gunfire and more Quazzga ships exploded. It didn't make sense. *"What the hell is going on?"*

It suddenly dawned on her that that madman from the hills must be attacking the base, but instead of helping them he was ruining everything. This wasn't how she'd expected him to help. *"Why not contact us first? Why not give us a chance to fight with them?"*

The next thing she knew, she couldn't move, no one could, and her frozen friends were being sprayed with some goo and being pushed together in clusters. Before they got to her, Ramsees took charge and set a dozen or so of them aside, handing the limp form of Isees to her. The other Quazzga appeared to balk at his actions, but something he chittered made them stay back. Then she heard, *"Come with me. I've told them you will follow me and be under my command!"*

Glad to be able to move again, they worked their way past the knot of aliens who were getting ready to fight something coming their way, while at the same time bundling up the remaining humans. She wondered again where Jax might be and hoped he was alive.

"Ramsees! I have to go find Jax!" she shouted to his back.

"I need you with me to take care of these children! We must enter the ship now! It's our only chance for safety!" he telepathed emphatically.

Torn as never before, her survival and nurturing instincts took over and regretfully she followed him, hoping all the while Jax would show up.

Once inside the craft, Ramsees chittered something that made the few remaining Quazzga exit. He sat down at the control console, commandeering Genree's last ship, and closed the entrance.

Del suddenly realized he was readying the ship for takeoff and shouted "No! We can't leave them behind! What are you doing? Stop!"

Ramsees stayed at the controls and only said, *"We must leave now. We cannot help the others. We will get them later, if we can."*

This did little to comfort her, 'though she knew he was right. Now her tears flowed freely. *"Jax, where are you? I need you! Oh, please let him be OK!"*

After what felt like an hour of crying, but was only minutes, she steeled herself, wiped her eyes, and collected herself enough to notice her surroundings and the wounded. "Are you hurt?" she asked Ramsees, "Is there anything I can do to help?"

"I will mend. You have others who need your attention. We will be stopped momentarily."

Since it was still dark out, she had no idea where they were. Indeed, the ship slowed, then stopped. The couches released them, lights grew brighter, and amidst several groans, she started to make rounds. Work, a useful purpose, was what she needed to keep her composure.

"You wouldn't have a first aid kit handy by any chance, would you?" she asked Ramsees.

As if reading her thoughts, which she knew he couldn't, he produced a backpack-sized cylinder and touched his wounded hands to her head. *"You now know what to do with this,"* he told her, his voice sounding tired, very tired.

And she did, the miraculous Quazzga mind meld teaching her in seconds what otherwise would take months. Her skill, his thoughts, and this cylinder, would do the trick. And fortunately, she didn't pass out this time.

Resisting his mental and physical protestations, she used the proper contents to heal Ramsees' most serious wounds, including a few drugs she wished humans had developed years before. And not giving him too much attention so as to support his unselfish dignity, she moved on to the other passengers. Del wished she had more than this remarkable med-kit, but it would have to do.

Isees was a particular challenge, as he appeared fine by all diagnosis, but was clearly unconscious and unresponsive. After several futile minutes, a weak Ramsees explained, *"Move on. He is repairing himself, but it will take some time."*

"What's wrong?" she asked.

"The shock of so many Quazzga deaths caused him to go into...hibernation...is the best way I can explain it. It was too much for him to assimilate in a conscious state. This is a defensive mechanism that will protect him from physical brain injury and psychological damage. He will be fine...in time."

Disappointed that she could not help him further, but accepting Ramsees' explanation, she moved around the ship. An hour later, with burns, breaks, and bruises attended, she finally had a chance to think about their current circumstances. "Where are we Ramsees?"

"We're on the floor of the ocean, off the California coast," he replied. *"I am uncomfortable here, but it is the safest place I could find for now."*

Remembering how poorly Ramsees could swim brought some levity to their dark situation, but she agreed with his strategy. "Can we look for Jax?" she added hopefully.

"I mourn your loss. I am not certain we can locate him to your satisfaction, and it would be unwise and dangerous to return to the base. But I assume you will want to try anyway."

"Please. We do need to try...if we can. Thank you." Del understood the likely futility, and the danger. They were fugitives from everyone on this rock. Clearly their cooperative utopia was finished and everyone from humans to Quazzga wanted a piece of their rears. It was still hard to believe what had just happened to them. Things had been going so well up until now.

Eric and Shandra had been very silent. They were physically in the best shape of everyone, apparently thanks to Ramsees. Psychologically, she wasn't too sure, 'though they acted calmly enough. Touching them on the shoulders, she asked, "You sure you're fine? No hurts anywhere?"

Eric answered calmly, "It's OK, Del." We've been talking with Ramsees. We feel safe and we're not hurt. Do you know what we're going to do now? We don't think it's safe to go back. Are we homeless?"

Del had forgotten how resilient kids could be and was surprised at his adult-like response and question. "No, I don't know what we'll do, but we'll figure something out. And also, we're never homeless as long as we have each other and some place to live. Do you have any ideas on what we should do next?"

Shandra spoke up first, "I'd like to go back to the base and start over, but I guess that's not gonna happen."

"Maybe we could find another place on Earth," suggested Eric.

"He is most perceptive, and that may be our only option, but not on this planet. We cannot stay here indefinitely. We cannot go back to the base to live. We are hidden from detection for now, but that will not last long," explained Ramsees.

Those few, sad words alerted everyone as they took stock of their unfortunate situation.

"Just what are you saying? Do you have a secret base nearby? Are we going to have to leave Earth?" asked Del, trembling a little thinking about the repercussions of the latter.

Ramsees was measured and solemn in his response. *"I do not have a place on this planet for us. You will not be allowed to live here with free minds, nor is it likely we will be given easy passage. I am...in trouble...and have...few allies. There are other places in space we could* live, 'though not as hospitable as Earth. We have...few options yet must decide soon."*

Everyone was silent for several minutes. Like being between a rock and hard place, their choices were minimal. They were running out of cards to play and it wasn't looking like a winning hand.

A middle-aged woman named Randi finally spoke up. "I, for one, think getting a controlling chip in my head is the same as death. I vote we get out of here. Tell us more about our options for a new home."

Several others nodded, so Ramsees explained, *"There are only two within reach by this vessel, which is limited in its range,"* he went on and laid out the differences and similarities to Earth so they could review their options. In the back of his mind, Ramsees wished they would never have come to Earth but chosen one of these two planets instead. In retrospect, it would have been better for humans, 'though not for Quazzga. The humans had certainly complicated matters, for him at least.

"Great, just great," grumbled Del. She couldn't believe they were even having this discussion, that it had come to this. But everyone was sober about their predicament. Ramsees' assessment was, unfortunately, correct. There would be hardships to face, but at least they'd be alive.

As for the planets, they were opposite in so many ways, 'though not unlike comparing Utah to Florida. Ramsees was bombarded with questions. What are the atmosphere and weather like? Are there seasons? Would they be safe from diseases? Are there any animals? What about gravity? How many planets are in the system? What resources will be available? What will they eat? After a brief discussion, they all agreed on the planet most like Florida in climate and topography, a planet they named New Florida for lack of a better idea. Ramsees appeared uncomfortable, probably because of all the water.

Shandra spoke up, "We'll have to teach Ramsees to swim." No one chuckled.

What bothered Del was that leaving Earth seemed like a cowards way out. And what would be accomplished by running away? A dozen people and two aliens weren't a sustaining colony. It seemed to be a dead end, literally.

Perhaps it was time to devise a new plan, find the soldier who attacked the base and join forces or take them to New Florida. Mulling over this option, she realized they'd probably be blown up before they could say hello. *"It'd be worth the trip if we just had more people,"* she reasoned.

That made her think of Jax. There had to be a way to find out if he was dead or alive. "Our implants!" Del exploded. "Ramsees, can you track the others? Jax?"

"Not from this ship," he responded flatly.

"Can we go look for Jax?" asked Adelle. "I have to know."

Several others voiced concerns for lost friends and a need for closure.

"That area is very unsafe and will have much activity, but I knew you would insist. Yes, it may risk us all, but we will make a brief stop there...as...I sense the importance...for your benefit...and perhaps us all. To make it safer...we should shut this vessel down and wait a night...maybe two. We will only have one chance, and if detected, we will have to abort any landing and leave immediately for New Florida. Is this acceptable?"

Heads nodded somberly, though Del's mind was still searching for another possibility. Systems were shut down, and everyone settled in for some rest and waiting. Returning to look for Jax couldn't come fast enough for Del, although what lay ahead for them at the airbase could be the end of the road or a new beginning. They would know only when they got there. If they had to wait a day more, it would be worth it. Her thoughts, and hopes, of Jax continued through the painfully long hours.

Lost Cause

It was two days, not one, they waited. A long time: too long for Del. But Ramsees' interpretations of sensors and his mental listening advised against quicker action. Del could only think the worst, even though that was not productive. She had to, however, trust his sixth, or seventh sense to lead them. In many ways, he had totally sacrificed himself for them. If other Quazzga before questioned him, he surely was an outlaw now. She thanked him often, both publicly and privately. He had lost as much as any of them.

Still, a melancholy mood slipped over her with each passing moment. She just wanted a conclusion, for better or worse. They wouldn't have much time when they arrived at the base. A cursory search and if no one was found, then goodbye to Jax and rest of the humans would likely be all they could spare. For her, that would have to be enough, though she needed to know for sure if Jax was dead or alive. Inwardly, she would stay behind if it meant finding out the truth. Leaving him once was bad enough. She wouldn't do it twice.

To pass the time and avoid unnecessary frustration as they waited, they discussed their upcoming trip.

"How long will it take to get there?" Del inquired.

"About 10 of your months," Ramsees answered levelly. *"This craft is very fast."*

Her mouth agape, Del blurted, "Ten months! What will we do for 10 months in this little thing?"

Exasperated, he explained, *"Please relax. I would have chosen a different vehicle for this journey, but we didn't have that option. It is much bigger than the ship you learned to pilot, and we have the resources aboard to travel much longer, even without use of stasis techniques. To avoid boredom and pass the time, I recommend putting all or most of you in stasis. I will remain awake to watch over you and guide our journey."*

Both Eric and Shandra popped up "We'll stay awake with you! You'll be too lonely if everyone is asleep."

"You are most perceptive and I thank you. It would be .... most difficult...without your thoughts. I welcome your company and promise to keep you...entertained," he replied.

The lighthearted banter relaxed everyone and discussions turned towards New Florida, particularly what they would do with the ship, how they would feed themselves, what kind of shelter they could make, and exactly where on the planet they'd live. While their discussion was mostly conjecture, it was more productive than worry and it got everyone thinking about the hardships they would face and how they would face them.

During their discussions, Isees awoke. This cheered Eric and Shandra who surrounded him with affection and support. Del checked him over anyway. Blinking, and gathering his strength, he told everyone, *"Give me more time. I'm very tired, and saddened by what I saw."*

Everyone understood. After a few minutes, he closed his eyes and rested while the children stayed by his side.

Finally, Ramsees signaled it was time. Securing themselves in couches, they rose off the pitch black seabed and sped towards an uncertain rendezvous. There was a gathering of anticipation as they headed east. Del wasn't the only one seeking closure. Their next destination after this uncertain rescue would be far away, an incomprehensible distance, and with an unpredictable result at best.

The darkness of night, with no moon even to guide their way, made the trip a sensory blank. There were hardly any ground lights for perspective where in the past Sacramento at night would have been easy to spot. Ramsees explained the Quazzga were conserving resources. Humans had been far to wasteful in using electricity. Work for the Quazzga was being done in Daylight. Del was glad he knew where they were going, and glad Ramsees hadn't restricted their use of power on the base.

When they landed, the humans practically poured out upon landing, care tossed to the wind. Ramsees gave the "all clear," but only after the ship was already empty. They peered through the darkness, each looking for someone. What they did see in the glow of ship lights caused all of them to halt just beyond the ship's ramp.

They had landed in nearly the exact spot from which they had left. Only there were no destroyed ships, no smell of weapons fire, no piles of dead Quazzga, no sign of any humans.

"Your friends work fast, Ramsees," commented Del.

One wouldn't have known there had even been a battle if not for scattered charred spots. The base had been scrubbed clean. Only their own heartbeats and breathing broke the silence. The base was deserted. There wasn't even a single light on. It was dead.

Shandra disagreed. "They are here! They survived! I'm asking them to show themselves."

Del called out, heedless of any possibility they might bring instant danger upon themselves. "Jax! Jax! Anybody!"

From one of the nearby barracks, a group of people rounded the corner, heading for the ship. In the dark, they were only shapes and Del moved back up the ramp, hesitating. *"What if it's soldiers? They'd shoot first and ask questions later,"* she fretted briefly. "Who are you! Identify yourselves!" she shouted.

"It's our friends! And Jax too!" Eric said from just behind her.

Indeed, the huddled group waved, though it looked like several people were injured and being carried which was slowing them down.

"We must leave now! We are being vectored!" apprised Ramsees. *"We have no time for this!"*

A group of lights broke over the western horizon and sped towards them. Del ignored Ramsees and the lights, and sprinted out towards the eight or so people 100 yards off who were working their way towards the ship. Several others took up the rescue with her as she closed the gap.

Smiles of relief broke out as she got closer and mutual recognition settled in. Her smile faded as she realized Jax was the one slowing them down, and badly injured from the looks of it. He wasn't even holding his head up.

"Oh Jax! What's wrong?" Del asked as she reached the group.

"He's burned and not very coherent, but he's alive," replied Ben.

"Hurry. Into the ship! We have to leave now!" she goaded. "Jax honey, hang in there!" The added support from Del and some others made the group move much faster. The lights ahead got brighter and closer, it looked like a dozen ships coming very fast. They had only seconds to get inside.

"Is there anyone else?" Del ventured, knowing they had precious little time as it was.

"No! Just us!" Ben shouted back. "The soldiers rounded up everyone else and headed for the hills. There's been a lot of alien activity that way last couple days, but no one's been back. I only hope they're OK!"

Ramsees was as frantic as she'd ever heard. *"We should not have come here! We have to leave now!"*

His urgency goaded them to even greater efforts and they practically threw themselves into the ship in a heap, Jax groaning as they did so.

The door irised shut a split second later and the ship rose quickly. Ramsees warned, *"Everyone take a seat, this will be a dangerous flight!"*

Del barely had time to settle into one of the couches with Jax and the med kit when they were both almost tossed to the floor. "Ramsees, what are you doing? I'm trying to assess and treat a patient here!"

"I'm attempting to escape, if that is still possible," he answered tersely.

Someone asked, "Will they shoot us down?"

"That is science fiction as you put it. We have not needed that capability, but we can be forced down or surrounded. Those ships are faster in the atmosphere. This will be...difficult, but this is an agile and fast ship once we get into space," he replied, fingers working like greased lightning across his control panel, the ship swerving dramatically in response.

Del gave up trying to treat Jax and concentrated on trying to keep them from being thrown off the couch. Jax was secure on his back and took up most of the couch. There was barely enough stickiness left to grab her side.

Jax had been seriously injured, his face red from 3rd degree burns, but his heartbeat was regular, breathing was steady, and she didn't see any signs of broken bones. His lack of consciousness worried her. She hugged him partly for stability, and mostly to give him what love and strength she could offer at this crazy moment.

The ship veered in every possible direction. It reminded Del of the one time she had flown in a jet simulator, and got sick in the process. Looking out the 360-degree view ports showed they were surrounded by a number of smaller ships which were matching Ramsees' moves with precision. And they were closing in. Judging by the sky, they were still close to the ground, but it was hard to tell from this most uncomfortable position.

One ship closed within feet, the proximity of its dark shape obscuring much of her view. Then it bumped into them roughly, stuck to the hull, and began to force them downward. Another ship completed the same maneuver seconds later. They were being corralled and captured.

"Ramsees! Do something!" Del shouted. It was only a matter of time now before the swarm of ships around them succeeded in bringing them down. Another two ships were closing in.

Ramsees' mind was nearly overloaded as he worked feverishly to maneuver the saucer out of danger and fend off thousands of barbed orders from his fellow Quazzga. It took all of his considerable talent to block the mental attacks and maintain control of himself and this craft.

Their ship suddenly braked and Del was thrown from the couch, hard. Nothing broke, but there would be some nasty bruising. She reached for something solid and realized it was a combination of Ramsees' leg and his chair.

The braking maneuver worked, and one of the attached ships was dislodged in a rather spectacular fashion, sparks noticeable in the view screen, other ships veering off in various directions to avoid collision. Their ship then punched straight up, pulling so many G's it hurt, leaving the Earth's atmosphere in seconds if the blue to black darkening sky was any indication. It was hard to see from her floor perspective.

One ship was still attached and there was no question that it was affecting Ramsees' flight path.

Now in deepening space, it was harder to see the ships trying to stop them. The next maneuver was proceeded only by a terse "Hold on!" warning from Ramsees. A second later, they were spinning like a top, an action which had everyone holding on for dear life, Del's arms feeling like they were near the breaking point. The lone ship clinging to them like a remora finally dislodged, stabilizing their ascent arc. Ramsees relaxed noticeably as their pursuers fell behind and the ship freely accelerated to a point where the stars blurred, then winked out.

They had folded into space, on their way to a new and very uncertain home. Whatever had happened up until now, nightmarish and unreal, this brought them to a new reality. This was their life now.

"New Florida had better live up to the travel brochures," thought Del.

Out loud she asked, "Can they track us?"

"It is possible, but very difficult," Ramsees replied.

"Will they try?" she retorted.

"Perhaps," was all he would say. He sounded tired and still worried.

Looking around briefly, she couldn't help but wonder what their future would hold. Less than two dozen humans and a couple aliens. What could this pathetic group accomplish? What about supplies? Would they just live out their lives as banished refugees? These thoughts were depressing her so she pushed them away, boxed them up, and threw away the key, for now.

It was also sad to realize so many friends, like Lady Henri, were gone forever, the fate of those left behind uncertain. Those thoughts were depressing too. Another mental box was filled and the key thrown away for the moment.

Once into folded space, the ship became even keeled and the ride was as smooth as silk. No one needed to be glued to couches, so she could release her death grip of Ramsees' leg. Painfully she worked her way towards Jax.

"OK, you big lummox, wake up and help me out here," she sighed over him as she brought the tools from the Quazzga med kit to bear. It was designed for alien physiologies, but the concepts were similar. She didn't like the interpretation of Jax's vital signs, but it was clear he would live. The brain trauma was most troubling, 'though the readings indicated that the simple brains of humans could be fixed. How she knew all this was a minor miracle she didn't begrudge. Fixing his melon became her top priority. A while later, his wakening groans let her know she had succeeded.

Tears coursed freely down her tanned cheeks. In all her years as a nurse this was her most important save. She loved this man, this savior of her psyche, this soul mate from out of the blue, a one-in-a-billion match, someone she was certain had been lost.

"I love you," were the first words he spoke weakly as his eyes became wet with the joy of seeing her.

That opened the floodgates from Del, as she stopped her ministrations and simply hugged her mate, sobbing freely. As uncertain was their future, their love was certain, a lighthouse in the fog.

From the corner of her eye, she noticed Ramsees slump forward. Letting go of Jax, she grabbed their savior and pulled him to the closest open couch, making sure the ship was on autopilot. Scanning him assured her there were no serious physical injuries. Like Isees, the trouble must be psychological.

"You need to rest. I can fly the ship for a while," she told him softly. His lidded eyes didn't open, but she heard him say weakly, *"Thank you. I'm sorry for all that has happened."*

"Don't worry about it. We're alive at least. Thank you for saving us. Just relax. You have new friends," she replied solemnly.

Taking the helm, she found that Ramsees had set the controls so there wasn't much to do. Looking around, she sensed both physical and psychological sighing as everyone let out the tension and took in their present situation. Each person seemed to be ruminating about what fate had dropped on his or her lap, perhaps contemplating now lost loved ones or friends they would never see again, perhaps just trying to compartmentalize this unbelievable string of events. There was mass silence though Del sensed gears churning in every head.

Opening one of those mental boxes she'd closed earlier, she put some thought to the future as she stared forward at the streaming starscape. There had to be a way, some way, to move beyond just escaping to New Florida. It could never be Earth. It could never be home. She was sure of it. She vowed then and there to return to Earth and make a stand, change things for the better. This seemingly futile hope instantly became a goal. It would give her courage. It would give her strength.

They had made it this far and were certain to make it a lot farther. And who knew if anything would have happened differently if the soldiers hadn't arrived. There was no telling now. Perhaps the cards they'd been dealt weren't so bad after all. Looking down at her beloved Jax, Del whispered with renewed hope, confidence, and love, "You're a royal flush, my dear."

His brow furrowed not understanding this sudden reference, then relaxed sensing the compliment. "Thank you my queen of hearts."

Greg Burke
About the Author

Greg Burke was born in 1956, and is an avid science fiction and non-fiction reader and published technical writer. Married over 20 years to Julia, they have three sons. He currently owns a leather and hat store and resides in Estes Park, Colorado.

Printed in the United States
4139